Praise for
Blood Kiss

"So many fierce images, so immediate and propulsive! There's huge energy in *Blood Kiss*—the energy of a performance, when the audience and the people on stage feed from one another, push each other past all boundaries, together."

—Kathe Koja, author of *The Cipher* and *Christopher Wild*

"It's the art-scene, it's the death-scene, the sex-scene, the meaning-scene. Some nightmare, but mostly bone-wide awake; Stone makes it feel like you are characters . . . in all those scenes. It's tempting to say, 'Keep an eye on this guy.' Because he's young. Because this is only his second book. But you'd only say something like that to mean one day he's gonna do something great. The thing is, he already has. It's right here. *Blood Kiss* is refreshing as hell. In a field where most are trying to out-thrill one another, Stone is riffing, philosophizing, writing . . . out loud.

—Josh Malerman, author of *Bird Box*

"Like Poppy Z. Brite, dark and sensuous and filled with artsy characters on the fringes of society. Like Clive Barker, even darker and viscerally sexual, where blood and love come together to paint a disturbing picture. But even more, entirely J. Daniel Stone, with a voice like no other new writer I've read. He drips this novel, *Blood Kiss*, with a bleak, disturbing sensuousness that oozes from the pages. Stone makes you feel the pain that goes into art--whether music or painting- and the pain that art causes. He'll make you believe that art has a life of its own--dark and dreadful. And love . . . oh love hurts."

—Bram Stoker Award-nominated author John F.D. Taff

"Once more Stone has taken readers into the crevices of Brooklyn, where dissolute artists stretch and suffer. Poetry and lyrics are as much opium as oxygen to his characters; it's a sin not to fall with them. I applaud him for telling it."

—Steve Berman, owner of Lethe Press

"J. Daniel Stone's writing possesses a mesmerizing, silken music. He's one of those rare storytellers who can draw you along irresistibly and thrill you with his artistry at the same time. His scrutiny of love and desire is fearless. *Blood Kiss* is a haunting journey through the dark labyrinth of the wounded heart, where obsession can fuel both creativity and destruction. Terrifying, beautiful and utterly unique, it will leave you hungry for more from this brilliant young author."

—Stephen T. Vessels, Thriller Award-nominated author of *The Mountain & The Vortex*

Praise for J. Daniel Stone's first novel, *The Absence of Light*

"*The Absence of Light* is lush and lyrical . . . a jangled and disturbing book that seeks to transcend through rituals and incantations. This book is highly recommended for anyone who wants dark prose that seeks to transgress boundaries though not designed to appeal to people who want streamlined plots, transparent prose, or simple stories. First novels are often ragbags where writers try to explain life, so Stone has clearly come across more dark wisdom than most people."

—*Hellnotes* (Review by Geoffrey H. Goodwin)

"J. Daniel Stone is a gifted young writer, capable of some of the most beautiful sentences about the most horrid things. [*The Absence of Light*] combines horror, the art world, the music world, the paranormal world, the young, displaced hipster world . . . and combines it all into a heady, trippy story that is sad at times, powerfully dark at others. I didn't just enjoy the book; I enjoyed the act of reading it."

—John F.D. Taff

"From the first few pages I was swept into a dark punky world of nightclubs, Jägermeister, craft beer, ghosts, and music. [Stone knows] what it feels like to grow up "different"—different being, queer, goth, fat, loser, outcast, whatever you want to call it. To me [*The Absence of Light*] became instantly important because it represents the power of so-called "outsider" fiction and it is with this power that this book will call its readers home."

—Drunk in a Graveyard

"*The Absence of Light* manages to walk the fine line between the suffocatingly eerie and tear-jerking beautiful. J. Daniel Stone gives his characters life in a bleak world resonating with song . . . which you will never want to leave."

—Jonathan Moon, author of *Heinous* and
Stories To Poke Your Eyes Out To

". . . one part ghost story, one part alternative lifestyle exploration that explores the themes of identity, loss, and the power of art through poetic language."

—Fanboy Comics

"What struck me immediately was Stone's ability to make the reader feel as if they're in an uninterrupted fevered dream. The characters were well drawn, flawed and in their own ways feeding off of one another, just as the invisible waits to feed off of them."

—Gemma Farrow

"J.D.'s style forces you into this fictitious world without remorse, without a chance to escape as you're propelled to turn each successive page. [*The Absence of Light*] rocks on so many levels."

—Charles Day, Bram Stoker Award nominated
author of *The Legend of the Pumpkin Thief*

"The world needs Goth boys and girls—who better to guide a reader into a good ghost story like that of a black-clad bearer of angst and pain? J. Daniel Stone's The Absence of Light offers a horde of such morbid youth as well as satisfying haunts."

—Steve Berman, author of *Red Caps*

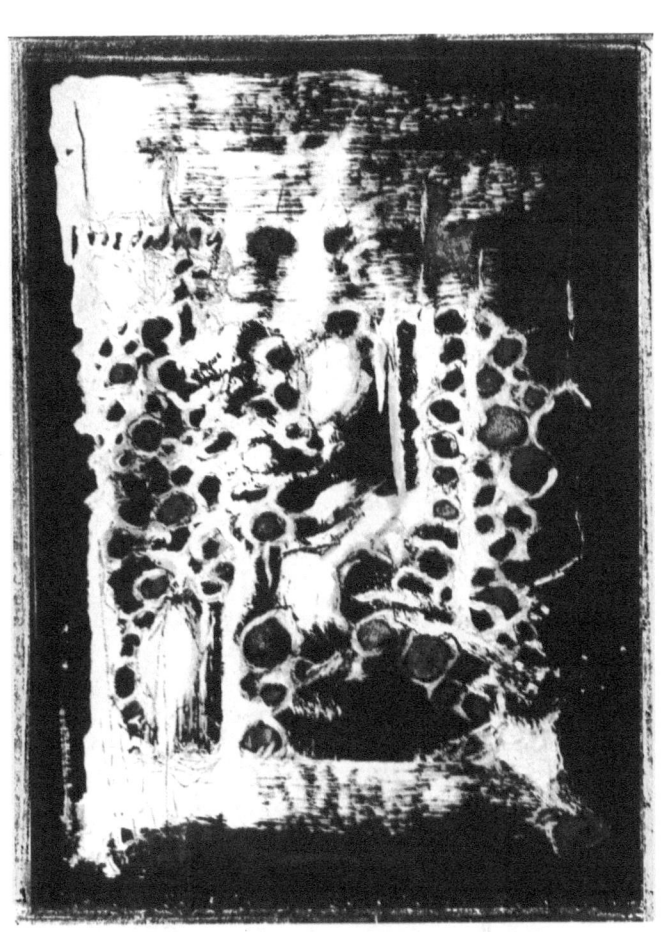

Published by **Villipede Publications**

Villipede Publications
Villipede.com

Special discounts are available on quantity purchases. For details, contact the publisher through the website.

Printed in the United States of America

ISBN-13: 978-0692715451
ISBN-10: 0692715452

1st edition October 2016
2nd edition August 2018

For Jessi,
the *light of my life, fire of my loins.*

And Kathe,
who has helped me longer than she's known me.

Most importantly, to Sonoye,
supporter of my madness.

BLOOD KISS

A Novel

by J. Daniel Stone

PART ONE

SYNERGY

"All colours will agree in the dark."

—Francis Bacon

Art is a blade so sharp you don't feel it penetrate your yielding flesh. Art is escape from this claustrophobic ghost-box we call reality. Art is a holy gift.

The past is no longer prologue and the future is a feral game. It is well known that fact is stranger than fiction. But do you know that the real world is full of monstrosities that no nightmare could ever create? To be desirous is to be criminal; to be unique is to be weak. If you find your voice they will take away your choice.

But I've always been a dark dreamer. What reality declares taboo I conceive through imagination, for the artist manifests what the naked eye has yet to see. My specialty? Studies of gloom and viscera, the contrast of cultural beauty to natural ugly. I remember one time a critic tried to offend me (though she failed) by referring to one of my pieces as a "paranoid awakening." I had entitled that one "Love . . . the greatest virus ever known."

With love comes the frightening notion of procreation. I often take a few minutes out of my day to try and fathom why my parents felt the compulsion to breed (I am the quintessential only child, and a failure in their eyes). If in the end all we make are skin and bone robots, what is the point of continuing our existence?

My father was an intolerant, dictatorial and censorious figure who demoralized life and imbedded into my head that I should evade it before it is too late. My mother, on the other hand, was gentle where it mattered, untrained in her intelligence and gregarious in nature.

Opposites attract.

I knew well into my adolescence how strange it was that my parents never touched each other, yet it still never made any sense as to why they withheld affection toward me. I am no longer hung up over such trivialities; I let go of hope and accepted my dark fate. I learned to be grateful for my curse as I was told with careful horror about miscarriages and foster homes. My father said that I was the luckiest zygote-glob on the planet to have successfully navigated my mother's fallopian tube.

It has been twenty-three years since my birth, and I'm still vexed by the process. I am prone to a more carnivorous memory than a rational one. An amalgamation of slimes and juices, gestation of red and black, birth of gelatin and meat; I am enchanted by the thought of my infant-self clawing out of my mother's canal for that first gulp of blood-tinged hospital air, my skin glazed with placenta, my eyes glued shut with gore. I know this not so, but it is a dream of mine.

By the time I hit my teens I was dark with desire and a curious fury burned in my eyes. The anger I held for everything spun into creativity. I had picked up my first skill: reading. I blasted through books, mostly beat poetry and classic novels of horror that challenged me to think outside of the box. William S. Burroughs once said *America is not so much a nightmare as a non-dream . . . precisely a move to wipe the dream out of existence. The dream is a spontaneous happening and therefore dangerous to a control system set up by the non-dreamers.*

That instantly opened my eyes. I saw through the printed lies, refusing to accept the paradigm that permeated every religion, billboard and television station. Reality TV did not lull me. Video games remained a Technicolor blur. I wanted my ideas to be my life. Drawing came naturally to me; all I had to do was pick up a pencil and let my mind control everything else.

I started my journey into solitude. Artists crave so much of it that we find ourselves often traveling the valleys of our own brain and envisioning new worlds, new universes. What

BLOOD KISS

I chose to give up in friends and lovers I made up for with art and literature. I needed not the wisdom and opinions of those around me. Books were comforting for brief spans, but it was drawing that saved me from self-affliction.

"Dorian." I remember my father's tone being tyrannical and drunk. "Stop trying to be *different.*"

"I don't want to be like you," I said.

I often wondered what was truly expected of me. Was I born to become a happy little slave for minimum wage? Or was I meant for another path? If I refuse to accept comfort does that make me a bad person? Knowledge grew into my power; antipathy became my inherent creed. That set me apart from the rest.

But I wanted so badly to be good.

I failed miserably.

One night my father caught me wearing my mother's under garments. There I stood pale and skinny in front of the mirror, my flaccid dick sticking out of a pair of panties he most certainly adored. Narrowed eyes and a drooped mouth, his hands craned toward me in an instant. The only thing I remember after that is waking up with the taste of blood on my tongue and my eyes bruised shut.

"He's a fairy," my father told my mother.

The next day I saw my black denim jacket draped over an empty suitcase with money in the pockets. My father couldn't accept that his own flesh and blood was not destined for his view of reality. But I knew something fragile about my father. Somewhere buried deep within his ego was a soul that so very much wanted to be free. But he was too comfortable with his silent rage to ever really feel. His suffering was an entity that everyone in his life had to share.

Misery loves company.

Still, I pitied my father in that moment when he asked me to leave. But I remember my mother's reaction. Her hair was greased with vegetable oil and her black eyes were wet with tears. But as much as she loved her son she knew that disobeying my father came with a heftier price. She stayed with me as I packed my things, not that I had much: a few tattered paperbacks, a pencil, and a pair of Converses. Her lips hit my forehead, burning, yearning, drunk. And then I was gone.

Outside the moony glow of night was my guide and the disregard I had for society kept me at bay. Freedom tasted fresh and clean; I was a man, finally, and it was time for me to make my own choices. For too long I'd seen people demonize art and obliterate freedom of speech. Entire identities had been burned at the temperature of 451 degrees Fahrenheit, the way paper burns.

But instead of collapsing in on myself and worrying about where I would sleep or what I would eat, I drew vertiginously, upholding my ideas of an anti-life, anti-society. It was a revelation to become one with these abominations, bringing them to life in the fashion of pure rebellion. Was it a dream? Had I lived too long in my own head?

I prayed to an unknown goddess, accepted her sickness and her plague. The cheap whiskey that had swirled my brain into a bitter soup made me realize that all salvation would lie within it. In my world nihilism became nascent reality, not discredited sociology.

That's when I saw the first sketch move.

A dark winged monstrosity with pins and needles for a face. It had shifted positions so unnaturally that I began to question my own skill. That night I dropped the pencil for the paintbrush and followed a new philosophy: to dip the brush into the color of the mind and stroke it across the canvas road was the only platform where imagination was to become reality.

It is a talent rarely appreciated.

When I tire myself out from drawing I think about Leland. Serious party-boy by night but furious dealer of art during the day. Through memory I feel his soft hand playing with my hair, the stark pallor of him dressed in all that bad black. I think about his velvet lips, my tongue spilling into his mouth in search of his tonsils. He tastes like long nights of drinking, dancing until dawn and hangover Sundays.

BLOOD KISS

I think of his legs scissoring open. I can see his ripe almond asshole throbbing fish-mouth hungry, taste the delicate sag of his balls. I touch myself at the thought of him. We've been lovers for three years, are markedly different from one another, but it's what brings us together. We appreciate one another's desires because it is something the other could never achieve.

Leland's vices lay within the fine-combed perfection that has brought Bosch and Ernst to fame, whereas I suffer the obsessions of the abstract, surreal and avant-garde. We dissertate, we argue, and then I'll imagine myself ripping into him or him ripping into me. When I stop dreaming I wipe the sticky spooge off of my nightmare-soaked skin. I see a handwritten note. *Dorian*, it said. *Don't be late*. The opening was at nine, I remembered.

Above me I see Dali's self-hating pose in photonegative, famous fetal position inspiring future madness, black eyes half open and thin mustache spilled across his face like ink. Dali speaks prophecies with his self-hating eyes. But oh, there's Pollock to the left raging over a murder scene of paint; Bacon lies adjacent, the only picture in color. He's licking a paintbrush that splits his tongue in two meaty chunks.

They were once misunderstood as I am today.

Because *I am* misunderstood. I do not contribute to society in the ways that are expected of me. I'm queer and outspoken, misguided and disconnected. I don't want a perfect life or a perfect wife. I just want to live. Consider my wasteful existence on this apathetic planet: sinewy and bent at all the wrong angles as I complete a new sketch, hair swaying cryptically dark and my pale bones stretching to lengths that could rewrite the Yoga books.

Sometimes I look in the mirror and wonder what I've become. Am I a joke of myself? Is the world laughing at me? Why define my work if no one, in the end, will understand it? I'm fully aware how unappreciated I am in my craft, but at the same time driven by a sickly compel to make my mark within a world that I cannot change.

Artwork is *work*, no matter what they say.

SAGE.

See it rise in smudging smoke, opaque tendrils to rid the air of bad energy, send it back to where it was born. Tight bundle burning in pretty little rings; sweet odor of it that gets under the skin.

Herbs. Spice. Sometimes everything is not so nice.

Tyria Vane writes in the spiral bound notebook opened like a pale mouth in her lap. The room is candlebright. Her pen swipes madly, bat's blood ink too comically red to be the real thing, yellow pages crumbling at the command of her rising prose. She writes when she gets weak.

Tonight's angry words beat in time to the rhythm of sex and blood. The Deftones record grumbles, cymbals crash and her vision becomes assaulted by color. Dark blue ribbons flap like Chinese dragons; power chords rattle the world black; heavy bass broods like grey storm clouds. This is a personal acid trip that the experts called synesthesia.

But even with the amazing sights she realizes how alone she is. Adelaide had been out since the afternoon peddling fun in little baggies, and so she thinks about taking a walk or having a drink, but instead gazes at the poetry stretched across the furniture like dead skin.

Pages perfectly flawed, pages with spider-ink deep as tattoos. Black downward spirals and erratic circles. The scrawl of denial and regret, of trying to make sense of the world that will never feel what you feel, see what you see. The mark of it clear on Tyria's hands, pen nib scars badly healed. Paper cuts beyond recognition.

She'd been writing all day.

To her left the shadow lay in wait, lissome in the scrollwork candelabra. The shadow has its own mind and its own desires, a fleshless symbiot. It is the dark twin to her bones.

BLOOD KISS *Daniel Stone*

It is invincible. You can step on the fucker or smash it with a hammer, but it will not move from its place until the light tells it to do so. The shadow is so demanding in the way it always wants to be next to you, behind you, *attached* to you.

You're never truly alone.

She sees it metamorphose. Across the red wall it goes, running beneath the sweaty bodies of rock singers, spilling hyssop water. It clatters against her beer bottle collection. *Hex* and *Heart of Darkness* hit the floor with a dark crunch. Tyria closes her eyes and counts to ten. But it did not vanish, so there was only one way to control it.

She's up on her feet—skull socks worn down to their last thread—and she chases her shadow like she has done since childhood. It spreads like the wings of an old black bird on the floor; she jumps on top of it, only to feel its snakeskin snap like rubber. It sails into another part of the room, making its own hideous music. The jigger filled with bone dust shivers and the metal plates etched with intricate Hindu deities cry in various languages; crystal dragons breathe glassy fire as the purple carving of ohm hums its gloaming enchantment.

Tyria shut off the stereo, focused all attention to her book collection. How many more books could she fit in here? Soon she'd be drowning in the dust that forms when one leaves a book unopened for months. Aleister Crowley caught her eye, then Charles Fort and Dostoyevsky. *Magick Without Tears* and *Book of the Damned;* below that a five-volume essay anthology about extraterrestrial phenomena called *DarkLore* opened by itself to a random page: "Eye Spirits."

Was it still watching her?

Though Adelaide had been complaining, space would never deter Tyria from buying books, especially when her own volume of self-published poetry sat on that shelf. *PrOsE to PrOpHeCy* was a 2012 failure she thought would be the best medium to get her art out to the public, a way to help people understand why her words could possibly drive them mad, or at least open their eyes wide enough to see that poetry was well and alive, even if it was declared long dead.

But self-publishing was just another business to drag creatives into a monetary hell. Books are the last things people want when they have video games, iPhones and television to choose from. Opening up a book these days is equivalent to digging your own social grave: no one understands the reader anymore.

But words, at least to Tyria, have not failed her. Words helped her forgive yesterday and accept today. But how many more years could she sweep it under the carpet? Many girls are victims of violence, but more so they are victims of silence. If you know someone being repeatedly hurt, that they have been scared into silence than you are doing them a disservice by not getting them help.

Now the shadow was gone; it no longer wanted to play, and so Tyria returned to writing a poem laced with blood and glory. She yawned, reached for a book, Anne Sexton's *Live or Die*. Poetry sank right down to the marrow in her bones. The book's company was soothing.

Tyria wanted a cigarette. She felt certain that tobacco had been the largest contributor as to why her voice was so deep, a voice that makes eyes wince, that makes air tremble; a voice that comes to a person who was born and bred into agony, someone who turned to screaming as a coping mechanism.

The cigarette was old and tasted like ash. And so she looked for fun of a different nature. The baggy Adelaide had left her was pure as Brooklyn. She saw crystals palely glowing, could feel the numbing of her tongue. This was Adelaide's finest trade, the only way she could make enough money for the two of them to survive. Spoken word poets cannot make ends meet, but drug dealers certainly can, especially when Brooklyn is always hungry for a spontaneous time.

Tyria took a bookend and smashed the bag, poured out the powder into a line and snorted. Snowflakes swelled into her head. Cocaine. It was the only drug that made her feel powerful. It snow-blinded the past and made Tyria's ex-

BLOOD KISS

istence worthy of actually existing. But cocaine is a trap. The high is so intense and short-lived that the user always comes back crawling for more.

At twenty-three she'd already exhausted all her teenage angst and frankly all her patience. The backs of her knees and wrists were a latticework of raised pink flesh from her cutting phase so that not even her intricate tattoos could hide them; the liquor dependency had faded to the cocaine habit and craft beer.

One indulges when one is lonely.

But it was not all her fault. Getting along with people was never her strong suit and holding down a conversation was always more work than fun. Most people wouldn't give her the time of day, and the ones who did claimed she was over-zealous, outspoken or rotting from the inside out. But never Adelaide. She was the only girl who understood Tyria.

The memories of the night they met had thinned over time, but Tyria could recall some images through the snowy blur. A poetry reading at a book store named Blue Stockings, brick and mortar haven for the punky, gothy, woe-is-me type that you don't hear about on social media or television. Tyria had worn her finest attire: a *House of Secrets* era Otep t-shirt and acid-green jeans that she had picked up from a vintage shoppe. The color of the jeans matched the streak in her hair and the ouroboros tattoo that encircled her left wrist.

"I know that," someone said from behind. "That's the eternal return."

Tyria saw black hair draped across lips as red as candy apple syrup. It was as if someone had drawn the girl with sidewalk chalk, then stuck a bad Halloween wig on her head. She was the most intriguing human that Tyria had ever seen, her eyes so black it reminded Tyria of Dario Argento's "Jenifer." The thing about people with Tyria was that she instantly hated them; deep inside she had built a wall to protect herself from giving away her trust too easily. But with Adelaide that wall came tumbling down.

"What do you know about the eternal return?" Tyria said.

"That the universe has been recurring, and will continue to recur, in a similar form an infinite number of times across time and space."

Respect granted. "I'm Tyria."

"Adelaide, but most people call me Addy."

They left Blue Stockings and hit up a local queer bar. The drinks flowed like honey and the flirting slowly morphed into the physical. Adelaide's tongue invaded Tyria's throat; she tasted cigarettes, hops and spice. Her hands were so knowing of the female body that Tyria's flesh suspended, automatically giving in to their sweet demand. It was like no touch, no kiss, no heart she had ever experienced.

Adelaide was the only girl who made all the wrongs of the world seem right. She believed in Tyria's talent almost immediately, began showing her off to all her friends, but most of all she gave Tyria a shoulder to cry on when she needed it. Though they were yin and yang, opposites in everything from clothes, piercings, to tattoos and music selection, they were truly, madly, deeply in love.

With no signs of stopping.

Tyria decided to write again, dipped her pen into the black reservoir and swiped it across her notebook. The ghost-gloom of ink mocked her, the well was very much dry, and now the fact that she might have to use a ballpoint pen grew infuriating. Tyria threw the quill to the other side of the room, black-feathered bullet.

A thought eclipsed her. She was sick of whining, sick of crying. It was time to make a change like Adelaide had said she should do a long time ago. Tyria would use her voice to propagate her choice. She would do something simple but poignant. An impromptu performance. Tyria grabbed her baggie of warm snow, her black Ray Bans and slipped on a pair of disintegrating sneakers.

Let's get ready to rumble.

BLOOD KISS

When I paint it feels more like an out-of-body experience. The mind I once controlled begins its kinky control of me. I am no longer a flesh and bone organism, yet I know that my cells are replicating and dying as they traverse the labyrinth of pale vessels. I can still feel my lungs soak in air like giant pink sponges; my brain throbs at excitement of a new idea.

But I am not myself.

Creativity seeds itself in the soil of my existence. What blossoms is more mysticism than reality. Senses change. I see with my hands and feel with my eyes; my tongue does not taste, but smells. I watch my hand grip the brush and move into the palette like chemistry. I draw with no mood or idea of what I want as I break the laws of color. I am a shadow, a bag of bones, stardust. I am seized into a stroke-like state.

"Are you in here?" I say.

The black hole eyes glisten and the lugubrious galaxies scream. I gaze into the mad gelatin movements of the lava lamps and fall into a psychedelic hypnosis. Grotesqueries spread into psychosexual patterns: squalid penises throb half-erect, torn vaginal lips demand to be kissed. When I do not oblige they drip a smelly stream of viscous urine in retort.

You might have made us but we will take you, I think I hear them say.

The muse is a mere germ in the garden of man and mind. It always changes. I begin to introspect. Acceptance is the hardest part of the ego to conquer; it is life's dénouement.

I thought of myriad ways to unify art, supernaturally and biologically. In my studio the walls are my personal palette; paint spreads about it like a plague. Sometimes I make my own paint. I have an acquaintance who takes people's blood for a living. She gives me butterfly needles and vacuum-sealed vials. *You have to sanitize your skin before each use*, she told me. But I do no such thing, for whatever disease lies within my epithelium must join the rich red party inside the vials. The one with the blue top thins the blood like oil paint and the gold top thickens it to the constancy of acrylic.

Some nights I use the local square as my cash flow. I fashion a big tent as if my own traveling gallery and hang art up on easels, some across the crummy table. I talk bullshit, I kiss major ass as Leland has taught me, and I manage to sometimes sell. The track marks that line my arm are turgescent, ugly, and they tend to magnetize the punkish runaway junkies whose eyes glow strangely. I am a man of vices; the respectable art crowds judge me.

When I get angry I party.

The children of the night flock to me like dark sheep blind to the shepherd. There is a small circle of art-fags that consider me their storybook leader, my very own children of the night. Not that I'm famous, not that they seek my advice, but we are like-minded and feed into each other: it is the assurance that someone will join them in the sorry game that life has in store as they suck down another bitter bottle.

Their pierced lips are wet with a child's desire to learn; their coprophilous tattoos run from shoulder to wrist. Sycophants, poseurs and trust-fund babies. Metal heads, punks and abusers. They're easy to win over. Drugs and craft beer are enough to stultify them with my worldview. Their minds are like sponges. They are lost souls draped in leather and wingtip boots who desire a leader, a lover, a friend.

Dark bars, taverns, and dives. Neon, craft beer, and stroboscopic light. Brooklyn, the Lower East Side, and Long Island City. We congregate. We crave revenge. We plot to conquer. We get nothing done.

BLOOD KISS *Daniel Stone*

In my apartment the vials are cold red bullets ready to be mixed into liquid vinyl. Mucus, semen and saliva add texture to paint; the clumps of hair I pulled out and dried by daylight are ground down to powder; the stardust I find in the streets give a gleam to my strangest portraits.

They let me know I'm never alone.

The floor chills unexpectedly and the brushes stand upright without so much as me touching them. The air is tainted with anger and there comes a dark static smell of living things so strong that I cannot bear it. I'm well aware of a greater force, but I've yet to witness its true evolution.

I write love notes so that it knows I see it, feel it, accept it. *WHAT DO YOU WANT?* is permanently scribbled across the moldy kitchen tile; *COME OUT! COME OUT!* is written in volatile longhand on my studio wall. *AM I YOUR VESSEL?* begs it to make contact.

I get back to work. I have nothing else to do and nowhere to go. I don't have a day job or any real responsibility. Like I said, I'm a loser by current societal standards. I'm out of cigarettes, but Leland might bring me some later. Until then, I'll work from my studio.

I unfold my triptych.

The first panel showcases an abyssal landscape flecked with the color of no color. I explore its depth with my mind's tongue; when I touch it a sudden vacuuming sensation takes over my hand, then clamps down. I know that if I'm to paint the abyss I must first to learn how to use the *color* of the abyss. But that little miracle still remains a mystery.

The second panel flourishes with masturbating mythological creatures; tumescent phalluses and drippy orifices. It's a rebel's version of reality, all without a cause. We don't appreciate sex in this country; we pretend it doesn't exist. A few minutes alone with this piece and one will find themselves turned on; the restrictive cotton of their clothing will become infuriating.

But it is the third panel that scares me the most.

The beginning of the end.

A bony paunch balances on chitinous legs; carrion arms spread as if inviting a passerby to sit within its darkly beaded depths; a slack-jaw skull screams with no voice; xylophone ribs glow like the most intricate spider webs under moonlight; a hand curled into a fist has no arm to support it.

Wet and lush as a kiss, it is my finest piece. Opinion would say it is too influenced by the surreal and the abstract, which makes it all the more confusing. The edges are dashed in black and the background is a never-ending swirl of silver, lapis lazuli, and shadow. The stars are eyes and they wink out fast as a butterfly's lifespan. Tell me what better way there is to show off the life of a star that is light years away, already dead before its ephemeral fire can touch the earth?

But it's all for good reasoning.

Like Fitzgerald wrote about the Jazz age I'm painting my own uninspired generation. I find that most people these days are fully disconnected from their souls, and I find it even scarier that they are perfectly fine with it. Follow the leader, play it safe. Don't rise above the law, just obey it. Perseverance? Does the principle exist?

It scares me to find out.

TYRIA HIT THE NIGHT AIR like a blade of starlight.

Ray Bans shielded her small jade eyes from the bright street lamps; kohl eyeliner dripped like sweat in the unmanageable heat. Feathery blonde hair swayed to the length of her angular face, skewing her vision of the world. The ripped band tank top she wore hadn't been washed in days and the black jeans were so tight they could be mistaken as desiccated flesh; a silver ohm necklace lay peacefully against her sternum.

Tyria's night vision was so sharp she could see as if it was daytime. But there was not much to see on Flushing Avenue. A graveyard of trucks and desolate group of stores; old tene-

BLOOD KISS Daniel Stone

ments refurbished into art studios; thrift shops enslaved to effulgent graffiti, party pin-ups, art galleries to support and rooms for rent.

Across the street hipsters fronted of a local dive called *Wreck Room*. The lush red glow of neon laved their twiggy bones and radical clothing, made their eyes a red web. Tyria saw leather and lace, Converses and Doc Marten boots, cigarette burns and beer in paper bags.

But on her side of the street it was rather lonely.

This part of Bushwick uses fear to empower curiosity, fear of not remaining safe inside the hipster hangouts or chatting with PBR groupies, or feasting upon the famous rice balls that melt butter-like in any drunken mouth from the Arancini Bros. This side of Flushing Avenue is safe; though just a few paces away you could easily become a victim of crime.

Tyria lit a hand-rolled cigarette and poured a fine white line along the ridge of her wrist, snorted it clean off and then drank back her Magic Hat Séance. The bump was amazingly pure. Hops and ripe fruit assaulted her tongue, washed down the dead flavor of the cocaine. She snorted the second bump off of her pinky nail, painted silver for effect.

The drug plowed into her skull and her chin began to jitter, tongue running endlessly across the labret piercing. She felt her pupils dilate. Steam practically shot out from her ears. But, she knew, it was time to show the world what she was all about.

Born in the visceral depths of being an outcast—be it your skin color, class, gender or sexual orientation—spoken word poetry came to be as a form of escape. Rhythmic and un-structured, the language used is more about slang melodies than straight-line reading. It was about letting go and translating the message to the masses because a poet's weapon is their words.

And so Tyria began to raise her voice in the middle of the street.

"I have something to say, and I don't request that you pay. My words are resistance to man's ignorance." Tyria spread her heavily tattooed arms wide. Thin muscles tensed; the sleeve of maniacally smiling caricatures swelled, the flames on her forearms glinted to life. She began the word-slam in her signature throaty voice that sounded as if she'd drunk a cup full of glass.

> *I am guilty of violence*
> *Yet still a victim of silence*
> *Evil has formed his alliance . . .*
> *In a bone yard to build my defiance*

The words shook in vibrato and lengthened like an echo. Each syllable popped as if falling stars. Tyria saw shades of yellow, rose, orchid red and eerie black. Behind her a shadow began to slither, nimble with premonition.

"I will not stay quiet. I will not feed from society's unhealthy diet."

A mass of oily hair marched toward the oral slaughter. Their eyes shimmered like insects in the dark. As they surrounded her Tyria caught the odors of patchouli and armpits, dirty feet. The smell of poverty.

It had been so long since she smiled naturally.

The gossip got louder and the curiosity thicker. Bodies jumped and heads nodded in unison. Skinny hands dug into pockets for money and moths. Coins flew at her like tiny diamonds, down into the wishing well of her mind. Pennies, quarters, and a half dollar, literally. Maybe they shared Tyria's story; maybe their lives were just as destructive. Maybe her poetry had reawakened something in them.

> *Umbilical lies tied me to this demise*
> *I am wasted, cast off like a parasite*
> *Deception is my only road to reflection*
> *Pain is the path to my resurrection*

By the time she hit the last line there came a natural flood of momentum. She hadn't felt this kind of useful rage

BLOOD KISS

in a very long time. Tyria clawed at her hair, her arms, as if something was coming over her. The duct tape holding her sneakers together gave way.

Blood surged into Tyria's throat and she let out a roar, so much like that first night he'd touched her where no father should ever touch his little girl; that first night she knew there would be many more nights of suffering. And so she let the animal out of the cage. The window to Catland shivered; the neon light of *Wreck Room* rippled like dripping blood.

"How could that sound come out of girl?" one young kid asked.

The crowd of ten began to sway wildly, throwing their flesh into one another. They became part of the show as much as they were patrons. A skinny girl took a hit to the face by a bony forearm; Tyria saw the blood glow black beneath the moonlight. Two wispy boys began to pull apart one another's clothes, their nails creating tiny little tracks in pale skin.

"Look what she did," said a mindless toad.

Tyria stopped screaming and caught her breath. The awed faces fell flat, eyes glazed in wonder. When she turned around her shadow was already filling the cracks in the glass. Silence followed, a few kids cackled, but she felt safe behind her Ray Bans.

"She's like magical or something . . ."

In the back of the crowd two kids argued. Their teeth were stained the ugly yellow of Parliament smoke and their hands rose in the air carelessly. *Performance art*, she heard. *I know a space*, the girl said. *Spoken word slam and a live canvas*, said the boy.

The moonlight turned them into creatures of silent black and white films as they made an exchange that looked like a drug deal. Skinny girl gave party boy a very serious looking book; they hugged and he split left as she turned right, barging through the crowd.

"There's more where that came from!" Hyping up the mystery as best she could. "See to it that you find out."

Familiar assertive snarl followed by a familiar peachy smell. Long, long dark hair and clothes so scrappy she could be mistaken for an Alphabet City squatter. Black dice in both eyebrows, green gauges in her ears, eyes so alien-bright they could blind you with one stare, and those soft, soft lips covered in rouge. Tyria had been worshiping them for two years.

Adelaide wrapped a skinny arm around Tyria and planted a deep girlish kiss on her lips that tasted faintly of rotgut. The rush of her girlfriend's touch illuminated her guts, made her feel embryonically safe.

"Out of our way, hipsters."

Adelaide made a few hand gestures to the crowd that only junkies would understand: you cross me and I won't sell to you. Junkies are easy to control. Dangle the baggies in front of their face and they will do anything in their power—sometimes more—to shoot it up, snort it, lick it, cook it in food. Anything. That was one thing that attracted Tyria to Adelaide: she had the natural capability to control a crowd, even if that crowd was a bunch of suckling little losers.

She thought about how Adelaide's principles always lived somewhere messily snug between the fringe and everyday normal life. The local art scene wasn't hardcore enough for her these days so she always threw art parties of her own. Her hunger for freedom of expression bordered on illusion.

Before they started walking away Tyria looked at Catland. It took her back to a time when she might have done the same thing with her voice, but the memory was blurred with blood and paralyzed by cocaine. She could only recall her hands steeped in a rich red sauce, the windows in her bedroom caved in as if broken with her bare hands, shadow slick below her little feet.

Then she heard the hoarse voice of her father . . .

"You're spacing out," Adelaide put a bogee between her lips. "You were a mess last night. Dreamed more violent than I've ever seen."

"When I dream, I dream *hard*."

BLOOD KISS Daniel Stone

"You're a natural," Adelaide said.

"It was time to speak up," gleam in her eyes like wet sugar.

"I knew one day you were going to mind-fuck these people."

"I'm sick of waiting for some miracle that doesn't fucking exist. God is dead. The sun lies and the moon is a cunt-whore."

They both walked arm in arm, set for a new kind of adventure. Their minds spiraled with the thrill of Tyria finally getting her words out to the people who wanted to hear it. The hardest part of any creative mission is convincing people that you actually *need* it as much as you claim.

You surrender your soul and your body for the stage.

But for now Adelaide's hand was entwined within hers, fingers the color of ice, nails black as beetles. Their cigarettes made angelic circles in the air. Life wasn't so bad when Tyria was with Adelaide. She could hardly remember how she survived before they'd met.

It was a harsh excuse for a warehouse. Boarded windows and glass sprinkled like a glittery carpet all the way to the front entrance; graffiti dripped fresh off the walls. But the J train was only a block away, which naturally attracted Brooklyn's worst.

RaBiD InTrIcAcIeS commanded the long silver banner, and on every table small red advertisements inked in charcoal. Tonight's theme the exploration of the unknown: fragments, entities and mutilations. Abyssal shadows and amorphic organs. There is no end and no beginning, just the construct of time: ruiner, death incarnate.

It was crowded inside. Perplexed faces swarmed and hands were pushed into pockets. I chivied past seersucker suits, hipster rags and costume jewelry. Their interpretations furiously bored me; their ideas of sustainable art relied too heavily on Google searches. Those who would not openly share their feelings busied themselves with stale cheese and cheap wine. Manischewitz.

"What the hell is this?" A troublemaker held up a bleeding finger. "The painting bit me."

"Clearly you can't read," Leland pointed to the DO NOT TOUCH sign.

Every corner a portrait was placed with the effect of carnival mirrors. I wanted them to mock the viewer, challenge them, assault their eyes.

BLOOD KISS *Daniel Stone*

"Is this the work of hypnotization?" A sullen lady said. "They have an attitude about them."

I snorted. "Is that all you see?"

"You're insane."

"But at least you *see* them."

The lady walked away and Leland frowned at my behavior. But I was all of a sudden filled with inspiration. I did another loop around the gallery. Everywhere I turned I knew that they were watching me. I was their catalyst no doubt, their creator, but that didn't mean I was not looking to sell them. I need to eat too, you sons of bitches.

I recalled a scene out of *The Picture of Dorian Gray*, how the man himself had locked the aging portrait in a secret room. Each time he entered he saw the cruel fate of his life's choices. What was once a budding flower of a man now looked haggard. It proceeded to drive him mad, and I like to think of my own paintings in that fashion: they might drive their owner mad.

"Hey," Leland said over the crowd. "Watch this."

Pointing to my immediate left, I stepped up on my tippy toes to see a man opening his checkbook and signing it with a silver pen. Both of them smiled contentiously; the deal was made. It was a small, decently priced portrait, a face swirling into itself, depending how long you looked at it.

The man chose his best wolf's smile. "I'm going to put this in my bedroom."

"Dorian's work is best hung in places of privacy."

"Do what you wish," I waved him off, focusing on my cigarette.

That's when the door slammed. Three girls had left, complaining about one of the first serious portraits I had ever made: a landscape of silver and black inspired by The Funhole—if you look hard enough at it your malevolent future might be revealed, so long as you can read the runes.

Two hours later the gallery was at full capacity. I drank more wine than I could stomach I was so bored. Leland introduced me to nameless faces and vacant bodies. I talked the talk and walked the walk. I smiled, nodded and pretended to care. It's what artists have to do if they want to sell.

Fake it until you make it.

That is, until you see something that catches your eye.

She seemed to shimmer and rot at the same time, her clothes hanging like strips of midnight. Yellow hair rippled across magnificent wrap around shades, and within them two eyes as green as jade stone. I sensed no pretense from this specimen, but I could not say the same of her companion. She was someone I had definitely met before; a girl that resembled what could only be a giant fang wearing a bunch of crow's feathers.

"You know who that is," Leland said.

"Not ringing a bell."

"What about her?" He pointed to the golden goddess.

I couldn't focus on what Leland was trying to tell me. The pale haired wraith demanded my full attention. I watched her scan my work uneasily, her moonface in serious thought. I noticed her jaw rapidly moving back and forth and a dab of powder at the corner of her nose. I saw tattoos odd and forsaken as my own.

Her female companion focused on a portrait of meat hooks; it seemed to speak volumes to her. And then she reached her hand out to touch it, only to be splattered by red acrylic. The sound she made was that of horror and repulsion as if what had just happened was the work of witchery. I walked as close as I could to not seem like a creep before her black eyes caught my own.

"Dangerous Dorian," she said. "It's been forever."

I could never forget that nickname. "Adelaide?"

"In the flesh."

"You've put on a little weight. It's been—"

She flipped me the bird. "Three years. Wasn't it sort of a night like this?"

"That's surely a time I want to forget," I felt myself getting angry.

BLOOD KISS

"Don't bring up bad times," Leland said. "Things have changed."

"From what I remember the only thing you two had in common was the needle," pointing to the crook of my arm.

"Looks like you've been busy as well," Adelaide said.

"Constructive wounds. Not like your useless abuse."

Adelaide looked at Leland. "Seriously? I didn't come here for this."

"She gave it up," Leland said to me. "Only sells it now."

Adelaide sighed. "I do like your work," she told me. "You've grown as an artist. The crowd seems to be spending and that's what I *really* like."

"Are you buying?"

"I'm making sure that what I'm looking at is the real deal. Tyria too."

Strange name for a strange girl. It gave me a momentous high. I admired how in one hand she held a spiral bound notebook and in the other a chewed pen. I watched her as she set it down on a table and lit a cigarette despite the unnerving New York City law about smoking indoors. That was a girl I wanted to learn more about. She expelled this powerful presence without even trying.

"I never paint for the sake of painting," I said.

"You had an attitude then, and you still have one now," Adelaide said.

"I've nothing to prove to you."

Adelaide sucked her teeth. "Actually you might."

"What do you mean, I might?"

Adelaide turned toward a nervous looking Leland. "He hasn't changed a day in his life, Landy. I don't think this is a good idea."

"But there's gold in our hands," Leland's fox grin so beautiful.

"What are you talking about?" I said to both of them.

"You'll *never* open your eyes up to see. You'll never know what it *is* to actually feel," Adelaide hissed.

"My art is—"

"Literally a *piece* of you. Don't look at me that way. You think I don't get it? You think I'm not good enough for your exclusive club?"

Her understanding stunned me. "Art is my sacred duty."

"I know how it can . . . make a room feel *very* eerie," Adelaide scratched her head. "Just standing here skeeves me out. Feels like they're *watching* me."

Leland cut in. "Dorian's work is an amalgamation. Limbs and torsos, downward spirals. Nothing is at any considerable stage of gestation or desecration. Inorganic mutations, devolution . . ."

Adelaide looked stunned. I felt my eyebrows go up, tapped my septum piercing on my wine cup. This is why I loved him. Leland *knew* without ever asking.

"I don't do it on purpose," I said.

Adelaide pointed to the princess in black. "And neither does she."

"Your girlfriend?" I asked.

"Yes. And her poetry will knock you off your feet."

"Introduce me to her," I said.

Adelaide's eyes narrowed. Suspicion behind them. Or jealousy. "Maybe some other time . . ."

Leland's eyes blazed black as coals. He stopped Adelaide short, but she would not hear him out. *She's tired*, I heard her say. *I have to make sure before we can commit.* Leland pulled at his hair and said *then why did you bring her here?* as he walked away to satisfy another client. I watched Adelaide scoop Tyria up into her skinny arms, whose face melted into pleasantries that were nice to see. True love can never die.

"Would've been nice if you two could've been introduced," Leland said.

"That Addy is still a regular old pistol."

"She is, but I love her anyway."

"When did you two start hanging out again?"

Leland shrugged. "We've been on and off, but somehow we always pick up where we left off. Our friendship is weird like that."

BLOOD KISS *Daniel Stone*

The girls out the door now, leaving behind their entwined smell of grease vapors, bad attitudes and cigarette smoke. It was then I spotted the book Tyria had been carrying atop a table, and the closer I came to it the more I wanted to open the thing and read it. *Poetry*, I remembered. In my hands, ready to crumble; the spirals were beginning to uncoil. I cradled it like a newborn, waiting for Tyria to come back and claim her private thoughts.

But she never did.

TYRIA'S DREAMS ARE NOT CONSTRICTED *to the storybook rules of sleep, and so she has given up trying to avoid them. If dreams feed from weakness rather than strength, is there really any point in trying to fight? Memories are forever; scars are what you have to show for them.*

This is how it always begins.

Rows of crumbling Brooklyn tenements jut like an arcane smile. People careen with beer on their breath; crack pipes wind through dirty fingers. They are disconnected from the world and too uninspired to change their ways. Poverty is the law of the land.

But then the world unhinges from its constrictive angles of physics. She is no longer a being bound by chemicals and law. Tyria soars above the candy-colored lights of the city with her eyes closed, a wingless bird to be shot down. When she opens them next she is in a place that she wants to forget, one of mirrors that reflect every memory she has ever rejected, everything she has been running away from since she's had the power to do such.

But Tyria knows that there is a time in everyone's life when they must make sense of the past. To conquer the moment that changes you—the moment where destiny becomes insipid reality—one must accept it. The cruelty of the world becomes smaller. Sustenance is the only way out.

Consider the anamorphosis of a little girl. Once upon a time she could smile, pretend and forget. Once upon a time trust was taken for granted; once upon a time family was everything. Bloodlines are supposed to take care of you, tuck you safely into bed, treat you right and never let you feel scared.

But it was a lie from birth.

Tyria's big comedown is called menstruation. Everything that is playful and delicate is replaced by judgment of character. A big black line drawn between gender, sex and childhood. At the switch of the biological clock she is suddenly a woman and expectations begin to degrade, replace, and erase her.

The womb is her infection and the warm red trickle between her thighs is the poison. The sore, budding tits and widening hips make her nature's whore. Suddenly innocent colors take on horrible connotations: pink is the color of her anatomy and purple the wrinkled lips that fold over it.

Eve fucked it up for all girls. The bitter apple breeds their disease.

In this dream Tyria Vane is eleven-years-old. She is sitting at the open window in her firetrap apartment. The city is alive with demise and the timorous sky wants to eat the streets below. The wind smells of rain and smog; the shadows from the alleyways come closer. And it still sounds like Doom out there.

She closes the window and falls back into the faded copy of L. Frank Baum's The Wonderful Wizard of Oz. Tyria absently flips through it, sees her notes scrawled across the pages. This is the book that opens her mind to the possibility of fantasy becoming reality if you wish for it hard enough. Mommy always says good girls get what they want. Maybe she if she taps her sneakers she will find a new home.

There has been no running water or electricity for three days. The roaches come out to play on these warm nights, fat black land mines; and the rats still claw at the wall behind her closet. Daddy says that the bills have been too high and that the money has not been coming in. Mommy can't take a job because Daddy says a proper woman needs to be home and care for the family.

And so Tyria reads by candlelight, road openers, Van Van and Blockbusters. A whole bunch of them on the windowsill and the glow against her hair mimics the color of dandelions; the shadows they

BLOOD KISS *Daniel Stone*

throw hide the bruises. The smell of them is like a clean slate, like opening the road to destiny.

Tyria thinks about going outside for a long walk, something to clear her mind. She assembles herself: a vintage t-shirt that smells like mothballs and jeans ripped at the knee. But then there is the sound of thunder, and the sky filling with veiny lights.

They are fighting again.

She wishes for them to stop once, twice, three times. Stop! Stop! Stop! And it is this moment when the shadow unhinges itself, a black skin shaped like her own bones. It wants attention, affection. For one delicious second it takes away the pain in her belly and the red wetness from between her legs. Why do girls have to undergo this punishment? Mommy said this would happen. Daddy said he'd be back when it did.

Louder now, vibrant through the thin walls. What follows is the crash of cassette tapes, the glass crunch of ceramic dishes. Her mother shrieks. Don't you fucking touch me! Tyria can do nothing, helpless until the final clap of fist to flesh silences her mother.

Tyria puts her hands on her ears and screams until she tastes blood.

In the aftermath Tyria sticks her hand into the darkness. She wonders if it will ever talk to her, wonders if one day she can simply trade places with it. What a life it would be to live in shadow, tucked safely away from all those that plan to hurt you.

The chase begins.

To her it was not about being crazy. She read about it in Peter Pan so many times. All she wants is to reattach it to her body, because the shadow is your first friend and will be your last. It was there when you were born and will be there with you in the coffin.

In her chase she knocks into the old boom box and Fleetwood Mac's Tusk sizzles out of the speakers. She can see the music pull itself off the instruments, can feel the vocal melodies rip into her like poetry. This is the first time it happens, the kaleidoscope colors, each syllable a shade of blue and red, each strum of the guitar a blueprint madness. Her own personal Wonderland.

But the shadow is still on the loose. Books hit the floor and the window shakes as it slides up the wall. A green Open Road candle spills its wax, the first sign of a bad hex. Finally, at the foot of her

bedroom door, her shadow strangely concedes defeat and is successfully reattached her feet; Tyria is surprised at how much weight
it bears, how cold it is.

Then the door slowly creaks open.

Another presence comes through.

Tall, dark and lanky. Eyes like hungry voids. He smells of laziness
and the sour amber of Wild Turkey whiskey. Tyria vicariously tastes
the liquid burn. She freezes in her tracks as he takes a step forward.

"Been runnin' around when I asked you to be quiet,"
Daddy says.

"Just trying to clean," a sweet little lie.

"You lying again," and she sees his five o' clock shadow, how
tired he looks, preemptively guilty.

"I'm sorry," and she leans on a pile of books for support.

"I told your mother to get rid of them," pointing at the
books. "And lower that hocus-pocus music."

Tyria acquiesces, even though she knows that once the music is
turned off all of those beautiful colors will die. Now Daddy sits on her
bed and removes his dirty shirt to reveal his scrawny form. His chest
has a light dusting of hair that is pale even in the darkest parts of the
room. Tyria can do nothing but stand frozen in terror, angst; any
innocence she had in her body would soon be lost.

"Take off your pants and your shirt," Daddy says. "Gunna
clean you up."

"No," the word comes out so fast she can't stand it herself.

Daddy's face changes, like something had come from hell and
pulled down his skin. He grabs Tyria by the arm hard enough to pop
the socket, doesn't stop pulling until she gives in. In this moment
Tyria feels a new kind of pain, the unhealthy stretch of fibers, a fire
in her joints.

"Do what I say when I say it!" he rumbles and roars.

Part of the problem with control is that the control freak craves
too much, and when they can't have it all they become crazier. Tyria
knew that Mommy only made it worse when she tried to defy Daddy.
The trick with abusers is to give in to their demands because the
consequences of evasion are far greater than that of consenting. If

BLOOD KISS

you challenge them they only want to hurt you more, and that will render them guilt free because you asked for it.

"This will only hurt for a minute."

Sweat like rotten rain; his smile empty. Her body shaking—he likes it that way—her shirt off, and then her pants. Now she is on the bed with her back to the sheets and her face to the ceiling. She focuses on the stars she's pinned there, wishing that they would save her like the storybooks say. But it is a useless distraction as his spit-greased finger grinds into her. Something like the ghost of pain, or the miscommunication of sensory receptors, makes everything shimmer.

There is this terrible feeling in her chest. Her mouth gawks and out comes a sound like an asteroid hitting into ice. It is the death of innocence and ignorance. It is war against betraying humanity as the world is suddenly colored in thin streams of red, until she is screaming so loud that the window blows clean out of the frame.

TWILIGHT.

Golden moment of reflection. Time not ticking but dripping; light from the sky sticky against the streets.

I awoke with a sore throat and the taste of blood on my palate; I'd been screaming in my sleep. When I ripped my head off the desk there lay a glittering puddle of sweat like a new kind of paint. I found that it made my morning pulse rise, made me fully aware that I could not shake the tantalizing smells of poison and darkness. But I longed to find meaning in it.

I drew furiously.

My hand dabbling in ink like witchcraft. A paper catastrophe slashed in black and gold and jade. My nightmare brought to life before me: boiling mushroom clouds, a galactic helter-skelter of slime and ash. So alive was this demise. My fingers suddenly bleeding and my wrist twisting to snap in order to complete the tawdry lines and red clots of clouds.

A hand reached out and smeared gore down my face. Smoke darkened my view, but through it I could see the lurching bodies. How cliché for me to be drawing the apocalypse . . . but the dead are not stupid and slow as you would think. They roam elegant and synchronized as a dark art. I saw a gang of them ripping into a passerby; they made horrible music with his bones. A woman cried in pain as her baby suckled. Dark strips of flesh filled the tiny mouth; pale blood marked its lips.

It helped me realize how easy it is to evolve from infancy to cruelty.

When I left my desk I rushed to the window in hopes to see some carnage, or at least a sky roiling with chemical plague. All I found was the same ugly Brooklyn streets that have done nothing but brood, its concrete tongue lapping at the East River.

The same city cursed by a different ray of light.

I sat for three hours not caring about nourishment or going to the bathroom (showering wasn't even an option). I watched the sun burn out like an ancient light bulb, let its rays warm my face and sticky hands. It would have been wise of me to start my day, but I had been invaded by one thought: Tyria.

I wiped the sweat off my brow, forced myself up on broomstick legs and attempted to eat a pathetic almond butter sandwich, but soon lost my appetite when I saw it. The sight struck me as forceful, yet rather odd; I hadn't realized how violent my nightmare was. *WILL I FIND MY WAY?* scratched deep into the painted window. A lost twinge of pain found my hands, and that's when I saw black caked under my nails, smelled the drying blood.

I threw the sandwich on the table, pushed my sketch onto the floor and chugged from the bottle of Stolichnaya. Warm vodka is heinous and should be illegal in the way it dries your throat and tears apart your insides. I decided to sweat it out instead, bathe in the juices of fear; let it trickle between my teeth.

BLOOD KISS

It had been a while since I consulted a mirror, but I thought it a fancy thing to do at this hour of the day. For the first time in a long time I was able to see my own tattoos in a light that made them seem more painted on than tattooed. Neat little funguses growing from my skin, and the sweat made them appear gelatinous, wet with desire.

The razor-brush dripped blood; the psychedelic easels shimmered; haunting musical notes fluttered as gently as moth wings. I wanted more ink and more piercings. I played with the septum in my nose, twisted the bar in my eyebrow and ran my fingers through the gauges in my ears.

Then I heard a knock. Before I could even will the person away the door was creaking open. Before me a scarecrow skinny body, eyes so black they could be mistaken for lumps of coal. Less malignant spirit and more hungover party monster. I knew the smell of that boy-sweat before I made sense of the filthy auburn hair concealed beneath a green snapback cap.

"You should straighten up," pointing to the endless clutter.

"Come *here*," I said.

Like clockwork—like knowing sex is the only thing in life that really matters—Leland ripped off his shirt and straddled my lap. I latched onto his flower petal lips, sailed my tongue down his chin. We found no reason to stop, no reason to allow the world to tell us our love was sin.

I realized that in this society we rely heavily on gender preferences, even if we render one form superior to the other. On a sexually appealing level Leland was that of a god. His ribs are like piano keys and his stomach is hard as a slab of marble. Pity his pierced nipples are too delicate to bite.

"Dorian, when's the last time you showered?"

"Two days ago."

"Smells like it."

Voice scarred by cigarettes and lack of sleep. Tobacco was Leland's main vice. When I stay home to draw he goes out to party. I pictured him huddled with his club queen friends strung out on GHB and creating clotted clouds of smoke in the cold October night. Their conversations would be mind-less, their tongues practically numb, but their needs would be plausible: sex, drugs and rock n' roll.

"I was so fucked the other night," he said.

"But you managed to sell a few of my pieces."

"Yes, though you're a strange sell, Dorian Wilde."

Bitchy, bitchy boy I have. I hated when he used my last name. It meant he wasn't in a playful mood.

"Hey—"

"But it's a good thing."

We stayed silent for a moment. I breathed in the air he breathed out.

"Too bad you couldn't talk to Tyria," he said.

"What's her deal anyway?"

"I don't really know her."

"Then why do you want us to meet?"

"Why not introduce two talented artists to one another? You might learn thing or two."

He lit a cigarette and placed it in an ashtray shaped like the ace of spades. We moved onto the next order of business without words. Something in me was raging. His dark jeans were already unzipped, and so I pulled them off easily. In his tight green underwear now, and I cocked my eyes perversely toward his boner, a holy gift between the hairless slide of his thighs. Morning sex was our wake up call, or call of duty.

"Let's make it quick," Leland said.

I am something ravenous after a nightmare. If I don't paint away the angst with art, I fuck it until it bleeds. I extricated my mind from responsibility, ran my hands up Leland's knobby spine. He put his arms around me softly, looked at me dead in the eye. His presence alone intoxicated me.

"You're different today," he said. "What are you thinking about?"

I ignored him, thrusting my pelvis into his ass. The delicate grind of his bones was heartbreaking; the weight of him atop me was pleasure and pain. We kissed with our eyes

BLOOD KISS *Daniel Stone*

closed. Our torsos melded, forming a language of lust that only two men could understand.

The rhythm of same-sex couples is more natural than any breeder would have you believe. Homosexuals don't need to inquire about tender spots; we are aware of our lover's body because we literally are in that body. To share the same anatomy is to almost share the same brain; we know the limits of our own meat, *understand* it.

Society might deem anal sex sodomy but it is the crux of male/male fornication. There is a walnut-sized gland just a few inches up every man's ass called the prostate—it is where the seed of sinful titillation lies—and so naturally we deem it a hedonistic practice the moment we prod it. Ask any straight man who receives a regular blowjob and he will turn red as he knows he might have once asked his girlfriend to slip a finger or two up his asshole.

"Stop thinking." Leland looked at me fiercely. "It slows you down."

I seized the back of his neck and shoved my tongue between his lips. We began to gyrate, bones into bones. Leland is a fierce nelly-bottom without reservation or constriction. It pains me to refuse him. In the heat of the moment I ripped his underwear in two; he gripped my hands in that soft-but-deadly way that made me fall in love with him: patience gets you between these legs, foreplay wins you the fleshy prize.

My cock raged. His hands sailed down my biceps; his tongue found mine in a wet explosion, forcing me to nearly fall out of my chair. His teeth tugged my lip until it bled. Gooseflesh pricked Leland's skin as I licked him from his smooth armpits to navel.

Then I saw that green underwear whisper off his legs and his cock come alive like the house of the rising sun. His scrotum sagged to the weight of his testicles. I lifted his hips so I could get my face between his fairy-winged legs. I felt the muscle between his balls and ass tense as I traced my tongue down to his sweaty pink hole.

I greased myself.

As Leland's sphincter accepted my cock I felt a strange warm sensation. His intestine pullulated. Something like electric and fire lit from my dick all the way to my brain as our bodies became one knotty tangle of flesh. When I came I howled; Leland pulled himself free and a white worm dribbled down his strong thigh. All those babies dead, all that potent passion exorcised.

We lay in heat and sweat. Leland brushed my knotty black hair behind my ears and then ran to the shower. In the mirror I saw him fade to black. I drifted off to sleep and did not dream. When I woke up I smelled the mingled scents of Arabica coffee, vanilla extract and whiskey. I lazily made my way to the kitchen, walking zombie-like in my early morning state of mind. Leland greeted me with a golden smile, then sat me down at the table where he laid out a luxurious breakfast of French toast and a special bourbon syrup.

"Are you trying to get me drunk this early?" I said.

Leland smirked. "It's five o' clock somewhere, right?"

I sat down at the table, to which I noticed there was a thin white vase with a single dandelion wilting towards me. I touched the velvet petals, squeezed them for its pollen, then sprinkled it on my French toast so that it was now dusted in yellow. Leland served my coffee black and my bourbon syrup very warm.

"I wanna talk about something."

I winced; this was immediate danger. "What did I do now?"

"Nothing. I just have an idea."

"You always do," I said after taking my first delightful bite. "Wow, this is good."

Leland took the seat next to me, placed his hands on my lap. "So . . . you're okay with me doing this; setting you up blind."

"Yeah, what do I have to lose?" My second bite was even more addicting. "This syrup is incredible."

"I knew you'd like it, Alchy!"

"Am I supposed to ask you questions about it?"

BLOOD KISS

"No," Leland said. "I don't expect that from you."

Leland kissed me goodbye and got right on his cell phone. I heard him talking through the walls as he was leaving, something about a painter and poet, landscape and prose. I fell in love with Leland all over again, mostly because he'd left behind an avant-garde advertisement that scared the hell out of me.

After that I went back to my room and curled myself into a ball on the bed. Being alone is dangerous for me. It leaves me to my own heinous thoughts. I heard susurrus and felt a queer vibration, like a heart beating its last beat. I looked over my shoulder and realized that it was the triptych staring me down . . . feeling needy. I turned my head away, stared into the dark. But what stared back at me was a head of yellow hair, a sharp pale face, and below the brow a dangerous glimmer of jade eyes.

4

A change in the weather, colder this week so that jackets, gloves and beanies became a necessity. Though summer thunder was nascent, the smell in the air was that of frost, the season's first threat of snow clear as the glowering clouds. The electric zap of neon was the only star in the sky.

Adelaide watched pedestrians scatter like sprinkles into cabs and subway stations. She took a shortcut through the neighborhood, undecided where she wanted to head to at first, then succumbed to the city's tunneled hell. She and Tyria waited quietly for the train, eyes fixed on the silly advertisements. So many ideas, so many ways there were to sell people. *Welcome to her Nightmare.* They boarded the number 6 and took a seat, Tyria's head on her shoulder, gloved hand resting on her lap.

Twenty minutes later the 6 train arrived at Astor Place. Tyria went out first, launching herself over the turnstile. A tongue of wind curled her hair, made the city stir slowly as soup. There came the sound of dripping musical notes and clinging beer cans, followed by a smoky clot of trucks. Adelaide smelled cinnamon and the viscous glaze of barbecue sauce.

"If this is the smell of hell, I don't welcome heaven at all," Tyria said.

"This part of the city is hardly hell anymore."

They were not teenagers, not by a long shot, but were hardly adults. Their insomniac lifestyle made their faces cadaverous; drugs only enhanced the look. Their style of dress hung dying in limbo, clothes so dark they could only have been fashioned from the absence of light. No smiles could be found upon their faces, but their eyes spoke of great things to come.

"I can't find my notebook," Tyria said.

"It's probably under your pillow, like always."

"I never misplace it. You know that."

Truth was that Adelaide hadn't seen it since the night of Dorian's gallery. Had he taken it? No, she didn't want to think of Tyria's reaction if some stranger's prying eyes were devouring her private thoughts, especially that of a man! She lit a hand-rolled cigarette, bright slash of light on the already bright streets, and took three hits trying not to think what consequences could arise. Who would she blame? Would she be up to even being in the same room as Dorian if this were so?

"Why are you so quiet?" Tyria's hand craned out to take a pull.

"Thinking . . . planning," Adelaide said.

"Yeah, but about what? You've been with Leland the past few days. I don't like surprises, so out with it!"

Adelaide stopped, looked at a graffiti tag on the adjacent brick wall. Tears filled her eyes, and Tyria wiped them away, rubbed the black liner into her jacket.

"What do you think about that?"

Tyria looked upon it with disgust. A tornado of uninspired words, unnecessary swirls in white, grey and yellow.

"You mean like, what do I feel it means?"

"I wasn't asking for your interpretation. I was asking if you liked it."

"Does it make you emotional?" Tyria asked. "I've never seen you cry over graffiti."

"What I mean is would you want to be part of something? Something *huge*."

Tyria smoked Adelaide's cigarette down to ashes. "I want to be part of something in this world, yes, but I just don't know what it is yet."

"You knew it out there on Flushing Avenue. You knew it when those words fell from your lips. Your voice, your choice."

"All I knew in that moment was that I was tired of being broke, tired of sitting around thinking and not acting. I want to perform, I want my words out there."

"So how do you feel about a collaboration?"

"I don't know what you're getting at," Tyria said.

"Imagine the music of instruments not yet invented, or a medium of art not yet pursued. Something so niche even the hipsters wouldn't like it."

Tyria scowled. "Why be part of something you can't share?"

"Because it will be yours, all yours, for you to manipulate, dissect, dictate, to murder or to create."

"You've been reading from my bookshelf I take it."

"I know that you're going to be big," Adelaide said. "We just need the right crowd to hear you."

"They don't want to hear me," Tyria said.

"Yes, they do."

"They think I'm crazy, outspoken, derivative."

"Derivative? Please. You're an original. A walking freak show."

"The freak show was at Dorian's gallery. If people think I'm insane, they need to simply look at one of his pieces and—"

Adelaide cut in. "Dorian is a goddamn cynic . . . but a genius with the paintbrush," dark hair covering her face, and Tyria brushed it back to kiss her. "I just wish he was normal enough to talk to."

"Artists aren't usually the most approachable people. They spend most of their time alone."

"Still, the idea of the both of you coming together and making something . . ."

"Is that why you wanted me to go to the gallery so badly?"

"Yes, but he was just as arrogant as I remembered."

BLOOD KISS *Daniel Stone*

"You looked at him as if he was the bubonic plague incarnate," Tyria said.

"He's an egotistical, narcissistic, members-only kind of artist. Dorian is tormented because he knows that no one will ever understand his work, but he also gets off to that."

"So what?" Tyria said, lighting a new cigarette.

"I guess you're right. He just makes me so mad."

Sailing down Bowery Adelaide thought about the start of their night. They pulled themselves out of a painful sleep to a PBR breakfast and a small prayer filled with sage smoke and Open Road candles. Best to start your day with a good flow of energy. Outside, Flushing Avenue was graveyard grim, a premonition of the things to come. Adelaide scoffed at the sights before her; Tyria focused on fixing her shoelaces. Sometimes, one can only marvel at the way a town can change before your very eyes.

A decade ago East Williamsburg was a certified shit-hole that no one wanted anything to do with. Today it was more crowded and more upscale than ever. Food trucks littered a once desolate Bogart Street; a too-bright liquor store spills light as if a rising sun; pseudo-vegan restaurants with fancy wood paneling took the place of local art.

They stopped at a food truck and purchased tacos. Vegetarian for Tyria and meat-lover for Adelaide. Tyria ate hers fast, but it took Adelaide a few bites as she remained distracted by a row of gutted brownstones being refurbished for the new money moving in. The "big business" culture of Manhattan had finally sunk its teeth into Brooklyn. Even though New York City is a place that thrives off of change—you get decades of prosperity just as much as poverty—it still hurt to see it.

Adelaide was well aware of the schedule of trends, and she wanted nothing more than to make a subterranean revolution of her own. She knew enough people to support a start-up, had the connections one needed to attract people. Those friends might be fake, a few might be real, but they would come at her beckon, and they would pay.

Drugs facilitated this process. The exchange would be rather simple. One transient tells the next, and before you know it another fiend is fighting for his place in line. Marketing done right. Word of mouth spread fast as the lice in this part of town, something she knew from past experience. It almost worried her about who would be the dominant group supporting her new plan, the junkies or the transients. The two are extremely different degrees of human scum: the transient is able to function with or without the drug; the junky cannot function with or without the drug.

"Have you any idea where you're taking me," Tyria said, butting out her cigarette on the cement.

"Of course, my love. Have faith in me."

They boarded the L train at Morgan Avenue. Adelaide began to sweat immediately; smudged makeup and naturally curled hair. The station was practically empty, and so Tyria stuck her head out, testing the darkness that surrounded them. Tyria nodded, grabbed her ohm necklace. Had something looked back at her? Something like a shadow.

"Fucking rats!" Tyria said.

Alas, nothing supernatural. The crazy black bodies darted for a place to hide from the oncoming train. When Tyria gave up yelling she lit a smoke even though it was illegal to do such down here. Adelaide took it away and put it out against the wall to the relief of the woman standing with her purse clutched white-knuckle tight to her body.

Tyria could not be blamed for her sickeningly selfish ways. You can't possibly slide into adulthood when your tormented childhood is still with you every day. You break the law or break someone's heart; you do it to just do it. You find yourself in irrational situations pulling off irrational stunts or taking useless drugs to halt reality; you kill yourself to live. In fact, it was with a great sigh of relief that Tyria had yet to confide in suicide like so many girls have done in the past.

"I'm thinking about revolutions," Adelaide said.

BLOOD KISS

"I *want* them to hear me," Tyria took the Ray Bans off her face and pierced Adelaide with her alien-green eyes. "I want to be *understood*."

Adelaide adored her eyes. "You and Dorian are alike in many ways."

"No. I'm alone in this big bad world."

When the train came Tyria fell asleep as quick as she found a seat. Adelaide saw a small dab of powder by her nostril and wondered how anyone could sleep with coke in his or her system. Regardless, she pulled Tyria's uneasy bones into her, saw the ink on her arms become carnival bright beneath the fluorescence. Adelaide knew it was her job to protect Tyria.

I won't leave you. Not even at the end of time.

This brought Leland to mind. Adelaide and Leland had the kind of friendship that defied separation by borders or by time, and so whenever they became united in the same room they picked up like time had stood still. They believed only in each other, especially now that they were sliding into the next phase of their friendship: building a business. Adelaide trusted Leland's hunger to make money, trusted his drive to succeed.

He had told her to gather everything they would need, all the ingredients for a spooky time. In the back room of Catland some kind of metaphysical ritual was taking place; there was the smell of frankincense, hyssop tea; skinny bodies encircled strange organic offerings. Eggs for fertility, pennyroyal for prosperity.

Adelaide packed a bag. Shredded paperbacks; Anne Sexton and Angela Carter; a bundle of sage, sweet grass and two neon lighters. All the magickal ephemera that Tyria had been using since they met.

"Got them free at the Mabon celebration," Adelaide had said.

Now they were ready to make war with art as Adelaide fell back into reality. A playground of posh hotels painstakingly sparkled; artists and stoners careened while the transplants took for granted the smile that comes so easily to them.

Adelaide found the address on the corner of Spring Street, a wide and ugly Renaissance Revival piercing the ugly sky. Before her was the elaborate scrollwork of the chéneau; stone gargoyles perched downward as if on the attack. Tuscan columns painted in pollution flanked the heavy metal door.

"A squatter hang out," Tyria said.

"I thought it might add authenticity."

Tyria ran her hands across the rusticated stonework, trying to feel the sentiment behind all the graffiti. White bubble letters, tags like *BAM* and *POET* and *ALONE*. A photo-negative of a sad looking old man; a boom box exploding with the sound of music.

"Wasn't this place a bank?" Tyria asked.

"Decades ago, but now it's owned by an artist."

The pillar candles in the windows reflected the shadows of plague masks and tentacles.

"Looks fucking cool," Tyria said.

As they approached the front door Adelaide nearly lost her breath. She could not believe Leland went this far without asking her. Tyria's eyes caught the advertisements before she could explain. Anamorphic creatures and bones, words dragged across. Not just any words, but Tyria's words! And then the title.

SyNeRgY: an alternative mix of poetry and art.

A hectic sound erupted from Tyria's throat. She pulled at her hair, smacked her own face. If not that, maybe Adelaide.

"Why did he do it to me?" Tyria howled.

At the height of Tyria's throaty protest the clouds began to part. A pale tongue of moonlight licked the street, bringing urchins out of the shadows. Long hair and the smell of beer wafted. Kohl rimmed eyes scanned Adelaide; pink tongues licked their lips hungrily for drugs. Adelaide willed them away and opened the front door.

BLOOD KISS

A Venetian mask appeared. Adelaide became startled and looked to Tyria for protection, but she was in her own world. That's when Adelaide noticed how different Tyria looked in the dark, that she took on a glow, was almost the color of starlight itself.

"Did I scare you?" Leland removed the mask and revealed himself.

"You creep," Adelaide said.

Skinny jeans ripped at the knees, wing-tipped boots and a pinstriped shirt that looked painted on. Curly hair and a smile sweeter than sugar.

"You didn't answer my question," Leland looked at Tyria.

"No," Tyria said with no emotion.

"Be nice," Adelaide said.

"It's not a problem. I have one of my own at home," Leland winked.

Tyria almost smiled, but failed. "Am I a dog?"

"Won't you come in?" Leland opened the door so that a cloud of dust swirled around them. "We've much to talk about."

I FOUND MYSELF INTROSPECTING at dangerous levels.

Why do we exist? Who is G – D? Is art the only salvation? Why were my days getting dimmer and my nights more vibrant? Tequila quelled the confusion, but mostly the boredom, yet I remained uneasy and filled with a fear a loathing. I fell back asleep, and when I woke my lips were still puckered around the tip of the bottle, my gums numb and my tongue sizzling.

I smoked a cigarette, marveling the power that nicotine had over me. There really was no reason to stop as I did not fear death or debilitating disease. On the last pull I wondered where Leland was; his menacing scent was everywhere. I felt heat rise from between my legs; I touched myself as every cell in my body yearned for him. Those lips and velvet tongue; his smooth thighs opening to my beckon and imprisoning me to his love. I wanted his body next to mine, but all I had was a ghost in the sheets.

At twilight the sky turned the color of a bruise. I watched *Donnie Darko*, curled up with an old blanket, a pack of smokes and two Dog Fish Head IPAs. Movie nights are so inspiring. I realized that no matter how many times I had seen it Frank the Rabbit still scared me, and I wanted to be the only one who could hear Grandma Death's whisper.

After the movie I leafed through some books. Harlan Ellison, and Le Fanu . . . but mostly Fitzgerald. I became weirded out by Ellison's prose and frightened by Le Fanu's ghosts, but Fitzgerald fixed all my feelings, replacing the weariness with Jazz music and flappers. Reading puts me in a neutral state of mind; its sex that turns me into the madman.

Being alone makes one realize how they crave the flesh of another. And so I took out my frustrations in my sketch-book, ideas twining out of the softest spot in my conscience. I had drawn a naughty thing, I wanted to destroy it: a shimmering, rotting girl with pale hair and eyes as green as Emerald City. Her voice flowed like liquid midnight.

Tyria.

My Black Madonna.

Her words are anathema. They thrive like pupae in her journal. One might think it is used and abused, its pages dog-eared as if held with angry hands, but it is a tome of destruction. When I first opened it a spray of sweet smelling dust hit my nose, something that reminded me of burning herbs. What began as innocent gazing turned into a gateway drug.

The fashion in which she pulls thoughts out of her head and smears them in ink vexes me. They transport the reader into a Technicolor delusion. My imagination swam between the pages of *Johnny the Homicidal Maniac* and *Sandman*. Death smelled sweet, Dream prophesied and Delirium got me drunk on neon and candy. Crazyskinny kids butchered one another; razor blades were their teeth; maggots fell out of their eyes.

BLOOD KISS

I knew their thoughts, understood the shattered dream of being told you are never good enough.

For three days I was unaware of sunrise and moonset. My breathing depended solely on her words. Leland even threatened to take the journal away from me.

"I know that's not yours," Leland said as he took the notebook.

"Give it back!"

"You shouldn't be snooping around in someone else's private thoughts."

"But I need those words," I said.

Grabbed it right out of his hands, and only then did I notice that my fingers had made permanent indents on the back and front cover. And why shouldn't they have? Her prose was the Rabbit Hole. Words weaved like a haunting cornucopia. *DECEPTION MOCKS MY REFLECTION* stuck out like thorns; *INNOCENCE LOST* and *LIFE IMITATES ART* dueled for fame and notoriety. Vignettes, haiku and short stories. I became her vicarious soldier. Painful memories—ones that I never had!—bloomed inside my head.

I couldn't help but to wonder what the effect of all these words would be if they were given a microphone. Would they come in the shape of a bullet? Would they shock its listeners into empathy? Tyria was certainly a poet of the bards.

But Leland's words ruminated. We could do something great together, but the only reason I know this is because I stole every opportunity I could to be inside her mind. For that she would hate me forever.

"You still reading that thing?" Leland asked me on day four.

I stunk so bad even I couldn't stand it. I showered and imagined Tyria standing outside the dirty plastic curtain in a blaze of anger, cursing my existence. When I re-claimed the couch I fell asleep with the journal clutched in my grip and dreamed viciously, but woke up to find myself in a fever sweat . . . and with a raging boner. That was day five. By then I was on my hundredth read.

"Can you paint this perverse poetry?" Leland asked.

I became strangely jealous, as if the words were written in a language that was meant for my eyes only.

"No," I said. "I cannot."

Truth was that Tyria had crushed my muse; maybe she had become it. But how could Tyria—a girl—get that far into my skin? On the sixth night Leland came back with the official advertisements. He could sell anything he put his mind to, even words that complained about a pain so inhuman that I nearly vomited from the thought of it.

"There's something odd about this book," Leland said.

I knew what he meant. I swore to myself, on my tattered living soul, that the thing was alive, that it had a mind and body buried deep within the pages; its eyes were crusted shut with blood, eyes that knew how to *see*, how to *process*. I looked over my shoulder, saw something fluid in the air. It was a mystical experience at best.

"Don't forget about tonight's arrangement," Leland said, flying out the door.

It was almost time to go. The sun was down and the stars lilted like tiny gas lamps in the October breeze. Air would do me good. I read the local newspaper to check out my competition, scoffed at the uninteresting clauses. Kids these days tried way too hard at their disconnection from the world; their art is a misrepresentation of feeling. I found no natural flow.

Tyria was all that mattered.

I lit a joint with my zippo lighter and sucked in the gracious herbal smoke. The immediate effect of THC made me want to return to my triptych, my thoughts afire, my hormones confused. But there was this annoying buzz in my head and my lungs hurt too much to even breathe. I wouldn't be able to stand the smell of paint at all.

Instead, I dallied in recollection, thought about Leland, how the night we met was full of so much unconventional circumstance. Though the cosmos decided that we should meet, it is this very night why I refuse to acknowledge Adelaide's existence.

BLOOD KISS

In those times clubbing was only cool if you did it four times a week; living in the moment was all that mattered. Drugs were dealt like fashion tips: pills, poppers, powder, grass and glass. If you overdosed or died you became a god. The lifestyle was one to aspire to: no rules, no etiquette. Ignorance was truly bliss.

It was a midsummer nightmare of no sales, snarky artfags with too much hair and no meat between their ears. I followed the wayward streets to a part of town where eyes stared strung-out and hungry; the warehouses stacked like smoggy pancakes. Inside the music was turned up too loud and the track lights were dangerously luminescent. Beer initiated all conversations. It was then I heard curious beings opine.

"What do all these terrible paintings mean?" a tall meth-head asked.

"Some of them feel . . . alive. Like if you could climb down tree rings," said a Skinny Boy. "Not just that . . . they're watching us."

I swallowed a purple pill and stared at Skinny Boy; he was the prettiest thing in the room. Moonlight skin and bones like a well-drawn stick figure. His brown hair was shaved at the sides and a green snapback cap covered the long curling bush at the top. His posture spoke of surety unlike the other tragic numbskulls in the room that took up way too much space. The cigarette in his hand was as black as his eyes; the Glassjaw t-shirt was all it took for me to fall in love.

Leland.

The lanky goon placed a protective hand on Leland's shoulder as they stared into one of my pieces. They seemed oddly stricken by my experimental acrylic, the thick clots of black bleeding into gold. *The Mindless Menace,* I had called it. Leland took one step back as if the portrait was going to yawn wide and eat him.

Then the X devoured me, slowed my heartbeat to a crawl and turned reality into an enemy. One of the downsides of ecstasy is that the power that makes you crave control disintegrates. Reality is no longer at your disposal; you become a servant to space. Most of the time you just humiliate your-self. I smoked a Camel Crush to freshen my breath; I wanted to talk to him so badly.

But then a new crowd arrived. Junkies! There were three of them, two guys and a girl with tits so small I knew she didn't need a bra to support them. She licked her cracked and bleeding lips; I dreaded the thought of someone kissing them. Their faces were parchment skulls and their eyes were filled with danger; they swarmed my pretty little boy with no intent on leaving him alone.

"You got the stuff?" I heard the girl weakly say.

Leland didn't answer.

"Hey!"

One of her goons pushed him against the wall. I imagined delicate muscle fibers separating, bruising, his delicious bones cracking. An instant rage reached out and collected me. I was not one who ever liked bullies.

"She asked you a fucking question, faggot."

Before I could react the lanky one acted out in violence. Fists swam in circles, to which I saw him immediately become set back with a single uppercut to the chin. The sound of his head meeting the floor made my groin tingle.

"I don't have shit for her. She fucking knows that," Leland said.

"Pussy." The girl raised her dirty hands as if to hit him.

"Go ahead. Hit me. Won't change a goddamn thing. You'll still be a junky and I'll keep moving on with my life."

"Fuck you."

Her nails became claws; she ripped furrows into Leland's shirt. I knew that they had to have had a deep personal relationship for this argument to turn so violent. Her hands seized his hair, Leland fell back but not before grabbing her face as they both crashed into my painting; someone's boot punctured it straight through the center.

Now it was my turn. Consequence was masked by anger for defacing my work. I grabbed one of the guys by his leather jacket and shattered his nose with my knee; bright

BLOOD KISS Daniel Stone

beads of blood sprayed my face. In a split second the other goon took out an X-acto blade and waved it. I raised my hand up to block it from hitting my face.

The pain was something like a demon being birthed from my hand. My skin delineated; tendon showed through. In my agony I kicked up my boot (the dude was just as skinny as I and no stronger), and slammed it into his thorax. As he lay in agony on the floor I stomped until his mouth looked like a platter of raw meat.

"You fucking asshole, you betrayed me!" the girl said unfazed by the blood.

"No. I just gave it up."

She cried unreasonably, and Leland tried to comfort her. I knew then there wasn't a bad bone in his body. Being in the presence of someone so perfect makes one feel inadequate, but as I stood there nursing my hand I couldn't help but to stare. Three minutes later the trio left, and that's when Leland came to my aide

"I'm so sorry about your painting," he said. "Adelaide can't help herself."

"Pretty name for such a violent girl," I said.

"I'm Leland."

"My name is—"

"Dorian Wilde, I know. It's your show isn't it?"

"At least someone knows who I am."

"You're not exactly hard to find. You stand out."

"Is that good or bad?" I winced.

"It's a characteristic that certainly interests me."

I smiled so big on the inside.

"And the girl, what's her deal?"

"Adelaide isn't so bad. We used to use together," Leland looked at the floor, sighed.

"Is that so?" I said.

"But I'm clean now. And I know she'll get better one day."

"Yeah, when she's six feet under."

"Don't say that," Leland grasped my arm. "Oh my gods, did they do that to you?"

Leland removed the rag to see for himself. The flesh of my hand suppurated. A few stitches were in order.

"Fucking pricks. Let me get you to the ER."

He insisted that he pay the bill and would purchase the broken art as well. It was an offer I couldn't refuse. I could tell the way in which he looked at my work that he understood it and genuinely wanted to learn more about it.

"What about your friend on the floor there?" pointing to the bag of bones.

"Morgan . . . my boyfriend."

My face went red.

"But don't worry he'll be fine."

A long pause followed.

"Do you like my work?" My tongue was never such a poet.

"I do," he said. "Do you have an agent?"

"A what?" The world spinning too fast now.

I felt a fiery twinge. We were lost in one another's gaze. Love at first sight? Nothing mattered. Not the stars, not the moon, not air or art or life. And then without a care in the world (and one of the many reasons why I fell in love with him), Leland leaned over and kissed me. I saw fireworks as our tongues played a wet game of tug o' war.

BLOOD KISS

5

Somewhere down a too dark street the bohemian music of zippo lighters and aerosol paint cans can be heard.

Misguided eyes collect moonlight and cigarettes burn like stars. A line forms and gossip swells.

The show is about to begin.

Tyria could see them, the children of the night. They looked hungry, afraid, but mostly curious. She set herself at the nearby window and let the cool threads of autumn roll off her skin. The wind felt black, looked black, and so she had to remind herself that not everything in this world is ensconced by shadow. Sometimes there is just not enough light.

"How many are out there?" Tyria said.

"About fifteen heads."

A delicious spill of streetlight dappled Adelaide's skin.

"Seems like there're more. Look at them."

"That's the plan."

Tyria heard voices, horrible and impatient; their angsty drawl spiraled into whorls of yellow, blue and red. She couldn't speak. Nerves had colonized her entire body; she felt chained to the silence, but somehow free. She could turn into a beautiful bird and fly into the night if she wanted. For what could come of this other than a dream fulfilled, a chance to escape? Leland had explained it all: she was to be herself and Dorian would paint along to her words.

But who said that she even wanted to do this? Yes, all Tyria wanted was to be heard, yet she never planned it to be this way. Being the center of attention was one of her worst fears, even though Adelaide kept reminding her that if she was to grow as an artist, she would need to face all of the fears.

"You girls know what to do, right?" Leland asked. Tyria noted his blessed bone structure; the kind of pretty that gets you beat up out of envy.

"What are we supposed to do?" Adelaide said.

"Be yourselves!" He was holding a bunch of papers in his hand, one eye closed and the other mapping out the size of the room. Not much space really, and there were boxes everywhere as if someone had just moved in.

"Come sit by me, Ty. I wanna do your makeup."

They took a spot by the bar. Adelaide ran her fingers through Tyria's hair and applied a thick coat of kohl liner to her eyes. Leland put some on as well, removed his drab leather jacket down to the tight white Deftones t-shirt.

"You think we did this right?" Adelaide said. "I feel like we're missing something."

Leland served everyone a cold beer, talking about things Tyria didn't understand. Logistics, statistics and future business.

"Yeah, more people," Tyria said.

"They'll come. Trust me," Leland smiled.

"How can you guarantee that?"

"I spent a lot of money on the ads, and I put them in all the right places."

Adeline swung her long black hair behind her shoulder. "Don't get ahead of yourself. We don't need that much money to survive."

"Oh, yes we do."

"Is that all this is to you? A night of numbers and figures?"

"Part of it is, yes. I'm a businessman at the end of the day. I crave success."

"This is about art, about Tyria voicing her choice," Adelaide said.

Leland chuckled. "Do you talk for her too?"

BLOOD KISS

Tyria summed up their friendship in a matter of seconds: they were close as they ever had been. Leland turned toward Tyria.

"Then there's only one thing left to do before we let them in," skeleton finger like an arrow in the dark.

Before Tyria the makeshift stage, a microphone draped in Victorian silk and chains like something Stevie Nicks would sing with. She took a careful step up; there lay a pair of fingerless gloves for her to wear so when she lifted her hands the chains would rattle and the silk would flap like wings.

She thought about the wind blowing and the moon rising.

Tyria could fly.

"I knew you'd be a natural," Leland said.

With Leland and Adelaide below her Tyria became a nascent goddess. She was no longer afraid of the dark being that her side of the stage was secured in light. But just a few inches away was where the shadows certainly lived. Tyria claimed the darkness for herself, knowing very well that soon she would soon become it.

"You feel it," Leland said. "It's beautiful."

"You look good," Adelaide said.

Tyria nodded. Words were precious to a newborn goddess. She stepped down from the stage, lit a pillar candle and then a cigarette to accompany her mini tour. The dilapidation was overtly noted, holes in the ceiling and glass scattered across the floor. Modern graffiti in giant letters. *ELECTRIC ORCHID!* in black and white; *HAPPINESS IN SLAVERY?* in bruise-purple. Every electrical socket was pulled from the wall exposing live wires; copper crackled like the shocking relationship between bug zappers and moths. It wasn't a nice place to be, aesthetically or literally, but it was rent-free and cloaked to the general public.

"We can fit at least thirty heads in here," Tyria heard Leland say. "Did I mention candlelight séances? I thought you might like that part."

"Because we're Pagans?" Adelaide slapped Leland playfully in the arm.

"I'm a confirmed agnostic," Leland said. "I'm not judging."

Tyria quickly grew tired of the conversation. "What time does Dorian make his grand appearance?"

That was the first time she had said his name out loud. It left a bitter taste in her mouth. A storybook character came to mind in Oscar Wilde's masterpiece, *The Picture of Dorian Gray*.

"In no time." Leland stroked his lips with an idle finger. "You and Dorian are the start of an awesome story."

PICTURE THE SCENE: me browsing a rag shop dollar store, half drunk on beer and wildly inspired to paint; nothing in sight but choking hazards and crap so cheap that not even the Chinese could take credit for it. Shelves of useless items and random household appliances. The tube paint was hard as a rock and the paintbrushes were all broken. An artist's nightmare!

I found some candles. Green, white and purple; pillars, votives and tapered. Leland told me to get as many as I could carry as there was no light at the performance space. At the counter a look of shock spread across the Indian lady's face. Had she never seen such a big purchase of candles before? We stared at one another; I could smell the sandalwood of her sweat, saw a dusting of tamarind powder on her red sari.

She asked in a heavy accent how many I had.

"Sixty," I pushed the box forward.

When I opened my wallet her countenance turned into great satisfaction; meanwhile, all I could do was stare at the red smudge on her forehead, which from what I knew meant that she was either married or forgot where to apply her lipstick.

"Twenty dollars," she said.

Outside the Bowery rippled like a bad acid trip. Lights became my enemy; the saw-toothed wind beat the shit out of everything. Above, the pale tear of night sky became sutured by gathering clouds, but the residing buildings shielded me from burgeoning thunder and lightning. I studied them, gothic and modern, gargoyles and slate. I thought for a moment what it would be like to paint a scene upon one of those skyscrapers. A worldly canvas of my own, creation's refuge. I've always envied the fearless graffiti artists who risk their lives to spread their message on the tallest buildings in sight.

I was running late. Not my fault entirely as the L train is a slow and horrible hunk of junk; but what's worse are the people who ride it. I love New York City, could not imagine living anywhere else in the world, but its MTA patrons are full of shameless abandon and can become too pushy at times. They beg for change, pull rabbits out of hats and won't give up their seat to the elderly. Courtesy is certainly dead.

I consulted Leland's directions. A few dizzying streets and broken solar-powered bulbs made the path too dark to see. Lightning sizzled the color of Tyria's hair; thunder growled like a caged animal. Rain began its all-out assault on the city. But something amazing came to mind. Rain: the very poetry of it. Life requires water for its continued survival, but does anyone ever stop to think about how rain comes to be, how all those vapors condense in the sky until the clouds burst?

It's the fact that no two raindrops are the same shape or size, like snowflakes, or the endless whorls of human finger-prints, that strikes me as beautiful. Each particle is unique. I'd never, ever in my life thought about rain in this fashion now that I was dashing through it. I became a student of poetry, Tyria's pupil.

Then I arrived.

The building of choice stuck out like a sore thumb on the corner of Spring Street. A line had already formed, vagabonds in black and dirty Converse sneakers, twiggy artists forever haunting.

"Finally!" Leland shouted.

Spider hands pulled me into a dark paradise. I felt the world play out like a stop-motion film as if I'd drunk a river of liquor. Hot lips against my own, and even though I knew it was Leland, I had hoped for another. He spun me around twice, threw a beer in my hand and dried my hair with a smelly bar towel. I felt like a big rat.

"Hello, handsome."

I blushed.

"You got what I need?" he asked.

I handed Leland the box. Something tapped my shoulder, but when I turned around nothing was there. Then I heard voices talking about stage lights, candles, curtains and amplifiers. A pair of bright eyes peered from behind the faux bar top, Adelaide in her usual thrift shop fashion, as another pair revealed themselves slowly. I saw that they were covered in Ray Bans, but a hurricane of prophecies and curses lived behind those eyes.

"You starstruck or something?" Leland asked.

Not starstruck. *Reverence*. No one had to tell me her name. It had been in my head all fucking week, and the revelation set like a stone around my neck so much so that I almost bowed.

"Tyria," backstage introduction of a rising star.

The light on her weak but the green fire in her eyes was strong. Her tiny feet dangled from the stage and her hands reached for the ceiling as if she could rip it open and search for the stars. I could not move; my throat was dry and my legs numb. There was this cold presence about her, a phenomenon I couldn't fathom. It was like meeting the one person you admire your entire life, that one person for whom you had a billion things to ask, but choke up at the moment of first contact.

"He's finally here," Adelaide said. "Candles and all."

"Hi Addy."

"So glad Landy has you wrapped around his finger."

She took the candles from Leland and began setting them around the space. Soon we were washed in yellow light and the smell of bland wax. I walked one step closer to Tyria, to which she brought her foot instinctively up to stop me. I noticed her eyes were closed and her lips were moving. She

BLOOD KISS

was praying, worshiping, incanting. Something of that nature. And so I respectfully backed off.

Leland took my hand. "She's something else, right?"

"Is she on something?"

"I don't know"

I nodded, then turned back to Tyria. She was staring right at me, reptile blink, and then stepped off the stage. The Hot Topic rings on her fingers clinked and the neon labret piercing spoke of teenage rebellion. She approached me cat-like, fully extricated from the darkness.

"This is him?" Tyria said. "This is the artist?"

I almost laughed at her voracity, for it was I who should've been saying such things. Instead I studied the outline of her Ray Ban sunglass, the bright orange burn of her clove; I saw the aquiline nose and hair so yellow it shined white. I wondered if she would ever take off the glasses, for it was an immediate rape of my immortal soul to tease me this way. Eye contact is everything.

"What were you expecting?" I asked.

Tyria shrugged her shoulders. "More."

She was so close I inhaled the smoke she exhaled. I began my own introspection to make sense of her caution. Oh, the torment in that moonface, the depression that put a great weight on her wilting spine. These were the sentiments in flesh that I had read cover to cover, the memories that I'd never had all of sudden began to make sense.

"Sorry to disappoint you," I said.

"I didn't say you disappointed me. I don't even know you."

"Hopefully we can change that."

Tyria rolled her eyes. "I doubt we will."

Before I could continue the conversation, I felt the natural compel in me that ruins everything surface. I'm such a bad liar.

"You left this at my show," I handed Tyria back the book, relieved of its possession.

Tyria froze. "How the hell—"

"*I said* you left it at my show."

She flipped through it with pithy, making sure each line was the same, making sure no word had been tarnished.

"Well, Dorian, thank you for returning it," shooting a terrible glance at Adelaide.

"I swear I didn't know where it was."

Tyria's relief was a surprise being that I expect animosity. That thing crippled me for a week straight, I wanted to say, but she had already taken of her sunglasses to further distract me. The look of disdain was chilling. I searched for any trace of innocence or ignorance, but could find none. I felt terrible that I'd violated her secret thoughts, but the recoil of horror germinated inside my head: the pain of child rape and abuse, of pills, alcohol, cocaine and worst of all, neglect.

And then I *saw* it.

A presence that put fiction stories to shame. It was the color of no color; the abyss in flesh. It had come to me, finally! And then moving, not for me, but Tyria! Same size, same shape, and *dense*. I could feel it weigh upon my heart with each stretch and billow. A cold silence fell over us like wet velvet

"Is it alive?" I asked.

"What?"

The thing had already faded away.

"Your journal . . . is it alive?"

Tyria looked at me profoundly. She knew I wasn't kidding. "I can ask the same question of you. Your pieces are *not normal.*"

"So you enjoyed my gallery?"

"When I look at art I expect to be the one defining it, not the other way around. Somehow your pieces study the viewers rather than the viewers studying them," she said.

"A trick of the hand, really."

For the next hour we chatted lightly about expectations and revelations. Tyria barely blinked; she seemed dead. I, however, remained a feral beast ready to learn civility, or chivalry. I focused on the graceful spread of her legs, the

BLOOD KISS

starlight skin and the strong curve of her chin. It drove me mad.

"What do you want from this?" I asked.

"To make money."

I knew she was lying. But Leland had already pulled me aside, shook my head to get me thinking rationally again. I wanted to tell him everything, wanted to confess my obsession with Tyria. But there was hair in my eyes and a lump in my throat. I could not figure out if it was ennui or vigor that I felt, I just knew that something was absolutely wrong, and Leland did as well; no one knew me like he did.

"You seriously look like you've seen a ghost."

"Am I not looking at one?" I joked.

"Hey. You fairies want a hit before the curtain goes down?"

Adelaide held a fat, fragrant joint that smelled of sugar and spice. I declined the offer so to not blur the trajectory I was on. Tyria denied it as well, but for another drug in the form of two fine white lines spread from thumb to wrist, then she took it up her nose. I watched her in silence as Leland and Adelaide smoked the blunt, who then led me to my easel that was set up next to the stage.

SOMETHING LIKE STAGE FRIGHT brought pins and needles over her entire body.

Dorian looked nervous as well. Was he feeling what she was feeling? To be so close to a person who had betrayed her before they had even met—but one who also was capable of so much promise—calmed her in ways she didn't expect. Why must the creatives always bear these kinds of tropes?

"You think we're crazy for doing this?" Tyria said. "No rehearsal and no plan."

"Improv doesn't suit you?"

Tyria froze, and then said, "It's where I thrive."

"Sometimes spontaneity brings out the best in art."

Maybe it was the fact that he was looking for a greater cause that made Tyria want to do this; maybe it was the fact that he seemed to *know* without her ever telling. In the end it's never fun to be completely alone. Sid had Nancy; Kurt had Courtney; Fitzgerald had Zelda.

Anima and Animus.

"I hope I don't frighten you," Dorian said.

"Why would anything you do frighten me?"

"It's just what people say about my work, is all."

She watched Dorian unravel his version of the truth, a black easel and a canvas big enough so that one could sketch the barebones of any dream. Brushes in neat little holders; a box filled with vials of the deepest red she'd ever seen, all capped and color coordinated. Blood. She'd noticed the track marks on his arm earlier, beaded horribly red even through the scrollwork of tattoos. Adelaide used to bear the same kind of scars.

"I'll take this corner." Dorian sat on a battered stool. "That's a good look on you," he said.

"I kind of feel like Stevie Nicks," Tyria shook the chains and lace.

Dorian laughed. "Start practicing your high kicks and twirls."

He added that her hair might have been the same blinding blonde, but that she was no Stevie Nicks. Tyria saw how thick and black Dorian's hair was, and at the ends were natural waves. The surgical steel studs in his lower lip accentuated his long face and the smell of him was like rain and sweat and paint swirled into a single vial of pain.

"Anyone ever tell you that you look like Maynard James Keenan . . . *A Perfect Circle* era?"

"Sometimes they call me Marilyn."

"You don't look like that fucking clown."

Tyria pulled Dorian onto the stage. "I want them to see you too."

"But you're the star."

BLOOD KISS *Daniel Stone*

His words came in the colors of comfortable blues and pinks; it made her question her natural hate for men, made her almost forgive their dangerous nature. Somehow his touch—though there was hardly that much *touch*—sent a bright atomic charge throughout her body. It was as if their physical chemistries were blending on the stage, gaining momentum before the curtain finally went down.

"Test the mic," Dorian said, dark eyed stare.

"Check one," Tyria's smoky voice took over the room.

"Louder."

Tyria let out a pitiful sound.

"You can do better than that," Dorian said.

Then Tyria clamped her teeth on the mic until a hectic wave of static flowed out the amps. Dorian held his ears and leaned back into the darkness. It had been so long since she'd heard any man ask her to scream, not since the night Daddy covered her mouth with his dirty hand and drove his dick into her.

"What have we gotten ourselves into?" Leland said from so far below it seemed.

Dorian grinned. "A message that needs to be spread."

"Then shall we let the monkeys in? I'm ready." Adelaide flashed little baggies in her hand. "I wouldn't want our party busted on the first night with all the noise they're making outside."

"What's tonight's vice?" Tyria asked.

"You name it I have it."

Adelaide spread a fine white line across a metal plate and Tyria took the blend up her nose in a quick sniff. Her heart underwent an arrhythmia, but everything would be fine so long as she had the snowflakes. Dorian behind her now, mapping out a sketch on the canvas, his hand fluttering like magic, the outline of something prehistoric, spreading itself in a masturbatory pose. And then the door squealed open to pour in the mélange of dirty bodies.

They filled the room looking for drugs and comfort, and with them came the stink of the street. Tyria felt right at home. She saw the wet flash of cash in everyone's hand, the drug exchange natural as it was illegal. Adelaide collected the money while Leland showed everyone where to stand, where to wait to be astounded.

BLOOD KISS *Daniel Stone*

Candlelight vigil for the setting of mood, wet movement of bodies sonorous and sweet.

Amplifiers for the illusion of sound or the reality of it. Chains and silk; a painter's easel spotlighted by weak light. The room smells of Nag Champa.

Sit back, relax and enjoy the show.

Tyria emerged onto the stage as if from a womb, tapped the mic until feedback demanded everyone to listen. The floorboards wobbled weakly beneath her, threatening to collapse, but she remained poignant in her goddess pose, soaring above an audience who looked upon her with eyes of boredom and confusion. What were they expecting?

But the stage was her land to claim, the sea of faces her army. She attached the gloves to her hands, stretched her arms up like the wings of a great raven until the chains hissed. She pressed her lips gently to the mic and a natural melody flowed from her throat; it gushed in an ugly color, smelled ugly too.

"Oh, children," whispering deep. "There are so many stories I want to tell you. Stories of tragedy that inspire my strategy."

She glanced at Dorian. Erudite, strong, his canvas clouded with lapis lazuli and a daring red that could pass for blood. The colors wavered and whined like the angry ooze in *Ghostbusters*. Something wanted out.

But something inside of her wanted out more.

Tyria eyed the audience. Electricity snapped like thaumaturgy. The collective held their breath as the music stopped and the candles blew out. Tyria let her lips touch the mic again, smeared it with black lipstick and cigarette ash.

"You know, a lot of people said I'd be nothing . . . that poetry is dead, that books have been bled dry. But I never believed them. You see, books have saved me; words have never betrayed me. Prose is my hero; it's constricting society that is the zero. Listen to what I have to say. This is my tirade."

> *I'm gunna take you back*
> *Where a girl must learn to attack*
> *Because she's on her back*
> *And he will do whatever it takes to make her crack*

Tyria found herself in an act of rage and perversion. The sexual jut of legs and groin, Elvis the female Pelvis. She stamped the floor with her tattered Converses; dust shot into the eyes of the first row onlookers. She had worked up a sweat so much so that her shirt was soaked and her vision blurry; so black behind the Ray Bans. But part of the culture of spoken word poetry is to play the part as much as you are the part. And so she continued her poetry of death.

> *The dark pulls up its curtain*
> *And this time she has never been more certain*
> *How can she love him so fucking much?*
> *How can she long for his betraying touch?*

A simple scream ended the line.

"There are memories that I don't want anymore. They once ruled my world, destroying that little girl. But without them I would not be able to see through the lies and its wretched paradigm," rising hate in her voice.

Feedback filled the room, ringing through the whorls of her brain. Though the eyes were astonished—blue, brown and green—Tyria thought that maybe she should stop as the faces did not seem the least bit amused.

BLOOD KISS *Daniel Stone*

But she could do no such thing when she saw Dorian.

A marbled god upon his dais. The shock spread across his face was violent as it was necessary. His hands shook, paint dripping off them like mercury into the dark spaces between them.

He reached out.

The shadow came begrudgingly, scarecrow swirl and teeth, tearing away from her bones; Dorian now on his feet, wing-tipped boots moving fast and arms wide to tackle the impossible black. To Tyria's surprise he *caught it*; a ripping ensued inside of her chest. But she was already back at the mic forgetting the pain.

> *Spilling innocence like rain*
> *Until nothing of her will remain—*
> *His hand descending like disdain*
> *To the center of her pain!*

At the crescendo her tongue became a knife that flayed the skin of her listeners. Everyone covered their faces, too dedicated to run, too enthralled to question the velocity. But she could take no more of this. Tyria released herself form the chains and lace, fell into the fetal position; her hands found the place between her thighs that Daddy had made his own, the smell of his Roadhouse whiskey fresh as a wasp sting.

"No," Adelaide cried.

Three boneheads in the crowd began to scream—less abhorrence and more consternation—at the sight of Tyria's downfall, beads of blood rolling down her neck and arms. Their faces became immediately wet with red, but their reaction was lazy with drugs.

"What's he doing?" a girl screamed. "Is it magick?"

Dorian in the pose of a wicked old witch, neck craned in deep thought, his paintbrush clotted black. Bony outline of something, a girl blotted by pain, her legs drawn open and dried as a wishbone. Double crimson smile as the shadow ascends like the absence of light. Its eyes watched her in anguish.

But it's the way that this painting takes charge that makes it so disturbing. One blink and her mouth gets wider, redder; blink again and the shadow moves in closer, creeping, crawling, drooling; the chitinous arms rise, the wishbone finally splinters—

As the voices of the crowd gather in a dizzying swirl and the painting rips itself off the easel, Dorian lost his balance, but not before screaming for Tyria to get up as her shadow crawled amorphously across the wall, then out the door.

The sole light bulb went *pop!* as it shattered. Tyria could barely see, but she heard the crowd clapping, whistling. Everyone pulled money out of their pockets to buy Dorian's paintings; they would surely sell their souls just to own them. Portraits in hand and money on the floor, satisfied and frightened all at once as they squeezed through the front door for sweet freedom.

"It's just a bit of blood."

Red clotted bright in Tyria's hair, streams of it down her face. Something about it looked delicious, a color I needed to paint with. My hand reached out before I knew what it was doing, but she swiped it away with such instinct and force that it knocked me backwards, mentally and physically.

"I don't need your help," Tyria growled. "I *am* an adult."

"Just wanna touch it," I said.

"You wanna touch something? Make it a drink because this shit is empty."

Quick chug of the PBR, crushing the can until it spliced open with a metallic cling. It cut into her hand for more of that exquisite blood. I handed her another, along with a rag, but she decided to swirl her pretty little hand in the stage dust until her wounds looked black.

BLOOD KISS

"Figures that they would drink the expensive beer when it's free."

"We scared them," I couldn't help but smile; it almost felt wrong to be doing so.

"You think they'll come back?"

"No matter the horrors *they will come back.*"

Tyria breathed out her exhaustion. "That, or Addy will have to reel them in with better stuff."

Now that the shadows had found their place again I thought about that creeping dark, living black or the embodiment of something far scarier. Black like no shadow I've ever seen. And oh, how I had to touch it, yet it was as if I was touching nothing at all, a nightmare made flesh, a bottled up scream.

"Is that me?"

Tyria eyed my new portrait. I sometimes surprise myself. Striking tableau, study of innocence lost. A girl with pale hair and eyes the color of jade stone. Fear was written across her face, but the vibrato of her body proved that she liked the pain because she didn't know any better. Sad truth in the world of Tyria's past abuse.

"Poor thing," Tyria said.

I saw anguish rape her face.

"What do you see?"

"A victim."

As she caressed the painting it moved slightly, as if the floor had drawn itself back like a tongue. That's when I heard the howl, deep within it, and Tyria grinned; but so did I. What was to become of us? We seemed a mad lot; we seemed to be the only two who understood this heinous brand of art.

Adelaide yawned. "It's a big rat."

"I see a beast," Leland said.

That was the first thing I heard him say since the last patron had walked out. His smile had never been more genuine; it had been a while since I'd seen it so natural. Then I saw why. Leland pulled bill after bill after crumbled bill from his pockets; on the table they were already categorized by Presidents. When each stack reached the threshold

Adelaide separated them into Ziploc bags and formed two piles.

"That one's yours and this one is mine," Adelaide said.

"Why is yours bigger?" Leland's sharp eye wasn't about to be fooled.

"Because I scored the drugs. You want a bigger cut next time, you score them."

"But I made the ads."

"Those cheap pieces of garbage couldn't attract flies to a pile of turd."

"That's real low," Leland muttered.

"You know the real reason why they came, and *paid*."

"I like to think it was to see art."

"Aw, poor naïve, Landy. The glass is still half full for you, ain't it?" Adelaide touched Leland's face.

"Fuck you."

"Well, I'm glad you understand. Business is business."

"Seriously? Fine. Next show, it's my way!" Leland said.

No one said a thing after that. We waited for the air to cool between them. Then Leland locked the front door and stared at all of us as if we all needed to have a private talk. The money now held by each respective camp, Leland pulled Adelaide to the table and resumed a bureaucratic conversation I wanted no part of. I took the time to think about what I wanted to do with these shows, how far I wanted them to go, and the buttons I wanted to push. Money would never be an object; art always took me higher.

I turned, put my hand on Tyria's shoulder. "You in it for the money?"

She shrugged. "If it means I can buy my smokes, so be it."

"You know what I mean."

Her green eyes locked wetly onto mine. "If you're insinuating that I'll become a sellout don't hold your breath. I don't have that in me."

And that was the end of that. We all sat in silence. I heard rats crawling through the ceiling and pigeons flying outside the windows. I lit a candle and placed it on the bar top; Tyria

BLOOD KISS *Daniel Stone*

sat near it and swished her finger through the yellow flame. I wanted to very much to hug her, to kiss her for a job well done, but I did no such thing. And then a fancy black cigarette was fitted between my lips. Upon the first pull I tasted vanilla and green spice.

"A celebratory high," Leland said.

"None for me," Tyria's voice sounded raw and tired.

Adelaide kissed Tyria's hand and then locked lips with her. I found myself marveling the sight of the love between two females. It invoked in me almost the same feelings as the love between two men does, the natural beauty of same sex relations, the superiority I assumed it over straight couples. To be of the same gender, to have the same curves, the same breasts and sex, is to know how to manipulate your lover without effort. And so there is no better pleasure than being with someone who knows the fleshy map of one's intimate needs as well one's personal wants.

"You're a rock star."

Leland's lips were suddenly on mine, his familiar smell of mouthwash and cigarettes so refreshing. I slipped my tongue inside his mouth, felt his teeth tug it as I swallowed some of his spit. I became instantly hard, but I admit my mind was not in its normal position of sex and art.

"What's wrong?" Leland asked me.

"Tired," I said.

"No, something else."

"What?"

"You look . . . drained."

Not really that. I just wanted to be on that stage again. The chemical reactions of Tyria and I, her voice spilling like pale midnight, broken and aching as if she'd gargled glass. Her shadow the fire in my loins. I wanted it more than I'd ever wanted anything in my life.

"You scared the fuck out of them." Leland's hand ran through my hair. "And your new piece is—"

"Such *is* the horror of art," Adelaide said. "Nobody knows the torture it takes to create it."

"Maybe they do now," I said.

More silence, but louder than ever, then—

"We have to do it again," Tyria said, strange glow in her eyes.

"I should get to my supplier."

Leland rubbed my back. "We need a DJ. Some beats would be good for next time."

"Would she approve?"

Adelaide tilted her mop-head toward me, "I do have a name."

"I like to think you don't."

Everyone began packing. Keys, cash, cigarettes and personal ephemera. Beer cans rolled wetly, ads were picked off the walls; Leland swept the garbage to one side of the room so that Addy could kick it all into big bags; fuck recycling, but to my silent disapproval. We all pitched in, took a separate part of the room. Adelaide lit a gray tea light and prayed for some irrational goddess to bless us all. Tyria and I studied our lovers respectively, and then one another. Fear of the future or fear of our new friendship? But then she turned away from me and put her Ray Bans back on.

"I almost broke them, and I can't afford another pair," she said.

"I'd buy you another pair if they broke," said it so fast I didn't even know what I was saying.

"These were a hundred-twenty bucks. You got money to drop like that?"

"Canal Street," I said

Tyria laughed awkwardly, then became quiet as if she had expressed the wrong emotion. I wanted to ask her more questions but it was not the right time. Leland put a moldy mop in my hand, Tyria cleaned off the bar top and windexed the big mirror. Adelaide folded up the poster boards and delivered them to the front door.

"Let's go," Leland said. "The sun is about to come up."

We shot out into bleeding dawn like rodents with bags upon our backs, beer on our breath and THC clouding our minds. New York City rose above us, a mountain of glass and

BLOOD KISS Daniel Stone

garbage; the sky began shifting colors. In the streets people were entranced by their cell phones, but I could think was how this was truly the city that never sleeps, and as the final waves of the marijuana hit me, I looked uptown and the skyline was nothing but a bed of nails.

PART TWO

SYNTHESIS

"Take me. I am the drug. Take me. I am hallucinogenic."

—Salvador Dali

The ghost of dirty hair, teenage dreams and the smell of lust. No sleep 'til Brooklyn. Now the group split into pre-destined halves: Adelaide and Leland to the road of pins, Tyria and Dorian to the road of needles. Old relationships to decay and new ones to blossom.

The October wind was too cold to fathom, a rat-tooth pain on Leland's skin. But October's colors were everywhere: candy detritus, cinnamon sticks and withered leaves dripping off the trees. On every windowsill sat a fanged pumpkin, on every tenement door fake cobwebs; in each window was an electric witch and fluorescent skeleton.

Bushwick was in full costume.

Leland followed Adelaide beneath a crumbling underpass and then through a block that reeked of ozone. They stopped for a pack of smokes and shot the shit with the storeowner. Not much to talk about besides the economy that wasn't recovering, or that the world was going to shit. Outside, two hipsters were flipping through a local art magazine called *Eyesore*.

"What month is that issue?" Adelaide said.

The hipster didn't even look up. "Was printed yesterday."

Adelaide turned to Leland. "You see what it says right?"

A gaudy headline, centerfold: INNOCENCE AND RAGE IN PERFORMANCE ART. Someone had written about *SyNeRgY*. Not just that, but there were a plethora of pictures. For a moment Adelaide was taken over by rage, cursing how their right to privacy was violated, but Leland redirected her attention.

The canvases seemed alive; Tyria remained forsaken and ashamed; Dorian's pose was that of a wraith.

"Can I see that real quick?" Adelaide said.

"It's free on the stand," the hipster said.

Adelaide vanished for one moment. "Here ya go."

It was beyond surreal to see their names in print. Leland cradled the glossy pages, his eyes rocketing back and forth. The review was generally positive, but lacked a thorough understanding. The writer was hidden behind a pseudonym, so there was no tracing it back to open a real discussion. *Silent and deadly*, Leland read. *Built upon a pretense that doesn't exist.* That one he liked. *Perverse, disturbing, wretched.* The writer seemed to love adjectives.

"How does one come into my show and write about it without asking permission? What about paying us?"

"Shh, Addy. Read it through."

Adelaide began to chuckle but Leland almost cried. Drugs, queers, candles and magick, he read aloud. *The show was everything that should have never been, but that's why you need to see it.* And as if the writer had known not to give it all away, he asked that the readers wait for advertisements rather than supplying the address.

"My ads *were* a hit!"

Adelaide rolled her eyes. "Guess this time I lose."

"Do you think this is a good or bad review?"

"It doesn't matter. Any press is good press! I'm just a little annoyed we weren't asked permission."

Leland remained in heavy thought. "I have an idea."

"Wait a minute," Adelaide pulled on her clove. "I just had a vision."

"Addy—"

"Of cutting up newspaper prints and pasting the text together randomly. We could do it with pictures too, but from horror magazines."

"That's how Kurt Cobain wrote his lyrics."

"He learned it from Burroughs, the cut-up method."

"But this time it'll be all about change," Adelaide said.

BLOOD KISS *Daniel Stone*

"You agreed this time would be all me."

"You're right, sorry."

Looking up into that Brooklyn night sky, they fell into a menacing silence. Leland took the moment to think about change. Brooklyn had certainly changed. The tattered hipster palace might have been loaded with transients and artists from all over the country, but it was slowly starting to show signs of gentrification. The storefronts were cleaner; the skin tone on the street was lightening. The poorest of the poor, the angel-headed hipsters raged in depression, would soon be kicked out. Bushwick was slowly diluting its art and its sense of community, all the things that made it safe to live here again.

"Let's walk," Adelaide said. "I know what you're thinking."

"You know me well."

"And grab a few of those!"

Leland pulled five copies off the shelf.

"Don't torture yourself with the 'what ifs' or the 'coulda-shoulda-woulda.' It's only going to work against you."

"It's a mixture of a lot of things."

"Like how you persuaded me to let my girlfriend hang out with Dangerous Dorian by herself."

"Why do you call him that?"

"Because that's how he makes me feel," Adelaide said.

"Well, that's not fair. He's a nice person."

"To a certain extent, Landy."

"I refuse to argue about this."

Adelaide smirked. "That's a good boy."

"I wish he was here to see the paper though, he would be so proud."

"I don't think one silly little article will change him. He has to do that for himself. Same goes for my baby girl, Tyria."

They headed south. Here every storefront window seemed to be plagued by ads for titty bars, art galleries and local theater shows. Leland saw the words HeAvEn? and MUSIC SAVES! but he knew these were the first signs of another culture being chased out by big business. When Adelaide cut left Leland saw something very familiar to him: a gaggle of gays laughing loudly and hitting one another playfully. The words *American Horror Story* and *Sashay Away* fell from their lips in tandem. Just as Leland was about to break their conversation a Mexican woman asked him for change, sipping languidly on a can of beer. Adelaide pulled him away.

"In here," she said.

Leland pointed to the dark entranceway. "This?"

"I'm trying to show you something cool, now come on."

Falling beneath a heavy duty curtain that felt like wet hair, and inside seemed to be made of solder and wood. Where did the fucking bricks go? The hot smell of piss and puke, the proof of it stagnant and slick beside them. Then through another hallway as if sneaking into Fort Knox, one light bulb flickering and Leland's ears popped like the change of pressure when diving into deep waters.

"Wow."

Roller coaster machines so high it couldn't be possible; the horrible squeal of rusted gears turning made his teeth chatter. Paper, so many reams of paper. Matte, gloss and business. Leland saw stacks being separated by machine hands to be packed into boxes. In the back a shapeless ghost was staring into a novel with no cover; it touched buttons nonchalantly.

"It's a paper factory," Addy pointed at the assembly line.

"How did you—"

"Pick any style you want. Shane will trade for Xanax."

Leland stamped his foot. "Addy I said I wanted to do this one on my own."

"Why don't you thank me instead of fighting? I did this for you."

"It's not the same," Leland said.

"Why do you have to be so proud?"

Leland bit his tongue and browsed the maze. He thought about how many types of paper there were in the world, all the way down to good old papyrus, the mother of them all. As he scanned the aisles he realized that the gloss was too

BLOOD KISS

bright and the business paper too posh. There had to be something that would be a better fit for an art ad. And then he saw one that immediately caught his attention: matte.

"I knew you'd like that," Adelaide smiled. "How many do you think?"

"At least a hundred."

"Double. This factory shits it out."

Swiveling into the shadows, Adelaide chatting with Shane, a pale baggie on the desk; his face peering out to take a good look at Leland resting his body against the matte stack of choice. Two hundred prints, two hundred different ways to advertise the next show. *SyNeRgY* would be so hard to top.

"It's all ours."

"How much?" Leland asked.

"Two stacks for a few pills. When I'm good I'm *good*."

They loaded their cart; Adelaide's smile was bright as coins, a sure sign into their lucrative future. She guided them back out, pulling and tugging; paper gets heavy after a while. They stopped for a cigarette.

"Where to now?" Leland said.

"I gotta pick up," she said as they came to the corner of Myrtle and Wyckoff. "I'll make the deal inside."

"Is it for you or . . . ?"

"Look, this is my livelihood now. You know I'm clean."

Leland rolled his eyes. "Don't take forever."

She winked. "If I'm not out in ten minutes come get me."

Drug deals made Leland nervous, even when he was a user.

Above, the J train arrived with a whine and whistle, spilling down dust glazed in moonlight. They both watched it come to a halt in silence. Imagine if a train were a living thing, prisoner to age and arthritis and plague. It could never last as long as these trains have been running. Adelaide huffed and puffed—a sound he knew all too well, that nothing good was about to happen—and then slipped herself into the bodega. Behind her, a crippled looking metal-head with huge gauges in his ears followed.

Now the J train roared its way to the next stop. Leland raked his hand through the curls upon his head, relaxed his body against a brick wall with one leg leaning upon it. He heard a jarring noise, looked to his left to see that a garbage can had been tipped over, and inside of it was a nomad looking for dinner. In New York, you either ignore the bums or feed into their habits.

Ignorance is such sweet bliss.

He rubbed his fingers across the pins on his messenger bag, all the geek fandom one could imagine: the Umbrella Corporation, Star Wars Sith insignia, The Strand and a skeletal face with the most radical Glasgow Smile he'd ever seen printed. Green blood smeared bright across its forever grin. But what he wanted was inside the bag, an old paperback copy of *Web of the City* by Harlan Ellison. He opened the book's yellowed pages, inhaled the smell of ink and fell headlong into Ellison's world of Brooklyn gangs, retribution and bad temptation.

New York City is a web that waits patiently to ensnare those who are stupid enough to fall prey to its hollow temptations. You should never trust a city that thrills you to the point that you only come to expect the good, for when you least expect it the bad catches up and opens its greedy maw.

Leland thought about the writing process of the book, how little Jewish boy Harlan disguised himself as an Italian and joined a Brooklyn gang for ten weeks so he could *be* the main character. Rusty was the kind of kid you wanted to be. No matter how big of a web that the Cougars spread, no matter how much they scared him, Rusty persevered.

Easier said than done.

Back then the gang life of 1950s Brooklyn was about as normal and moral for any teenager as getting an education and being clean cut is in today's society. To go against the trend, the *family*, was to betray yourself and your loyal brothers. To take a stand against wrong doings deemed you crazy. But Rusty knew it was wrong to stay; being bad would

BLOOD KISS

get him nowhere as an adult, and he especially found that out when the gang fatally involved his sister.

This got Leland thinking about how if the five boroughs are a web, then Manhattan must be its dream-catcher core as the outer boroughs are the spiraling inward strands. Brooklyn was where its thickest strands of silk were certainly spun. It's the city's most populated borough and home to some of the largest ethnic enclaves outside of their respective countries.

Leland knew that Brooklyn could be a dream so long as one let it be, though it severely lacked the street-cred of Manhattan. Its skyline is far-less grandiose; there are no fifty story rooftops to party on, but it's a dream no less, once you realize that you never have to look back.

What were Leland's dreams these days? Empty concepts and incredulous introspections. How would these shows go on? What were the consequences of putting together two titans of art? According to the article it was *magick*. But who had authority to say such? The patrons? His friends? To dream of real friends was a joke. Cell phones are a person's best friend now; the internet is everyone's escape. To know that people used this wonderful technology to search for the stupidest shit was crippling.

But maybe this was part of growing up. Friends deplete to day jobs and families and lovers; what interests you all shared in your teens have no say in your adult lives. The extremity of these differences changes your opinions of the world, of each other. This can ultimately cut all ties.

Yet within all these crooked realities there was Adelaide.

The only friend Leland had that lasted through all the years of addiction and leeches. She might have once lost herself in the needle, might have once been considered an enemy, but she had cleaned herself up and found that she could lose herself in Tyria instead of losing herself in dope; found that flesh and blood is what really matters and not the quick fix.

Leland checked his watch. Fifteen minutes had passed, a taxi honked at him for a ride and young girl looked horrified as if his stack of paper were dildos. Leland put the book back in his bag and walked beneath the bodega's bright fluorescence, straight into the mouth of a white hell. Shelves of the worst brands of chips, a sloppy counter of rolling papers, cigarettes, lotto, and behind it the clueless Arab storeowner.

"Two loose." Leland handed over four quarters for the Newports.

He saw the commotion out of the corner of his eye. That same crazy metal head, denim jacket and ripped jeans, his shoulders maniacal in their movement and his voice scratchy with withdrawal. But it was the sight of his hand gripping Adelaide's unwashed hair and the switchblade pressed against her throat that made Leland see red. Her eyes were filled with tears but her face was soured with rage.

If there was anything Leland learned being born and bred in Brooklyn, it was that you had to protect yourself, even if that meant getting hurt. If you let them win, the assholes would never stop.

"You ain't getting my stuff," the metal head said languidly.

Leland couldn't hear Adelaide's reply, but she'd eyed him desperately. He paced himself, didn't want to scare the guy off or scare him into doing something tragic. He opened one of the refrigerators, grabbed hold of a twenty-two-ounce bottle of Old E. There were times when downing that crappy beer was heavenly in the way it made his body feel, but his years of teenage abandon were over. This bottle was now a weapon.

He swung.

The glass exploded against the junky's head like a Christmas ornament. Beer and blood soaked Leland's pant leg, and the junky collapsed instantly. Adelaide wiped a few tears from her eyes, then spit on the motionless body and gave Leland the signal.

Run.

BLOOD KISS

The storeowner screamed about the cops but they were already gone, didn't have time have time to discuss what had happened; they just had to get the hell out of there.

"If we're gunna make some money, we gotta burn some money," Adelaide said clutching the money and bag of drugs.

IN THE LANGUOROUS DAYS THAT FOLLOWED Tyria remained dressed the part of the stage, a dusty black wardrobe and too many rings on her fingers.

Dorian forfeited any chance to change his clothes. His white t-shirt remained yellow around the armpits, and his hair was like that of jellyfish tentacles. What was the point of cleaning up when one is destined to be on the stage again?

"Your scratches are healing," Dorian said.

Tyria dabbed the wounds with a small napkin. "They weren't that deep."

The café was quiet, smelled of burning wood and coffee grounds. The tables were vintage and the chairs all fresh-picked from around the neighborhood. For a Tuesday afternoon it was surprisingly full, everyone hypnotized by laptops, cell phones and ear buds. A minority of nerds were knuckle deep into novels and comic books.

"I'm going to go get a coffee. You want one?"

"Sure," Tyria said with her eyes focused on the window.

Dorian chatted up the barista, but Tyria could not make out what they were talking about. She did notice that the drink he ordered was called an "All Nighter" and it supposedly kept one up all night so said the menu. Ten minutes had passed before Tyria realized that she was still transfixed on the window, that beautiful landscape of Brooklyn desolate as ever. Dreaming. Thinking.

"Lonely out there," Dorian said.

"Bleak. That's the word I'd use."

"And cold. I can't stand the cold."

"Me too. But I love New York, so I deal with it."

"Don't we all?"

Silence as Dorian put his drink down. "So did anyone tell you?"

"Tell me what?"

"They wrote about us."

"Who?" Tyria cocked her head.

"There's an article. *Synergy* was a hit!"

The memory of that night gummy bear bright, colors whirling in her head like Dorian's bestial palette. But she didn't want to talk about it, not even as Dorian put the glossy magazine in her hand with a wolfish smile. The pages felt laminated, even a little frilly. She saw myriad photos of the performance space enhanced by Photoshop; every crack in the wall and every spider web in high resolution made the article even spookier. She even saw herself screaming into the microphone, a goddess made of wings and metal.

She smacked it off the table. "I don't need a pretentious article to justify my feelings for art."

"Neither do I, but I think it's cool that someone decided to use their own time to write about us. They even know our names."

"Funny, I don't remember being interviewed, or even being asked permission to have my name printed."

"It's a local art 'zine, not the *New York Times*."

"It's still against the law."

Dorian rolled his eyes. "Come on, cheer up."

How could she cheer up? There were too many sentiments weighing down any rationale she had left in her soul. So as she has always done in the heat of the moment, Tyria pulled out a fresh notebook and wrote out her feelings, the muse demanding and the ink wetting her fingers from pressing the pen too hard.

"I'm a little grumpy."

"I think you need some caffeine."

"I asked for a cup and you never brought one back."

Dorian's sharp face reddened. "Oh, crap. I'll be right back."

BLOOD KISS *Daniel Stone*

"Get me something bitter and black."

Tyria pulled a twenty out of her pocket but Dorian would not accept it. Chivalry or fleeting guilt for forgetting her drink? He came back with two hot mugs and Tyria sipped hers slowly, careful not to burn her tongue. The coffee seized her taste buds, woke up her soul. For what's the difference between a caffeine high and a coke high? They both make you feel powerful, focused, and both are very short-lived. Dorian picked up the magazine from the floor, glanced at it again, then slipped it into the pocket of his coat.

"What's Adelaide been doing these days? Haven't heard from her in a while."

"She's been up my ass."

"That's not such a bad thing . . . that she's been up your ass. She cares about—"

"I know." Tyria felt terrible for what she was about to say next. "But I feel suffocated. Unfortunately for me, I crave a lot of time to myself."

"It's a strange dichotomy . . . being an artist and being in love. Trust me, I understand."

"So you don't think I'm evil for saying that?"

"You want to be loved, you want to spend time with your lover, but you also want to be alone. Why is that so hard for people to understand?"

Now his mouth moving faster than his actions, opening up about himself, perhaps for himself. Too many questions, assumptions and opinions. What did they have in common? Why was the art world so stagnant lately? Boundaries are no longer being pushed because the artists have lost their vision.

"Where's the fucking sustainability?"

"Within each generation the human mind molds accordingly," Tyria said.

"So then what *is* this generation's clause?"

"Apparently to not fill any hollows."

"That's not what the article said about us. We are perverse and gloomy."

"Yeah but to what extent? Maybe the writer is predisposed to say that about everything. We can't just accept that."

"My gods, you *are* a Negative Nancy."

More weird questions, quickly passing over the formalities that help ease the path to a new friendship. Their shared inherent queerness, how same sex relationships outweigh that of heterosexuals, but how the breeders will always be in charge; that it will be a century before the gays can have a grand white wedding without hesitations in thought.

"The fact that society still doesn't talk openly about sex is probably why the writer of that article thinks we're perverse. And gay sex . . . well, just forget it!"

"How can people possibly understand it if they still shy away from straight sex as our Puritan founders did?"

"Don't get me started on that. I once saw a performance where a girl split her hymen on stage in an act of virginal ecstasy. She called it art," Dorian said.

"Destroying one's vagina is *hardly* art. To me, something has to be *created*, something that is unique to *you* . . . to *your* voice."

"But then again *somebody* has to please the voyeurs."

"Listen to yourself. Mammals have been having sex in order to survive for thousands of years. How is that innovative? Are their hearts in it?"

Tyria turned her head sharply. "Do you even have one?"

Why was she asking him that?

"No, but I have a *spine*."

And the days rolled on. They went about their business like ghosts, perusing the dustbowl streets of Brooklyn and the neon-scarred skyline of Manhattan. Antique shoppes of Victorian and Medieval flare, beer gardens and poetry readings. Tyria plowed through the cavernous aisles of The Strand, eighteen miles of books, her eyes fixated upon all those paper universes. Only the constricting store hours stopped her from reading everything in sight.

BLOOD KISS

Dorian dissertated about mostly Wilde and Fitzgerald, but somewhere between he spoke about Kerouac and Burroughs. While Tyria loved to listen to Dorian split prose apart for its inner meat, she counter argued with the value of poetry, how it was elliptical and lyrical, reflecting inner states and processes of thought, feelings. The structure and character events of prose was too confining for her. Plot was an unholy construct in her eyes.

"How can you bash a book for having a plot? Isn't that the basis of a story?" Dorian said.

"Plot is for writers who don't know how to dream."

"That's harsh."

"When you read the Beat Poets do you even understand what you're reading?"

Dorian almost looked insulted. "So who are your heroes?"

"Sylvia Plath, Anne Sexton and Otep Shamaya come to mind."

"Never heard of Otep."

"You're certainly missing out!"

All women, all the time. Sexton was one of her personal favorites. Tyria had never been so confounded by someone else's words, the proof now in Dorian's hands as Tyria pulled the great dusty text from the thrift shop shelf, noting the highly personal and confessional verse.

"She knows how to get me into her head, trap me there. It's a power I'm aspiring to achieve."

The hours slipped away coldly, but not lonely. Making a new friend had never been this easy or surreal. Though her expectations were less than nothing, Dorian was truly a pleasure to be around. He liked live music like her, read a shit ton of books like her, wanted to aspire to new heights like her. His opinions were sharp and assertive; he didn't have time to feel bad for anyone—just like her!

"Why should I filter my feelings for the sake of others? That would be hurting myself!" Dorian said.

"It's called class."

Dorian smirked. "Consider me crass."

And then, *Are you a witch? Is being a Pagan worth the hate?* It was time for a lesson on the semantics of Wicca and being Pagan. Tyria explained it all, the phalanx goddesses, the tarot and burning of herbs. Mabon, Ostara and Samhain. The Fool's unmolded potential, The Devil's cancer that devours you from within, how The Moon's light can turn all that was once benevolent into something malicious, how The Five of Cups is the warning sign to change your ways.

"It's not really a *witch* thing," Tyria said. "Please tell me you don't believe that shit."

"You mean you're not wearing a mask to cover your green skin and long nose?"

"Do I look like an asshole to you?"

Two more nights drained away, so fast but so fulfilling. This time Dorian dragged her to the intimate galleries of Brooklyn, and then the fine-combed galleries of SOHO. Tyria learned about the abstract and the surreal, the difference between Dali, Bacon and Pollock, a diptych, triptych and single canvas; how the same portrait painted with different mediums could evoke contrasted emotions.

"It's all about the colors, our personal *perception* of it," Dorian said. "And the panels, well, those tell a story."

"In some of them I see madness. In others I see nothing."

"The viewer is god. But what god are you when viewing?"

More nights separated from Adelaide than ever before. Tyria would come home at sunrise, black-out-drunk, but still thinking about Dorian. She would find Adelaide passed out on the couch, the anger clear in her uneasy face. But it wasn't about Adelaide anymore; it was about Tyria becoming complete, even if she had to suffer Adelaide's scorn, all teeth and hair.

"You're spending too much time with him," Adelaide would say.

"We're just friends." Tyria wouldn't let Addy see her flushed face.

"Then look at me when you say it," Adelaide's hands were cold on her cheek.

BLOOD KISS

Tyria still didn't look up.

Adelaide sighed. "I want you to be careful."

"It was your idea anyway," Tyria said flat.

And it was no different tonight. Behind her Catland's shattered window reflected a billion Dorians, a billion stars. The mystical books were toppled over and the candles melted by an invisible flame. Tyria didn't even bother to tell Dorian that she had done this with the sound of her voice. Somehow, he knew she was responsible.

"Your voice is ferocious."

Did this guy ever shut up?

"A singer's touch, no doubt," Dorian said.

"But I'm a poet."

"You could sing if you wanted."

"Why would I ever want to do that?"

Dorian walked into the dark street, Tyria's hands creeping like Dracula's shadow changing Harker's ignorance to monsters. *Sing.* With what voice? It had been destroyed in her childhood. Sing with the voice that only caused harm. *Scream.* Scream to escape; scream to swallow blood; scream to breathe.

Dorian broke her concentration, put another Camel between her lips, and brought her hands back down at her side.

"Easy there."

"I'm sorry. A bad memory found me."

"Not a problem. You can be yourself in front of me."

Tyria discovered something very important in this moment. She never had to bat an eye or explain herself to justify her actions with Dorian around. He was a man of understanding. Suddenly, her innermost fears and complications were no longer solitary confinements, but the cornerstone of some strange philosophy that she could begin to share.

"We honestly don't fit in," Dorian said. "But that article will help launch us."

"It'll always be us against them."

They were eating at a vegetarian restaurant now, garden wallpaper, clear glass plates and mason jars. The food was spicy and fresh—no traces of unwanted hormones or additives—blackened vegetables and steamed rice like the cool blue neon of Chinatown.

"This is my cuisine of choice," Tyria said.

Dorian noted aloud how he'd never felt so connected to Mother Earth in his life, had never thought about food being so important. His motto was that so long as one could eat it, then it was good. But Tyria would not hear it.

"Food is not just food anymore. Capitalism profits off our slow demise."

"Are you talking about high fructose corn syrup, thiamine mononitrate and sugar?" Dorian felt suddenly smart, but saddened that he let himself eat synthesized food ingredients.

"Our bodies are our temple," Tyria said. "Nothing in food should be fake or sweetened to the point where it just makes us grossly obese. Yet there are laws that allow this consumption."

"Are you one of those vegans?" Dorian said, regular question sounding suddenly stupid.

"*A vegan*? Like we're some weird alien race?"

He held up his hands in mock surrender. "I didn't mean for it to sound so . . . ignorant—"

"It's *my* choice. Why does everyone look at me like I'm nuts when I sit down to order food? They say *she's a dyke and a vegetarian*? It's fucking annoying."

"You're doing something most people cannot or will not," Dorian said. "For that you've earned my respect."

They paid the bill and went back to walking. For twenty blocks the moon remained a dead cold eye, drippy with color as it washed upon Dorian's face. Flushing Avenue came and went. The bar across the street was an empty red pulse of light, the rice balls lackluster in white, the diesel trucks oddly quiet. Hipsters in Raggedy Ann fashion walked slowly past them. Their voices flowed in the colors of bright blue and fluffy yellows. To the left a big wall full of advertise-

BLOOD KISS

ments and caricature graffiti. Tyria saw *SyNeRgY* in silver and ripped it off the wall to see Dorian shaking his head.

"Leland spent a lot of time on that."

"It could have been done better," Tyria said.

"First gigs are always cheap. It'll be better next time."

"Why is it that some are born to the silver spoon while others to pennies?"

Tyria's questions were coming off too fast. Dorian was taken back.

"If we were born to the spoon, we'd be quite ordinary, and that's my biggest fear."

"They're *spoon* fed their reality. Pun intended."

"That, or they don't have the balls to choose anything for themselves."

Dorian stared at her for nearly five minutes, the longest five minutes Tyria had ever experienced. Smoke nearly came out of his ears he was thinking so hard.

"I want to go vegetarian," Dorian said. "I want to do something radical."

Tyria's ears itched. "Life is all about *change* and there's no better time than now."

The lounge was on the border of Williamsburg and Bushwick.

Long yawning windows, long dance floor and too much art on the walls. Ripped leather seats bulged with bodies, and in the center the line for the pool table was already two people thick. Though the beer was served warm, it was cheap, and you could smoke inside. Yeah, at least that.

At the bar palms were turned upward for drinks. As usual, people sulked in useless gossip and indulgence. Four mouths crowded around a hookah of red and gold to puff watermelon flavored smoke. A sad, but brilliant drag queen was preparing for a long night's set. But it was the DJ booth that Leland set his sights on, and behind it someone familiar, tall and lanky, eyes too hollow to be awake, clothes too baggy to be taken seriously.

"I want music," Leland said.

Adelaide had just finished lighting her smoke. "What kind?"

"The kind that will heighten the intimacy between the viewers and the performers," Leland said. "I want what he's playing."

She took a moment to listen, unimpressed.

"You want a more immersive experience?"

"Yes," licking his lips wildly.

"What if I disagree?"

"You won't, and not because you're afraid, but because you owe him."

"I owe him?"

Leland smiled. "You don't remember, do you?"

"Doesn't ring a bell," Adelaide squinted her eyes again toward the DJ.

"That's Morgan."

Adelaide's head snapped back. "*Shit*. Your ex?"

He chuckled.

"What a loser," Adelaide said.

"He might be a loser, but he's a talented DJ."

"And what do I owe him?"

Leland looked at Morgan, then back at Adelaide. "The night I met Dorian, the night you were under your spell, one of your dopehead friends punched him in the face . . . knocked him right the fuck out."

"Oh . . . right!" Lips above her teeth.

"We broke up after that."

"And let me guess, you haven't talked to him since."

"Something like that."

"So then why do I owe him anything?"

Leland looked at her sharply. "I met Dorian that night. If not for that, I might still be with Morgan."

"That's your issue, not mine," she said.

"True. But you earned your spot in hell along with me for that."

Adelaide took a big pull of the cigarette. "He's staring right at you."

Leland turned to see Morgan staring wide-eyed. He felt the cold heat of vindication before he heard the music skip a beat. Memories spilled into reality, meth-induced nights, glassy eyes, and lots of loneliness. How could their relationship have been so empty when they always had one another? How could they have been so stupid?

"Shit, what do I do?"

"I don't know, Landy. Talk to him if you're so convinced he has talent."

Leland waved, but Morgan did not return the gesture. He placed big headphones over his ears and deep-dived back into the music. Heavy Metal, progressive, and indie-pop.

"Doesn't look like he wants to make friends." Adelaide pushed a lukewarm Genesee into Leland's hand. "A peace offering."

"He won't understand what we're doing."

"Then why are you bothering with this silly idea?"

"It's not a silly idea. I just want to expand our little world."

"Morgan breathes and eats and shits like the rest of us. He's capable of understanding art so long as he opens his heart."

"But I never really explained myself. I just wanted Dorian. Do you know what I'm talking about?"

"Oh, Landy. Your hormones always betray you."

"Morgan was a lie from the start, at least for me."

"Do go on."

"We were so clouded by meth and sex, at one point it was literally all we were doing."

"Look, I totally get it. But what's done is done. It's been three years! I'm sure he's softened up."

"Not by the look he just gave me. He knows exactly who I am."

"Yeah, but is that really stopping you? You said you want this more than anything. Think about the money rolling in. Having some kind of noise for the show would be good. That silence almost drove me crazy."

Two big black eyes that meant business, then pointing to Morgan as she swept plastic beer cups off the table and spread magazines around. Transgressive prose was placed next to photos of casual horror. Leland left her to do what she wanted and thought heavily about what he was about to do himself. A can of scorpions would surely be opened.

"Attention everyone."

A young girl took the stage, and to her right a man set up his canvas and easel. Poetry came out of her mouth smooth as whipped cream; the man drew to the beat of her words. Leland was surprised at first, felt almost a little bit ripped off. But the biggest form of flattery is imitation.

BLOOD KISS

Yet it was the music that made his mind move in too many directions. The bodies on the stage were in a peristaltic rhythm so practiced, so perfect, it was almost like watching a movie unfold. It's what he wanted for Dorian and Tyria.

"Go," Adelaide said.

But Morgan's baggy eyes were on his Mac screen, and Otep's "Blowtorch Nightlight" crushed sound waves until bodies segued into a dance that made no sense in this lounge. Then came a freestyle dance beat, and Leland remembered that Morgan used to play these beats when he wanted to make nice after a big fight. Morgan was sweet in his own way.

What am I about to do? Leland thought. *Dorian is going to kill me.*

No matter the clues Morgan was sending through the music, he could easily dismiss Leland's attempt at rekindling a friendship, and he had every right to. But could he also accept him? Maybe he was overthinking the entire situation. Maybe Dorian was still in his head, knowing very well that he would never approve of Morgan walking back into Leland's life. Nevertheless, Leland downed the last of his cup, and when the beer kicked in the world suddenly was a warm jellybean. Somehow that reminded him of Fitzgerald.

"Hey," Leland said to the telephone pole covered in clothes. "This is for you."

Morgan didn't look at him but said, "I hate Genesee."

"Since when?"

"It's been a real long fucking time, yo."

Not as strung out as Leland remembered, and he even smelled cleaner.

"I'll put this beat on repeat," Morgan said and stepped down from his podium.

"You look different."

Was that all Leland could account for? He hadn't seen or heard from Morgan in three years, and his attempt to pick up right where they left off failed. This moment was *not* the next day of their life, if he hadn't met Dorian.

"I've had a lot of time to clean up."

"That's not what I meant."

"Sure you did. I know you, Landy. Know you too well."

The floodgates opened. Three years to make sense of the anger, three years to get over the hurt. Three years to realize that he'd lost the love of his life to a fancy-pants artist who looked more dead than alive. Leland offered Morgan a seat near Adelaide to talk, but he chose the bar. Drinks were free for employees, another Genesee for Leland and Blue Moon for Morgan.

"Why are you here?" moon eyes, deft lips.

"To make friends, of course."

"You're not innocent, Leland. To be frank, you're quite calculated."

Morgan must have been waiting for the alcohol to kick in as too many feelings had already surged. You never want to start a new beginning by saying things you immediately regret. But Morgan's hands were on his head now, an overt headache long come and gone, then sudden surprise on his face.

Elation or conquering fear? Vengeance? It was some sort of flashback, and Leland almost craved defeat upon himself for what he had done. All Morgan did was stare as if Leland was some sculpture to be marveled at. The worst kind of punishment is to sit in silence; he wanted very much for Morgan to hit him, to make the emotional pain go away.

"I still care about you," Leland said.

"I can't say I feel the same."

"Come on . . ." His hand slipped over Morgan's skinny wrist. "Let's not do this."

"Then tell me why are you here, yo?"

"I actually wanted to hire you for a gig."

"You think I'm that stupid?"

"What?"

"I said do you think I'm stupid?" Morgan asked. "I'm not into spooky shit, yo. I read the article about your show."

"How did you know it was me?"

BLOOD KISS

"By the name. Sentiments, sins ... whatever it was called. Plus, I saw Dorian—"

"*Synergy.*"

"Whatever. I also know *she* is running shit." Morgan pointed at Adelaide. "I don't want anything to do with her or your boyfriend."

Leland was taken back by his anger. "I'm in charge of the shows, Morgan."

"She's your partner."

"Oh, come off it!" Leland said. "My *partner* is Dorian."

"Your *business* partner, smart ass!" Morgan eased out a long breath. "I have nothing against you. You were the best thing I ever had."

Morgan took back a well shot. It seemed that the fires of the past were still burning hot. But after venting he seemed to feel better. They cleared some of the air and picked up where they left off. Sometimes relationships work that way: you fight, you break up and become physically distant, but the moment you are put back in the same room with that person you immediately connect as if nothing had changed.

"You never told me that. Never *showed* me that," Leland said.

"I was in a dark place back then. Now, I'm not."

"Too late."

"*I know* I can never have you again, knew it the night you left me. I was so fucked up then."

"You were."

"But why should I be your friend, especially after all this time? It would only torture me."

"Listen, it wasn't right to do what we did to one another. We enabled bad habits."

"You mean I enabled. I was weak."

"I have so much to live for now," Leland said, serious. "So do you it seems."

"I still love you," Morgan was beginning to slur.

"And I have love for you too, Morgan. But I'm not in love with you."

Leland looked at his watch and realized that he had been talking to Morgan for an hour, and that the room was beginning to spin. How many drinks were there? Now Morgan became friendlier, drunk. He talked about how he got clean, no better incentive than getting beat up and practically left for dead, no better wake up call like breaking up: to lose the one you're most fond of will get anyone to put their life back on track. You never want to feel that more than once.

"Still, there's no reason for me to be in the same room as her," pointing to Adelaide. "She makes me nervous."

"But there is," Leland choked down the last of his piss beer. "You know music. She knows how to get people's attention."

"All she knows is how to hurt people. There's a black cloud over her head, yo."

"She's changed and so have you."

"How has she changed? She looks just as evil."

"The drugs are not in her system. She only deals. Ya gotta understand that she can bring in a crowd . . . and they *spend*."

"Don't give her all the fucking credit. You're a dedicated and intelligent person. You're hardworking. You have a whole article written about a show you created!"

Leland cut Morgan off. "The gig is paid . . . well paid."

Morgan took the moment to think. "Well then, cheers."

Morgan, no matter how unsure he is of something, was always intrigued by the dollar. When you don't know where money is coming in from, when you have no secure job or pretty little degree to get you ahead in life, you take a gig wherever and whenever you can. Especially if it pays.

"I'm broke as a joke, yo."

"Take my number," giving away the digits so freely. "We've always been friends, at least in my eyes."

"On my own terms, though. I don't want to get back into any bullshit. My methadone is at the lowest dosage, and I want to get off of it soon."

"Glad to know that tax dollars have served you."

BLOOD KISS

Morgan blushed, then scurried back to the DJ booth. Leland felt accomplished. He squeezed through a serious clot of bodies and smoke, saw Adelaide in strict work mode: the papers around her a murder scene, glue stick everywhere. Her hair sprinkled with tiny balls of what looked like dust, her madness spilling over into this new advertisement. Kids hung over her like groupies, their opinions and observations something she took to heart.

"They won't get away from me," Adelaide said.

"Isn't that the first rule of junkies?"

"All for the sake networking. And this!" Holding up the new advertisement.

SyNtHeSiS, kelvin-bright, a broken pen dripping ink onto a canvas, but smeared by a ravenous looking paintbrush.

"Psychedelic," Leland said. "Dorian would love it."

"And Tyria would hate it, but that's the point. Nothing inspires her more than anger."

"How sadistic of you."

"What did Morgan say?"

"Well, he still hates you."

"What a surprise," Adelaide said.

"And let me guess . . . you could care less?"

Adelaide nodded, pushed the ads into Leland's hands and performed a new song and dance. *I want it on Facebook and Twitter*, she said. *We gotta get the word out fast!* They flew into the lavender night to catch the J train to Marcy Avenue.

The glass clink of Old E brought back a bad memory, but the slow weekend crawl was soothing. Leland gripped the handrail, then Adelaide's sharp shoulder for balance. He eyed a hipster who was reading Nabokov's *Lolita* and began to hum "Off to the Races."

A black man caught onto Leland's song, deciding no better time than now to make a performance all his own: he swallowed his cigarette and made the tequila in his bottle disappear in two gulps. Everyone clutched their wallets and purses. You could never be too careful with the Brooklyn bums. One wrong move and all of a sudden five filthy fingers will claim what you have worked so hard for: your cell phone, your wallet, your fucking shirt if they felt like it.

"I wonder what they're doing," Leland said in reference to Dorian and Tyria.

"She's been on some massive scavenger hunt with Dorian. All they do is spend time together. It's making me uncomfortable."

"Oh, stop it. They're becoming good friends."

"That's exactly what I'm afraid of," Adelaide said.

"You have to let them bond. It's important"

"It's not just that, Landy."

"What is it then?"

"This is strictly between you and I, but I *felt* something that night."

"What do you mean?"

"There is so much energy between them I'm afraid that they might kill one another."

Leland didn't react. "We get out here."

Down familiar stairs, a labyrinth of windows and heavy doors, the warehouses reflecting badly against the cobblestone streets. In the vista was the skeletal phosphorescence of New York City, but it was the dark glow of Brooklyn that awed them, no matter how many times they had seen it. Leland ran his hand nervously through his brown wave of hair, the signature signal that he wanted to get high. He always felt nervous walking here, as any gay man would; someone was always going to pick on you. Adelaide caught his weariness, lit her swirly glass pipe and took the first toke.

"Me next."

The Sour D pistoned into his head. Life was now a cushion rather than a pin. He leaned upon a wall, then looked down at the puddle by his boots. That roll-out-of-bed look is getting old, he thought to himself.

"It took me leaving Morgan for him to clean up," Leland said. "Isn't that ironic?"

"As long as he's clean, that's all that matters."

BLOOD KISS

Leland crossed his arms; his leather jacket made a strange stretching noise.

"Funny how far we've made it as friends. You know, it's been like five years. But for sixteen months out of those years we had our fair share of bad times."

"I never liked the drugs, but they sure fucking liked me."

It was no secret that for as young as they were, Adelaide and Leland had lost a lot of their youth to addiction. But while the drugs completely took over Adelaide's existence, Leland resisted as much as he could, never letting the needle whisper lovingly in his ear like it did to Adelaide. Often he had to remind himself that women are emotional creatures and fall prey to their own mind easier than men.

"You were a true dopehead."

"That all depends on how you deduce."

"Who taught you that word?"

"I read a lot."

Leland began searching through his cell phone.

"What the hell are you looking for?"

"Dictionary.com."

Now they weaseled their way through the cobblestone streets, switched to hand-rolled cigarettes to cover the smell of the weed. Leland's head felt fuzzy but his mind was relaxed; ideas came at him like paper airplanes. When he looked at Adelaide the outline of her was something like a caricature out of a scary comic book.

"Look!"

The club was called Death by Audio. Here you could find every caste of the indifferent and detached conglomerating, gossiping, abusing, drinking and exploring their bottomless hate for the world. Their vacant faces were pierced, poked, gauged and prodded in every orifice; hair pricked like a crown of thorns atop every head. And that's when Leland heard the sounds of local punk rising through the concrete walls like a scratched and broken record.

"Look at all these kids," Adelaide said. "A goldmine."

Leland saw high heels, Doc Marten boots and cruddy Converse sneakers. He thought briefly about that metal head that had put the knife to Adelaide's throat, the blood oozing slow and wet. Would he be here?

"We're certainly in for a treat tonight."

"I can make three bills easily."

Leland could see the water now, fat black belly, hardly a tide, but the smell in the air was that of muscles and seaweed. A beach that could have been. Addy made a quick exchange with two fiends, and when they left something passed *through* Leland. Nothing of true substance or sensation, but something like he saw at the *SyNeRgY* show. Adelaide met him on top of the hill, saw Leland's confused, cold look.

"What did you just see?"

"Nothing . . . it was nothing."

"We're alone, you can tell me."

"No, it's bad."

Tell me, Leland. Tell me so *I don't* have to say it."

"No."

"So you're gunna make me say it?"

Leland put out his cigarette. "I didn't see anything . . . . I felt it."

"I can't explain what it is either. The weed's making me paranoid!"

"Hell, it *was* Tyria for all I know."

"Landy—"

"I know I sound crazy, so I just want to try and forget it."

"You ain't crazy. I felt it too. Cold, damp, depthless."

"And Dorian's after it," Leland said.

Adelaide stopped, gripped Leland's hand hard. "No. His painting was after it."

The blackest cloud Leland had ever seen rose before them, disjointed and big as a warehouse. It writhed to the sound of the music coming from down the block. Leland pulled Adelaide close to him, and just as they were going to run, the blackness broke into a billion leggy bodies and crawled down the first sewer it found.

"Let's get inside," Leland said.

BLOOD KISS

WE GOT OFF THE J TRAIN AT KOSCIUSKO.

The first thing I noticed was the smell, herbal smoke laced with diesel fumes. Tyria lit a cigarette, offered me one, but I was too inspired to ruin my body in that moment. I knew that eventually I would meet my damnation, but I would not bring it willfully upon myself tonight.

"This area is quiet once the train leaves," Tyria said.

"I'm not usually in this part of Brooklyn, so I wouldn't know."

I took a panoramic view of the ugly neighborhood. The boulevard was too long to comprehend, and its name was like that in Manhattan: Broadway. But the Brooklyn version hardly lived up to its big sister. For every dazzle and dream come true in the big city there are drug deals and dollar store robberies on this side. And then I saw the sign. *GOODBYE BLUE MONDAY* displayed like the bottom of a trash can.

"Music. Art. Antiques. Coffee. Beer. Wine. Stuff," Tyria said. "You'll enjoy it."

"Stuff?"

Tyria took the last pull of her cigarette, flicked it into the street. "Yeah, stuff."

We ducked beneath cool blue neon. Once inside Tyria immediately approached a crowd that she was friendly with: a jaded bartender and a few scrungy musicians who were setting up for a show, their shit everywhere, paperbacks, post its and equipment.

"You gunna read tonight?" A baby dyke said.

Tyria shook her head.

"Why not? You're famous now."

"Because it's my night off."

"Oh, so who's your friend?"

"This is Dorian," Tyria said stern. "He's an artist."

"Omigod! The one from the show."

I nodded; the dyke took a step closer as if I was some strange museum statue.

"Thought he would be bigger, well, I mean from what I read in the paper."

"Get lost, will you?" Tyria said, then looked at me. "Ignore these people. I only come here for the good beer, maybe the music."

Inside was lengthy rather than wide. The smell of dust, spiders and beer was assaulting. To my immediate left was a wall of vinyls, paperbacks, pre-world war toys and strange trinkets. Antiques indeed, and all for sale. Did I want to buy something? Yes. Everything. But I am always weary of second hand expenditures as I don't enjoy inheriting someone else's ghost. I have too many of my own.

"So many vinyls," I said. "It's like a musical library."

"There must be over a thousand bands."

"Do you care if I take a walk around?"

"By all means feel free."

Right next to the front door were two small chests, and inside were very special records. I held them as if buried treasure. Black Sabbath's *Masters of Reality*, Fleetwood Mac's *Tusk*, The Cure's *17 Seconds* and Tool's *Lateralus*. I imagined all this music conglomerating, fusing. There came the sight of golden ribbons; I felt my blood vibrate. I had worked myself into a daze, not realizing that I was staring at a selection of instruments hanging from above. A lone violin and keyboard on fishing line, an acoustic guitar layered in cobweb. Perhaps they were the cause of the psilocybin images.

"Are they for sale too?"

"Yes," Tyria said. "And look here."

She slipped herself into shadow. The only reason why I knew she was even there was by the starlight tinge of her hair, glimmering jade of her eyes. She pulled me into the main section, pushed a shelf back as if a secret passageway so that I could see the massive amount of books. There were numerous titles about sex, drugs and rock n' roll, the swinging sixties and Stonewall. Horror, Dark Fantasy and

BLOOD KISS

Mythology. *House of Leaves, The Modern Prometheus, Strange Angels* and *Wuthering Heights.*

"Makes you want to read forever," Tyria said.

"I wish I had the time to do such."

"Why don't you?"

Before I could answer a drugged transient with glossy eyes rudely interrupted us. "Hey, you're that painter."

"I am."

"Saw your show."

"And?"

I just had to know.

"Word's getting around fast."

"Why's that?" Tyria said.

The kid licked his scabbed lips. "I was there. I felt the power."

All of a sudden I couldn't breathe, and as I grabbed Tyria for help I saw her face go red as fire. Though the walls felt like they were closing in, I came to slowly realize that bar was almost at full capacity, and the wave of heat was just that of gathering bodies. I watched the kids doodle in their notebooks with bloodied and calloused fingers, fell in love as Tyria introduced me to their world of poetry, music, passion and treachery. It made me dizzy; the smell of their body odor was horrendous.

"You look like you need a drink."

"That is definitely in order," I said.

Tyria led me to the bar, ordered two PBRs and two well shots. The bartender's hair hung in front of her face like cobweb, a typical Brooklyn dyke that liked to be called "dude" and "bro" but didn't want the sex change. When I took down the Wild Turkey battery acid filled my guts, making me almost spit it back out.

As the girls chatted I began a strange telepathic conversation with Salvador Dali. It was a statuette on the bar top, and I bowed before my master like a pauper does to the king. But he was pointing at something, an ancient film reel spinning as if it wanted to play a movie: one of a painter and a poet, of a stage too dark to see, and so they must use one another as a fulcrum to perform.

"Wild Turkey ain't your thing?" Tyria interrupted my daydream.

"It's pretty cheap."

"Who the fuck has money for the good stuff? We're artists."

"Amen."

My vision began to breakaway; everything went drippy. The lampshade that housed a patient Buddha layered in strange drunken makeup began to laugh at me. The beer taps vomited flames.

"Addy came by today," I heard the bartender say.

Tyria snapped her head to the side. "If she wants to find me, she can catch me at home."

"She says you haven't been home in a long time."

"That's a fucking lie," Tyria said.

"She seemed pretty strung out. Her hair was a mess, and she smelled like she hadn't showered in a while. I begged her to stay with me, but . . ."

Tyria clicked her dark nails against the bar. "What does this have to do with me?"

"She's worried about you. She said you're with some guy all the time, an artist. She thinks you're—"

And then the girl shut her mouth, her pale eyes sailing my way. I froze with the beer to my lips.

"I'm Shelley."

"Dorian," I said.

I licked my viper bites nervously, played with my black ear project that stuck out through my hair like a needle. We unanimously agreed that more alcohol was in order. Shelley dropped the conversation and gave us the next two drinks on the house. Might it be that the Wild Turkey had changed my way of thinking (and after Shelley's suspicions I should have better controlled myself) but I was overcome with a wanton need. My hand reached out and gripped Tyria's arm ever so slightly. Her skin was not scaly as I once thought, not

BLOOD KISS

hardened by a life of pain. It was tender and inviting. Shelley looked at me like I was a rapist.

Tyria pulled away; her jade eyes sparked with rage.

"We're not on a fucking date."

"I—"

Tyria took a handful of my shirt. "Don't ever touch me like that again."

But the reality in her face was that my touch might have sparked an interest, and oh, how it almost made her head spin! Because, she knew, my hand was not Adelaide's; not soft, not aware of another girl's needs, not intelligent or even gentle. But she might have liked it.

"Didn't mean to do that."

Liar.

"You're fucking wasted. I'm going outside."

Tyria flew from her seat, a tornado wrapped in skin. She knocked over her can of beer and flipped a table. I bulleted after her. Outside it was so cold I couldn't stand it, but I caught her body heat. She was raging. I knew it was in my best interest to let her cool down, so I bummed a loosie and waited for her to talk.

"You can't touch me like that," she said.

I apologized again.

"I don't accept."

The streetlight dazzled. An aureole was her shadow. She was in need of being worshiped. She needed the stage. And then the emotional levy broke. She took me back to a vertiginous time when a little girl never felt safe, always too scared to sleep because that's when Daddy came into her room and touched her. A little girl who had no one to protect her. Her story was instant poetry, born from her dark history; the madness and sadness brought tears to my eyes. I almost vomited. How could someone have hurt this fallen angel so? I could not fathom it. I felt suddenly murderous.

"He's long dead," Tyria said. "So don't get any ideas."

"I was contemplating slicing off his prick and painting with it."

"Yeah, well, his heart exploded in his chest a few years ago. I would have loved to see that," smoke shrouding her face.

"I hope it was a painful death."

"The goddesses answer one's prayers in queer ways." Tyria gripped her ohm necklace, the triple moon and trident glowing.

"Did you put a spell on him?"

"I'm not a witch."

"What about your mom?" I asked.

"She died with the bottle still wrapped around her lips."

I had no words for her. A lump formed in my throat thinking about parents, skin to skin contact, love, affection. I never had it from my own, and neither did she. We had that much more in common. And then some goony broke our conversation in half. He talked as if we had asked to hear what his opinions were of the world, said how he was going to read some poetry and how he wanted to see the queer band play tonight but didn't know if he liked punk or not. Tyria blew smoke into his face; I didn't make eye contact.

"They can't help it," she said

But I couldn't get the thought of her childhood out of my head.

"I don't know if I can even dream of that kind of pain. My gods, how did you survive it?"

"By challenging everything."

She lifted up her pant leg so that I could see the tattooed palette of her skin. A vortex of black and green, but not just that: burns and keloid scars, so many of them, a dream catcher made flesh. On her left wrist the acid-green tattoo of the ouroboros could not hide the deepest markings. She let me touch them. The raised skin was hard, but tender. When I looked up Tyria's face gleamed like the tip of a knife.

"You want a taste of the pain?" Grave matters in her voice.

"Yes," I said.

BLOOD KISS Daniel Stone

How could I not? To vicariously live through her past was a sudden must. She took a great pull on her cigarette, brought my palm up and then put the burning tip right on it. I'd already had a glossy keloid scar of my own thanks to Adelaide, and so the pain didn't touch me at first; I simply loved the sight of the orange corona exploding, the smell of my skin burning. But as Tyria pushed the cigarette deeper there came the faint twinge of pain, the realization that my skin was rolling back two layers.

"Terrible," I said. "Heartbreaking."

"You don't see me at all."

Before I could justify the pain more bodies arrived and stole my attention, bad kids in denim and nylon who looked at us like we were on display.

"You're the poet and you're the painter," a girl said.

"We're an official commodity." Tyria almost spat the words.

The girl looked suddenly disgusted. "You're just as vile as your performance."

"Worse," I said.

"You got another gig coming up?"

Tyria and I remained quiet.

"Are you deaf?"

"We do," I said ignorantly. "Spookiest gig in the city."

My usual hate for these Brooklynites was instantly abated. Every day is a learning experience. I knew that they were to be my new source of income; everything that I once knew about them, their precarious lifestyles, their hollow opinions, was gone. I kicked myself for judging them so harshly.

"Please come out," I said.

Tyria added. "We enjoy when like-minded people get together."

One girl stepped forward. "I don't know how you can top the first."

"Improvement is part of art. Each emotion is different," Tyria said.

I handed them a *SyNeRgY* ad for effect as I had no new ones to give out.

"Same place, different theme."

Cigarette's stamped out by ugly sneakers and the red burn on my hand blistering, but we headed inside. Shaking like a leaf, I looked up and saw the lights begin to dim. On the miniature stage a queer band was setting up. Amps everywhere, chords, a microphone and cigarettes.

"They're so androgynous," Tyria said.

The music began. I thought to myself that there is nothing more soothing than a live show. To see the world through the eyes of musicians is a wonderful vacation from my own head. We sat at the closest table where I studied the traceries of veins on Tyria's hand like a mystic on the verge of seeing the jaded future.

"I understand this negativity, and how we can use it to our benefit," I said. "But we'll have to do things that others won't want us to do."

"As in Addy and Landy."

I nodded

"So what is it exactly you want to do?"

"Take chances."

The queer band played another song, an explosion of punk and thrash that shook the foundation. Tyria bobbed her head up and down; I soaked in the tunes. The next song was called "Sever," an ambient musical circus. The song depressed me entirely, the lead singer hopeless in her forever need of the sweet sounds her former lover makes. The words sat heavy with me. Could Tyria and I use music for our own show?

"Music is everything," she said. "Brings a crowd together."

Her gaze dropped away. She was obviously weary of spending so much time with me. I wanted to shake her, my meat-doll. Why was she so hard on herself? Sometimes a woman must undress the ego in order to let the conscious metamorphose. Sometimes one has to leave behind the scorn

BLOOD KISS

to let their garden-mind be pollinated with the mind of another.

Life Imitates Art.

"I like this band," I said.

The lights a mad flicker and the band cut into their third song. And then it made itself known. Tyria's shadow, oddly calm—expanding monster yawn—not alive as I'd seen it before. She pretended it wasn't there, flicking her zippo lighter down her black pant leg so that I could see the engravement: *T&A*.

Small minded nymphs would read it as tits and ass, but the sentiment, I knew, was one of early lust: Tyria and Adelaide. A romantic gesture; Landy had given me many as well. Perhaps that was the moment they knew they had found the one. There is a stark difference between being in love and finding *the one*. But the way Tyria was staring into the flame spoke of a life without Adelaide. A life of rot.

"I think I'm drunk," Tyria said.

Indeed the beer was taking control. Everything lilted, the lights became too bright. Ghostly inebriation and the soon-to-be hangover spread fast and heavy in my head, fire down my neck. The memory of the stage plowed into my skull, forming a deep ravine of shadow as my lust for Tyria bloomed.

Just knowing we would be on the stage again soon soothed my soul. To imagine commanding a crowd, the thought of all those frightened faces, those hands in the air, was almost as exciting as deciphering Tyria's brain. We had just become friends, and I was still trying to understand her wants and needs, her fetishes, her vices and virtues, preferences, doubts and inspirations. The human psyche is the strangest puzzle of all, and we have yet to truly figure it out. So many roads to travel, so many pathways to genius or madness.

"I saw that sparkle in your eye," breaking the silence. "You want it like me," I said.

"If the stage is willing, so am I."

The lights falling like a hot nosebleed on her skin. It was time to go; we'd already killed four hours. The train ride home was slow and gruesome; someone had puked on the seat across from us. Tyria fell asleep but dreamed uneasily. She awoke with a weak scream and gave into icy temptation as she spread a fine white line across her hand and snorted.

Cocaine, she had told me, was the only drug that made all that was wrong evanescently right. I'd never tried it before and was deathly curious. Before I could even ask for a bump she had put away her stash, slapped on headphones and closed her eyes. The train light accentuated the freckles on her skin and the wrong angles of her face.

"Hush little baby," I said.

But the song in her ears was so loud she didn't hear me, hard-boiled bass, devilish chords of drop D tuning and a touch of synth.

I shook her. "You're a Deftones fan?"

Tyria remained in her daze. I bathed in the black rainbows of the lyrics, listening to the world explode beneath my clothes, thinking of all those horrors creeping across my skull; I fell asleep to dream the melodies, as did Tyria, nightmare worlds divided. Violent visions found me, oils and acrylic slathered like meat across a canvas; death was rampant. How I had touched the dark, accepting the fact that it touched me back. Dragon scales and orchid petals.

"It's been with me forever," Tyria said, awakening. "So has this color thing. Your aura is purple."

"Is that good?"

"It's comfortable. Just like when I read, I'm comfortable."

"Why don't we read anymore, as a society?" I said. "It's the work of miracles how much of an escape reading is."

"A lot of people don't understand the benefit. But if we rewound time to before television, people read their asses off."

"But why can't we evolve with all this awesome new technology and still read?"

BLOOD KISS

"I think attention spans have shortened. Twitter and Facebook might have done that."

Her jaw quivered, the cocaine crash soon to come.

"You shouldn't put that shit up your nose. It'll freeze your brain."

"That's half the point."

"And what's the other half?"

"Addiction, I guess.

Back out on the street the conversation took a jagged turn, less art and more literature, sex and death; the webby cosmos that links all books together, much like how it links life itself. How waking up each day is a joyful curse. You spend your hours hoping that nothing will bog you down, that no one will hurt you, but somehow it always happens.

"I don't plan on hurting you," I said.

"*Plan* is the scariest word in the world."

And then back to square one. I do not know how much time it took or how far we walked, but I now saw Catland smiling at me, and Tyria eyeing it like a holy sight. She pulled out a great set of keys, rubber skeletons, a Magic Hat bottle opener and a something that reminded me of a lightsaber.

"This is it," I said. When did this feel like returning a date home to her worried parents?

"Why don't you come in?"

I was surprised she asked. "Are you sure? You know Addy wouldn't want me in there."

"It's my apartment. I can have friends over if I want."

We walked into the land of esoterica and incense. Before me was a table littered with candles and herbs; books of masochism, decadence and Deities filled the shelves. The shelves along the wall to my left had jars of herbs on them. *Anise* said one, and when I opened it I swear I could smell Italian cookies. Another jar was labeled *sage*, thus which the odor was wonderfully sweet. Tyria stuck her hand in jar labeled *Wormwood* and pulled out potent green leaves for me to see, to feel. But it was the yellow-green seeds of *Asafoetida* that sparked my interest the most.

"What do you know about these fantastic herbs?"

"I can teach you, if you want."

"Make me a believer then."

Tyria pointed to a black door. "My place is downstairs."

I'd never seen a frown stretch so sidelong. It was the most interesting facial expression I'd ever encountered.

BLOOD KISS

9

hrough the heavy metal door to greet the young hipster dressed in rags, her tobacco stained fingers ready to take seven of your dollars, but those busy blue eyes widening at the sight of Adelaide. A revelation claimed her face. She returned the money without thought.

"Free for you," she said. "Curators of the macabre."

"Thanks," Adelaide said.

"Just keep the art coming."

She waived them off and went back to reading Angela Carter's *Wise Children*. Leland had read that book twice, smiled that someone else was genuinely lost inside the world of Dora and Nora. The hallway was long, the brick walls dusted in fog; neon ads were spilled across the floor like confetti. The smell of aerosol fumes became sickening as some of the graffiti was still wet and dripping *ElEcTrIc OrChId* and *REVELATION mother EARTH.*

"This is like something out of a bad 80's film."

"It's all about the music," Adelaide said. "Plus, this is how we'll make ourselves get noticed."

"Free advertising?" Leland questioned her motif.

"Exactly."

The inner core of Death By Audio was populated with a shit-ton of badassery. Perfectly flawed boys and girls somewhat damaged. Death heads, punks, thrashers, leather and lace. It was a crowd that knew Leland and Adelaide, and so they were greeted with bows, hand shakes, business cards and even hugs. Pinnacle gods inside these walls.

"What you got tonight?" The kids said in unison.

"Can you people let her breathe please?"

But Adelaide's hand was already fishing inside her bag for the goods. Eyes brighten and teeth showing. Leland had no place in drug dealing, didn't very much like to live in the past, so he felt free to look around. On the main floor the strobe lights turned faces into skulls, made eyes endless black holes. Cigarettes were banned but no one batted an eye to glass pipes or hookahs. The stage was draped in duct tape, flower petals and horror ephemera. It was all dizzying, and by the time Leland found his way back to Adelaide the crowd had dispersed and she was smiling.

"One sniff and they all come begging." Adelaide stuffed the cash into her jacket pocket.

"I never said I didn't believe you. But I don't want anything to do with that shit. I'm over it."

Adelaide rolled her eyes. "Quit being so high and mighty."

"You quit trying to be a rock star."

"I'm trying to make a living."

Leland remained quiet for one moment, unsure of what to say next. The room filled with a small ripple of laughter, and it was with that sudden sound that he knew it was time to unveil the ads to their new source of income. Adelaide handed him half the stack. Leland took a good look at a few, deciding that they were something that could have been made from the junk-sick brain of William S. Burroughs. Being that they were handcrafted made them all the more special.

SyNtHeSiS dripping like quill ink, and snapping a paintbrush in half was a mighty microphone. The images would haunt their viewer for a long time.

"*Synthesis*. The perfect storm." Leland turned his snapback hat around.

"What did I tell you about that hat?"

"Just shaddap about it will ya."

"You think you're some party boy, don't you? Devilish little bastard."

"It looks good on me."

BLOOD KISS *Daniel Stone*

"Makes you look like a slutty twink."

"And you think I don't like that?"

"You should be seen as a strong person in the public eye."

"Jesus H. Christ, Addy. Get over yourself. We have business minds, but we can also have a good time. I'm gunna get a drink. You in?"

"Whatever you're having," Adelaide said reluctantly. "Oh, and Landy?"

"Yeah?"

"It wouldn't be such a bad idea to put on a show here, eh?"

"The stage is perfect and so is the lighting . . . but I can almost guarantee that it'll cost too much. The Bowery space is f-r-e-e."

"You always have your head on straight . . . for such a homo!"

The back room was a war zone of graffiti. It all seemed to blend without effort into one huge mural inspired by the psychedelic days of The Magical Mystery Tour. The images brought songs like "Lucy in the Sky with Diamonds" and "I am the Walrus" into Leland's head.

He passed a table fronted by two boys. They were selling pins, patches and t-shirts for a band called Electric Orchid. One boy had a face like a bird and was wearing a TOOL t-shirt; his black hair was cropped eyebrow length and tipped in red. The copy of *Naked Lunch* he held looked like it had been read over fifty times. The other boy was so androgynous with his high cheekbones, multicolored hair and black on black clothes that Leland had to study him to the point of embarrassment to realize that he actually *was* a boy.

"Hey," Leland said. "I like those pins."

Four eyes met his, two green insects and two sapphire balls of fire.

"Name your price," the androgyne said.

Leland smiled.

"I'd be a hypocrite if I said I wanted to spend little when I have a business mind of my own."

"Dollar for everything on the table," the bookworm said. "Just for you."

"You selling for the band?"

"I *am* the band," the androgyne said. "This is Electric Orchid's first gig in Brooklyn."

"What about the t-shirts?"

"Those are five."

Leland gazed at the mythological print, Cthulhu-like creature hovering above a nameless city; the band's insignia crisscrossed in hellfire.

"See anything you like?"

"Oh yes," Leland said with his eyes on the boys.

"I'm Rez and this is Alex."

"Do you play in the band too?"

"No."

"I've never seen Electric Orchid, but I've definitely heard of them."

"Get ready to be mind-fucked," Alex's sotto voce voice was assertive but friendly.

But I want more than a mind-fuck.

Leland was just unfolding a bill when two gothlings levitated toward the table. They had their own deal in mind, slipped a crisp twenty-dollar bill into Alex's hand. Leland watched Alex open his trench coat—wafting spicy licorice—to take out a silver cigarette case. It was filled with very thin sheets marked with a black rose. Acid, Leland knew, maybe LSD. He didn't know people even did the stuff anymore with the competition of more modern drugs like Molly and K.

"What are you staring at?" Rez said. "Haven't you ever seen a deal go down?"

"You don't even know," Leland laughed.

He remembered trying the stuff a few times but could never figure out why people liked it. The drug is best taken with a group of friends because hallucinating isn't safe when you do it unsupervised or you're likely to wind up streaking the neighborhood or masturbating in a police precinct. Acid can open the floodgate to your madness.

BLOOD KISS

"I see your little girlfriend pushing for a show. But she's got it all wrong," Alex said.

"Her name is Adelaide and she's just a friend."

"That's good to know," Rez's smile was sharp as a bird beak. "What are you promoting?"

"Spoken word poetry."

"Your own?" Alex and Rez asked together.

"Someone I'm managing."

"Maybe we ought to come by and check it out."

"If you like art, yeah."

"Count us in,"

"Dorian, my boyfriend, he's an artist that paints to the poet's words."

"Boyfriend!" Rez said as he opened a flask. "Is he a Dali enthusiast?"

"He practically worships him. Bacon too."

"Your boyfriend sounds like everything I want in a new friend," Alex said.

"Well, I do hope to see you there," Leland handed the boys a flyer. "And I'll take two pins please."

"Two bucks," Rez said in his Queens accent.

Leland put them directly on his t-shirt. Colored red and black was the mountainous terrain, and in the center of a rotted moon were a colony of bats. It was the best two bucks he had spent in a long time. Leland waved to the boys and then went to the bar. But something was lingering, his thoughts were betraying him. He couldn't help his hormones, wanted so badly to get right between the legs of those marbled and pierced beauties. He suddenly hoped that if he turned around four heartbreakingly beautiful eyes would be watching his every move. But he was too scared to find out.

At the bar three kids jabbered about Electric Orchid. Leland heard words alive and *heart*, but didn't know what to make of them. He saw other people lazing on soccer mom car seats, drowning in the newest excitement that their iPhones and Androids could provide. Did they not care about bed bugs or mites? But what did it matter when the images those cell phones provided were everything in that moment.

This made him realize that he hadn't talked to Dorian all day. What was he doing with Tyria that was so special anyway? Were they really getting to be good friends? Were they painting the town red? Maybe—and this could be true—they couldn't stand the sight of one another anymore. Some people are made only for the stage, forging no relationship once they exit.

Leland felt guilty for being needy, but his love for Dorian was so deep he couldn't *not* talk to him. For the last two weeks there had been nothing more than a hello in the morning and then out the door to see Tyria. Sometimes he would get a good fucking, a wet and passionate session; other nights there was nothing but Dorian's cold body to cuddle, his hair in his face and his heart barely beating. It was like Tyria had Dorian possessed!

Life had changed so quickly since *SyNeRgY*.

And so Leland gave into automatic privilege via text message and sent a simple *Are you okay? What have you been doing?* He typed as fast as he could think, turning around to make sure no one was looking at him for fear of appearing clingy. Leland liked to look as neutral and free as possible.

For the boys, mostly.

No immediate answer, but his iMessage said that Dorian had at least read it. Worry seized his brain, but then released him when he absently ordered a well shot and two PBRs from the young bartender. He took the first syrupy shot down and chugged the PBR. His face warmed as did his loins, and just as he had hoped, four eyes were staring *right* at him from the Electric Orchid table. Naturally Leland was attracted to Rez and Alex. He had a thing for skinny artistic boys; it was one of the reasons why he was still with Dorian.

And as it goes through every man's head gay or straight, he wondered what a three way would be like with Rez and Alex. Their exquisitely skinny bodies pressed into his own, their curtains of hair, smoker's breath, wet and warm tongues, their eyes unraveling universes. New smells and new flesh to taste, new bones to learn.

BLOOD KISS

But something smashed that image.

It was the voice of an angel, or its fallen cousin. A short girl with pink and black hair swinging like spider's legs, dreads half undone, and she berated the bartender for a drink, hard stuff, Jägermeister straight up. Her arms were covered in jet-black tattoos of bats and some kind of archaic map; her clothes were torn and her Doc Martens were peeling like snakeskin, but she wore them proud. Leland all of a sudden smelled clove cigarettes, and when he saw her face he thought that she looked exactly like Rez. That's when Alex called her to the table.

"Delilah!" he said. "Jäger bombs!"

"Don't ya think I fucking know?"

Her mouth twisted into something like a rictus grin, the smile that comes with the peace you find in death. She was a girl that would not regale you with her life's story, would not make friends easily. If you wanted to find out more about her, you had to see her on the stage.

" 'Scuse me, comin' through."

Delilah's body brushed against Leland's as she crossed over to get to the merchandise table, and through that iota of touch he could feel her feral energy like fire and ice. She made it clear that he better stay and watch her perform, to learn something. When he looked at Rez and Alex they were downing their shot and beer with their best friend, their lead singer.

"You gunna give me my damn beer or what? I'm thirsty."

Adelaide's warm hand on his face, her smile safe, familiar. Cash flowed out of her pockets, and the word on the street now was that *SyNtHeSiS* would top *SyNeRgY* so hard! *This time we're charging a door fee*, she said. *They love the ads!* As soon as she finished the PBR hands came for her and she made her secret exchanges.

"Electric Orchid is about to go on," Leland said.

"What is that in your hand?"

Leland hadn't realized it, but two tabs were sitting in his palm.

"Acid, I guess."

"You guess?"

"Here, put one on your tongue."

Adelaide stepped back.

"It's not addictive."

"What are you the narcotic guru all of a sudden?"

"Acid isn't a narcotic. Now watch," Leland placed a thin tab on his tongue, felt it dissolve like a Listerine breath strip but without the cool taste; it was more like a wet fungus. "See?"

Adelaide was hesitant at first. "Okay now me." She stuck out her tongue and let the tab dissolve. "Tastes terrible."

"It'll relax us. You know the lead singer is a chic right?" Leland said.

"Yeah, and funny story: the music business can't stand female-fronted bands."

"Fuck all that shit and fuck the majority," Leland put up his hands. "It's time we let them *really* know why they all call us freaks, weirdoes and outcasts."

"SO THIS IS MY PLACE," Tyria said.

"Is Adelaide home?" I hated myself for asking that. How could those be the first words I utter inside of Tyria's personal living quarters?

"She won't be back for a while." Tyria looked me right in the eyes. "I hope this doesn't disappoint."

How could I be disappointed when it was everything I ever wanted? You know you're in an artist's space when there is shit piled upon shit, how blatantly obvious it is that the person who resides here has no time to think about the upkeep. Creativity can do that to people, make them forget about life and the things we need to do in order to be classified as human. The only responsibility we feel is to that of the art.

"Reminds me of a cave," I said.

BLOOD KISS

"Is it the darkness?"

"The dankness, is more like it."

We walked into the center. I smelled the mingled dust of ambrosia, rose petals and sage, but also the horrid stench of filth, saw the proof of it in the unwashed piles of black clothing. Tyria lit a candle and set it on the coffee table, and as the light fingered each part of the room I scanned the ephemera lying around.

Myriad books scrunched together and in no fucking order; some had never been opened and some had been read until the spine was unrecognizable. Dust and cigarette ash scabbed everything. I found the walls with my hands, attracted to what at first I thought were thumb tacks but which turned out to be the eyes of fallen rock stars, posters and magazine cut outs everywhere.

"What are these?" I said.

But my hands knew before my eyes: beer bottle caps revealing bleak fortunes and rare facts. I found a label with the words ARROGANT BASTARD, dared to take a sip from the bottle and nearly spit out the warm fuzz. After that I followed a path of cobwebs to find guitar picks and a quill pen sitting in a jar labeled BAT'S BLOOD.

"As you can see I'm a bit of a hoarder," Tyria said.

"Some things are not meant to be parted with."

"Especially when they have priceless sentimental value."

I lit a cigarette. "We're in a constant battle of collecting moments versus things, but these things *are* my moments."

I absently looked through more shit. Pages crumbled beneath my grip; ash kicked up into my face. I walked the perimeter of her bed, which was cloaked in black and silver, only to be pulled back angrily. Tyria didn't want me to see what lay at the foot of her bed, but how could I not investigate? Curiosity might have killed the cat, but it would make a believer out of me. What exactly lay beyond the periphery of her mattress? Was it a hole in the earth, a taxidermy nightmare, a carnival trick?

It was an altar.

"I said don't look, but you just had to."

A small table draped in red velvet, gold chains and flower petals. Herb bundles and a bowl of sweet ash banked by candelabras and incense sticks. A tapestry of fine Indian silk fronted the altar with the symbol of Ohm in its center. Tyria found me gazing, but so was she. We sat opposite one another, legs folded, our hearts stammering. She lit a cone-shaped incense that threw spirals of smoke in the air, reminding me of summer nights.

"Be careful," Tyria said.

"It looks like a simple place of worship."

Nothing prepared me to see the thing that lay in the center. Upon first glance it was just a clay glob partly molded into something sinister, but clearly feminine. Then it began to throb, molt. Blue skin broke out of the shell, wet and sore, its great tongue striped red as it swung out of the fanged mouth. Four tiny arms beaded in gold gyrated to a rhythm I could not hear.

Tyria snapped her fingers to jar my attention, but I could not look away from the queer sight as every time I blinked the thing changed positions! In one moment the arms wrapped like a pretzel, in the next they were sinuous as worms, torturing my immortal soul with sex, blood and darkness.

"What is this?"

In that moment I smelled death. But this was not the smell of wasting away. William S. Burroughs once said that death smells worse than carrion, cordite and burnt flesh. Yes it does. Death smells real. Death smells like the one thing everyone has in common.

"Kali," Tyria said.

She had startled me. My bones shook madly.

"Don't be afraid."

Now the Indian deity was fanning open her legs so wide I could see all the way into her volcanic cavity. Was she to tell me my fortune, or did she want that I succumb to her evils? I had no reason not to indulge, but every rational cell in my body was screaming in defiance. I reached my hand

BLOOD KISS

out, fingered the fiery cleft until I was knuckle deep, until it felt like my skin was melting.

"You can't touch her like that," Tyria said.

"Leland was right, you are a witch."

I watched the little demon for a few more minutes, deciding that it was in my best interest to not test the limits of my faith. I didn't know if I had any and I was in no shape to challenge the supranatural. I asked Tyria to walk me to the other side of her bed so that I could sink into her black and silver world. But my eyes deceived me. I was witnessing another miracle.

"Please, no."

"Goddess," Tyria said.

She was less macabre and more elegance, but for some reason I knew she held twice the power Kali. A molding so exquisite it could have been carved from a tree in Eden. She wore an eloquent Greek dress of white and green; amethyst crystals hung upon her breasts, and in her hands three flames were shaped like crescent moons. Not just one woman, but three. Three faces, three minds, three hearts.

"Hecate," Tyria said. "Goddess of the crossroads."

"What do you want me to do?"

"Obey."

I was ignorant to Hecate's history, and so I felt no strong need to respect or worship her, but I found myself bowing before all that beauty and rage. Tyria had done the same, and I noticed that her hand was on my back, converting me to her beliefs. I broke my trance and immediately stood up.

"I need a drink."

"I know you think this is strange," Tyria said.

"Please," I begged. "Get me a drink."

"What do you want?"

"Something replenishing."

Tyria left me alone with the little dancing demons and I almost felt the need to ingest them like some sacred candy. When she came back she handed me a bottle of sparkling water. I drank until I felt clarity reach me. Then the music in my head stopped, the dancing halted. I stood up and changed the subject.

"Some of this stuff is so old," I pointed to a stack of magazines. "Have you ever considered downsizing?"

Tyria knifed me with her eyes. "These things are not just material; they're my memories."

"It was a simple question."

"And now you got your simple answer."

She pointed to the CD rack. "What do you wanna hear?"

I twisted my head, felt my hair glide past my ears. "You got any Down? Glassjaw maybe?"

"Tool?" Tyria said.

I shook my head. "How about something with a little more pain?"

"Alice in Chains it is."

Tyria placed the CD into an old fashioned stereo where you had to twist a knob to control the volume. You know, the kind we all had before Spotify and Apple Music took over our lives. It struck me rather odd, the record of choice, but it was perhaps an album that had brought solace to Tyria when she was in a dark place.

Alice in Chains' *Unplugged* was recorded when the band had reached their apex, which was simultaneously a time when Layne Staley had dug the heroin hole so deep there was no coming back. It was most depressing album I'd ever known a band to make.

Tyria swayed to the sound of "Nutshell," seeing the color of music as she had already explained to me. I closed my eyes, following the lyrics like I was on another plane, all the way to the throes of my own depression. When I opened them I couldn't find Tyria, even though I heard her voice call from the shadows that brought her sustenance, and smelled the sweet bundle of leaves she was burning.

I was so in love.

"What is that?"

"Sweet grass and white sage."

BLOOD KISS

She lit a match. In the next moment we were washing the room in sugary smoke. With each inhale I felt anew, clean, like my spirit had just been reconstructed. Tyria smiled.

"Positive energy," she said.

"What's the point of it?"

"You've never done a sage cleanse?"

"No," I said, almost embarrassed.

"Then you don't believe."

"I don't believe in God. You're right."

"You don't have to believe in God to believe. Faith is not belief in God," Tyria said.

"Faith is a fictional entity."

"To you, maybe, but to me it's everything."

I thought about that for a moment. Maybe I was judging, but I could not hold back my opinion. I think it made us better friends, arguing, debating . . . learning from one another.

"We don't have to agree on everything."

"I would be so bored if we did."

"Let me tell you something. I once prayed to a goddess of glum and misfortune, but it got me nowhere. I learned fast that if I want something in life I have to do it myself and not wait on the power of prayer."

"What about what you just saw?" Tyria said.

"I haven't had time to process it."

I felt horrible for saying that. Had I just denied the wicked sight of Kali? Had I denied her faith?

"Then you don't get it."

I pulled my hair into my mouth nervously.

"I know one thing," referencing her shadow.

Tyria caught on. "He doesn't like the smell of sage."

"He?"

"*He* also hates that I don't keep the lights on down here either. You can't cast a shadow without light," Tyria so close to me now we could kiss. "It's so *he* can't find me."

The idea of a gendered insubstantiality vexed me so. I became irreparably quiet.

"You've *felt* it. I don't care what your iconoclastic mind believes, or your bureaucratic brain calculates—"

"Take that back!"

"You need to open your eyes!"

She grabbed me, and in that moment I recalled the emptiness I felt, recalled how blinded I became to the color of no color. In my hands, then slathered across my portrait . . . it reaching out for me or my portrait reaching for it. But as quick as I had it trapped the damn thing slipped away. What had come over me? Who was I to challenge it so quickly?

"You think I'm bat-shit crazy don't you?"

I was startled by her assumption. "Maybe I just don't want to know."

"You're afraid of what you can't control," Tyria said.

"No, Ty. I'm attracted to it."

"Then why don't you do something?" Tyria became frustrated. "There are things that exist beyond the single reality we've all been trained to believe. You shouldn't be so closed off."

It wasn't that I was closed off, it was more that I didn't know how to comprehend another human being who was more fucked up than myself. We sat on the floor, and between us Tyria placed a small black candle, it's weak light crawling over her silver ohm necklace, dripping over the rings on her fingers. The light was so vivid that I attempted to touch it, bring it to my mouth like candy until I felt the heat biting into my fingertips.

"Shit that's hot."

Tyria laughed. "You know what they say about those who play with fire."

I rolled my eyes, got back to the conversation. "I'm not denying your faith, Ty."

"Yeah well I still don't believe that you want to trust in things that exist far beyond mammalian knowledge of time and space."

"I know what I see and believe," I said firmly.

BLOOD KISS

"Yeah? What about your own art? I know that your paintings want it."

There was a cryptic pause; I knew very well that I'd just set off Tyria's trip wire.

"How can you come here and insult me like this? I've become so comfortable with you."

Tyria faded into the candlelight. I hoped to catch a glimpse of shadow, but no luck. *It will come when it wants*, I thought. Then she confronted me with a big sack and dumped it on the bed. A hundred little baggies landed on my lap, dusted me in powder.

"I don't want to think anymore," Tyria said.

"What is this?"

"You know."

Tyria handed me a tiny mirror and spread two fine lines across it; the dollar bill was already rolled. Rather than putting a damper on the moment, I acquiesced to peer pressure and took a line up my nose. My how the storybooks got it all wrong. The cocaine suffused my brain with numbing ice, coated the back of my throat. I felt my teeth clatter, chin twist; my skin lifted from the pale skeleton beneath. The world became a masquerade of beauty.

I felt powerful and instantly addicted.

"I want to dance," Tyria said.

She brought me to my feet and pressed her torso into me. I became hyper aware of our racing hearts. Tyria took two more bumps up her nose and tossed her head back as if she was driving down an endless ribbon of highway. Her pale hair looked marvelous in the dark. The stage reenacted.

But the next moment was chaotic blur. All of sudden my hand was not my own. It reached for the back of her neck, climbed into her hair and tugged gently. Then her fingers slithered into my hair, scraping furrows into the scalp. Tyria wasn't thinking or judging; it felt so weird but so right.

"Do you understand what you're doing?" Tyria said.

"I'm spending time with my muse."

We danced recklessly and sung the heartbreaking lyrics. We marveled at one another's mouth, one another's intentions. The moment leaked into an unattainable perfection, then slowly receded to leave me hopelessly devoted to feeling it again, much like a drug addict. It was then I saw the first dribble of blood worm out of her nose, smelled it fresh as meat on a butcher block.

"Is it the blood of God?" I said.

"*Goddess*," she corrected me.

My lips darted for that sweet ichor. As her tongue accepted mine, reality exploded into red pins and needles. I closed my eyes to do away with this feeling of shame, until I felt pain take me.

Tyria bit down so that we were now entangled in a blood kiss.

"NO! NO! NO!"

She released me. I fell to the floor; a pile of magazines buried my legs. The candlelight flickered; Tyria bared her red teeth, defying a presence that wasn't there.

"I DON'T LIKE IT! I DON'T LIKE IT! I DON'T LIKE IT!"

She didn't stop screaming. Her anger extricated me from the high like closing the curtain over the stage. There would be no finale. My head felt heavy, but exorcised, and just like that I was a rational thinker again. But it was a harsh reality to see her so hurt. What had I done?

"GET OUT OF MY HEAD."

Black tears fell down Tyria's face. I got up off the floor and tried to apologize for my actions but my tongue was bleeding too heavily. I found the coke mirror and saw how red my grin was. Grinning in this aftermath?

"This can't be."

Tyria became a shrew, a monster inherent. But I empathized because I knew that this was the only way a little girl could protect herself from a force that could not be stopped. How could I have let human temptation get in the way everything?

"He did this to me," she said. "And I remember wanting it."

"Talk to me," I said

BLOOD KISS

"I used to dream. I used to laugh. I used to want to be somebody!" She tore her Hot Topic tank top at the shoulders so that I could see the jut of her small tits and her heaving chest. Showing skin or shedding it? Save that for the stage.

"Why do I still touch myself?"

"I can't answer that."

"Why did you do this?" She slammed her fist into the wall.

"Please stop," I begged her.

"I've always been a danger . . . whether to someone else or myself. You're no different. In the end I will hurt you."

"No, you won't."

"It's always my fault!"

Right in the middle of this madness I received a text from Leland. *Are you okay? What have you been doing?* Oh, if I could only answer him at that moment, if I could only beg him to send Adelaide home to see Tyria clawing at the walls. There was an angry trail of blood-glitter in the candlelight. She did not wince, did not cry out in pain. Rather, it was this physical trauma that helped ease the mental instability. I grabbed her by the shoulders and shook that tiny form, felt the bones crack beneath her skin, felt them *change*.

Tyria was no longer in my hands. I noticed the smudge had stopped burning and that the Open Road candles had blown out. Cold now, the dark twin of her, and it played tricks on my sense of touch, telling me it was Tyria, but then not at all.

So I stuck my hand into the shadow.

It filled me with images: a warm spill of blood, loneliness, seduction. The dark is always a temptress.

I ran.

Nowhere fast as my head found the wall. In my daze I heard her crying. No little girl deserves such torment. But I could take no more. I held Tyria in my arms, told her that everything would be okay even though she was bleeding and afraid, the smell of pain and shame too real, too strong.

Everything was her fault.

10

ights down to make the world a better place, always prettier in the dark. The stage was the altar, and as the first band crashed their way into their final song, Electric Orchid's strobe lights were already as bright as fireworks. Feedback exploded from the speakers and sparks turned into smoke. Everyone stood attention, awaiting patiently and gazing as *O Fortuna* rang out like a diabolical choir.

Sors salutis, et virtutis, michi nunc contraria. At the last chorus Adelaide held her ears. *Mecum omnes plangite!*

The band spilled onto the stage like inkblots, eyes rimmed in doom and hair dyed too many colors. Instruments were strapped to their torsos like extra limbs and they barely acknowledged the crowd before the creepy pianist began his gloomy tune.

Adelaide felt the wave of bodies unite, but then ignite. A sudden energy took over the room. It was an elemental force she wished that Tyria and Dorian could inspire within their show. This song, an obvious fan favorite, haunted her. It was a tune that could only be if Black Sabbath and Nine Inch Nails had an illegitimate child.

That's when the lead singer rose like a hydra from the smoke and neon, ripped fishnets and hair like rope. *DELILAH! DELILAH!* the audience preached. *MAKE THEM RISE!* Delilah heard their call, and as her sapphire eyes darted toward the crowd she smiled sharply, placed her teeth against the vector microphone and unleashed her voice.

> *She's a prisoner of the mind*
> *Unable to fight this sickening paradigm*
> *Too weak to be complete*
> *Too stubborn to weep*

The words melted over Adelaide. She wished Tyria was with her so that she could witness this blazing lead singer. The way that Delilah controlled her audience made Adelaide think differently about power. Tyria lacked Delilah's confidence, the I-don't-give-a-fuck grace, but it was something that could be learned.

Where Delilah was practiced, but natural, Tyria was still finding herself. Where Delilah's voice cut the room in two, Tyria's shattered it. If Adelaide could only show Tyria such power existed, only then could she rule the underground.

Adelaide opened the messenger screen in her cell phone, realizing that she had not received a call or text from Tyria all day. I have a plan, she wrote. *Bowery, tomorrow night. See you at home. Love you.* She waited to see that the message was delivered, taken back that Tyria didn't respond right away. What could she have been doing with Dorian that was more important than texting back the love of her life?

But Delilah's voice whined through the amps now, flecked and bruised roar that died at the end of a harsh lyric. She ripped the vector mic from the stand and ran it back and forth against her face, smearing lipstick and powder, pulsating it against her lips so it made the natural sound of reverb. Adelaide could see the pain in her eyes.

Then the magic happened

Behind Delilah something rose to life. Not her band, not a stage prop—though there were plenty of horrific dummies and puppets—but stilted arms and a half gaping jaw. It crawled backward, up the broken ceiling and then down into the mass of heads. Everyone raised their hands in dark prayer; it scared Adelaide out of her wits.

She tried to escape, but they wouldn't let her, too pious in their incantation, too mystified by Delilah's commanding stage presence. Whatever it was, she had to get Leland and get the fuck out. Something not of this world had been let loose, something that wanted to hurt people. Adelaide jumped up to locate Leland; unfortunately he was nowhere to be found, so she jumped again with all her might.

But this time two guys grabbed her by the hips and thrust her into the air. She slammed into a pile of heads, her body rolling and her teeth bared, but the people knew this practice like they knew how to breathe. Adelaide was crowd surfing. She saw the world through a different light, saw Delilah locking eyes with her, eyes of blue fire, and then she sang another lyric.

> *Today is about corruption*
> *Tomorrow is my self-destruction*
> *Resurrection is an act of seduction*
> *To feed the cannibals of compulsion*

Just as she thought she might enjoy surfacing into oblivion the crowd let her down. But the words kept ringing until she spotted the only brown head of hair in the room—the only head of hair was that wasn't dyed with Manic Panic—the only body not covered in tattoos, dressed in ripped jeans and a plain white t-shirt.

Leland was in front of the bathroom stall talking with a boy in black who was rubbing his finger across his face, then grabbing the graceful curve of neck, sliding that pale finger down his torso until he ended at Leland's waist line. They kissed long and hard; Adelaide almost had to smack herself to truly believe in the sight she was seeing.

"Landy, what the fuck?"

But with the music so loud her voice could not be heard. She pressed forward and was just about to break the two up when her phone vibrated: Tyria. I'm home. Don't feel good at all. I need you.

"This is the last song," Delilah said. "So if you want to get kicked out . . . now's the time!"

BLOOD KISS *Daniel Stone*

Adelaide reached over and broke the kiss. Leland didn't fight it. He was too fucked up to even know what he was doing. As soon as they found the exit Electric Orchid and their dedicated following began tearing the room apart.

THEY HAD SKIPPED OUT ON SMALL TALK because memory is the worst enemy. Moving forward is how you defeat it. At the table Dorian was bent over fetal-tight, his hand moving like the conductor of a grand orchestra through his sketchbook. Tyria could hear the slide and glide of delicate bones beneath parchment skin, the sound of the pencil gliding across brand new paper. Images destroying to create, which reminded Tyria of the birth of a new star.

"I gotta get this out of my head," Dorian said.

"What is it?" Tyria said.

"You'll see."

The resent in his voice was hurtful but necessary. With her head righted and her heart no longer dangerously beating, Tyria was able to process Dorian in his element. The way he drew was not calculated or contrived; he conducted his macabre portraits like a symphony, truthful to his craft because art was true to him.

"I'm most inspired after terrible events," Dorian said.

"And it was terrible."

Now Tyria wanted to write, wanted to heal in this quiet aftermath. There is something to be said about art: the pathway in which it starts is something that cannot be taught like a technical trade. It is earned through the pain and suffering we feel from the external world. To understand art is to fully understand your biology, and then transcend it by blending your physical cells and your ethereal mind into one fluid being.

"What are we going to do?" Tyria said.

"Nothing," Dorian said flat.

"Why nothing?"

"Because what's done is done."

"Am I supposed to sit here and smile, pretend and forget?"

"You have the choice to feel whatever you want."

"No, I actually don't."

"Yeah, you do," Dorian's eyes met hers, a fresh cigarette between his lips.

"If you don't want to talk . . . if you don't want to make sense of this mess, I think you should leave."

Dorian didn't argue, packed up his stuff and flew up the stairs. She followed on instinct, not wanting him to leave this fast. Why had she allowed her emotions control her words? Why do we say things we don't mean in the heat of the moment?

The winter air hit Tyria's lungs heavily, almost choked her. She reached for Dorian's shirt, his matted hair, and did not realize that it was night until she saw the moon's corrugated surface, so close she didn't need binoculars. She remembered that tonight a special elliptical dance was about to begin. Astronomers called it perigee-syzygy, but her kind called it a Super Moon. It was the telltale sign that the harvest was at its end and the darkest half of the year was upon the Northeast.

"Dorian, please stop. I didn't mean what I said."

He didn't turn around, but said, "I guess I'll see you around."

"No, please. I won't ask again."

A pathetic amount of leaves stirred. Brooklyn was quiet. She wanted to scream at him. *WHY DID YOU FUCK IT UP! WHY DID YOU DO IT TO ME?* But he was already in front of Wreck Room, turning his head as if he wanted to say something, but then continued walking. Tyria raged with insult and violation.

"It can't be this way," Tyria said. "I have a girlfriend!"

But Dorian was getting smaller and smaller, his outline blending into darkness. This was partly her fault, just like everything else, but he didn't have to leave when she needed

BLOOD KISS Daniel Stone

him. Daddy always left after he touched her. Was Dorian not ashamed or embarrassed for himself, his weakness of character? She wondered how badly his tongue was hurting as the smoky flavor of his blood still lingered on her palate.

The night could not end this way. She had to do something more.

Tyria bolted across Flushing Avenue to find Dorian sitting on a small bench. He would not acknowledge her, and she knew exactly why: a true artist cannot be disturbed when the muse calls. But why did it come to this? Now her notebook opened, a pale maw, and her mind spinning, her hand shaking to jot these fresh images into legible prose. Nothing of value, not even with the hurt so big and blinding inside her.

Not just that, but his kiss still haunting her, *changing* her. Not invasion or even true sensation, but the missing puzzle piece. The thought of exploring everything that cannot be—everything that should not be—was complicated as much as it made sense. How far could their relationship literally go when it was only meant to be for show? Could it defy the societal laws of sexual orientation and monogamy? Could there be a far greater performance off the stage than on it?

"I didn't mean to get crazy," Tyria said, not noticing her hand had landed upon his shoulder.

"I never said that I didn't like it. But I can do without the attitude," Dorian remained focused on his sketchbook.

"I'm fully aware how unstable I am."

"And I love that about you."

Love. You.

A cockroach crawled near them and Dorian squashed it with his fist. "What's your issue?"

Tyria was disgusted that he'd killed a roach with his bare hands, but then said, "Look. You and I—"

"Can become something more than the stage. A *living* art," Dorian's eyes rising like the moon.

"We aren't supposed to break people's hearts."

"It's not about that. Mammalian emotions are below us."

It hurt to hear him say this, and to admit that she liked him was to betray all she had built with Adelaide. To admit that it felt natural would be adding insult to injury.

"I've never done anything like this before," Dorian said. "But never in my life have I felt so . . . *alive*."

"You take one silly snort of coke and all of a sudden you're into girls?"

"Not girls. *You*. A person, a soul, a conscious. Tyria Vane. That's it."

Better to learn it now than later.

"What do we do now?" Tyria said. " I can't live with this secret."

"Take it to the stage," Dorian said it so naturally it was as if he planned it the whole time.

"I don't know if I can do that. I don't have it in me."

"All you have to do is let go. Let the moment take over. I've already seen it happen."

Tyria lit a cigarette. "Still, the repercussions will be astronomical."

"Do you fear that our visions will be tampered with?"

"Are you listening to yourself Dorian?"

He sipped from a flask that reeked of tequila. "The audience wants a show, and we're going to give it to them."

"But this is not how it's supposed to be. You paint. I spit poetry. That's it. Whatever else happens is impromptu."

"*Impromptu*, Tyria. Why can't you see that?"

"I actually want to see *that*," Tyria pointed at the sketchbook.

Dorian pocketed his pencil and brought his sketch into the hazy streetlight. Two bodies twisted into one another like some mystical manifesto, and they could not have been more real as if he'd taken a photo and developed it himself. A boy with hair so black it made the girl's skin appear albino. Their arms sleeved with tattoos, their hands clasped in unison and their mouths open wide, but between them a curtain.

BLOOD KISS Daniel Stone

Somehow, someway, the photo quivered. Not wind, not Dorian's shaking hand, but the lead itself rippling, the bodies yearning for one another. Luckily she had the Ray Bans on to conceal her reddening face as she looked to the sky for answers, only to see through her peripheral vision that the two bodies in the sketch were now entangled in a drippy kiss.

"Your brand of faith is quite different from my own," Dorian said. "But this doesn't lie."

Before she could answer a familiar rumbling began in her stomach. Sudden pain rolling into knots; a warm trickle slid down her thighs. Fertility calling.

"I don't feel good."

"What's the matter?"

"I don't know."

"But I *have* to know."

Dorian grabbed her by the shoulders, and something like an electrical charge billowed through her chest, setting fire to her blood. His lips covered hers, and this time she gave into sweet temptation. This time the kiss was not filled with blood, but of revelation.

THERE WAS NO TELLING HOW LONG we had parted. I remembered walking home defeated and filled with angst, barging through my front door to see Leland opening his arms for me, but I blew him off and fell asleep for what felt like a millennia. The next thing I remembered was Leland covering my mouth from the scream, my head pounding and a crimson worm sliding out of my nose. An awkward silence followed so that I could recollect the visions.

A room so big it swallowed sound and light, and in the center Tyria: Queen of the Night. Words dripped like stars from her lips, stars of red, gold and white. But there was so much pain in her face, in this act of madness, her bare legs wishbone-wide so that I could see her fingers spread the gloomy cleft like mandala petals.

Red grin, red cheeks, red eyes.

Menstrual blood, the richest, darkest of all.

"This is what he liked," she said over and over. "This is how he knew I was pure."

Was it an act of mockery the way she dipped my paintbrush into the rich menstrual spill? Was it nightmare incarnate to see her spread the red arc across my canvas? I found myself bowing before my Black Madonna. I drove my face deep between her legs, lips to catatonic lips, and when I came up for air my grin was red as hers.

And then it showed me its teeth.

I found a calendar that I'd been keeping my schedule on, saw that we had parted for three days. There was no attempt at contact. I conjectured that we'd taken one step too far, so this time apart was necessary. But she stayed on my mind, no matter if she was with Adelaide tucked safely in her bed, or shrouded in sage smoke; worry kept her in my head.

I made up for the lost days by staying with Leland as much as I could. I didn't mention Tyria at all and Leland didn't ask me any questions. Adelaide's name didn't leave his mouth, better for me. He knew I was in a bad mood. We ate pita chips and drank warm beer in front of the television, switching between *The X-Files* and *Xena: Warrior Princess*. Both shows had a cult following, and both shows starred very dominant and intelligent female characters. Dana Scully was my alter ego, as Xena was Leland's.

When the sun came up Leland went back to work. I knew that something was bothering him, but I dared not ask. I didn't want to get caught in a lie. The silence between us remained mutual and masked the issues at hand. He focused on the new gig; I drew my ass off. He asked me a few times to go free style, but all the sketches wound up being of Tyria. After that we'd have sex, but the passion was lacking.

After another day I was able to erase most of my guilt while simultaneously fueling my affection for Tyria. I missed her terribly—I didn't want to admit that to myself—but it was true. Maybe it was that I felt lonely being that Leland was off

BLOOD KISS *Daniel Stone*

doing his own thing all the time, which I would never blame him for. And so as the hours droned on all I did was think of our potential and our possible destruction. We had a long road ahead of us, but we also had our loyalty to art: the show had to go on.

I knew I was to see her tonight, and so I prepared for our collision mentally. Leland had given me strict orders to show my face at the Bowery space by 9pm. I got dressed, grabbed my metro card and perused the streets. It was a clear night. Moonlight glazed the vista of spires and gargoyles; all the little trees glowed like ghosts in the post Halloween fervor.

The weather was less than seasonable, and the people were even worse. Nobody looked up from their cell phones to see to the street signs or traffic signals. The crummy black jacket I had on was so useless I might as well have worn a t-shirt. Down an alleyway there was a band of bums careening around a fire pit (illegal, but not uncommon) and so I made use of that source of heat.

I was acknowledged as the random company made them happy. The conversations I heard were mindless. I yawned, scratched my oily hair, tasted something expired in the back of my mouth. How long had I been walking? My feet ached, the back of my ankles were raw and stripped of flesh; my wingtip boots ate right through the socks. I took one off and the smell was terrible. One of the squatters nodded, an understanding of this hard-knock life, and then unzipped his pants to pee on the steps of the Bowery space.

I found myself gawking. Were they here for the show?

"I can smell pussy from a mile away," one of them said.

I touched myself and found that I was aroused. The red dream took me again, all that glorious wetness, the smell of Tyria's pussy so strong, my dick getting *harder*. I looked at my crotch; it was dripping blood. The sight reminded me of all my vials: if you leave blood long enough the plasma and the erythrocytes will separate like oil and water. Is that what would happened to Tyria and I? But then a sudden squirming, and oh fuck, I creamed myself.

"I don't know what kind of night I had," I said.

"Look, kid, I know how to make it all go away," taking a careful look around before he brought out the glass pipe and lighter.

"Not a meth head," I said.

"But you is too young to be so . . . questionable."

The man studied me carefully. Dirt spiraled into his eyes, his lips cracked upon the first pull of his pipe. I knew my appearance didn't scream gay, but my voice, my poor little voice, was not acceptable to society's male prototype. This bum was no idiot, he'd probably seen so many LGBT runaways who were no longer welcome in their homes for being exactly who they are.

"You a queer, ain't you? This city is full of them."

But was I still queer? My mind was prisoner to Tyria's forbidden fruit. How can something so bad feel so good?

"I don't know who I am anymore," I answered.

"Welcome to the club, young man. We all lost folk in this part of town."

He fell asleep with the pipe in his lips. I hated myself for feeling this way, restricting myself of such pleasure. The realization that in life we only exist to play a game of exquisite corpse with death saddened me. Why do we resist temptation when we'll all be together in the end? That's when my phone buzzed, and I noticed that it was 9:25pm. Leland's text message came in. *You here?* I felt a calming relief knowing I'd be at his side again. I craved only his love. *You're late!* my phone buzzed again.

When I searched my pocket for the keys I felt something warm and thick like syrup, pulled my hand out to see that it was blood. So much of it, but it was not mine. Blood beneath my fingernails. Bright little beads that smelled of fertility and innocence lost. I pocketed my hand for fear someone would see me, then wiped it across the graffiti covered stairs, and walked through the door.

BLOOD KISS *Daniel Stone*

"SOMETHING'S CHANGED," Adelaide said.

The bathroom smells like stagnant water and the candles are lined like a funeral pyre to mourn the loss of cleanliness. There is too much pain to talk anymore. This brand of suffering was only supposed to happen when Daddy was still alive, his lanky body dark as smoke above hers, his hand riding her moon-dappled skin down to the tender cleft between her legs to pluck her fertile flower from the garden.

"Please, Goddess!" Tyria said.

Biology can sometimes be a punishment, especially for those who have evolved past certain processes. A woman's biology is utter torment. They cramp and bleed until a man plants his seed so that she can nurture the next assassin, the next power hungry drone, or worse, the next girl doomed to a societal hell.

"You've been bleeding like this for days," Adelaide said. "I should take you to a hospital."

"I can't afford—"

"But I can't let you bleed to death!"

"It'll pass. Just stay with me."

Adelaide pulled Tyria into her arms even though Adelaide was well aware that she and Dorian had become slightly more than friends over the past few weeks. Soon she would be asking a hundred questions and expecting the answer that would never come. But for now she held Tyria tight, kept her safe. Her mouth sought for a kiss; her hair poured over Tyria's face like spider legs.

"You've been drinking non-stop," Adelaide said. "Trying to cover for something?" She was prying, and it almost worked.

"Just let me sleep." Tyria felt the tears come quick and hot.

"No! You have to be on stage tonight."

"Stop telling me what I need to do. Just be with me."

"I'm not telling you what to do. I'm telling you what you must do," Addy's eyes were black with worry.

"Get me a damn beer and I'll be okay."

"I said no drinking!"

"But it's the only thing that takes away the pain. It's the only thing that makes it right."

"Makes what right, Ty?"

"That I don't rip out my fucking uterus," fetal position now, and the tiles on the floor so cold.

Adelaide's eyes narrowed. "We're dykes and yet we still get punished with this monthly nuisance."

"Nature calls," Tyria managed a half-smile.

"But we have evolved beyond our nature. We don't want kids. Never will."

"I fucking hate kids," Tyria said. "They're the most selfish things in the world. They take and take. They suck everyone dry."

This put a foul thought into Tyria's head. What were the chances she'd ever have a child of her own? Would she love it? Would she care for it like the mammals she had evolved from have done since their ascension out of the water? Would it be Dorian's?

"You smell," Adelaide said.

"Like what?" Tyria feared the answer.

"Like *him*," baring her teeth now, and Adelaide began to cry. "Something happened between you and Dorian."

Tyria froze. Adelaide pointed her finger like a gun.

"Whatever it is . . . it stops right now. I put too much on the line for this to happen. How can you be so weak?"

"We didn't do anything," the lie so smooth flying off her tongue.

"BULLSHIT! I know you, Ty."

"Maybe you don't, Addy. Maybe you don't know me at all."

"And he was in *our* apartment. How could you?"

"How could I . . . what? Make a friend?"

"Do you think I deserve this? After all I've done for you?"

Adelaide reached for Tyria, but slowly retreated. Instead, her hand found the outline of the bathroom mirror, shook it until the wall gave in and the entire thing was in her hands.

BLOOD KISS *Daniel Stone*

Tyria could see her own guilty reflection pale and sad as Adelaide's vengeful one was coarse and hairy. Then Adelaide let it go. The sound of the glass smashing enveloped everything in the bathroom. Tyria covered her face as bits of silver flew everywhere, screaming at the top of her lungs for Adelaide, but she was already seeking something in the pile, a shard that was almost the size of a kitchen knife. She put it up to her own throat, and then Tyria's.

"I'll kill him first, then you, then me. I won't be sabotaged by this bullshit!"

Tyria pushed Adelaide's hand away. "I'd rather you go back to the needle than resort to murder."

"Since when are you so rational?"

But Tyria could take no more, was already on her feet. The menstrual pain was nothing compared to this freak show. She wobbled into the living room and slipped on a smelly pair of black jeans and a band shirt so old it would not even be sellable at a vintage shoppe. Anything was better than being trapped indoors with a lunatic. But Adelaide was already after her, the sliver of glass so tight in her hand the surface was slicked red.

"They want a good spook . . . the audience. You are powerful," Adelaide said.

"No, I'm actually not."

"Don't destroy all I've created because you have the hots for some boy."

"He's not just some boy!"

Adelaide was heaving. "Do you know Delilah?"

Tyria had no idea why she said that.

"Who?"

"She's the lead singer of Electric Orchid. And she knows how to command a crowd."

"What are you getting at?"

"That's who I want you to be. I want you to control them. I want them to see!"

"But all I can be is myself, Addy."

Adelaide let go of the mirror shard, looked at her mangled hand, and then sat on the bed, suddenly released from her angry trance. There was an assortment of papers there, ones that Dorian had drawn on, a beast with four arms, a goddess with a serpentine tongue tipped in gore. There was nothing Tyria could say to salvage any last bit of Adelaide's sanity. Her weakest characteristic was her jealousy. And so Tyria wasted her breath in trying to explain some of the moments she shared with Dorian.

"That shit should be for show only."

Adelaide's bloodied hand stroked Tyria's hair until she fell into a horrible sleep. Dorian was laying on a bed as big a car, his arms and legs spread like Da Vinci's Vitruvian Man and his skin was white as eyeballs. She did not choose this; desire embraced her, stripped her of divinity. She saw herself standing above him, her hips opening like doors, knees bending and her pussy greased in blood. Dorian went inside her like a knife, and when he came Tyria tightened her pussy to lock the juices inside.

Keep every bit and piece of him.

BLOOD KISS

11

I opened the door to a world of low light and chaos. Shadows erupted, roaches slipped into the cracks of the wooden floor. The smell was smokier than I remembered, reminiscent of sage and sweet grass, and there were voices mingling, arguments and laughter, all the sounds friends make, old and new.

Candles encircled the periphery of the room, Open Road, pillars and votives from every hue of the rainbow. Such a different look from the last time I performed here, and now that I could see above me there were fancy spiral bulbs of black, blue and red installed. When they flickered to life I saw the banner in photonegative.

SyNtHeSis .

A catastrophic advertisement to say the least. It showed me things I did not want to imagine even though I knew that I was the maker of that heinous art. Swirled through the vortex was Tyria's poetry, mangled and ferocious.

"He's gunna be here soon," said a low voice in the dark.

"Practice makes perfect," a different voice, feet taping.

I knew one of the voices like I knew my own, knew it before I smelled the Old Spice deodorant and clean sweat. I followed the familiar odors until my hand was on his shoulder, sliding down his torso to pull his tender body into my own. Leland accepted my lips, letting me caress his neck, then his cheek.

"Hey babe."

He was in a good mood tonight. Sweet black eyes met mine; his flower petal lips glimmered and his unwashed hair swam in chaotic waves. I kissed Leland deeply. It was as if we'd been separated for a full year the way he kissed me back. Physically we'd been close, but emotionally we'd been distant and so this was a wonderful reunion.

"Is that who I think it is?"

A toneless voice to break apart our embrace. I paid it no mind. My focus was only Leland. I placed my bloodied hand on the back of his neck; my other pulled up his shirt. Our chests pressed together; his slatted ribs felt like piano keys. My tongue crawled into his mouth; our teeth clinked. But then suddenly his boner vanished.

"Stop it, Dorian. We have a special guest."

"Who?" I said that rhetorically at best.

"Morgan."

The name instantly enraged me. It had been years since I'd even heard it. The last thing I'd come to understand was that he was holed up in a shanty off the J train Kosciusko stop.

"Where is he then?"

"Don't catch an attitude. This is business."

"I said where is he?"

"Dorian, he's not going to come out if you keep this up."

"Why can't you kiss me?"

Fuck it. With Morgan nowhere to be found I forced myself upon Leland, unbuttoning his pants and biting his lips. He was willing before even I was, propping himself up as I greased my hand in spit, sliding his asshole onto the head of my penis so fast he elbowed me in the mouth. But I was fine with the taste of blood. It had become a familiar flavor.

"Dorian, oh, we can't—"

"Shh!"

We made love in the dark, his head falling into the crook of my collar bone, me licking his neck, biting that white, white skin. But it wasn't Leland who I fucking. Tyria was in my head. Oh, the thought of those bloodied folds, of us violating the sanctity of friendships; it turned me on madly. My orgasm arrived quicker than I thought; I held Leland tight

BLOOD KISS

to let my seed settle and fester inside him. And then we were pulling up our pants as a standing ovation ensued and the sound of footsteps came our way.

"Now that's true love, yo!"

He was just as tall and malnourished as I'd remembered. In the low light I saw the gray beanie covering his shaggy hair and that he still wore clothes that were two sizes too big.

"To what do I owe the pleasure?" I said. "Surely you're not here to contribute to anything."

"I did read about you in the paper, yo. But is sarcasm the way to start off our new business venture?"

I looked straight at Leland. "Please clarify."

"He's a DJ and we need music."

"He's also a fucking meth head."

Morgan took a step toward me. "I didn't ask for your opinion, bitch."

I pushed my finger into Morgan's skinny chest. "Take a step back."

"Don't do this here," Leland said.

"Might I add, yo, I believed in what that article said. Something big is happening here and I want to be part of it."

I was thankful he understood that much.

"This is personal, I don't know why you're involved."

"Ask your boyfriend, he's the one who hired me."

"What?"

"Morgan's on the pay roll," Leland said.

"Now we have payroll?"

"Yeah yo," Morgan lit a cigarette. "Like a J-O-B."

The sound that escaped my throat was more mockery than actual laughter. At first Leland laughed along with me, nervous, breaking the ice. Morgan didn't catch on at all. He was still the dumbest person I had ever met.

"You would never understand what I've created here. You could never even DREAM of Tyria's worst days."

"Who?" Morgan said.

"My point exactly. Landy get him—"

"What's gotten into you?"

"Nothing," I lied.

"No. Your eyes are different."

"He looks spooked," Morgan said.

"I'm *tired*. And if I wanted your opinion, I'd ask."

"Whatever."

I turned away from both of them and went straight to the bar. There was never a better excuse to have drink than having to deal with your lover's ex-lover coming back into your life for good. If Morgan was here for as long as these shows would go on I would need to be in a constant state of inebriation. So I grabbed a Genesee, chugged half the can and then sat my ass down on a stool to smoke one of Leland's hand-rolled cigarettes.

"I brought everything I have," Morgan said.

"Your crack pipe too?"

"Enough," Leland said.

Did I have any right to be this jealous?

"What kind of equipment could you possibly have?" I just had to know.

"My Mac and a few amps, yo."

I found that it truly tested my humanity to tolerate a person that ended every sentence in "yo."

"I'm talking about a system. What do you use to make music?"

"I use Dream Synth and a few other platforms," Morgan said.

"Never heard of it."

Morgan turned toward Leland. "I told you he wouldn't like this idea."

"He'll get over it. Always does."

And so the truth came out, how they had met up after all these years, how Leland had all these ideas. Music at this point during the show, strobe lights when given the signal, smoke machine in all four corners to enhance Tyria's stage presence and ensconce my own. Keep it spooky.

Morgan read from a pre-scribed notepad, to which shocked me. I never knew that he could think rational

BLOOD KISS *Daniel Stone*

thoughts, let alone jot them down on paper. But even so, it was Leland who was our fearless leader. He had that natural ability to take charge. If a fire broke out, if a bomb exploded, Leland would find a way to abate the disarray and lead everyone to a safe destination. I loved that about him.

But Morgan was a class D loser. Born and bred in the project housings of Flushing, Queens, his IQ was no higher than that is attributed to children. One could say that it was not his fault. According to Leland he lacked proper education and the requisite stability in the adolescent years it takes to become an honorable person of society.

His best attribute was his Queens accent; his worst was that he did not turn his life's hardships into any kind of creativity. He let the drugs in and they never left. Regardless, he had but one simple talent that I could not deny: manipulating sounds and weaving them into distinct beats. But he also talked more than he produced; Meth can do that to its users, make your mouth move faster than your brain.

"You do know that I'm clean," Morgan said.

"For how long?" I said.

"Two years, yo."

"There is never any *clean*. You know that. There is only recovery. Every day is a battle."

Leland stepped between us. "So then we're all in the right mind set."

"I guess so."

"Look. Putting on a show takes more than two people. We need production, music, we need better equipment."

"You're right."

"Don't you dare start agreeing so I shut up."

"I'm not. I just want this thing to work."

I ran my hand through my hair nervously, all but forgetting about the blood until I smelled it. I bolted to the sink to wash away the evidence of . . . what evidence? Dream leaking into reality? When I dried my hands Leland began spinning himself around, arms out wide; Morgan squatted behind his crappy DJ booth. The speakers crackled with white noise, the rave lights pulsed.

"Yo man, can't wait to witness it. Psychedelic and shit. We need lava lamps."

"That's an awesome idea."

"What colors?" trying too hard to crack a smile.

"Black and green! Like the lights, yo."

"Why would you want to match the lava lamps with the lights? That's like wearing stripes with plaid. It can't be."

"I don't know what that means, yo."

Then Leland walked over to the window.

"They're coming! So many of them."

"Light more candles!"

I looked outside. They all inspired me, and so I grabbed a pencil and began to sketch, nothing formulaic but nothing random. A swollen vagina, and something poking out of the molten center. A delicate cranium, new born baby with teeth in its scalp. I showed it to Morgan and something like a dry click sounded in his throat; he nearly puked.

"What time is she showing up?" Morgan said in reference to Tyria. "Can't wait to meet her."

"Not sure what time, but be prepared. Tyria is a bomb with a very, very short fuse."

THE CROWD THIS TIME was of a different nature. All classes of the jaded and exasperated; groupies, art-fags, hipsters, drag queens and druggies. Brooklyn's glam to Manhattan's worst. The human pollution that society has created.

Tyria entered through the back door. A few people from the crowd saw her and began clapping, and so she put her Ray Bans on for safety. On ground level Adelaide passed out the ads, each one of them concealing a special kind of drug for the night.

Behind the stage stood Dorian, who barely acknowledged her. She felt like it had been months since she had seen him. Her heart wanted to burst, but she remained calm just like

BLOOD KISS *Daniel Stone*

him, even though his kiss still lingered darkly on her lips. Adelaide did not even look his way, too encompassed by the new DJ booth of cardboard and jagged pieces of sheetrock.

"We have about ten minutes," Leland said.

The smoke machine began its inevitable fog. From what she saw behind the curtain the crowd was engaged and pious, the sign of the psychosis to come. Leland hugged a bunch of people he knew, then put his arm around Dorian and whispered into his ear.

To her right a lanky guy with moons for eyes—they said his name was Morgan—filled the DJ booth with his tall presence. Would she need to even meet him? It was well known that some members of rock bands would only be in the same place with one another if it was on the stage; after the show they went back to their separate lives devoid of contractual agreements and greedy lawyers.

Leland saw Tyria and waved, then pulled Morgan out to initiate the half-ass introduction. *Tyria this is Morgan . . . Morgan this is Tyria.* They shook hands, made nice, played the game. Morgan said that he was excited to play music for her.

"Now be friends," Adelaide said.

Tyria, Dorian and Morgan sized one another up, too nervous to talk, too into their own problems to even care. Then came the pre-performance jitters as Tyria counted dozens of heads. Everyone was tripped out, their glassy eyes abound for the stage; cigarettes ringed their red lips. Adelaide shut the door and collected the last of the cash, more than fifty people no doubt, fifty curious hearts, fifty open minds.

"Ready?" Leland said

Tyria tapped the microphone for the requisite feedback. But before she could muster up the courage to perform, she measured out two tiny white lines on her hand and snorted. Snowflakes began their ascent through her; white stars dripped and drained. Nothing could stop her now, not even the tiny dribble of blood from her nose; not even the memory of happiness and the future of betrayal.

"Morgan, go," Leland said.

The room so quiet as the music dipped and rose, a ritual clangor weaseling into guitar chords and a well-skilled whammy bar; diesel truck bass made teeth clatter. There came the shifting rainbow of color, both living and synthetic as the new stage lights set a gloomy mood. The sickly scene of light masked Tyria's face in sonic silver as she stepped onto the stage and pressed her lips against the microphone.

"Ladies and gentlemen, we are gathered here today to become one with art and words," voice low and hypnotic, raged in speed. "We live in a time where we are not taken seriously, where we are expected, inherently, to follow rather than lead."

A roaring applause ensued.

"Freedom of expression is looked at with disdain. Alternative vices have been castrated; art is unappreciated. Choice is how we *should* rejoice, but yet they pin us against each other. Brother against brother. Sister against sister."

That was Leland's cue to light more candles for the séance.

"These are sheepish times, children. Uniqueness has waned to the power of smart phones and video games. They want *not* that you rebel, but to rot in their hell. So I ask all of you, creatures of the night, do you want to take back what's rightfully yours?"

In the back of the room, swirling above everyone's head, was a great black ectoplasm. It was amorphous, made up of some sort of skin, scales even, and it grew to the size of the room. *Missed you.* But before Tyria could process the sight power chords crashed into a storm of synthesizers. Dorian finally revealed himself fronting a bright canvas and began a new sketch.

Tyria spread her arms as wide as a big black bird. The chains and lace whipped to her holy dance. She wanted Dorian to see her without saying anything. But not just him . . . the crowd. They took a step back in unison. She spit out the lyric.

BLOOD KISS

It's in a world of deceit
Where I will finally be complete
And so I tear out this membrane of shame
To blot out this memory of pain

Tyria's voice slid into the microphone like mercury. She was never more alive than now. Tyria the phoenix. Dorian the prodigy. Morgan became confused; Leland closed his eyes and Adelaide chewed her cigarette whole. The crowd was vexed, satisfied, amazed.

A wishbone hard as stone
I'm nothing but a clone
Decline me of my dignity
AS YOU SLOWLY SLIDE INSIDE OF ME!

Tyria screamed so loud that one of amps blew out. Her throat felt like rug burn. But that was nothing compared to what Dorian was doing. He had begun dripping paint across the canvas the way Pollock did to create abstract expressionist portraits. His fingers were bleeding, the smell of it delicious as much as it was rank. He threw blood at the crowd; a few girls rubbed it on their tits. When Dorian turned the wet sketch toward the audience Tyria saw it throb like a severed artery.

She almost fell over when she made sense of it.

Two souls entwined in a blood kiss. One made of shadow, the other of hunger. Tyria looked up to see her own shadow begin its reptilian crawl. But suddenly Dorian's fingers grasped the back of her neck, pulling her down so that she kissed his red lips.

Tyria could not resist. The pain in her pussy died; the taste of his tongue was like that of a lie. Back up for breath and Adelaide's face gawked long as a carpet; Leland raised his hands in shock and awe. On the dance floor the faces were bleak, confused. What had they seen? Was it different for each viewer? But her hands were back on the mic; she had another story to tell. This time it was all impromptu.

Been waiting for the hearse
Because I am ultimately perverse
As I live this curse
All alone in my own head
It's he who I dread
But no one I need more
To make me a whore

The show had reached its crescendo. Tyria's wolfish howl shattered the other amp to sparks and smoke. And then pandemonium. The crowd was no longer viewing but participating. The sea of flesh rose in a vertiginous wave, their voices enraged. Fists fell and piercings ripped through various orifices. Chaos in the drugged atmosphere.

Bodies hit the floor, overdosed and drunk in the mosh pit. Not as much blood as you would think, but enough to dye eyes red and clot beneath fingernails. They clawed at the stage for more, but Tyria had nothing left. Security was in order but what did that matter at this point?

Morgan cut the music and ducked beneath the curtain with his Mac as two girls began ripping into one another's faces, knocking candles into the drapes. The fire was instant. Her hands went up and the pseudo wings looked like that of a fallen angel. Her voice became carnage, but there was no more a wicked sight than that of Dorian enveloped within her shadow. He was smiling.

The crowd was now clawing for the door—their hands violently clapping—satisfied, relieved. Tyria jumped off the stage, straight on top of some unsuspecting bodies. She moshed her way to the center, grabbed an Open Road candle and hurtled herself toward the horn-shaped flames, just as an unsuspecting embrace pulled her down to pray. Kali, Isis, Lilith, Ishtar. Powerful women that would save her—

—as all the lights cut out.

Everything burned.

The darkness lived on; creepy smiles all around.

BLOOD KISS *Daniel Stone*

We're fucking done!"

Adelaide's chagrin aimed directly at me. No spontaneity in her decision, no reason to stop screaming. Jealousy. Rage. Wrath. Three hours later, the clean up halfway done, and she was still pointing the finger of blame at me, as if my efforts in those last seconds before the fire truly spread—before Tyria almost threw herself into it—mattered nothing to her. Maybe I should've just let the place burn. That would have ended this art.

"I didn't start this to pimp out my girlfriend."

"At least they were satisfied," Tyria said. "The crowd, I mean."

"Fuck the crowd, Ty."

"Isn't this what you wanted?"

"In the end nothing matters but you and me. Not the show, not the money, not him!"

My eyes seemed to burn. But no flame could compare to Adelaide's fury, or Leland's pensive face as I watched it move between the emotions of shock and awe. He put his hand out to Adelaide, but she smacked it away and grabbed her own hair, yanking out clumps and scratching her scalp raw. She was stressed about all the wrong things, her overzealousness making us all uncomfortable. You can tell a person is truly in love when they freely embarrass themselves.

"Was it magick?" Morgan said.

I could hear the click of the K in that word.

"Maybe," I said.

"But I didn't come here to hurt people, yo." His beanie had been singed by the fire, half the scruff on his face as well.

"You said that you wanted to get *paid*."

"Not this way." Now Morgan's serious face on the verge of tears. His words came out sharp and judging about how he could not touch, taste or feel what he had seen.

I found his lack of faith disturbing. I explained to Morgan that reality, especially the one we so comfortably live in, can be altered very easily. Tyria had proved this to me. After everyone caught their breath no one spoke, too confused or occupied with their thoughts.

I had no time for such dalliances. Instead, I calculated the damage. Not as bad I thought, though there were considerable burn marks across the floor, and the windowsills had been eaten beyond repair. I looked up and saw that more than half the ceiling had vanished, and that the holes were as big as my head. An electrical socket spit sparkles of light.

At eye level smoke rose from the weeping wood panel; Leland had thrown buckets of water everywhere, and the smell of the dirty water rose thick as the smoke. Looking back, I am able to reason that the fire wound up being more smoke than flame. Fire is only dangerous if you let it get out of control. Still, all this damage required a new start.

"I'm not waiting on you people hand and foot. Do you think I'm a fucking fool?"

Adelaide was in my face now, and I almost wanted to hit her, but I restrained myself out of respect for Tyria.

"Sit down, Addy," Leland said. "You're off the charts."

"No, they're off the charts, Landy. Don't you get it? They've made fools out of us!"

"You're over thinking it."

"You're naïve."

"What about art?"

"If art means to destroy my relationship with Tyria, then I don't want any part of it."

"You're wrong."

BLOOD KISS

I was confused by Leland's defense. Devil's advocate or loyal boyfriend? I don't think I wanted to know the truth.

"LOOK AT THIS PLACE? HOW WILL WE FIND THE MONEY TO FIX IT?"

When Adelaide pulled her hands out of her thin coat a wad of cash fell to the floor. I chuckled, Tyria sighed and Morgan shook his head. Leland said that taking our business elsewhere would be simple, that we had the following now to go wherever we wanted—to the road, a traveling mystical manifesto—because money and cornerstones were no object to the important statement we were making. He was always full of dreams.

"We just witnessed the majesty," Leland said.

"Don't talk in fancy terms," Adelaide said. "Treat us like the idiots we are."

Nobody spoke then. Morgan moved himself to the bar and Tyria curled into a ball on the dilapidated stage and fell asleep. It seemed she was too controlled by memory to remain in this reality. It had become so quiet that it creeped me out. I could hear all the critters and roaches beneath the floorboards skittering.

I gathered my thoughts, postulating what I had seen. The ugly glow of moonlight melting over the crowd like cream, filling the tiny crevices of my skin. Tyria: a deity in all that dull brilliance, but out of the corner of my eye I saw it. The shadow came back haunted.

I wanted so badly to hold it in my hands, to use it like paint, but realized quickly that it wasn't an object of substance.

I stuck my hand into its depths and searched its guts. When it released me I saw my hands steeped in paint; they had become things of their own mind that drew what I never saw coming. To my right Tyria was raging, her voice melodic, molten. Her control of the crowd was astounding, devil horns raised and their screams getting louder.

I painted the rhythmic nightmares of her words. And then without warning I grabbed her face and opened my mouth to drink down that prosaic flood. The universe did not exist; we were black holes to light. Leland was an ash of memory, and Adelaide nothing but a badly shaped skin job. All that mattered was this moment, us twisting into this drunken hypnosis until the fire stopped us.

"What's really going on?" Leland broke my trance. "I knew something was up, but not anything like this."

His face was drained of color, disappointed. It broke my heart to see him this way.

"I don't know how it happened."

"Save it," he said. "I'm not doing this here."

At the bar Adelaide and Morgan were arguing. Apparently he had bad mouthed Tyria—who was still passed out on the stage—and Adelaide was not going to let that one slide. A beer bottle fell to the floor, vomiting froth and glass.

"Impromptu, yo?" Morgan said. "She's a joke."

Addy pulled Morgan down by his shirt and they rolled around on the floor like a couple of fighting dogs. He whined and she growled, and when he stood up to run she tackled him into the wall so hard they exploded through the sheet rock. *Much better you than I*, I thought, but as Leland came between them Adelaide's hand rose high with a liquor bottle gripped tight.

I saw red for fear of Leland's safety, pulled Adelaide down by her shoulders and stole the bottle out of her hand. She clawed at my arm relentlessly, money fell out of her pockets, and I realized than that money is the dirtiest thing on the planet. Blood is spilled for it, lovers separate because of it and families are destroyed over it. Money equals everything.

"What the hell is going on?"

The commotion had woken Tyria. She pushed me to the side and brought Adelaide to her feet. I ran to Leland and put my arm protectively around him.

"I can take care of myself," he said. " I don't need your help."

"Everyone needs to calm down," Tyria said. "We just made underground history."

BLOOD KISS *Daniel Stone*

"I don't have to do anything I don't want to," Adelaide said.

We were all exacerbated, and rightfully so as the sky was starting to lighten. I felt my hangover kicking in. I wanted to go home. I took in the smell of Leland's dirty hair and put my hand on the back of his pants. He kissed me back hollowly. I always looked forward to a soft-lip kiss, but he simply pecked me and began to mop.

"Leave it, Landy. It's done," I said.

"It's done when I say so. I put this gig together and I'm the one who's responsible for this mess."

"I want to know what that was," Adelaide said.

"It was nothing," Tyria said, the obvious lie.

"It was art," I said.

"Art? There's no art in kissing."

"It was a simple kiss," Leland said.

"But their eyes were closed."

"The crowd *loved* it."

Adelaide's face grew red; her piercings could burn through the skin. "You didn't like it, did you Ty? I mean . . . he's a guy . . . *he's not me*."

Tyria took a step back, lit a cigarette and inhaled slowly. Everyone stared at her, waiting for the answer. Two crystal beads welled in the corner of her eyes, but never did they fall down her cheeks. I wanted to lick them clean from her face.

"I just don't know anymore," she said.

Before Adelaide burst Leland cut in. "Nothing was out of order until you got all pissy."

"So said the kid who was kissing all up on some rock star poseur last night."

I felt a vessel in my brain snap in two. The spiral wound deeper.

"Is that true?" Did I have a right to be jealous?

"He gave me a hit of acid. It was innocent."

"*Innocent*, unlike Tyria and Dorian," Adelaide said.

"You're ruining this with all your bitching."

"Are you saying that you're willing to pimp out your boyfriend for the stage? I sure as hell will not do *that* to Tyria!"

But then Morgan cut in. "Yo, you attacked me like a caged animal."

"The wounded animal will kill you before any other," I said.

"Wounded?" Adelaide said. "Who the fuck are you? What purpose do you have for this show? Tyria is the star."

"He's as much part of this show as I am," Tyria snapped at her.

I lit a cigarette, Camel Crush . . . that or I was about to crush Adelaide's head.

"I'm going to break everything in this room with my hands if you all don't stop."

"What's her problem?" Morgan said.

"If you all knew anything about her you'd know that she is sick," Adelaide said. "And you, Dorian, with your fucking paint and stupid pencil . . . you take advantage of her!"

"I *care* about Tyria. I want to see her reach her full potential."

"I don't think you know the gun you're playing with. You don't know her like I do."

Adelaide was quick to come at me, her hands open, hair wild and her mouth snarled so I could see her yellow teeth. Dark daggered eyes caught mine, and it reminded me of that same crazed look she had on the night I met Leland. But I was ready for her this time. On instinct my hand caught her wrist, gripped it tight enough to feel the tiny bones splice so that the Bowie knife hit the floor, as did her body.

"Stop it!"

Leland pulled my shirt until it ripped; Tyria held Adelaide down. My vision was red and my attitude black with hate. I wanted to kill her. But instead I found an inner Zen. I knew this was no deal breaker for Tyria and I. We held something deep together.

"I want him out of my life," Adelaide said. "Want him dead and gone."

BLOOD KISS *Daniel Stone*

"A knife, Addy? You still have this stupid knife?" Leland's obvious disappointment. "What the fuck is wrong with you?"

"I want him gone!"

"I'll go no problem," I said, and then added the kicker so fast I nearly choked. "But not without Tyria."

Leland's faced dropped. The hurt in him was clear, but he respected my decision. Tyria's jade eyes glowered with thought. Adelaide began to cry. Everyone was nervous for Tyria's answer, including myself. She blinked once, twice, put on her Ray Bans and pushed her yellow bangs away from her face.

"Take me out of here, Dorian."

Lover on the left; sinner on the right.

And just like that we were gone.

DAWN.

Another day survived; another struggle until night. Dawn is for realization. No matter how bright the world may seem, darkness abuts like a shadow, a betrayal, a lie.

Consider Adelaide, consumed by the sickest dark of all. Weak, needy, with no end in sight. Tyria gone for three days now, busy with her new life and new dreams. Good thing Leland had stayed with her; but he didn't have any need to see Dorian, didn't want to believe that his own heart was broken.

But Adelaide had taken it the worst. When certain situations are removed from her control, she is unable to cope. The decisions she makes are deleterious, such as the rocks she is now melting on a spoon, the vintage syringe and needle ready to do the dirty deed.

Don't you do this. You've been clean for sixteen months.

The needle smiled like a vampire.

All it takes is one person to fuck it all up and the recovering addict falls back to square one. Junkies are never really clean, are they? Every day is a struggle as a little devil on their shoulder is always whispering in one ear, the angel in the other. The reality is that sobriety is never truly the goal; it's about placating the ones they love.

"Addy, don't," Leland said.

She stopped the needle mid-landing in the crook of her arm.

"Tyria doesn't love me anymore."

"Yes, she does."

"No, she abandoned me."

Leland's careful glance in front and Morgan's skull-face in back. He reached his hands out, but Morgan held them back. Nothing was going to stop her, not the public disdain, not the personal shame. The needle's prick—the sweet revelation of dope imbuing in her veins—was everything. What was the point of living if you've been robbed of happiness? What was the point of becoming a functional human being again? Every junky knows that loneliness is their only true friend.

"Why are you fucking doing this?" Leland couldn't help the tears, so many of them dripping hot onto Adelaide's face.

"She hasn't called or text in days. Without her I'm nothing."

"You haven't exactly reached out."

"And what about Dorian?" Adelaide's tongue was beginning to bleed from biting it.

"I don't want to see him right now."

"So you stay here and babysit me, how sweet."

Leland kicked the coffee table. "I'm so sick of saving you from yourself."

"She was my everything," bringing the needle into the candlelight. "But now this is."

"Gods, I hate it down here. Smells like mildew and incense," Leland said.

"Please go. And take that walking skeleton with you."

Morgan didn't move from his position on the couch. He looked ready for sleep.

"You look like utter shit," Leland said.

"I *am* utter shit," Adelaide said.

BLOOD KISS *Daniel Stone*

"I won't do this pity party. I've no patience for it. I love you too much."

"So what?" Adelaide let her head roll back.

"You have me, Addy, but without that you'd really have nothing."

She rose to wobbly feet. "What have I got to really fucking lose, Landy?"

"Everything."

"She chose Dorian over me," nails in her mouth.

"She did what she had to do. The stage is her life now."

"Do you know how hard I had to work to gain Tyria's trust over the years?" Her fist came down on the coffee table, spilling cigarette ash and beer.

"Stop," Leland gritted his teeth.

"To know that Dorian gained it in the snap of a finger, to know she let him into her life so easily. That hurts the most."

Leland sat next to Adelaide as she manipulated a piece of cloth around her arm. Leland knew this maneuver quite well, could tie a slipknot with his eyes closed. But instead of arguing with Adelaide, instead of trying his patience to the point of smashing her in the face, Leland helped her fit the cloth snugly. You don't forget the little things, no matter how long you've been sober.

"Tell me how you do it," Adelaide said.

"Do what?"

"Smile and pretend . . ."

Adelaide tapped the crook of her arm until a small, but strong vein surfaced like a pale worm. She pushed the needle in softly and pulled back to see a dollop of blood fill the syringe before she shot herself full of Brooklyn's best heroin. In no time she became comfortably numb.

"This is horrible," Leland said.

"What does she mean that you smile and pretend?" Morgan said.

"Adelaide wears her heart on her sleeve, and I guess I don't, so she thinks I'm too controlled."

"You kind of are though. I mean, look what you did to me, yo."

"Let's not get into that. You know damn well we weren't meant to be."

"Well, it looks like the same is about to happen with you and Dorian."

"That has yet to be determined."

Morgan averted his eyes to the now sleeping Adelaide; her hair covered her face like a black spider web.

"She looks awful, yo."

"I need to make sure she doesn't die."

"You know you can always stay at my place, since you hate it here."

"No. I'm staying with her."

Time passed, but there was no telling how long they'd been talking as the clocks in the room were all dead. Then Adelaide began to shiver, her body rejecting the dope as fast as it entered her system. Leland tried to assist as she darted for the garbage can and vomited directly inside of it. Leland brought her a glass of water and she downed it without a second thought.

"I feel like shit," she said.

"Smell like it too."

When she was able to stand without her head spinning, Adelaide turned up the music. Guitar chords panged is if played by spiders; a poet's frustration boiled over into painful screaming. From the stereo speakers Adelaide caught the liquid darkness spilling out, reaching for her as Otep's "Where the River Ends" tore apart every molecule in the air.

"Turn it down," Leland demanded.

"No."

Adelaide turned the music louder to kill the image of Tyria and to annoy Leland, but he wouldn't give her the satisfaction of the argument. Instead, he focused on his cell phone, running his fingers across Dorian's name, most likely hoping that somewhere out there in the dark he would telepathically hear his call. When the song ended Adelaide shook her head like a dog.

"I feel better now."

BLOOD KISS

Leland took a deep breath in and closed his eyes. "I'll tell you how I deal with it."

"I'd love to hear it."

"Trust."

"You're just as sad as I am. The thing is that you don't want to admit it to yourself."

"Oh, I'm sad, but I'm not going to let it take over my rationality."

"Landy, we have a forebrain for a reason! We feel, we hurt, we cry, we break!"

"But they haven't essentially done anything wrong. They're living the life they've always dreamed of."

Adelaide turned, vicious. "And what is that?"

"They're rock stars."

"Oh, fuck me! How could you be so naïve?"

"I see the glass half full."

Adelaide jumped to her feet. "Well, let me school you. The glass is *always* half empty!

For Leland to believe that Dorian was not up to anything sinister was to make a fool of himself. Adelaide couldn't bare it. Leland was soft where Adelaide was hard as stone. Maybe her heart was marble and his all marshmallow. But she was not going to sit here and nod her head in agreement. A real friend deals in truths.

"You got any beer?" Morgan said.

"Somewhere. And get me one when you find it."

Morgan found the little fridge, opened three PBRs and served them accordingly. They all sipped quietly. It's always five o' clock somewhere. In her silence Adelaide noticed the pale brown spot on the floor, not her blood and not Tyria's, so most likely Dorian's. The thought of them creating blood bonds brought fatal thoughts into her head.

"You guys mind if I?" Morgan said.

"Thought you were clean?"

"It's just grass, yo."

He produced a psychedelic glass instrument from his coat. Nothing like another junky to bring out the worst in you. Morgan lit it up and the sound of bubbling water ensued. Smoke sketched ephemeral shapes in the air, brought with it the verdant and spicy smell of marijuana.

"Yo, Addy, you need a hit," Morgan's baggy eyes above her.

"She isn't coming home, is she?" Adelaide said.

"She's not," Leland said. "The quicker you come to terms with that, the quicker your mental state will heal."

"Does he have a spell on her?" tears now, hot and pathetic and desperate.

Leland put his arm around Adelaide. "You really need to let go."

"But I love her."

"You can love Tyria and still let her do what she wants, you know."

"Tyria needs me. She's fragile."

"You ain't doing anyone any good by sitting here and shooting up. I won't stand for it," Leland said.

"I'm already a fucking monster, might as well be the *real* monster."

"That's right. You were a monster when you were on that shit. You were a loser and you tried to kill me."

"I was stupid and young then."

"No. You were a fucking junky. You lost two of your molars. You went to jail for trying to pawn a television that didn't belong to you. How much will it take for you to wake up?"

"My deathbed."

Leland removed his arm. "Real cool of you to say."

"Get away from me." Adelaide pushed herself off the couch.

"See what I mean. You're an animal," Leland said.

"She *betrayed* me. She promised to love me. But like all cunts in this world, they get fucking wet for cock."

She felt her top lip tear and brought her tongue to the open flesh, licking away the blood. Adelaide proceeded to cry until it physically hurt, until she could produce no more tears. When she wiped her face clean she looked up at the

BLOOD KISS Daniel Stone

only window in the basement where sunlight was seeping in slowly, warming the tops of her shaking hands and drying the sweat in her hair.

"We've been up all fucking night," Morgan said.

Mornings were always prologue to the day's discord. The notion that one has to face all that she has lost, all that she has fought for, was too depressing to think about. Only death can release one from this great pressure we call life. You would never have to feel again, which is far better a reward than feeling too much.

"Tyria didn't leave you. Dorian didn't leave me. You just don't trust them."

"How can you be so *stupid*, Landy? They've obviously outgrown us."

"If you love her, let her do what she wants."

"Easy for you to say. You have a fallback plan."

"What do you mean?" Leland lit a fancy black cigarette.

"You're in love with those Electric Orchid boys. Once again you have it all, and I have shit."

"We're just friends. Why are you being so fucking judgmental?"

He wasn't going to get this one over on her, not now. Adelaide spun herself around and began to destroy the room. She ripped the posters from the walls and kicked down Tyria's altar. Gold crunched beneath her feet, ash spit into her face. The statue of Kali roared; Hecate bled rainbows. The bookshelves were next, kicking at them with all her might until they gave out and the books were all over the floor. Adelaide spit on them.

But something had woken up, sprouting stilted legs and long arms. A shadow's crescendo into another shadow. Morgan jumped so high his head hit the ceiling.

"She ain't here, you got it? She ain't fucking *here*!"

"What is that?" Morgan asked.

"Nothing. Let's go," Adelaide said. "I need to find my girlfriend."

13

Time brought a queer winter spell across the city. The sky had never seemed so dark and the days never so short.

Upon every sidewalk was a scummy coat of snow, footprints and cigarette butts rippling within the glaze; snow angels dusted in soot.

The hours fell like flurries all around us. Three weeks had separated Tyria and I from our lovers. We spent every second of it together, gothic and pure as Heathcliff and Catherine. We drifted into the five boroughs as if the moors, knowing very well that as much as we wanted to be free, it could never be. We would soon be summoned back to Wuthering Heights.

But that would mean imprisonment, and to avoid such a fate we began to couch surf. It was a lifestyle not frowned upon nor eschewed since the hipsters of Brooklyn made us feel right at home. They were our most devoted followers. We had reached the point of superstardom where fans followed us wherever we went; the train, the supermarket, or even the bathroom, asking for photos and signatures, beseeching to pick our brains. Whatever Tyria and I needed they made sure it happened. All they asked in exchange was our company.

I remember a girl named Jenny. Black hair, eyes frigid as ice and a face like that of the Black Dahlia. If I didn't know any better I would have asked her if she had starred in a Showtime series about Lesbians. But she was no actress, no artist; just an admirer of the strange and hopelessly devoted to our cause, our message. She had said that Tyria possessed the power to create Vibhuti ash out of "thin air" which is essentially the debris from when a spirit is brought into the physical world from their eternal slumber.

We met in a typical Williamsburg craft beer sanctuary and somehow all wound up going back to her place in Red Hook. The building she lived in swarmed high for Brooklyn's standards, and I found it strange that in the not too far east stood a fairly new Ikea. Strange juxtapositions for such a dreary, empty part of the borough. Jenny thought nothing of it, worried only about an increase in rent as she had no real job to speak of.

I remember that one time or another one of our "landlords" asked for sex in exchange for housing us, and I was okay with that. Freezing to death outside would not have helped our artistic mission at all. But Jenny didn't want any of that, though her studio had no windows and it smelled like dirty laundry. I never knew what time it was while inside, not that it really mattered. I think that was the point of it all. Jenny wanted to keep us locked up.

After a week Tyria grew tired of Jenny's clinginess as I grew tired of her mouth. She had this gross talent for talking, and I mean not just talking, but babbling about the stupidest shit. Whatever subject Tyria and I brought up, no matter the circumstance, Jenny would find a way to "one up" us. She had a brother or a cousin or a friend's grandmother that made her portion of the conversation relevant. I so very badly wanted to put tape over her mouth, but Tyria reminded me that I should not be so cruel. Instead, we left for the streets again.

When the money ran out we knew that we could not ask Leland or Adelaide for more, so we cashed cans or borrowed it from our fans. I did not draw and Tyria did not write. We had never felt so alone even though we were together.

But the phone calls and text messages were relentless. Landy wanted to know if I was alive. *Please write anything to me, a dot, an emoji, just something!* and even though Adelaide cried on every voicemail, Tyria would not give into the temptation of calling her.

"Adelaide sounds sick," I said to Tyria.

"Sick in her own way."

"Do you not care?"

"I do, but I just don't want to see her right now."

Tyria turned away from me. A dozen snowflakes had landed upon her face and melted across her furious cheek. The hazy starlight cascaded down her yellow hair, gleamed bright as her jade eyes. Though the night felt young, dawn was just around the corner. We both were wayward, condemned to either keep running or face reality. We hadn't slept normally in days.

"I don't think I've ever lost this much sleep in my life," Tyria said.

"What is sleep anyway?"

"Perchance to dream?"

"Very funny," I said.

Were walked fast through distinct Brooklyn neighborhoods. I saw food trucks and brownstones, apartment buildings in shambles and the ghosts of the old Hebrew Orphan Asylum. But mostly there were factories and warehouses. As we arrived in South Williamsburg I found myself severely out of breath but craving a cigarette; the cold had seeped down to my bone marrow, threatening to freeze my heart.

"I just can't keep up with you," I said.

"Keep walking, you wimp."

Tyria had the energy level of a star athlete, despite being a heavy smoker. She sprinted down Grand Street while I lagged behind and soaked in the glitter of the hip stores, antique shoppes and endless bars. I put my foot down halfway around the next corner for fear of death by Mother Nature. I refused to end up like Jack Torrence in Kubrik's version of *The Shining* as I saw that my fingertips were blue and Tyria's lips colorless.

"My feet hurt," I said. "I need warmth."

"Let's go somewhere where people don't know us."

BLOOD KISS *Daniel Stone*

"Fine," I said in a great breathy cloud.

"I don't want Addy to be able to track me."

"I said *fine*, so long as we're warm."

We settled into a dive bar and book shoppe. The lighting scheme was so terrible I could barely read the titles. Maybe it was to trick the consumer, but I was not one who bought books blindly. Tyria sat on a stool and rubbed her hands together as if finally remembering that it was below ten degrees outside. I browsed the books and pulled a peculiar title off a shelf, flipped through the words absently waiting for my Magic Hat. When it arrived my hands felt like they were on fire; Tyria's face was red as a bouquet of roses.

"We shouldn't stay here too long."

Tyria seemed nervous now. Her hands had curled into fists.

"Why?"

"I have something special to show you."

A long ribbon of silence ensued. We looked over our shoulders for something, perhaps Adelaide or Leland—were they even looking for us?—then at each other. The music switched between Guns n' Roses and Queen.

"Why do we always find ourselves at bars?" I said.

"To feel a sense of community."

We cheered to art and freedom from pain. I put the book I was reading back on the shelf and picked up another. It was a self-published memoir written by a man who lived in the neighborhood. From page one I was swept into a world of heroin, prostitution and gentrification. The author's idea was that all this change had turned Bushwick and Williamsburg into flavorless black holes.

But I could not sympathize with him as it has been the trend of wealthy people to colonize squalor in New York City since I could remember. They come in and claim it for their own without thinking about the people that were there first. They expect everyone to conform to their special hole in hell. I stopped reading.

"What a crappy book," I said.

"Bet you wanna read mine."

"Once was enough."

For the first time in weeks I saw it. The heat from those pages was refreshing; I could swear those holy words were screaming at me, watching me, blaming me. Something had come over Tyria now; she escaped into her own head, forgetting about the world around her. I thought how selfish it was of her to do such a thing, but how magnificent she looked in her element. She nearly glowed. To see her discover herself through words was the true magick, and if I had any faith in the world, the power of words was where it laid.

Yet she was not writing words, but drawing a map.

"What is that?" I said.

"The way."

"To what?"

"The Moors."

"Now Ty, you can't trick me with your literary knowledge."

"But this is how I remember it."

"But what is it exactly?"

"The path to the books."

I looked behind me to see that a group of hipsters had walked in. I smelled funeral lilies and frankincense. They seemed unhappy but focused on something, a memory perhaps, a friend. When they warmed up and headed back out I took Tyria with me to follow. There was some sort of huddle, their feet in pointed out but in a star-like shape I knew very well. Tyria fell to her knees—an immediate sign of respect—in front of a picture of the trust fund baby gone urban renegade.

"He was robbed and killed right here," A girl said.

"Brooklyn is a piece of shit," I said.

Tyria kissed her necklace, looked into the night sky and then we were off into the river of night. Four blocks later we lost the light of the city—though the snow was white enough to keep our path clear—but we did not fear the streets. We

BLOOD KISS *Daniel Stone*

had been nurtured by the cobblestone and tarmac, where a quick fix is nothing but a normal night out, where beer is the mediocre high.

"I don't really feel any sense of community," Tyria said without looking at me. "I hate most of these people."

"Were you not sad about what you just saw?"

"Honestly no."

"Why? What do you feel?"

"Like I always have to *fight* to fit in," her voice was soft as flowers.

Tyria drew out her cell phone. She had missed three more calls and a flood of texts had arrived. *I'm with Landy. We're worried. I'm calling the police.* I looked at her phone in horror. The police were the last thing we needed.

"She's drunk, and she's trying to keep me caged."

"I think it's more than drunk."

"Like what?" Tyria furrowed her brow.

"If she wants to be down in a hole, that's her choice. But she can't take you with her."

The cell phone vibrated again. *Why are you doing this to me?* Tyria almost caved in and called—I nearly made her do it to at least let Landy know everything was fine—but instead we sought the map she had drawn and kept walking.

"I have this to forget about her," opening her hand to show me three baggies filled with powder.

"You remember what happened last time I did that shit."

"But we might find ourselves in a lot of trouble," Tyria said.

"With what?"

"Our feelings."

Despite the weather Brooklyn had never seemed so perfect. The uneven pavement might be morbid to most, but it was a quite normal to us. The stragglers looking to score might be looked down upon, but we were sympathetic to their stories. The chintzy outline of Manhattan from this side of the water was something that always made me sad: the notion that you are poor and they are rich.

"What feelings are you talking about?"

"*Change*. I'm changing and so are you. The world is getting smaller; our shows are getting bigger."

"We won't have another show if we don't call them."

"To hell with that."

"No."

"Say it, Dorian. Say it."

We arrived at the cross streets of Grand and Driggs Avenue, nothing here but drifting pieces of snow and detritus encased in ice. I found myself a bit dizzy, vexed even, for I had no clue where she was taking me. To my death, to the Grand fucking Canyon with all the walking we were doing.

"You won't believe me until I show you," Tyria said. "I wonder if we could stay there forever . . . away from it all."

"Show me what?"

Pointing to the cluttered row of warehouses, big painted windows reminiscent of old abandoned temples, metal doors so heavy I could never imagine them opening by our pitiful strength. The art on the walls read *GHoSTS iN MY HeAD* and *SeX CHAnGES EVERyTHING*. I thought about the potential to attract a decent following, us torpid on the stage, Tyria a pale deity spreading the night's fallen gospel; me off to the side to draw up their nightmares.

"We could just break into it," Tyria said.

"But that's illegal, even if they're abandoned."

"They're not abandoned."

I pointed at the giant POISON sign with the big computerized rat.

"Too dangerous."

Now that I had gotten a good look each window scintillated. Tyria spoke lovingly about fireflies and mole people. *Warehouse children*, she called them. Kids living off their parent's checkbook. But I was in harsh refusal, for how do you come from such privilege to live in all this destitution?

"And in we go," sharp smile.

She lit a cigarette as we ducked beneath a brick archway that seemed to play a trick on the eye the way it stretched into the sky. The hallway was long and dark as a secret. It

BLOOD KISS Daniel Stone

had a negative smell but parted like butter as I lit my lighter so that I could see how truly a mind-fuck it was, that it seemed to go on forever.

Tyria was my beacon in this umbrage; her eyes were two green markers. I followed the scent of sage, cigarettes and candle flame; I heard the high-pitched squeal of bats and the call of ravens in long maddening caws. A great quilt wrapped about my face, but when I put my hands up to grab it I saw that it was a giant cobweb. When I freed myself from the silky chains I saw the antiquated sign.

BOOKS and DREAMS.

"Just as I remember it."

"What is this place?"

"It'll make you a believer."

We fed ourselves to the labyrinth. Stone walls rose to my left and to my right, walls taller than any height I could fathom. The pavement suddenly became a dirt road banked by red wood trees as if we had fallen straight into a Brother's Grimm fairytale. Tyria stopped for one moment and looked up; I took a gulp of the misty air, tasted the life in it like static electric.

"It's still alive," jade eyes wide with wonder.

A sudden change in scenery. We ran like children through fields of pretty little ghostflowers to catch the scents of summer and fireflies. I imagined jars with eyeballs floating in formaldehyde, and then jars full of dandelion wine. The ceiling—what I conceived to be a ceiling—billowed like a carnival mirror trick. Tyria's reflection was that of a little girl I did not know, and mine of a boy I used to know. My hair short as Tyria's was long, dark as hers was light. She screamed as loud as she could and we followed the echo to the spiral staircase.

Tyria stopped and looked right at me. "You still think *believing* is stupid?"

I couldn't speak.

"Whatever you do don't look down."

Twisting upward—so fast it defied my own heartbeat—one could swim the sounds and drink the colors. A floating dazzle of moonlight; a gushing, burning orange sun rose high. Night on my left and daylight on my right. Bushwick's pathetic skyline to Manhattan's dreamy glow. We ascended too fast for our wheezing lungs, building heat and sweat and breaking physical laws to finally find the door at the top of the stairs.

A grand door.

It opened with a creak.

Behind it the starry glow of books, each one fastened with little bits of dream and nightmare, universes long forgotten. I had no real vision inside this place; it was replaced by that of a child's. I saw rocking chairs too big to describe, hammocks and lawns and picnic baskets. There were cobwebs and dust mites, pencil shavings and dribbles of ink everywhere. I imagined disheartened authors crooning over their pens and papers like junkies do the spoon and lighter. They do it until they bleed, until they get it right.

"You have to open them find out," Tyria said.

"What do you mean?"

"Think of your favorite writer and then pull a book off the shelf."

Fitzgerald was the first name that came to mind. I pulled a thick blank book off the shelf, found that it was warm as a beating heart.

"Open it," Tyria said.

Words weaved themselves onto the pages, *THE GREAT GATSBY* in a jazzy swirl. Suddenly I was vacuumed into a world of party. Fireworks exploded to the rhythmic jive of the roaring twenties; a Rolls-Royce became omnibus for dames. Cocktail music droned to the smell of Parliaments and hors d'oeuvres. Confetti of blue and gold fluttered into my face like moths.

"This is too real," I said.

Couples danced in eternal graceful circles. A huge orchestra led the night into sweat and tears and sex. I understood how intimate a big party was and how there isn't any privacy at small parties. Gatsby's hurt lived through me, and I found myself reaching for the light: Tyria.

BLOOD KISS

"What do you feel?" She asked me.

"Shock," I could only say. "Are you seeing this?"

"No."

"What do you mean?" I pointed to a laughing man throwing confetti everywhere.

"I believe you," Tyria said. "This is where my mother used to take to me escape."

"Still can't understand how you don't see it."

"Because you opened the book."

It took me while to understand what she meant. I closed the book, still tasting champagne.

"Books are the only things that *don't* kill me and still make me feel alive."

I pulled another down. I was drugged. I wanted to live another dream. WUTHERING HEIGHTS stitched onto the pages in gothic cursive. The smell of the moors rolled into my senses. A great mist swallowed my body and led me to a giant house where a gypsy child and a girl too mischievous to ever be her father's favorite became brother and sister, best friends and inanimate lovers.

But on the eve of one of their usual escapades they had stepped onto someone else's land the dogs were let out. The wounded girl was locked up for months and upon her return she had become a lady while the boy remained wild at heart. Though the girl would marry another, her love for the gypsy would always be first.

I cried my eyes out.

Tyria was twirling now. She had pulled down a book but we opened it together, the title swirling itself into a Victorian fervor, THE MERCURY WALTZ. Thus we danced to theater music and drank tea at sunset, unveiling our futures in tarot. We strapped plague masks on our faces; puppets became our hands, bits of bone to be wood, flesh to be weaved into leather and velvet. Horse carriages delivered moribund whores to well off tourists. We indulged in the drama of lost boys, suicide, aging lovers and the unholy threat that a theater can weigh upon the good mannered people of Rottermond Square.

"You can't just come here and find magic. It has to find you."

"Can I do this with a million books?"

"Do you believe now?"

"Yes."

I took her hand, unable to stop myself because I was so inspired. I wanted to draw her, rip into her soul. We back peddled toward the door, knocked a few titles off a shelf to see their pages spring open with the sounds of tendrils and endless ocean hearts. I could have fallen into their depths forever.

"I want you to believe in me too," I said.

Outside it had become even colder, but we were darting fast toward the East River. I was taking a big chance to bring her to my home, but I knew that Leland would not be there. We came up to my building on the left; it looked crippled, and Tyria turned toward me, a curious innocence overtaking her face.

"What do you want me to believe about you?"

"My art."

Though my hand reached out to hold Tyria, I saw that she had changed, saw something black and fluid. Her shadow exploded into its carrion bloom, the delineation of it clear as the rings of a tree. It had shrouded the street, but alas it broke the fall as Tyria collapsed to her knees. And then I talked to it.

"Come to me, you fuck."

We became entangled in act of violation. No sufficient word exists so that I could describe the sensation one feels when they cradle decadence, a beating heart, how it feels to crush the soft skull of a newborn, to stick a finger into the rotted vein of an addict. Too much electric; too much dark.

"No," Tyria screamed.

She broke my hypnosis. I realized that my thoughts in the moment before had been possessed with violence: I wanted to hurt Tyria; I wanted to make her mine. But we were

BLOOD KISS

running for my building now. The windows were rattling and the front door was covered in ooze.

I turned my head to make sure it was not following us, saw it slide back into the garden darkness of the sewer. We ran inside, fully aware that the real world is scarier than anything we could ever imagine, but still safer than any nightmare.

LELAND DREAMS WHILE HE IS AWAKE, the sort of dream that causes discord or paranoia: lizard bodies in a dangerous pirouette upon the stage and their eyes gleaming mean. Dorian wholly entranced by his art while the microphone draws blood upon Tyria's lips.

"Landy . . ." a voice said.

But he cannot wake. The show is too intense and Tyria's smile too red. The crowd surges, bathing the room in sweat. But this is what it was all about, the music and the poetry and the art. Nothing else really mattered.

"Leland!" Morgan's hungover voice.

As he slowly was ciphered out of the dream he opened his eyes to see Morgan's long, tired face, his eyes nothing but hollows. He was waving a copy of the local art newspaper, and lo and behold another article! He could barely read the title, it was still too dark down here, but Leland knew it to be true. Another underground success.

"How long was I out?"

"At least two days."

Leland shot up. "Two days?" The taste in his mouth was horrible. "I need a toothbrush."

"I never minded your morning breath."

"Why did you let me sleep so long?"

"You needed the rest and I wanted the alone time. Don't worry, I made sure you didn't wet the bed."

Leland ran his hand though his hair. "I need a shower."

"Nah, leave it, yo."

"You're gross."

But then a sudden pain in his head. "Where's Addy?"

"Relax yo, she's right there."

Leland looked at Adelaide, who had pulled her legs into her chest like a fetus, sleeping a horrible sleep. Her hair was wild and alive as serpents, eyes like rockets inside her head. He knew that she was haunted by nightmares old and new, sins that had yet to be committed long since discovered in her sleep.

"She looks like shit."

"I wouldn't dare wake her. I have no clue if she peed herself or not. All I know is that she hasn't moved, except for that terrible grinding of her teeth."

Leland brushed Adelaide's hair away from her face. "She's so sad."

"She puked everywhere," fixing the crooked beanie on top of his head. "I thought she was gunna explode, yo."

"Is that what that smell is?"

"Trust, Landy, she'll be fine once she reads this," holding the magazine for Leland to see.

"Let me see it," drawing a candle close.

A fancy title and a center spread. There was but one picture, unremarkably blurred for effect. A shadow, a canvas and a microphone. Leland followed the words like a downward spiral.

"They're all talking, Landy. A bunch of kids are outside worshiping this place."

"Worshiping?"

"They know Tyria lives here."

Leland was quiet for another minute, then said, "Let's go."

"Wait, what about—"

"I don't wanna disturb her. She needs the rest . . . for detox purposes."

Morgan placed a copy of the art magazine on the coffee table as Leland extended Adelaide's legs by her ankles, twisted her body so that she was fully on her side for a more

BLOOD KISS

comfortable rest. Still, she looked wrong. Sleep seemed so unnatural for Adelaide. Eventually she'd wake up, feeling defeated, but alive no less. Leland wrote her a note to text him when she woke up, that he would come pick her up when she was ready.

"Where we going?" Morgan said.

"I wanna see some new friends."

14

The air in Dorian's warehouse loft was warm and wet as menstrual blood.

What else should she have expected? Moving in there was a huge floor fit for dancing, an open kitchen and a sink full of dishes. All the walls were exposed brick, and hanging upon them was the art of Dali, Bacon, Pollock and Dorian's own pieces.

"Welcome to my nightmare," Dorian said.

"I think I'm gunna like it."

Dorian took off his boots and Tyria her disintegrating sneakers. Of all the things Dorian was particular about, it was keeping the hardwood floors clean. Not that the place was clean with the piles of clothes, paint stains and of course a towering shelf of books that was arranged in no order.

On that same shelf Tyria noticed that there was a picture of Dorian and Leland, one that was taken many years ago. Dorian was skinnier, if that was even possible, and Leland's face was that of a curious youth. The two of them stared at one another, behind them a fresh and wet canvas. They hadn't really changed, but she could tell this was a purer time for the couple; such is the purpose of a photograph, to stop time and keep it that way.

"That was the first show Landy set up for me."

"Looks like a special moment."

"We've never taken a better picture."

"Did you sell that night?"

"Enough to score this place."

He was leading her toward a room guarded by a bad sheetrock job, and in the center a wobbly door that took up half the space adjacent to the kitchen. *My studio*, Dorian said, but she was not invited into his world, not yet. Tyria touched the doorknob and felt something wet crawl up her arm, but decided not to inquire about such a spook.

"Mind tricks," Dorian said. "I saw you pull your hand back."

Tyria didn't say anything. She looked up and saw light bulbs in the shape of tiny spiraled moons. Everything glowed; teeth, nails and eyes the color of deep sea scales. Black streamers zigzagged like clotheslines in Calcutta; every window was covered in black drapes for the feel of permanent night.

"Sunlight can ruin paintings," Dorian whispered.

"Didn't know that," Tyria said. "Sure makes it cozy."

"Cozy, as one is hardly able to afford luxury on a crappy art salary," Dorian grinned that fascinating rock star grin.

The bed was shrouded in dust and feathers; the sheets were undone exposing piles of sneakers, underwear and jeans. Tyria took a deep breath in, the smell in here dirty but laced with that special spice of creation. At the sight of her curiosity Dorian lit a stick of sandalwood incense.

"Never anytime to clean," Dorian smirked.

"You can't cover up the smell with that."

In the gloomy light Tyria found dog-eared posters and drawings. Absinthe Robette in Victorian green, Darren Aronofsky's Black Swan and Frank the Rabbit in charcoal black. There was also the early stages of a sketch, then the final painted product. Transgression, aggression and deception. A diptych that was hinged together mocked the flapping of wings.

"I remember that from your gallery."

"We never really got to talk about that night."

"It's behind us now," Tyria said. "And it wasn't something we could control."

"You don't have to control *everything*."

She could feel a presence amongst them. Something about Dorian's drawings, their non-eyes seeing what she could not, their tongues tasting things she could not even imagine. Tyria closed her eyes and willed the feelings away, to open them directly in front of a poster for a band called Electric Orchid. She remembered Adelaide spoke of this band, especially of their lead singer Delilah. Something about power.

"You into this band?" Tyria said.

"Landy is. I don't know too much about them. He has a record of theirs somewhere in here."

"I want to hear it," Tyria said. "Addy talks about them."

Dorian rolled his eyes. "Supposedly they sound like the love child of Black Sabbath and Nine Inch Nails."

"I'm all for that."

Dorian went into a frenzy to look for the disc. His hands dug into a pile of jewel cases, the CDs in no apparent order, spilling them everywhere. Artwork for The Cure's *Bloodflowers* and Tool's *Aenima* settled by her feet. Cam de Leon's *Ocular Orifice* blinked once, then twice, before Tyria looked away.

"No luck, but there's this," Dorian said.

"Stevie Nicks?"

"You a fan?"

"Of course."

The record was Nicks' 1989 Alice in Wonderland inspired *The Other Side of the Mirror*. Dorian set the volume to a comfortable level as a song called "Doing the Best I Can" changed the feeling of the room.

"Let's relax," Dorian said.

Tyria found the floor fast, so good to sit after all that walking. Dorian lit a joint, filled his lungs with spicy smoke. When he passed it over Tyria pulled on it with a slow-moving force, and then let herself fall into the music. She could hear it travel up the walls, get lost between the cracks in the floor like water. It was a solitary, but timorous feeling.

The future came to her.

BLOOD KISS

She was seated at the head of a great crossroads. A triplicate road. Dorian, Adelaide, Daddy. The road of pins, the one of needles, and the one less taken. One will prick until you bleed, the other will fasten everything together, but the last will chew you from the inside out.

Tyria removed her jacket because it was just too hot now. She put out her arms, black bracelets jingling, the rings on her fingers all of a sudden too tight, and she turned them up toward her in seductive worship. Hecate called out to her. The twin torches twined into each other like overgrown vegetation. Goddess of entranceways, daughter of night and keeper of herbs. Self-made statue dressed in skin.

"Are you praying?" Dorian asked.

He was rising above her, and she didn't even realize that she was on her knees until she saw his crotch getting hard. Tyria reached up and tugged on his forearm for him to come down. His skin was cold, but accepting, and his eyes were like pieces of dark stone. Dorian was her living sex dream.

"Pray with me," Tyria said in a hoarse voice. "There's bad energy in here."

Dorian looked at her like she was nuts.

"I mean it."

He kneeled next to her and removed his shirt. She saw his little nipples, slatted ribs and scrawny shoulders. There was no hair on his torso and his tattoos seemed to grin with bad intent.

"I need a garlic clove, an onion and a few eggs, if you have it."

"Eggs?"

"For fertility."

Dorian did as he was told and came back with everything in a bowl. He didn't hand it over at first as there was a question burning on his tongue.

"What is all this for?"

"This place is a magnet for bad energy. I won't spend another second in here feeling like this."

"What are you talking about?"

"It's a dark moon tonight."

Tyria found the sage in her pocket and ignited the leaves. She took Dorian by the hand and began cleansing to room. She swayed their arms and chanted pagan prayers until the loft was one thick swirl of smoke like some night club.

Dorian stopped in his tracks, fell to the floor, and then pulled his arms and legs into the fetal position. Tyria put the sage bundle into an ashtray, straddled Dorian and unfurled his limbs one by one. He looked like the Vitruvian man as she unbuttoned his jeans. The muscled V of his groin was sharp as a knife, a knife she could not resist for the intricacy of intimacy was too strong. But for a split-second a whole bunch of thoughts invaded her brain. Why would she allow *any* man to touch her? Why would she allow herself to become weak enough to question her queerness?

It's bad enough to live in a straight world where a woman's role is that of the breeder and non-thinker, where the man is the bread winner and never the sinner. Tyria had fought long and hard to distinguish herself from everyone else—be it gay, be it an artist—and so why would she give all that up now?

"I'm not doing this for fun," she said.

Dorian didn't respond.

Tyria only knew one way to crush her thoughts. She poured a fine white line and snorted it right off the floor; Dorian's bump was twice the size of hers, and so his nose began to bleed and his pupils dilated enormously. Numbness veiled her rationality. She dreamed of the stage, dreamed of Daddy. The road less taken was Hecate's gift, the road of the future. Gone was her self-made gloom; gone was Daddy's rough touch. Gone was all judgment.

Her skin against his completed the meaty circuit.

Tyria slid her pants down in a fury. She felt a strange heat crawl out of her like a living thing, claiming the prize below. At the same time Dorian's hand moved up her thigh, calloused fingers manipulating the folds of her pussy.

"It's as if I already know you," Dorian said.

BLOOD KISS

She brought her pelvis down swaying, craving. Juices dripped like soup over their bodies; their mouths went on a mission to reach the back of one another's throat. It was a strange journey, but necessary.

Dorian slid into her like a knife.

The sensation erupted into violence. Colors bled like a rainbow scraped raw across concrete. The feeling was unlike anything she ever knew: if you could taste mystery incarnate, if fever dream were a flavor. The proboscis of his erection plucked her flower for nectar; delicate bones rolled like thunder. Secret slimes mixed into one smelly fluid.

"Don't stop," Tyria commanded as if on stage.

His hands gripped the back of her neck, fingers in her hair; their lip rings clinked like bells. His tongue was a lengthy worm wriggling into her throat, his touch suddenly knowing. Dorian was gentle enough so that she felt comfortable in this surreal exchange, but also aware of the animal inside her.

"He's not you . . . he's not you!" Tyria whined.

It was almost too much to bear as Dorian turned her over to go filthy doggy-style. Her tongue stained with tears, her lips tore in agony. The thrill of intimate contact was just too strong. There came a raucous pain throughout her body; a meaty soup became her guts. She smelled blood, saw it grease Dorian's dick, leaving Tyria to fear that it might spill the secrets of her womb.

"I don't care about the blood," Dorian said.

And then it came.

Huge and batty, it had wings as great as any gargoyle. The shadow had found its way back to her. Its dark tongue stroked her sweaty back, ran down the bony beads of her spine. But Dorian had caught sight of it; she felt it in the way his body shifted, how he pulled out of her so roughly. His hand gripped her hair while the other firmly violated the drippy dark.

Tyria saw that it touched Dorian right back.

And then he slid himself back inside her and howled. His black eyes rolled up until she saw the whites, the hairs on his legs rose in pleasure. His hands tensed so hard against her hips they almost broke through her skin. For one holy second his heartbeat swelled inside of her.

And then she knew the mistake they'd made.

She could feel the millions of opaque swimmers invading her garden womb. But rather than scrambling for a morning after pill or shoving a vacuum up her vagina, Tyria found herself clenching, didn't want to let any part of Dorian go. For the first time in a long time she felt worshiped like the goddess that she always wanted to be. Tyria became immortal.

The shadow shed its final skin.

HELL LIVES IN A HANGOVER.

Heaven is a lie. It was not the kind of headache that lingers after a bad dream or a night of blackout drinking. Adelaide hadn't dreamed at all. The pain in her head was attributed to loss and confusion; she couldn't even recall passing out or Leland and Morgan leaving. Time was non-existent during her rest.

She lit a cigarette to get the bad taste off her palate. Vomit. Beer. Cotton mouth. All good junkies know that flavor. She rubbed her tongue across her lips, then reached for a beer, knocking a stack of newspapers off of the table. Two small red pills miraculously slid toward her. She popped them in her mouth, and after the first sip the headache seemed to dissipate. There was this moment where a sensible thought almost took over her brain, but instead she grabbed the magazine and read the new article.

"Power in numbers. A cause the art world hasn't seen in a generation," Adelaide said out loud.

Something like pride built up inside of her. She was certain Leland was happy as well, and perhaps despite all of this confusion, he was sorting out the plans for the next show. Still, she could not help but to feel sad and lonely. Down by her feet the needle and syringe rolled away ghostly. *All you do is fuck with everyone who touches you*, Adelaide said. *You're the ruiner.* She didn't want it anymore; the high wasn't like it used to be. It no longer floated her away from her problems, but spit them back in her face.

There was a note from Leland. *Take a shower and text me when you wake up.* But she didn't want to contact him, not yet. What she wanted was to read the article a hundred times. Front to back. The writer this time around was deeply critical. Apparently the addition of the music didn't make the show better; it was a forceful distraction. Did Leland know this?

It was on the fifth read when Adelaide realized that the criticism was actually harsh. The writer's choice of words was sharp and listless. *Hopeless* and *depraved* were some, *reductive* and *contrived* were some others. She could fully agree with hopeless and depraved, but reductive and contrived was something she would not stand for. What they had was something new and innovative, especially now that the show had ended in blood and fire—though it hurt to think about that, she smiled. Words like *mystical* and *abrasive* and *unique* filled the last half of the article to make up for the insulting beginning. For that alone Adelaide could live happily. Tyria's gospel was being heard.

But this didn't stop the black tears from rolling down her face. The thought of spending one more morning without knowing if Tyria would ever come home—if she ever wanted to see her again—was the worst feeling in the world. What did Dorian have that she didn't? What was so thrilling about him?

Adelaide opened her cheap flip phone and sent a text to Tyria. *I miss you* and *Life doesn't matter if I'm alone.* She then called Tyria but it went straight to voicemail and Adelaide let out a groggy, hateful speech kissed with her smoky voice.

She checked the time, ripped herself off the couch and began to clean up. Her hair was matted, so she combed it straight; her makeup was horrendous so she washed her face and applied it again. Upstairs a musical manifesto had begun. She heard choreographed stomping and the hollow clicking of sun-dried bones shaking in a bowl. She smelled Hyssop water boiling as the voices sang in reverence to Tehuti and Kali. Catland's pinnacle gods. All the banging and chanting reminded her of Tyria. If she were here she would have run up the stairs with sage in her hand and Zen in her heart.

But there was no Zen in the destruction at the hand of Adelaide. She looked at what she had done, the altar smashed, beads of red and gold spilled like candy all over the floor. The statues of Kali and Hecate were broken, sluiced in ooze, but still strangely vibrant.

Adelaide's eyes now caught sight of a *SyNtHeSiS* advertisement and thus every thought that was on a trajectory had now fallen into deep space. There was Tyria's name in bold and Dorian's in monotone; she grabbed it off the table, tore it up and rained paper all around her. It felt good to strip herself of those two little demons. Now she desired to go out, slipped a black beanie on her head and unlocked the door with a new mission in mind.

ANOTHER DAY GONE, so much like the lifespan of a fly or moth, and Leland didn't even remember falling asleep on the L train, or why he was dreaming of them again. Sleep paralysis was pure torture as he could feel the train beneath him, could hear the people talking, but he could not escape this fuzzy world no matter how hard he tried.

Dorian was wearing only a pair of black underwear and Tyria was praying to an unnamed goddess. They both looked sweaty and tired, but every time they touched, kissed, a rocket dropped down from the sky. Dorian's heart was

BLOOD KISS

beating like a bird looking to break out of a cage; Tyria's tears were blood-red, falling from the stage.

"Yo, get up," he heard Morgan say.

"I can't," he mumbled.

Skinny fingers probed his torso, then tugged his hair. When they began shaking him like a hollow doll, Leland pulled himself out of the dream and heard the conductor announce that they had arrived at 1st avenue. Was Morgan the one holding him down in that dream? His eye sight was still cloudy, but he jumped to his feet, then up the crumbling staircase and into the empty streets. Leland smelled the threat of snow sure as that of diesel fumes and roasting lamb from the Halal carts.

"Thanks for letting me get cleaned up at your place," Leland said.

"It's nothing, yo. Anything for you."

"How long was I out for?"

"The whole train ride from Brooklyn. Seems like you can't get enough sleep these days yo."

Leland disregarded what he said.

"I hope you like Alex and Rez. They're chill."

"How long have you known them?"

"Not long at all, but they know art, and they want to help me."

"Are they in that band you like, Electric—"

"Orchid, yeah. Alex is the pianist. But Rez is a writer."

Morgan halted. "Maybe Alex can work with me on some beats I've been putting together. Experimental . . . but it's mad cool."

"What kind of music?"

"Basically anything that inspires me. Sounds. Echoes. A lighter's flint, the hiss of someone puffing a cigarette; a car motor in idle, a train passing and the awkward silence that follows."

"Would these sounds enhance the experience?"

"I imagine so," Morgan said with a cigarette in his lips.

"Also, is there anyway we can cloak the speakers and add them to all parts of the room. I don't want anyone to know where the music comes from."

"That's a lot of work, but it can be done. Maybe your new friends can help us."

"So long as we keep it experimental, then yes."

Morgan showed Leland a small black device that almost looked like a gun. "Just pop this puppy into my Mac and I can manipulate any sound into a song."

"We're gunna use that at the next show."

Morgan sucked in smoke, and Leland noticed he held it in for a dangerous amount of time. "Do you really want to put together another one of those disasters?"

"Absolutely."

Each block they passed was like a river gone dry. Somehow the world felt different. Maybe Leland was too tired, or maybe it was the feeling of dread all these dreams left him. But the thought of Dorian and Tyria's next act—even if they were bound to kill each other—put Leland's business mind at ease. The knowledge that he could present this brand of lunacy to a new audience enlightened him.

"You okay, Landy? You're thinking very hard. Your eyes are here but your mind . . ."

"It seems all I do is dream these days. But that's why I wanna see Alex and Rez. They help me *not* to dream."

"Do you even know where they live or are we just circling in this cold?"

"Stuyvesant Town," Leland said.

Dusk caught up with them. Leland saw a purple curtain close over the city, iridescent and soft as silk. Though warm in color the weather was still bitterly cold. Morgan was shivering beyond control, and every person on the street breathed out plumes like smoke. But then the light of a bodega caught Leland's eye.

"We can't show up empty handed," Leland said.

"What do they drink?"

"Beer."

BLOOD KISS

Once inside Leland requested four loose cigarettes and then scanned the beer selection for something cheap. A twenty-two ounce of Colt 45 for Leland and St. Ides for Morgan; a six-pack of Natty Ice for Rez and Alex. So cheap is the hangover too, the kind that keeps you sick all day. Back outside the air was heavy with the smell of snow.

Then came the big fat drifts, the wind kicking up. Flakes beating into flakes, crushing down upon one another until the city was covered once again in white. Leland looked north, high as his eyesight could take him. Midtown was pale and spiky; the tops of the buildings were iced over, giant crystal knives slicing the atmosphere.

"We've had enough snow this winter," Leland said.

"Hate shoveling that shit, yo," Morgan returned.

"But it's so beautiful to watch falling from the sky."

Leland saw an abandoned store window covered in snow and wrote his name in it. At this point Morgan began to publicly complain. He was very cold and his nose was numb. So Leland marched ahead, turning through blocks unknown, losing his way at some points, but never letting Morgan know. The last thing he needed was for Morgan to freak out.

"How many more blocks we got?"

Leland pointed. "It's right across the street."

"That big thing?" Referencing the large apartment complex.

"Can't wait to spend time with new friends."

"Yo, what about spending time with an old one?"

Leland kicked snow toward Morgan. "If you keep saying *yo* I'm gunna stick your face in the snow and bury it!"

"You haven't lost your charm."

Sweet little smile, and then running across Avenue A together. For Leland winter was the worst time to start thinking about the poverty, but he couldn't help but to notice. The bums were everywhere and they had no jackets or blankets to cover their shivering bodies. Leland felt so sad for them. If he could rip his own clothes off and give it to them he would. How could they survive another night like this? But the truth is that they do. They find their way, they live to see another day.

"Alex and Rez have major contacts. They can bring us to new heights. You know that right?"

"But you've been doing a good job on your own. They're writing about you."

"I know that, but I want to cover all my bases."

"What I don't understand is why you want to help Dorian so badly."

"I love him, Morgan."

"I know that. But he betrayed you. He hasn't talked to you in over two weeks."

"But he will, once I figure this shit out."

"He will?"

"I haven't exactly been diligent. I haven't been home. He could be there right now waiting for me. He could be a corpse."

"Leland—"

"Let me finish. I know he means well. He's just stuck in this sort of dangerous fascination. It'll pass. I *have* to believe that."

But the warning light of love had already been lit in his mechanical heart. Leland knew that his relationship was down the crapper, even though nothing was said officially. One can feel it when the end of something good is near. But a pleasant surprise vibrated from his pocket. *Planning the next show?* said the text. Leland text him right back. *You're forgiven. Miss you.* And immediately after he got an answer: *Tyria is sick no time to explain.*

"That was him, yo. Can see it in your face."

Leland's finger slid across the touch-screen. A river of consonants, a sea of capitals and vowels. It was like he was typing with his tongue. Who did his tongue belong these days? Fuck if he knew where Dorian was even putting his tongue. But Leland refused to let that bother him.

"What is it, Landy?"

"He's at least thinking of me."

BLOOD KISS *Daniel Stone*

"Are you listening to yourself, yo? He's taking advantage of ."

"Do you even know what you're saying?"

Morgan stopped, flat grey eyes stared into Leland. "I'd never do that to you."

"No, you'd only toke until you choke."

The malice in that statement hurt, so he immediately apologized. Morgan loved him, for sure, and he would go to great lengths to get Leland back. But it just could never be. That spark had died three years ago. But now Morgan's hand took his, and he pulled Leland into an alleyway filled with garbage bags and two bums. Leland rested his head against the side of a building and closed his eyes to think. When he opened them he noticed *REZ* carved into the brick.

When Leland brushed his finger across the letters something magical happened. There was the image of a voluminous dark thing; red eyes blinked fervently beneath a fedora. Camera flashes blinded him as the music of Electric Orchid flooded his senses.

"I'm dizzy," Leland said.

It had been a while since he'd eaten, but worrying about Dorian didn't help; neither did worrying about Adelaide. Where was she anyway? But his knees were buckling faster than expected. He felt too weak to brace himself, knowing very well how horrible it would be when the cement smeared his facial features. Luckily Morgan caught him in mid-fall, and like some movie scene, his cold lips found Leland's like when the classic dame is saved. Leland fell right into the trap.

The familiar taste of Morgan's tongue, the unwashed mouth and cigarette smoke. It was a sudden realization for Leland that what he really wanted out of Alex and Rez was not networking, but sexual. He wanted to build something like Dorian was building with Tyria, three fleshy instruments making the natural music of the body, even if it was purely out of spite.

His phone vibrated again.

Almost here? said the text from Alex. *U like Italian Splatter?* Finally, Morgan let him go. What did it really matter? Would Dorian honestly give a shit that Morgan's hand was down the back of Leland's pants, their dicks hardening, grinding furiously with abandon?

Leland was about to respond to Alex when the text from Adelaide came crashing in. *WHERE R U ?!?!?!* and Morgan laughed out loud; Leland sent her a text right back. *Working on music and a possible new venue.* Adelaide's response was *ALL U DO IS THINK WITH UR DICK!!!!*

"She ain't happy," a frown took over Leland's face.

Morgan took the phone and pocketed it. Leland didn't even care.

"She'll survive."

Stumbling into the big courtyard, the benches were filled with squatters and teenage troublemakers. Stuyvesant Town stuck out like a big sore thumb against the city's grey backdrop. A hundred thousand windows loomed; the fire escapes were falling apart. Graffiti was sparse and so were drug deals.

Alex buzzed them in. Morgan inquired about an elevator but Leland was already going up the stairs. Three flights, the smell of fried food and marijuana clung to everything; grease vapors stained the walls. Upkeep wasn't part of Stuyvesant Town's charm.

Rez's apartment door was at the end of the hallway. Do Not Enter read the horror-themed carpet at their feet, and *Electric Orchid* was written in marker. Heavy metal music pounded, Pantera's "Great Southern Trendkill." Phil Anselmo's voice sounded like it could start fires.

"Are they metal heads?" Morgan asked.

Leland knocked. The door swung open with no one there. He caught the spicy-sweet odor of clove cigarettes as he walked in. The stroboscopic brilliance of the television was blinding; Morgan turned his head in defeat. He never was one for gory movies. *Lo Squartatore di New York* was at the part of the infamous movie theater scene, the volume ridiculously

BLOOD KISS

turned up. The sound of Fay's murder was enough to get people to complain.

Then Alex appeared ghostly in front of them, dressed only in a skull and crossbones pair of pajama pants, his multi-colored hair down to his shoulders and his intricate tattoos glowing: an Electric Orchid insignia and a scarlet swirled orchid on his skinny biceps; something like vines crawled on his bladed collar bones.

"So good to see you, Leland," Alex winked one girly green eye. "And you brought a friend."

"Yeah yo, the name's Morgan."

"And what do you do, Morgan?" Alex's voice traveled the air like particles of dust.

"I make music."

"Is that them?" a voice screamed from inside.

"Come boys, Rez is waiting."

15

nstincts are everything. We ignore them at our own peril.

I'm a firm believer that life is too short. Why do we allow ourselves to get caught up in day jobs and responsibility so that we forget how to live? What happened to our youth, to having no perception of the clock and of things like sickness and death and morals? The sad truth is that within the blink of an eye we're transformed from an invincible child to an ill-prepared adult who cannot bear the cruelty of the world.

When we accept that life *does* have to eventually end, there comes this sudden need for spontaneity rather than organization. But by the time this is realized, it is too late. Our youth has fled our mortal DNA; we've become too old to dream, too fragile to endure a trip around the world, too tired to stay up all night and spend time with those we love.

The Grim Reaper stretches his death-head grin.

We begin to measure time in seasons. How many more summers will we get? How many more winters will we see? Have we made a unique mark upon our generation, or will it scar the next? We panic. We dwell. We yearn. We accept that living on this borrowed time will really never allow us to be all that we can possibly be. We ruminate over a terrible truth: that we have lived our lives to the wonted expectations of others rather that what truly fulfills us.

Some find themselves reaching deep into mythology to understand an impossible concept: Zen. Though the state of a thoughtless mind is something that is rarely achieved, I knew Zen so long as Tyria was by my side. She was now an official piece of me, invading the sacrosanct territory of my free will.

Together, we could evade the clock and skip out on death! I remember this moment of shear elemental force, of fire and electric that sowed the seed of friendship to bloom into our carrion flower. I think back and try to make sense of how far we've come, where are lives are currently going, and I am thankful for the stage.

But in my dreams I feel Leland's hands upon my face, searching for the map to my heart as Adelaide's hate for me grows colder. Gone are the memories of my past life and my restrictions upon carnal attraction. The walls of gender and sex had been torn down to fall prey to my impulsive needs. Changed are the days when I convinced myself that being alone would be the ultimate freedom, regardless of my being with Leland. I have fallen in love, slowly, but assuredly.

"Is it wrong?" Tyria asked me.

"Come again?"

"You know exactly what I'm talking about," she said.

The reference was to how we had become one body, one mind, one ghost; our souls melding into a single essence. I didn't question it because I simply didn't want to hear the answer. But Tyria was rather delirious. She had slept for two days to escape the pain. I kept a strict vigil over her body during that time, and when I mentioned that to her she giggled.

"It's wrong only if you make it," I said.

"You're not even sure yourself. I can see it in your eyes."

"But that's who I am. The incredible man of questions."

"So then why don't you question this?" Tyria pointed to herself, than me. "Afraid of the answer?"

"Yes," I lit a cigarette and gave it to her.

"But the pain . . . it's gone."

I looked across my loft. I looked at her. As wretched as she was, Tyria was also very pure. I couldn't bear the thought of us separating, whether by jealous lovers or artistic differences. My life would be useless without her. She was the Anima to my Animus.

And then I read the review of *SyNtHeSiS* in *Eyesore* again. There were things written in there that might put Adelaide on an even deeper hunt for Tyria and more murderous rampage for me. There would be no escaping her warpath unless Leland kept her close to him at all times. If she wanted a fight, I would be ready for only death could part me from Tyria at this point. I knew Adelaide understood that, and so she would make it come true.

"How many times have you read it?" I said.

"Twice," Tyria said. "Better this time around."

Her smile was queer, but proud, and I could not help but to feel the same. During the two days she slept I had gone back and forth through the article. It was indeed so much more in depth than the first. This time the writer took a keen interest in the show, in us as a pair of showmen. The music, the magic, but most of all the immersive content. Someone educated, someone with a sharp eye who knew the right adjectives and who knew how to control a yellow journalism narrative.

"Do you see how the writer understands the need for freedom of speech in the shows?" I said.

"Not just that, but the importance of impromptu, especially for spoken word." Tyria said, simultaneously taking a bite of a peanut butter sandwich.

"You think this name is fake?"

"Well, it's different from the last, and I still can't tell if the writer is male or female. But what I do know is that this article is written better."

"Maybe the performances have gotten into their head," I said.

"Indeed. I wonder if Addy's read this."

A laborious thought. I wondered not about Leland or Adelaide. I was still haunted by the moment of our ascension: Tyria's body a fleshy crescendo, pale bones and yellow hair dull as flame. In my memory her pussy has teeth, and the precious pink lips are starred in blood. I am not turned on by

BLOOD KISS

a female, but a process. The proverbial key had finally fit into the lock.

"I don't want to remember it," she said.

"The show?" I asked.

"Everything, Dorian. You know what I mean."

"How did you know what I was thinking?"

"Your face is red and you're losing your breath."

"I need a bogee."

A single tear welled in the corner of her eyes. She had no reason to bring that moment back to life, but it was currently messing with her. I took Tyria's hand, kissed it, but she pulled away and wiped her tears, then curled into a ball and became lost inside her head.

"Just leave me," she said.

There was no comforting her. I thought about the sexual phantom only to feel the pain between my legs catch up with me. My cock was rubbed raw as rug burn; my neck was bitten and bruised. Had sex became our shared drug? I judged myself harshly for dropping my queerness like dead weight for heterosexuality.

Gays sometimes ask themselves if we actually choose to be this way. I remember witnessing countless arguments between people who swore that being gay was a learned behavior rather than an inherited one. I could not help but to pity their mindset. Nobody chooses opposition so freely, especially when it puts one's life in danger.

And so queers are privy to spend a good portion of their life trying to self-abort, clawing at their skin in hopes it will rip away the old layer and give way to a newer, more acceptable flesh. Social norms bring us to that brink. When someone tries too hard to blend in—knowing very well they cannot—they are driven mad.

All my life I knew that I never wanted to be like straight people; did not want to follow their dogmas or their constrictions. I actually declared, one spontaneous day, that their eyes were not worthy of my presence. I even went as far as to test my luck and plucked a random person from the street. I asked her of her opinion on gay culture. *It's cool, but it's not normal*, the girl said. Her answer proved that we are tolerated but never accepted. The white picket fence is dark on our end of the block.

I once read something and it has never left my head. *In order for gay people to make a case for equality, they must adapt to the dominant culture.* That is a morbid, but infuriating truth. A lot us have fallen prisoner to this, and by the time we realize it we're already divorcing our wives and husbands and tearing our families apart. Queer liberation may be at its peak, but for others an ominous reality looms. Countries all over the world still stone gays to death, perform public humiliation and convict gays like witches in Salem. Some governments believe that homosexuals do not even exist.

Thus which brings me back to Tyria.

Was I a traitor for loving her so? Why was switching teams such an absolute horror to come to terms with? But as I lay dying in my thoughts, a miracle came to save me.

Black it was always meant to be, and it wanted nobody to touch his little girl. But I was too quick for him. Tyria need not explain it. When you keep cutting the same spot, the scars will never heal. I grabbed him so that he could see change had come, that Tyria was *mine*. I saw her eyes bolt open and her limbs go taut.

"Stay away!"

I was entangled, strangled by its power. Somehow it put me into a haphazard sleep. I woke up in a daze, my limbs roped and wet around hers and cigarettes between our lips. How had we become naked again? My teeth hurt and my crotch felt like it was on fire.

We moved to the kitchen, kept our eyes closed. The sun came up and then went down, Leland text me and Adelaide would not stop calling. We listened to countless voicemails of disapproving silence and tears. We listened to no music.

"Can't you just call her already?"

"No," Tyria said. "Gimme another Camel."

"You just smoked one."

BLOOD KISS

"Ever hear of chain smoking?"

She got the cigarette herself, then cut up a line with her pocket blade and snorted it right off the edge. The bags beneath her eyes suddenly grew, but there were no wrinkles on her porcelain face to accompany that dead stare.

"What do we do now?" I said. "You can't keep putting that shit up your nose."

"I can do whatever I damn well please," as she snorted another bump.

"Fine, do what you want," I wasn't about to argue.

"Maybe you should give me a proper tour. I sort of just barged in and made myself feel at home."

Her chin was jittering, her pupils were getting larger

"What's mine is yours," I said.

Her hand extended toward my studio door, jade eyes wide with wonder.

"That's what I want to see."

"After we eat."

"But I just had peanut butter—"

I cut her off with a simple wave, served runny eggs and lots of coffee. Black for me and almond milk for Tyria. She nibbled the food like a bird, but I wolfed mine down. We didn't talk over breakfast like most people do. Tyria found solace in an old 'zine about ghost hunters dated back to 1994 as I absently flipped through *This Side of Paradise*.

"I know you're not focusing on that book," Tyria said.

I smirked.

"There's really nothing to talk about," she continued. "If that's what you're thinking, I mean."

"Yup," slurping my hot coffee.

"I do feel like he's gone," forced grin, forced wince in sunlight. "The ghost of him . . . he's not in me anymore."

I didn't say a word. I just let her talk.

"It's . . . somewhere safe, tucked someplace where it can't haunt me anymore."

"Just like that?" I said

She was lying, hiding something.

"How many ways should I say it?"

A real argument. It felt good. You can't always see eye to eye with the one you love. Sometimes your opposite points of view can teach one another. But in her anger Tyria pushed her mug off the table. Before the crash I saw it play out like one of those slow motion moments in a movie. I wanted to press pause, but instead scalding coffee found its way to my lap and the mug bashed to a billion pieces of on the floor.

I knew not to get out of my chair; she was like a rabid animal the way her eyes found mine. One wrong move and she'd either attack or run away. And as if she expected that I was going to yell—going to hurt her—Tyria began to hold her ears and closed her eyes. Her rings caught the light. I put my arms around her shoulders and pulled her into me. We rocked back and forth until she fell into a torpid sleep.

LELAND HELD UP THE SIX PACK of Natty Ice. "We come in peace."

Alex accepted the beer, cracked one open and enjoyed the brew silently. As the door closed behind them the first thing Leland noticed—aside from the clutter—was the smell. It was reminiscent of every bar he'd ever hung out in: spilled beer, cigarettes and a whole 'lotta trouble.

"Do you need a formal tour?"

Alex was not shy about how messy his place was, and thus they were pulled through the apartment as if swimming into a deep ocean. This was everything Leland imagined pseudo-rock stars would be living in. An open arrangement so that the kitchen, dining and living room were all in one, where upon a glass table lay Light Sabers and McFarlane Horror figurines. Alex crossed over the mattress, then put his hand out for Leland to come but for Morgan to stop.

"We need to make more room," Alex said as the mattress sprung back into the wall.

BLOOD KISS

"For what?" Leland said.

"Anything."

Alex's gorgeous multicolored hair fell across his face like expensive silk. Leland wanted to run his fingers through it, wanted to pull this fallen angel close to him and drink his essence. But now that Alex made space Leland saw a broken door leading to the horrendously dirty bathroom. The smell of stagnant water was so strong it reminded Leland of low tide.

"Pretty scary in here," Leland said.

"Believe it or not they want to raise our rent. We may move out," Alex said.

Leland wondered who would even move in this dump if Alex and Rez left. The Neon rope above his head was practically part of the ceiling it had been there so long, and the walls were marked with nails, staples, pins and posters that had long lost their relevance. This was the certified work of the lazy, of the creators too busy to be bothered to clean, or even care. That, or Rez and Alex have accepted the fact that one cannot be ogled by dust, mildew or even dirty dishes, cannot fight it knowing that dust and dirt always wins. We are all stardust in the end.

"Ever consider Brooklyn?"

"Once, but even though it's so close, it's still so far."

Alex led them back into the living room, and this time he took Leland's hand softly. Leland felt fire reach his face and blood flood his dick. Why was this stranger so gentle, so welcoming? He hadn't felt skin so perfect, so soft, since Dorian. He knew what he was doing was wrong. But why did it feel so good? When he looked back Morgan was sneering like jealous dog.

"This is where the magic happens," Alex said.

In the living room nothing was in order. It was as if a schizophrenic had decorated the place. The mantle was taken over by wine bottles, votive candles, and a dream catcher. Amps, chords, a guitar with a devil-horned head and piano keys were strewn around like teeth knocked out of smile. In the low light Leland finally found out what that mushy feeling beneath his feet was: the entire apartment was carpeted with a strange black fabric.

"Hey, come over here."

Rez was cross legged on the couch, mesmerized by the splatter movie. He was wearing a red and black onesie, tight as the skin covering his bones, but nowhere near as fancy as the tattoos on his neck, things that Leland could not make out in this light, but he knew they were related to writing, to art.

"I guess I'm a long way from Brooklyn," Leland said.

"Brooklyn is for chilling, Manhattan is for living," Rez said. "Plus, it's so quiet there, it would drive me mad."

Now the television flashed violently and Alex giggled insanely. Morgan covered his eyes as the screen filled with cheap movie blood. He turned white as ghost and ran to the bathroom. Leland sat next to Rez, lit a smoke and watched the rest of the movie in silence. By the time Morgan came back he seemed refreshed and ready to do business.

Introductions all around, where are you from, what do you do, how do you do it. Alex sat on the other side of Leland, and now he was finally feeling the heat of the boys, unable to control himself. His cock was rock solid and his mouth too dry to talk; the cigarette tasted stale all of a sudden. He could not see what the boys were thinking given the dark hollows around their eyes. It hid all emotion and that confused him even more.

"Yo man, it's like the twilight zone in here," Morgan said. "I kinda like it."

"Where do you live Morgan?" Rez said.

"Bushwick. Right off the J."

"The ghetto," Alex said.

"It's not that bad."

Leland looked at Rez, his sapphire eyes taking in light brightly, and then found Alex's green eyes that reminded him of the color a clover in the sun. Morgan sat on the floor and drank a beer down without taking a breath. It made Leland dizzy, made all the blood in his body fall to his feet.

BLOOD KISS

"You look flushed, Landy."

Was that Dorian's voice he heard?

Now Alex's hands were coming for him; Rez's lips were on his neck. The smell of hair dye and Jägermeister was on their breath. Alex's tongue ran into his mouth warm and wet and knowing. Though Leland kissed him back deeply he was not in control. Something seized his tendons, pulled them into rigor mortis. He wanted that they devour him, take all they wanted until he was nothing but a bag of bones. Then there were teeth, hands in his pants, gripping too hard. When he opened his eyes he saw the faces of Tyria and Dorian . . . and he screamed.

"Hey!" Rez said.

Hands shook him awake. Morgan was cradling his face; Alex brought him a glass of water and a falafel sandwich. What the hell had just happened? Was he so tired he could not remember how he fell asleep? The smell of the sandwich was fresh, warm. Leland could not refuse food, and not because falafel was his favorite, but because he could not remember the last time he took down a decent meal.

"When's the last time you slept, cutie?" Alex said.

"He hasn't caught a good rest in over a week, yo. He goes in and out of sleep."

"Anyone else hungry? We have extra falafel," Rez said.

"Nah, yo. That shit goes right through me," Morgan motioned the universal sign for diarrhea. "But I *am* fiending."

"No," Leland said. "Not here."

"Drugs are cool with me," Alex said. "I'd be a hypocrite if I said otherwise."

Alex jumped off the couch and cleared the coffee table. Morgan setup shop while Rez rubbed Alex's shoulders lovingly. Those white fingers filed into white, white skin, and only now did Leland notice how skinny they were. Rez's torso resembled a birdcage in the half-glowing light; Alex looked more and more like a peacock with that wild hair and knife-like face.

"A water bong? Who carries those around anymore?" Alex said.

"I do, yo. Better than meth, no doubt."

"Word."

Rez set the mood to Black Sabbath's *Sabotage* album. "Hole in the Sky" shredded the airwaves; Ozzy's vocals gashed everyone's ears and Geezer's bass invoked a demon.

"You know, I didn't want to say anything, but I just have to because I'm not sure if you saw it," Rez held up the latest issue of Eyesore.

"I didn't want to gloat but—"

"Oh, do gloat! We're all artists here. Creation is our life-blood. Any praise is good praise, but if it's literally good praise . . . WOW!" Alex laughed.

"Nothing inspires me more than knowing there are young people out there doing good things."

"I agree."

"I hear you write, Rez," Leland said.

"Fiction. Mostly beat poet inspired vignettes."

"Have any to share?"

"If you look around you'll find words."

Rez swirled his finger in the air, which brought Leland's attention to what he at first thought was garbage, realizing now that they were pieces of Rez's fictional worlds scrawled in hopeless longhand of blue, black and red ink. There were pages underneath the couch cushions, stuffed into the pillows, there were even pages in the refrigerator. Rez had written so much there was no physical way he could file these papers in a proper place.

"Don't you have a computer so you don't have to have all this paper lying around?"

"Used to, until a friend broke it."

"Let's not even get into that," Alex said. "Too many bad memories."

"Are you curious?" Rez said to Leland.

"Very curious."

"Don't fall into that trap," Alex warned Leland. "Rez doesn't want you to read it, trust me."

"Yes, I do."

BLOOD KISS

Alex covered Rez's mouth. "He's just being nice."

Leland took a handful of pages anyway. He read fast but efficiently, until his eyes began to hurt. The words were that of a natural, the passion and drive clear. Rez was writing the dark prose of the future. Leland wondered what had compromised Rez's life for him to write such emotionally driven stories. Could it be as bad as the life that Tyria described through her poetry? But as soon as the words were making sense in his head, Alex's strong piano fingers lifted the pages out of Leland's hands.

"Why'd you do that?" Leland said.

"Rez doesn't like people reading his work until it's actually published."

"But it's so creepy."

"You sure it's just that?"

"Alex, it's fine," Rez said.

"Since when? You just think he's cute, and well, you're right about that."

Alex's eyes were clear, hungry; in the shadows Rez gleamed like a fallen star. Leland could not believe what he heard. Could it be that he would play with them both tonight, even with jealous Morgan in the way? Leland held his tongue, trying so hard to play coy, naïve, but Morgan butted into the moment, pulling hard on his bong and spitting large plumes of smoke out of his mouth. Alex joined him, then Rez.

"I have to say something, yo."

"What?" Rez said.

"Why do you like these stupid movies? How can you believe that there is any substance in them when it's only about shocking the audience?" Morgan licked his lips.

"Do you boys even like scary movies?" Alex said.

"Italian Splatter is all visceral, all blood. I can see what Morgan means," Leland said.

"But physical hurt penetrates our emotional core. All of our fears and dreads and longings spring up from horror. It can be gore or it can be supernatural," Rez said.

"We just prefer the gore," Alex added.

"So, what say you about the supernatural. Do you believe in it?" Leland said, wanting to know more and more about these boys than ever.

"You wouldn't believe me if I told you about all the ghosts and goblins that haunt our past."

"I want to know," Leland said. "But first can I have a beer, a smoke too maybe."

Alex handed Leland both and said, "Rez was once a ghost hunter."

"A ghost hunter?"

"Yeah, you know, like someone who knows that there is more than one reality in the universe," Alex said.

"We live in a giant void, and if you really think that we are the only conscious beings, whether organic or not, you're a damn fool."

"He's also a bit . . . *sensitive*."

Rez's ears perked up and his sapphire eyes grew huge. "Sorry to say it, but you two have your own hauntings. I smelled it the second you walked into my apartment."

"Like what?"

"No, I knew it the moment I laid eyes on you in Death by Audio. You're playing a bad game of exquisite corpse. Be careful."

Leland was about to explain that Tyria was the haunted one, and that Dorian was only tagging along because he is attracted to the unknown, but just as the words left his lips Rez turned up the stereo and put on a new movie. "Megalomania" began to play along with "Suspiria." Did he not want to know the answer?

Alex nestled himself into Rez's arms as a pair of yellow eyes hit the screen and a grotesque hand broke through a window pane to slice some poor dame's chest open, revealing her ridiculous beating heart. Morgan covered his eyes again and Rez laughed, then shut the television off and lowered the music. Still, Leland found Ozzy's voice the most haunting thing of all.

"I love that scene," Rez said.

BLOOD KISS

"Why didn't you let me answer you?"

Rez looked at Leland but didn't acknowledge what he just said.

"I've been meaning to ask *you* something Landy—only because this article has me hooked—does the show have supernatural elements?"

Leland's heart froze. "I'm not sure I have the answer."

"Are you part of it?"

"I am on the business side of things. I'm not a performer."

"Oh, but you are!" Alex said. "I really wanna see it."

"I honestly can't tell you when the next one is going to be. There was a mishap at the last show, some candles—"

"Fire," Rez interrupted softly. "We know."

"How?"

"Why, gossip of course! We all belong to the same dying breed."

"Word *does* get around fast, yo."

"We too have a strange history with fire and ghosts. You're preaching to the choir."

"And Rez is completely ignoring all my questions."

"I assure you I'm not. I just don't want to disturb any natural peace. My life has been very easy without *them* in it."

"Them?"

"Ghosts, Landy. You gotta keep up!"

"If you asked Delilah she would say that Electric Orchid's music talks to the dead," Alex said.

"But if you saw what I saw," Morgan said in reference to living paintings and shadow play. "You'd be very afraid."

"That's why I'm not inquiring," Rez said. "They latch onto me like I'm going to start doing them favors."

"All I know, yo, is that something strange is going on between Tyria and Dorian. Something deeper than the actual performances."

"Dorian is your boyfriend Leland, right?"

"Yes."

Morgan cut right in. "When we make music, as you boys would know, we have all these minds coming together, satisfying one another's needs."

"Go on," Alex said.

"But not with art and poetry. No, this is the strangest combination I've ever seen. It's as solitary as much as it is a symbiosis."

"And you play the background music for them?"

"Just one show so far."

"We really wanna go to the next."

"You've been warned," Leland said.

"I wanna buy a ticket right now," Alex said.

"Landy usually does all the talking, but when I think about what I saw, I'm loquacious as I have ever been."

"You don't even know the meaning of that word," Leland said.

"Do so, *bitch*. I read it in a book once."

"Oh man. I *need* to see this. Delilah too," Alex said.

"My sister isn't in the best state of mind right now. She's too unhappy where the band is going," Rez said.

"Doesn't matter, we're not ready. We have no place to do it and I have no idea where to go. Addy and I haven't even drawn up the new ads."

"I know a place," Rez said. "You just have to trust me."

"And we can throw some ideas around, then put up the ads on Electric Orchid's Twitter and Facebook," Alex said. "All we gotta do is draw it and name it."

"I already have a name in mind," Leland said. "*Symbiosis*, thanks to Morgan."

"Sounds amazing."

All was agreeing and quiet, and then Leland said, "But this isn't really why I came."

"Why did you, then?" Rez asked.

Came here to get Dorian out of my head, he wanted to say.

"I wanted to fuck," Leland said it outright.

Silence wrapped around them like cemetery fog. Rez and Alex looked perplexed; Leland covered his face.

"We're not judging, but I think I sent the wrong message at Death by Audio," Rez said.

"What's hurting you?" Alex was so knowing, so gentle.

BLOOD KISS *Daniel Stone*

"I . . . I'm scared to know what they're doing."

"Who?"

"Tyria and Dorian. Bringing them together was the biggest mistake in the world. I'm not the jealous type . . . but—"

Tears now, fresh tears. The first time he'd cried in a long, long time.

"How long have they run off for?"

"I lost count," Leland said.

"And what about that crazy, angry girl?"

"Adelaide," Morgan said.

Leland let out a long sigh. "She's become homicidal and suicidal at the same time."

"Say no more. We get it. Look, I know Rez kissed you in Brooklyn, but that's as far as it goes."

"So you guys hook up with random boys but never take them home?"

"Yup."

"So then why did you give me your number?"

"Somehow I knew something about you was different, and that a wonderful friendship could come of it. I know I'm not wrong."

"I'm sorry I made a fool of myself."

"Did not," Alex said.

"The way I see it, Leland, is that if you want something to last, if you want *you and Dorian* to last, you have to fix what's broken rather than throw it away," Alex smiled.

"Yeah. Let him get this out of his system. If he truly loves you, it will work out."

Leland let it go. The moment took a new turn. Morgan and Alex began brainstorming music ideas, mixing the sounds on Alex's DJ system while Rez and Leland wrote up the new ads and posted it to Facebook and Twitter. Leland sent a quick text to Adelaide and Dorian.

BROOKLYN. SyMbIoSiS.

After, Alex brought out the Jägermeister and made everyone drink from the bottle. The future suddenly brightened. New things were happening, and as Leland took his first chug of the licorice tasting liquor, he was more excited than ever to create a new show.

BLOOD KISS *Daniel Stone*

16

Tyria pulled herself out of a fascinating dream and found herself nestled into Dorian's torso.

Long arms engulfed her like a fleshy blanket, black hair fell across her face. She yawned, turned her face into the crook of his arm, and took in the smell of him. She was unable to decide if she was well rested or not, and with the dream not too long gone, it was unable to be determined as something lingered in her memory, something alive, pale and hungry.

"Feeling any better?" Dorian said.

"Not as rested as I want to be. But life goes on . . ."

"You were out for two full days."

"And you just let me sleep?"

"I did."

"Don't you know that the more sleep we get the less rested we feel?"

Dorian lifted his arms as Tyria stood. The world went black for a second, but once her equilibrium settled she saw that the sky was bright, unraveling like a carpet threaded with the dizzying shades of pale blue and blood orange. It infiltrated the entire loft like magic. Outside, the snow had settled and the river was partly iced over, especially toward the shore. Maybe today would be a good day.

"What time is it?" Tyria said.

"Seven in the morning."

Dorian was behind her, glowing god-like in the sun's reflection. The toned muscles of his groin were oiled in sweat; his ribs stuck out like butter knives. He put his arms around her again, nestled his nose into her hair as they watched the sun creep higher and higher into the sky. This blazing moment could be summed up to bliss if they wanted it.

"Are you hungry?" Dorian said.

"Slightly."

Dorian extricated himself, kicking renegade canvases and paintbrushes out of their path. What was he doing while she slept? How long had he been painting? Had he been drawing her? Tyria located the answer in the sketchbook writhing with new art.

"I couldn't sleep at all," Dorian said.

"Why not?"

"Thinking too much. Plus, I like the sound of your breathing. It's delicate."

Tyria never found any facet of her existence delicate. The word irked her.

"Can I look at that book?"

"Which one?"

"The one that's moving."

Dorian froze in an awkward pose. His black eyes jetted toward the small sketchbook, then Tyria. They both acknowledged that it was in fact moving. He nodded, and as she bent down to pick it up she smelled brimstone, felt a strange pain trickle through her gut. Upon opening the first page she saw a great cloud of chaos engulfing a mass of unsuspecting people. When she turned it over there was a girl that looked like she had passed through an X-ray, skeleton face and bones revealed, and within her womb a gelatinous blob was stretching and growing.

"What is this?" Tyria said.

"A rotten gestation."

She lit a cigarette to save herself the conversation. The feeling was all too familiar. Dorian lit a cigarette too, and just as he was about to speak the words he wanted to say dissolved into the smoke that exited his mouth. She thought about Adelaide all of a sudden, thought about how nothing

BLOOD KISS Daniel Stone

good was to become of this. She wanted to call her, wanted to say that she was sorry, but could not dredge up the courage to do it.

So much for a good day.

Then her stomach gurgled. Not hunger, not pain, but as if something was changing inside of her. She stretched to let the sun light warm her body, saw it scatter across all her tattoos. The ouroboros continued to eat itself, the Invader Zim characters glared madly.

Maybe food would do her good. She could smell something was on the stove, maybe oatmeal, or waffles, something laced with cinnamon and vanilla. But when she got to the table there was only fresh muffins and coffee. Dorian's work was everywhere, a few advertisements for *SyNeRgY* and *SyNtHeSiS* as well. That was when she saw the scratches on her arms.

"How deep of a sleep was I in?"

Dorian stared at the scratch marks on her arm

"You tossed and turned and tried to hurt yourself. I stopped you as much as I could."

The proof of it still red and sore. *Does it hurt?* and *Tell me!* Why was she hurting herself now? Shouldn't all this energy should be used for the stage? But maybe she needed this, maybe she needed to hurt in order to accept the fact that loving someone new while her first love atrophies should not be this easy, and that being with Dorian should not feel this good. That was the hardest part to come to terms with.

"You okay?" Dorian said.

"Yeah. Just a headache."

He changed the subject. "Coffee?"

"Black," Tyria said.

Dorian served her a steaming cup where the color of Darth Vader's light saber became redder and redder with the heat, looking ever so lovely—but she would never say that out loud. Tyria dunked her blueberry muffin in the coffee, then pulled a rainbow-colored pen and a blank notebook toward her. She began to retrace a dream, something to do with broken hearts, a small venomous family and a burning stage.

They didn't talk while they ate. Dorian sat back and played with a muffin, his legs crossed and his bare foot touching her bare leg. Some part of this moment made her think about how content she had been feeling. *Not some regular straight couple,* Tyria wanted to say. *We're above that.* Then Tyria took her first scalding sip.

"Very strong."

"Once you have this, you'll never settle for dollar store coffee again."

"That's never really my choice. I go with what I can afford."

"We're together now, so you won't have to choose that ever again."

"We're not together at all."

Somewhere the ghost of Adelaide was gnawing her guilty conscience. She could hear her words: *You like his coffee but not mine? You want to be a fancy pants like him?* Long black hair trickled across her memory like rain. But where Adelaide was skilled in anger she lacked in rational thinking. Did she not understand the first rule of metamorphosis? That an artist must change, for if they don't, they die. But guilt is a marvelous emotion. It can tear your soul apart. It can rule you if you let it.

"I've had a lot of time to think," Dorian said.

"About what?" Deathly little stare.

"About us."

"There's really nothing to think about. It's wrong, plain and simple."

"Don't you see how guarded by contemporary morals you are, by societal chains?"

"No. I just can't do this, Dorian. I'm not made to be content."

"This is what content feels like? You're placing judgment based on norms you don't even believe in!"

BLOOD KISS

Tyria sipped her coffee again, and this time it found its way to her air pipe. Dorian patted her back, wiped the hair out of her eyes. No matter how loving he was, there was evil between them, and they were spreading its disease fast.

"What do we do now?"

"I got a text from Landy. Things are moving forward."

"As in a new gig?"

"You got that right. People want to see us."

"That's good. But what about Adelaide?"

"I honestly do not know."

Before she could worry about Addy the swirling in her stomach rocketed down to her bladder. Sweat, fever. She felt delirious. She thought about that dream scene in *Aliens* when Ripley was gutted. As the pain forced her vision to go grey, she knew then that something was blooming inside of her, curling her intestine into a meaty knot. The cross she has to bear for being a woman.

"You okay?" Dorian said.

"Not sure. I'm afraid to move."

Two dry heaves, a third seeming to start at her toes until all the blood vessels exploded in her eyes; hazy red stars clotted her vision. Her mouth filled with the taste of beer and bile.

"It's all my fault."

"It's no one's fault," Dorian said.

"This can't be happening again."

"What? Tell me?"

Tyria pointed to her stomach. "I do not want this."

"What are you talking about?"

Dorian's hands seized her, witchy fingers traced the crook of her neck, ran them across her clavicles and then stopped momentously to twist her nipple ring, sending tendrils of flame across her skin. Tyria looked up at his bladed face, eyes blinking wetly, and kissed him.

"There is nothing we *can't* do as long as we're together." Dorian's smile lay on the border between joy and madness.

"We can never be, Dorian."

"But I *love* you."

The earth stopped spinning. Physics became an aberration. Every cell in her body rejected evolution and chemistry. A door that had been closed since she could remember opened, letting out a great hidden heat. She almost vomited as she said it back.

"I love you too."

He made her stand up and drink down a cup of water. The coolness soothed her belly, but wouldn't do the trick like a good old beer. She took a PBR off the counter, then grabbed Dorian's face and kissed him. Tyria found new avenues for her tongue to travel; the flowery taste of his mouth and skin was too good to stop. It usually takes time to get used to a new lover's smell and taste, but with Dorian that never crossed her mind.

"You want to tell me what's going on?" Dorian said.

"No. I want to relax and I want to write."

"You're leaving something out."

But the words were already here, screaming. She filled up two loose leaf pages. Tyria could not see their colors and that made her sad, but she knew another way to trip. She found the baggie in her jacket, cut up a single white rock and snorted it right off the floor. Dorian denied his share, but it mattered not once the amazing feeling of power coursed through her blood.

"I have so many ideas now," she said.

"Let's go to my studio."

"Yes. I want to know what the fuck is in your head."

He took her hand, and just as she was about to smile something passed through her, a dark gift not wanted.

"No. Please no!"

The sudden recollection of a child that could have been.

"Talk to me," Dorian said.

She screamed so loud that Dorian fell to his knees holding his ears. A rat that was running to the other side of the room collapsed in death and a few insects exploded into ash.

"I remember him fucking me," Tyria cried out

BLOOD KISS

Adrenaline possessed her to grab Dorian by the neck and dig her nails into him. *Son of a bitch,* she clenched her teeth whispering. *I can't have this again.* Tiny furrows gave way to bright and angry blood, the skin flaying back too sweet. But the story fell harshly from her lips. His face was wet with tears, his chest smeared in red and his tattoos completely covered in it.

ADELAIDE WANTED SO BADLY to leave her dream at home, but this time it rises from the abyss while she is awake: a stage burning bright, and the flames like a halo slipping down to choke Tyria. Red smile, red between her legs and red spattered across Dorian's canvas.

Love is the worst feeling in the world. No matter how good it makes you feel—no matter how happy you become—when it gets bad, it's *bad.* Love will make people do crazy things, because to be in love with someone is to ultimately surrender yourself to them. You're all of a sudden not yourself. You cannot be spontaneous anymore, you cannot be independent. You must always seek your lover's guidance and assurance, a certain permission that you would not need if you were single.

Sometimes when you love someone so fucking much it just simply hurts. Sometimes love is the worst drug of all.

"IF YOU SCREAM, I'LL KILL YOU," *he said.*

This time Brooklyn is moonless and the sky pulses in time with her angry heart. The stars are jagged pieces of glass. He's come later than usual but his whiskey breath is strong as ever. She knows it is the smell of tomorrow's excuse.

"Don't resist me."

red sin that covers her legs, feeling more broken than ever, but somehow hardened.

Six weeks pass. She has not seen Daddy other than the flicker of a shadow, or the sour smell of his morning whiskey. Why would he not hug her? Why would he not acknowledge her?

That was when she realized her monthly blood was late.

Somehow a girl knows before the doctor or drug-store test. She understands the natural shift into motherhood. The body changes, the mind begins to become protective of herself for the benefit of the fetus.

But Tyria knows this thing inside her was an abomination.

She does not want to carry a child created in anguish. It would most likely grow into a monster, follow rather than lead. It would drain her of every dream and longing. Tyria did not want to see her belly perk or her tits become tumescent with milk. To think that the meat-bean inside of her would sprout a brain for doing wrong sickened her. The worst part was to think that it might be a girl. And so there was only one way to pull this darkness out of her.

She unwinds the wire hangar, sharp as a spear. How far would it have to go in order to scramble her uterus into a rich red soup? Would it be sweet freedom?

She inserts it into her cavity blindly, passing muscled walls and feeble flesh until she sees the dark blood before she can feel the pain. Half of the wire is inside her, the smelly puddle beneath her black as arterial blood, and she gives it one last push until she feels a pop. When she pulls it out a tiny glob of meat is spliced at the tip and she smears it on the rug.

LELAND HAD FINALLY CALLED ADELAIDE TO MEET.

A strange smile stretched across his impossibly cute face, eyes smeared in dark lines and his hair twisted into patterns she had not seen before. This was the first time he'd worn make up in front of her, and it almost freaked her out. Morgan was at his side, and he smelled different too, like cloves and liquor laced with licorice. Where the hell had they been?

They walked without talking at first, streets not the black tarmac she was used to, but wavering like appendages. They were the only souls out in this cold. Adelaide lit a cigarette to keep warm and powdered her shoulders with anise to ward off the bad dreams. Morgan complained about the tiny cloud of herb dust, but she ignored him. Italians have used anise seeds for generations to find happiness, stimulate psychic ability and keep the bad dreams away. There was nothing Adelaide needed more than for the dreams to go away.

"Addy, you look like shit," Leland said.

"Who am I trying to look good for these days?" spite in her voice.

"Yo, do you ever not have an attitude?"

"I guess I'm always 'PMS-ing', as they say."

And then two more bodies slipping free out of the dark. Creepy excuses for boys, androgynous to the point of confusion, stilted legs reminiscent of a Dali painting. Soft and knowing voices. One had sapphire eyes like blue fire; the other had eyes green and pale as a gemstone. She knew them the moment she saw them, the boys from Death by Audio, the Electric Orchid groupies.

"You brought some friends," Adelaide said.

These days very few kids dared to pull off this version of black fashion and Manic Panic hair dye. Who had time to put themselves together like this aside from the clowns? Life is so much simpler rolling out of bed in the same clothes you passed out in.

"This is Rez and this Alex, do you remember them?"

"I know who they are," grinding her teeth. "Now where are we walking to in this damn cold?"

"I remember you from Death by Audio," Rez said. "You still seem just as angry."

"Rez, be nice," Alex said.

BLOOD KISS

Leland went through all the stale introductions again. *Alex plays piano for Electric Orchid and Rez is a very talented author.* When all was said and done Alex smiled and lit a clove cigarette. Adelaide noticed that for the first time ever Leland was no longer the ring leader. Everyone was following Rez and his red-tipped hair that looked like bloodied fingernails; the old sneakers that barely covered his feet made funny music against the pavement.

Their trajectory set them down an alleyway, then a few stormy city blocks. The smell of static was in the air. Rez would not stop talking about William Burroughs, as if he was trying to avoid any other conversation. At some point in passing he had said that the look within Adelaide's eyes was pure murder.

"I don't give a shit about Burroughs or music or art right now. I want to know where she is."

"Who?" Rez said.

"Addy! She will come," Leland said.

"Is she even alive, Landy?"

Hands clenched his jacket.

"She's alive," Leland said.

"I just want to see her, is that so hard to ask?"

"You'll see her at the show."

"Is she safe?"

Leland's hands held hers assuredly, the calming effect of a good friend. In the end he was her only friend, the only one who would crack a bottle of Old E over the head of anyone who threatened her.

"I'll do anything to see her right now."

"Not going to happen."

"Why not?"

"Because we still haven't seen the new venue or laid down any official plans."

"I'm fresh out of ideas, Landy. I'm a fucking wreck."

"At least you admit it . . ."

"Don't play reverse psychology on me, please, not now."

Leland stopped walking. "This is why I brought Rez and Alex along. Not only are they interested in seeing the show, but they are going to help us rebuild our brand."

"We never even had a brand. It was just all this jumbled bullshit, a pretense that we could never translate into something meaningful."

"I call bullshit," Leland said. "Your heart and soul are in this. You're just bitter."

"Mind if I interrupt?" Alex said.

"My hands are numb, my face feels like it's about to fall off and I'm contemplating pissing myself to keep warm. So make it fast," Adelaide said.

"We have the place picked out."

"Where?" Adelaide was curious all of a sudden.

"Bushwick."

"We're already in Bushwick," Adelaide howled. "Oh, Goddess, why did I ever want to do this? Everything is all fucked up."

"Not fucked up, yo," Morgan said. "We got new music now, Alex and I worked hard on it. Haven't you seen that we have Electric Orchid's official support."

Adelaide held her temples. "Someone please shut him up."

"I want to say something," Rez was holding up the article. "This piece, and the one before it, proved to me there's something special between the two stars of the show."

You have no fucking idea, Adelaide thought.

"From what I've read it's unlike anything that has ever happened at any Electric Orchid show. And believe me when I say it, they have a reputation. But this . . . is sorcery."

Adelaide closed her eyes—naturally the world went black—but it was as if she had fallen right to sleep since the sounds around her pulled away. She was not able to see where she was falling, but she knew it was somewhere down into the rabbit hole, and maybe she'd wake up in Wonderland, or Oz; maybe the darkness that she felt pressing down upon her would let up in a land of dreams.

BLOOD KISS *Daniel Stone*

Leland was shaking her. "You passed out."

"I . . . I'm so dizzy."

"You alright, yo?"

"I'm fine Morgan, fuck off."

Rez stood in front of her. "May I finish before you fall asleep again?"

"By all means, Rez, by all fucking means."

"You people have gold in your hands. Stop trying to sort out who loves who. Just try to support the art, the beauty in it."

"He's right," Alex said.

"Artists will do anything, and I mean fucking anything, to live their art . . . even if that means destroying something or someone. Art must go on."

"WHAT!" Adelaide shrieked.

"Please don't yell."

Overzealous and blinded by malice, she didn't realize that she had grabbed Rez by his coat hard enough to make him lose his balance. Face first onto the pavement, their bodies repelling one another like magnets of the same attraction. Alex pulled her hands off Rez, who suddenly fell into a manic state.

"It's you," Rez said.

"Baby, calm down," Alex was holding Rez's wet head.

"Me?" Adelaide said.

"Ow, my brain!"

"Say it, Rez. It's the only way to stop the pain," Alex said.

"You're the haunted one, Adelaide. You're the beacon."

"I don't want to hear that kind of shit."

But somehow Adelaide knew it too. She saw the iridescent wings, the oily roll of eyes. Everything she knew Tyria was afraid of—everything that had haunted her since she could remember—was with her now.

"I can hear them. They want you to free her."

"What do you mean?"

"Rez was drooling, his eyes were bloodshot. "You're holding her back from her full potential."

"Okay, that's enough," Leland said. "We're here."

It was a building that seemed to be picked out of Burton's Gotham City. Black brick and windows as big as the devil's eyes. Chock-full of ominous realities. It was perfect. The L train was down the block, so transit here would be a piece of cake, and from what Adelaide could see a couple of kids were already hanging out on the corner smoking and laughing.

"This?" Adelaide sneered.

"An old factory, but completely operational," Alex said.

"Let's get this party started."

"Always thinking about money, Landy."

Just before they walked in Rez cried out. "No! Please gods help me!"

His face was sullen, as if he had seen a future so dystopian that the guilt of it all was about to crush him. Alex rubbed his temples to rid him of the headache.

"What is it?" Leland said.

Rez sobbed. "It's *here*, and it wants to be freed."

BLOOD KISS <Daniel Stone>

PART THREE

SYMBIOSIS

"*Keep your face always toward the sunshine—
and shadows will fall behind you.*"

—Walt Whitman

17

Symbiosis: the interaction between two dissimilar organisms that live in a close physical association, typically to the advantage of both parties. Ideally the relationship would be mutual, or even commensal, but as with everything else we come to discover about this selfish world, we are all in this fleshy game for ourselves. And so what once was a mutual trade off turns parasitic. One begins to suck while the other withers.

Surviving is only for the fittest.

THE THOUGHT OF A GELATINOUS BLOB growing inside of Tyria, all teeth and fists and conscientious, scared me into seldom reached sanity. The notion that half of my DNA was the cause of the greatest magic I've ever come to know distributed a massive amount of clarity upon my self-judgment.

I'd committed the ultimate sin.

We as people try so hard to not get ourselves into trouble; we typically avoid it like the plague, but in the end it seems that it's all we know how to do. Now there was a price to pay. To see Tyria in such pain and filled with regret broke my heart. The way she squirmed and vomited and cursed made it seem as if her body was self-aborting the zygote rather than nourishing it.

"I wish this upon myself," I said to her.

Tyria looked at me with disdain. "You could never bear it."

She made me go out and buy a root of glorious ginger to quell the nausea, a bushel of mint for flavor and a mandrake root for decadence. While she squirmed on the couch I boiled the herbs into a dark tea. We drank until our minds reveled in psilocybin swirls, my heart aching and Tyria's face twisted with lunacy. The secret juices did not stop churning and the smelly gases continued hissing out of myriad orifices.

I admit I was happy at first.

I wanted nothing to do with any living, breathing clone of my own. I willed the blastocyst away and imagined my old life back, where my only responsibility was to art and my boyfriend. I am selfish, I admit. But then I thought about a life without Tyria and had a sudden change of heart. To be without her is to live in perpetual nightmare.

It took three days for Tyria to find peace, mentally and physically. It took me the same amount of time to even consider letting her keep the damn thing. At the same time I wondered if the devil would ever stop playing games; I begged the evil to come into me, spare my porcelain queen. But it remained inside of her.

When she finally passed out from pure exhaustion I dared not move. I watched shadows cascade down her face and her skinny belly, covered her shivering body with my winter blanket. At random times my bed would sink in with an unexplained weight. When I touched the indent it was *warm* as if someone had just sat down. I cursed the night.

And then one day she woke, inspired, as if she'd forgotten all about the living plague inside her.

"I still want to see it," Tyria whispered. "I want to know who you really are."

"I'm the father of your child."

"Don't fucking say that!"

"Why not?"

Tyria gritted her teeth. "I'm ripping it out of me first chance I get."

BLOOD KISS

The twilight sky was overcast; threaded through the clouds came a mystical spill of purple and orange light. Tyria lit a cigarette in the evanescence, and after refusing the one she offered me she didn't look at me for twenty minutes. I thought about quitting smoking right then and there. Isn't that what a father-to-be should do? My life was not my own to destroy anymore.

"Can't believe this," hand in my hair, pulling it until my neck cracked.

"Well, believe it," Tyria was showing her teeth again. "But trust, it won't be in me for long."

"You don't have to be so extreme."

"How is this extreme? I've been through it before."

Hearing Tyria say it out loud, that we were going to kill this thing, made me almost empathetic, if not sympathetic. What if my parents had thought to do the same when I was conceived and sucked me out of the womb with a powerful vacuum? What if Tyria's father had beaten her mother so badly that she pissed her baby-to-be out in blood? We would not be here and that made me so sad.

Had I not been born I'd not been able to discover the chaos and wonder of the world. There would be no art or poetry. I'd never have known what love and heartache was. I'd never know Yin and Yang. I'd never have met Tyria, or Leland, never have tasted another's flesh in the heat of the moment. I'd never have *lived*.

"Stop thinking. It's making you sweat," Tyria said.

I was indeed, what we call, clammy.

"Is it that obvious?"

"Yes," and she planted a dry kiss on my cheek. "Can't men ever, for once in their damned existence, trust a woman's instincts?"

"I trust you," I said. "I just don't want to lose control."

"Therein lies the issue," Ray Bans on her face again. "Men always have to feel in charge to satisfy their little dicks."

"I'm not a stereotype."

"But, you are a man."

Utter silence. There was no point in feeding into her man-hating, menocide attitude. I would never convince her any different, and the fact that she even slept in the same bed as me meant that she had lost a part of who she used to be. Maybe that was why she was looking for the argument.

"Now then, let's have a look," Tyria said, eyeing my studio. "I won't wait any longer."

I ran my hand through my hair nervously; a great clump separated itself from my scalp. Tyria sensed my unease, winked, and then blew the hair out of my hand and made some kind of a wish as if she was blowing on a dandelion in the middle of spring.

"Open it now," she said. "No more games."

"I'm scared," I finally admitted.

"Of what?"

"They request bad things of me."

The door opened by itself. *Come*, something said. *We need you.* Hair on the back of my neck rose in time with my own fear and loathing. Tyria's green eyes were a pair of weird stars. If anything was in there, something beyond my view of reality and science, it was going to have its way with me no matter how hard I resisted it. To indulge it was the only way.

Tyria took the first step in. Nothing had really changed in the weeks that I had abandoned it. A thin coating of dust settled atop every crook and corner; the smell remained that of old paint and energies wasted. The lava lamps were still swirling like neon invertebrates, anthropomorphic shadows spilling down the wall as if a surreal portrait by Dorothea Tanning.

"So much art," Tyria said.

I nodded.

The walls were slaughtered with color. Everything is my palette when I paint. There were piles of unfinished canvases; the ones ready to be sold had been placed on easels. A heavy whisper rang throughout the room; reptilian voices implored that we listen. I stepped over broken pencils and dozens of sketchbooks to keep up with Tyria's curiosity.

BLOOD KISS

"What is this one?" she said.

It was a portrait of something perverse, but elegant in its execution in that it tricked the viewer into thinking it was a nose, or even a baseball bat. Might it have been a mythical phallus? I'll never know. To be surreal is to trawl the psyche for its secrets, but glorify its deviance. We cannot deny ourselves of that impossible thought process.

"Not sure where I was going with that," I said.

Tyria looked at me, and then acknowledged the painting as if it was talking to her.

"Can you try to recall?"

I tried, but came up empty. "Nothing's coming to me."

Tyria shook her head so that her golden hair danced.

"Do you hear that?"

"Hear what?"

"You mean you don't hear them?" Tyria's arms filled with gooseflesh.

"I think you're hormonal," I said.

"Not funny. It feels like I'm being watched."

"Better to befriend evil than be ignorant to its existence," I said.

She pointed at the canvas, which was now *changing*. The caged phallus twisted, rising wet with white desire. I put my hand out for it, but immediately pulled away for fear it would take me. Might it slip into the first orifice it found, or perhaps penetrate the soft tissue of the brain.

"It's just art," I reminded her.

"No. I mean *seeing*, as if with my mind, not my eyes. The sound of them . . . it's a color I can't describe. It's a taste and it's a smell. It's everything you can't imagine."

"Can you teach me this power?" I immediately inquired.

"I was born this way, so no."

"Please," I pleaded. "I need to know."

She pushed me back, her hands exploring every single canvas and tube of paint as if she was Sherlock and I, Watson the standby. I saw her fingers sink into a portrait knuckle-deep beyond the borderline. She put a few drops of yellow paint on her tongue—which reminded me of Van Gogh's notorious habits—until her lips shined like tiger lilies in the sun. Tyria was like a blind person trying to see.

"I can *feel* all the strange colors, Dorian. They're lonely, needy."

"That's exactly it," I said with a grin taking over my face.

I recalled an inspiring moment in the movie *Mask* when Rocky was teaching his girlfriend—who had been blind from birth—how to understand colors. He used cotton balls to describe white clouds and a cold rock to describe the color of icy blue. I found that to be some of the most brilliant screen writing I had ever come across. Tyria was almost doing the same thing. How could she not as each portrait was a universe away from the next?

"Lapiz lazuli, cerulean . . . rotten apple."

"Rotten apple?" Tyria said.

"It's a shade of red."

The acceptance in horror that had taken me years to come to terms with only took Tyria fifteen minutes. Though I'd left my paintings for too long, now that I was here they wanted the attention they deserved. I had no explanation, no fragrant white lie to tell. She had me pinned down so fast, and I loved her more for it. Memories attacked me, made me see what I'd blocked out subconsciously, the toxic green mutations and viperfish faces, shimmering jellyfish tentacles.

I heard them call out to me too, not voices like you'd think, not any language you could imagine. If paint could articulate, if the smell of acrylic could be explained in sound, if paper could bleed . . . that would be the only way to explain it.

"Dorian?" Tyria said, licking her labret piercing.

"Yeah?"

"How the fuck do you do it?" She took off her Ray Bans; there were tears in her eyes.

"I could ask the same of you."

Colorful light lilted on the sharp frame of Tyria's face. "I never think. I just write."

BLOOD KISS *Daniel Stone*

My fingers do all the seeing, I wanted to say. *My arm does all the thinking.* Brain does not compute. I jump off the point and go. In the end I am but a viewer like everyone else, and that is necessary to the artist's survival.

"I have to see more," Tyria said.

She began to peer beneath the black sheets that I had put over a certain piece. I didn't want to see it, could not even begin to explain the wet and beating heart, or the charcoal eyes that cried slimy tears. But Tyria was not vexed. She grabbed the heart and demanded it to beat faster; she challenged the eyes with her own. A leggy thing wrapped itself up in a silky cocoon until it molted into an aberrant butterfly, though that was no aberrant reality for her.

Then she found the triptych.

I had neglected that one on purpose. It was expertly hid amongst the duds that I had painted, but for some reason it spoke to her. I knew by the look of disgust that it was still the most haunting thing I'd ever created. The arid zone of black and silver, the countless bones. What was I trying to do with it? I knew that the eyes of death's head were watching me, and I felt an ectoplasmic tongue reach for my hand. It wanted me back.

"This is the one," Tyria said.

"But it's not done."

"So then you'll have to finish it on stage."

"I don't think I can do that," and I meant it.

"What? Why?"

"I don't have it in me anymore."

"Have what?"

"The rage."

"Yes, you do, you just don't know it."

Her words made something inside of me open up its eyes. The skull beneath my skin began its eternal grin. I hadn't realized how much I missed them, my forever fallen angels. But I was taken back, and so I rested my head on Tyria's shoulder; she caressed my hair carefully. Her touch was lust, and the heat of her skin was love. I thought how easy for her it could have been to claw open my scalp and climb inside my brain. It's always a nice vacation from one's own madness while living through another's.

"What the hell?"

She released me to pick up a red vial from the floor. The opaque plasma jiggled atop packed red blood cells. And then Tyria did something I didn't expect: she poured it all over her bare stomach.

"Blood for blood," she said.

"Why would you do that? It's everywhere now."

"I wanted it," and she rubbed a red finger across her teeth.

"Fuck, it reeks."

There lay a mission in her eyes that I did not understand. Maybe the reality of motherhood had changed her.

"Ty?"

My thoughts were toxic.

"It's a heinous thing. We're not keeping it."

"How did you—"

"Men are weak. It's why they destroy everything around them. Compensation for their mental debilitation."

I sat on a stool and tossed her words around in my head. Something rose in time with my quickening heart, then exploded. We became covered in the iridescence of anthracite and the smell of ozone. Tyria must have felt my horror for she began a sage cleanse right away.

"Isis, Ishtar, Hecate . . . come to me," she incanted. "I need your strength and your guidance."

If magic was her only salvation, if it lay in the delicious, herbal smell of the smoke, I gladly tagged along.

"Is he here?" I said

"He's trying, but this keeps *him* at bay," Tyria said.

"Just don't go all *Croatoan* on me."

"Please try to be serious."

"Sorry." I took a step back, scratched my arm.

"He's my residual haunting."

"Infestation. Oppression. Possession," I said.

"What I'm talking about is manifestation."

BLOOD KISS Daniel Stone

"And so how do we get rid of this manifestation?" I said.

Tyria turned her head and cracked her neck. "There is no getting rid of it. You just have to find new ways to live, new ways to cope."

"What do you mean?"

"We have to learn to live with it rather than killing ourselves to get rid of it."

We were silent, unanimously deciding that it was time to go. We ventured back into the main floor of the loft, alone and safe—for now—and so Tyria changed the subject. She wanted a pregnancy test just to make sure. There was a bodega down the street and so I jetted out and came back with two of them.

"Will only take a minute. Been holding my pee in since I drank that horrible PBR," she said.

She closed the bathroom door and left me to the silence. My thoughts were way too loud so I put on *Down III: Over the Under*, a highly underrated album where front man Phil Anselmo descended to his most emotional lyrical depths. Everything from his addictive personality, to Dimebag Darrell and his fury over hurricane Katrina was let loose on that record.

I let the music engulf me like the velvet night. I drank Pinnacle vodka straight from the bottle, waiting for the effects to pull my consciousness into a downward spiral. When the bathroom door opened Tyria emerged with her face shamed and her little tits perking.

"Instincts never lie."

She held it up so I could see the tiny positive sign. I wished it away. But the gavel had come down, the future guillotined, and like the flick of a switch Tyria began to reject that knowledge. *Have to call Adelaide*, she said as tears smeared makeup down her face.

"Don't call her," I said. "Let's perform first . . . one last time before we make any decisions."

"But it'll kill me."

"Not while I'm around."

Tyria ran—so fast my little black cat—to the kitchen first and threw everything on the floor, pots and pans, my jar of almond butter and a twenty-two ounce of Colt 45. She stepped on the shards of glass without flinching. I saw the blood bead through her socks brightly. But it wasn't enough to satiate her rage.

"You did this to me!" With the blood from her foot she wrote me a love letter on the wall.

I don't dEsErVe ThIs!

And then the cell phone was in her hand, dripping wet; she dialed so fast I could not possibly have stopped her. When I tried to take the phone she knocked me back, sending the vile stench of that blood up my nose. Next thing I knew the phone was on speaker and to my surprise it wasn't Adelaide's voice, but Leland's!

"Hello?"

Awkward static crackling. Heavy breathing.

"Where is she?" Tyria growled.

A troika of strange voices in the background. Male, female and one that I could not classify with a gender. Maybe the sounds weren't voices at all, maybe they were signals picked up from television wires or other disturbances, things that you can only hear between the crackling lines of satellites.

"Hey, Ty. How are you?"

"Adelaide. Where the fuck is she?"

"Busy."

"Doing what? I have to talk to her. NOW!" Biting her lip harder.

"I don't think that's a good idea," Leland said.

"Don't fuck with me."

"Man, you sound just like her," Leland said nervously.

"Put her on now!"

"Calm down. She's finally come to terms with what's going on. I don't want anyone to start her up."

"What does that mean?"

Tyria's howl sent me back with a ghostly push. But it wasn't just me. The foundation beneath my feet succumbed

BLOOD KISS *Daniel Stone*

to the violent sound; the windows cracked. I braced myself for the ceiling to cave in, for the damn building to collapse as there was a great rumbling beneath me. But then Tyria threw the phone at me.

"Hey, Landy. What's going on?"

"Babe, how are you?"

The sound of his soft voice was soothing. Guilt instantly ate me alive.

"I'm fine. And you?"

"Great. I mean, a few hiccups here and there, but you know."

"Who are those people I hear?"

"Morgan, Alex and Rez. They're helping set up the new gig."

"Alex, from Electric Orchid?"

"That's him. You think he'd have an ego, but he's amazing."

Knot in my stomach. "How amazing?"

Something crashed in the background, and I heard a girl scream. Tyria's ears perked up; the tears rolling down her face were almost the same jade color of her eyes. She took one look at me and then ran back to the bathroom, and I instinctively reached for her like Gatsby to the green light.

Don't start breaking shit, Leland yelled.

We need ladders! I heard Adelaide say.

"Landy . . . hello? Landy"

"Don't get jealous. Nothing happened."

"How can you tell?"

"I know you better than you know yourself."

"I love you."

"Love you more," Leland said.

And then I changed the subject. "What are we going to do about the next show?"

"I'm at the place on Thames. You always dreamed of having your own art show in a real warehouse, and I'm giving it to you."

"What do you need me to do?"

"You and Tyria just bring your bodies here tomorrow night."

"See you soon, Landy."

"Brooklyn will burn, if you catch my drift."

We hung up at the same time.

THE MINUTES GLIDED INTO HOURS, his phone call with Dorian long since over, yet inside Leland's head felt like a meaty merry go 'round. Dorian had sounded great, happy even, but guilt was on his voice. Maybe Adelaide was right, that Dorian was essentially feeding off of Tyria, breaking her down, taking all he can take until she withered away.

But what was stopping Tyria from doing the same?

Dangerous as it was to leave them to each other's madness, Leland knew it was essential to the cause. Surely things could go awry, and they would all learn from this pain; surely they could all be friends in the end.

He willed Adelaide to accept this circumstance, wishing she could take a step back to judge the situation objectively now that they were all in this together. Even if the alchemy was to remain dark, it would light a road to new beginnings. No matter how deep you go, you can always climb back up. Then Leland stopped thinking. They would be here soon.

"I got some guys to bring everything so we wouldn't have to do much manual labor," Alex said. "It's good to have fans who'll do anything for you, even in this weather."

"They still have to pay to get in," Adelaide said.

"I know that," Alex said. "Don't you think that I understand the logistics of these things."

"Just making sure."

Adelaide stood on her tippy toes to look in all the cardboard boxes holding advertisements, band equipment, magic markers and glow sticks. She labeled each box with a hot pink marker, then unloaded them. It was almost as if this

BLOOD KISS *Daniel Stone*

night would end up being a rave; all that was missing was the day glow paint and fancy blue drinks.

Leland began marking off the supplies. Chords on the floor and electronic gadgets piling high. Though there was enough space in here to conceal the new amps, the factory style windows spilled in streetlight so that in every corner there was shadow. It made him feel unsafe, for nothing can stay alive long within the absence of light.

It was a frightening thought.

"Is there anything more to log?" Leland said.

"Nope. Unless you want props or something."

"Nah, this'll do. I don't know where to even begin."

"Let's begin by camouflaging the speakers," Morgan said. "Noise from every corner of this room would be sick."

As Morgan and Leland hoisted up the speakers on small metal cables, Adelaide paced back and forth, her temper thick as the cigarette smoke clouding her. Leland knew that if he didn't give her an assignment she would ruin everything. Maybe she could set up the stage, maybe she could place the candles on the appropriate mantle.

"What's on your mind now?" Leland said.

"I really miss her. I want to see her."

Adelaide turned, distracted by her own thoughts; her spirits were confused by the understanding that she'd soon see Tyria.

"Can't you at least pretend you have your shit together? Do you want Tyria to see you looking like you've been doing nothing but worrying about her?"

"What's wrong with that?"

"It makes you look weak."

"Maybe my pride isn't as big as yours."

"You need to *at least* pretend it is when you see her."

Morgan made mocking gestures, then pulled a heavy box with Rez over to his DJ booth. It seemed they were getting along gaily; the way they took out the machines and cables from the box almost made Leland dizzy. He knew nothing about modern technology, but Rez seemed to be a computer genius, inherently knowing what plug went into what machine, which chord fit into the ridiculously heavy speakers. They browsed the set list through a program called Serum Soft Synth; the light turned their faces into sharp portraits of dusk and dawn.

They finished plugging everything in and continued hoisting up the amps, but were now dressing the cables in black lace. When they were done Leland counted five speakers, one in each corner of the room and one in the center of the ceiling. Rez took a quick cigarette break and Morgan cracked open two PBRs to start the night's party. They had caught Leland staring and threw him one, and Adelaide as well. She opened it with her teeth.

"Take it easy Wonder Woman," Rez said. "Who opens a can with their teeth?"

"I do when I'm pissed off!"

"But that's all day every day,"

"Whatever."

"Come with me outside," Leland said. "We have to make sure these are at the entrance."

The advertisements were stacked high as Adelaide's waste and were almost the same color as her ragged clothes. She took one out of the pile and examined it, her black eyes pleased but confused, hopeless. *SyMbIoSiS*. The word whorled, and around it shapeless vertebrates in love and transformation. Silhouettes and shadows, a backdrop of screaming vaginas. Themes of growth, dependence, resurrection and infection.

Leland grabbed the pile, then Adelaide's hand and they sashayed down the scraggy stairs to see all the wonderful squatter sites. Beer cans, detritus of take out cartons and cigarette boxes. A body wrapped in its cardboard blanket and flea-infested cats. No wonder there were hardly any rats in the building. Leland remained cautious of the reflective eyes, all knowing, waiting to strike.

"How did you manage to get this place?" Adelaide said.

"The building is abandoned except the top floor. Some hipsters live up there and decided to give up their space."

BLOOD KISS *Daniel Stone*

"But how did you convince them?"

"It seems they owed Alex a favor."

"And he decided to waste that favor on us?"

"Yes, you negative ninny. Because look."

The graffiti was less talent and more drunken rage. *MiSaNtHrOpIc* and *FUCK LIFE*, adjacent to *GO HOME ALONE*. Adelaide gazed into the spirals and tendrils. Leland concluded that the work was more spontaneity while Adelaide argued it was carefully put there. *It's all circles and dull ends, I don't see any precision*, Leland said. *But that's exactly why they drew it like that, for people like you to question their talent*, Adelaide said. It felt good to dissent about art instead of the hardships of life.

Leland's grip on her arm clamped tighter as they glided out the heavy metal door and settled at the lone table where Rez said he'd be willing to sit and collect the ten dollar entrance fee. The cold didn't bother him like it did Leland. When Adelaide complained about the temperature, Leland gave her a cigarette to keep her occupied.

He studied his surroundings while Adelaide busied herself with the smoke. Barred windows, broken construction boards and a light dusting of snow. The block was desolate in both directions and the cobblestone streets were beginning to ice over. He heard the roar of the Morgan Avenue L train, which was a great sigh of relief as it would not be hard for people to get here.

"Landy?" Adelaide whispered.

"Yeah?" He felt the air prickling down his spine like a dead finger.

"I need to know what I'm supposed to do when she shows up."

"You let her do her thing . . . and then if you wanna talk to her, feel free, but only when the audience is gone."

"I don't know if I can hold myself for that long."

"Well, you have to. Tonight is the night where we make real headlines. Imagine a spread in The Village Voice or The New York Times? The money will roll right in!"

"What is it with you and the money? Where are your emotions?"

"I'm running a business. My financial future is my only concern right now."

"That's low, even for you," Adelaide scraped her sneaker across the pavement.

"Don't argue with me just for the sake of arguing. How the fuck do you expect me to eat without money in this soul-sucking city?"

"Fuck you, Landy. You've changed."

"Oh yeah? And what about this?"

Leland tugged her by the arm, but what was supposed to be a hug suddenly transformed into malice. Adelaide's fist rained down on his wrist, *let me go you fuck, let me go*, but the red fire in his mind needed to burn, needed to make Adelaide see. He ripped her cheap pleather coat at the arm, pulling hard as he could. Her arm tensed, the track marks so vivid on that white skin; he wanted to embarrass her, to make her realize that she was heading down into a hole again.

"You promised me no matter what happened that you'd only sell it."

"Fucking bastard," snatching her arm away, lifting it to strike.

"I'm your friend," Leland said. "I won't let you do this again."

"I should cut your throat."

Adelaide slipped the Bowie knife out of her waist line. The edge gleamed like a distant star, formed a patch of dying light across her face. Leland remembered how that metal felt pressed against his neck three years ago, and a hidden anger he had not felt in years erupted from the depths of his conscience and took control.

Everything that had been building over the past few weeks had reached the tipping point in this moment. Rationality dissolved as he launched her with his fists and his mind on overdrive. Their bodies collided; he took a handful of her hair, tugging as hard as he could. Her skull shook like

BLOOD KISS

a maraca and the thin skin shifted nastily as he pulled her down to the cobblestone.

The Bowie knife grazed his right deltoid, slicing down to the softness of his skin. Adelaide wailed murderously, then dropped the knife and began clawing his throat and eyes. But just like that their energy had been expunged, their spleens vented. When Leland released her she spit in his face, but he spit in hers right back.

"You ripped my jacket, you prick," Adelaide said.

"Why are you doing this?"

And then he cried, didn't even know it was coming, so unlike him. All composure lost, all hope gone. He'd turned into one of them. Why couldn't he rewind time, why couldn't he get Dorian back? But you can't ever get time back. If it were that easy to make all the wrongs right, we'd never learn.

"Stop crying, Landy. I don't want to see you hurt."

"I'm so sorry." Leland hugged Adelaide. "It's just that I miss Dorian. I miss us. I miss the past."

"The past is dead, Landy. All you do is remind me of that." Moonlight leaked into the hollows of her face. "Please don't cry it hurts me."

"You said that nothing could turn you back to those dark times."

"I slipped up. I mean . . . you know how it is. Once a junky, always a fucking junky."

"Admitting it doesn't make you a better person. Your actions speak for themselves."

Adelaide picked up the Bowie knife and placed it back into her waistline.

"I don't know what I'd do without you, Addy. You're my best friend, my confidant and all that cheesy shit. I love you."

"I love you too, Landy."

They embraced, then headed back up the stairs. As soon as they made it to the top three pale and confused faces unearthed themselves from the dark. Leland smelled liquor, cigarettes and spray paint even through the blanketing cold.

"Yo, what the hell happened down there?" Morgan asked.

"Nothing of your concern," Adelaide spit.

"Why's Landy bleeding?"

"Can you get me a rag, Morgan?"

"We heard screaming," Alex said.

"Just get me a fucking rag!"

Leland heard his voice hiss like fire, a strange sound. Morgan caught his drift, disappeared into shadow and returned with paper towels. He applied the right amount of pressure to make the blood stop and for some reason Morgan felt taller, his basketball shoes looked bigger and his hands felt all of a sudden nicer.

"Shit it's deep," Morgan said.

Leland saw the thin pink layers of flesh.

"It's not deep at all."

"Here, let me help you."

"Blood smells so bad," Leland said.

Morgan held an impossible amount of pressure, and before he knew it the cut stopped bleeding. Little jellied clots had formed a weird looking smile across his biceps.

"Now that I'm all cleaned up, let's get the final preparations done."

"The ads look good down there," Adelaide said.

"I drew them myself . . . from the descriptions Leland gave me," Alex said. "I figured anything spooky would do the trick."

Alex was not only knowing of the piano, but had a second talent for drawing. That made him all the more special.

Adelaide said, "Not bad for a—"

"A girl? A boy?" Alex conjectured.

"What are you anyway?"

Leland tsked. "That's not nice, Addy."

" 'S okay. I like to keep people guessing," Alex guffawed.

"It's not a guess, because you're definitely a boy. I just want to know why."

"Why what?"

"Why do you hide who you are?"

BLOOD KISS *Daniel Stone*

Leland took a good look at Alex again. Those high cheek-bones, multicolored hair and that razor smile, it nearly broke his heart. He indeed could pass for a teenage girl if he wanted. But now Rez's bony hand reached out for his lover, caressed that sweet face as if in redemption for what Adelaide had said even though Alex seemed excited. He wanted to talk about it.

"Genderqueer is what they call it now. It used to be androgynous," Alex said. "But I hate labels; they're just another bureaucratic construct to categorize people, being that we live in a world of shelves, where everything and everybody must have a cozy spot."

"Ever hear of QUILTBAG?" Leland said.

"QUILTBAG is a bad joke."

Morgan's face scrunched. "What does it mean?"

"Queer/Questioning, Undecided, Intersex, Lesbian, Trans-gender/Transsexual, Bisexual, Allied/Asexual, Gay/Gender-queer."

"That's a whole lot of fucking description," Leland said.

Adelaide clapped. "I need a joint right about now."

Alex opened a box of Djarum Vanilla, *salvia*, he said, *not weed*. Adelaide took a joint cautiously, never having smoked salvia before. She had only burned it for smudges. In no time the room was hazy with fruity smoke, the taste of cherry and blueberry on everyone's tongue.

"You did amazing with the ads, Alex. Holding them in my hand is like a dream. It's as if every gallery I put together in the past never happened. This is the *real* reason why I want to promote art," Leland said.

"And I believe in your vision, wholeheartedly."

"Does any one wanna get warm the old fashioned way?"

Rez had a bottle of Jägermeister in his hand. He cracked it open and passed it around the circle. Leland took two swigs, then Morgan, then Adelaide. A brown explosion hit Leland's stomach, but his senses flooded with ease. He became more sensitive to the world around him, hearing the electric sizzle of neon and becoming dazed by the strobe lights. It was almost grounds for a seizure.

Somehow the warehouse elongated, yawned wide with shadow. On this end he could see his crew, but turn his head the other way and they were gone, lost within the color of no color, that abyssal tease. If this was any precursor to the night's show, he was now looking more forward to it, wanted to understand that uncomfortable darkness like Dorian did.

"Spooky in here, yo," Morgan said. "I can hear the dust settling."

Leland just realized that moonlight was spiraling into the windows. It shined upon the thrift shop shelves of candles as if they were already lit; it traveled reptilian and cold down the cinderblock walls. It made you question the dark, made you wonder what was looking back at you.

"It's best for effect," Leland said.

"This place is antiquated," Alex said. "Delilah would love it."

"She ain't coming," Rez returned. "Not as far as I know."

"I sent her a text. Hopefully she'll make it."

"Delilah . . . the singer of your band?" Adelaide asked.

"Yeah. Spookiest girl in the world," Rez said. "And the toughest bitch you'll ever meet."

"I know. She was amazing on stage."

Alex jumped in their conversation. "Plus, you know what happens when you two are put in the same room together."

Rez remained quiet.

"I want to know what happens when you two are put in the same room together," Adelaide said. "Has Leland told you about Dorian and Tyria and the supernatural shit that happens between them?"

Rez said, "You shouldn't be so hostile when it comes to magical moments like this."

"Like I said before, yo," Morgan chimed in. "I almost bounced last time. If something crazy happens again I'm out for good."

"It's her shadow," Adelaide said.

"No, it's you."

BLOOD KISS

Rez's pale eyes were wide and blaming. Adelaide brushed him off, convinced that he was in need of a straitjacket. It wasn't time to focus on the spooks. There was work to be done.

Leland made sure that the little stage was sturdy and then set up Dorian's easel next to it; there was a stool for him to sit on and a razor-tipped paintbrush. Leland stood atop it, knew right away that it would serve its purpose. Tyria would be Queen of the Night.

"Make everything psychedelic," Leland said.

Adelaide nodded as Rez put up the local ads they had collected on the way. Catland and 983 and random house parties. Electric Orchid posters glowed a deep sensual red. It was sensory overload. All things slowed, changed. The cinderblock walls pulsed; the ceiling sagged like a lazy tongue. In the end, the patrons would feel certainly at home.

"What time you expecting the stars of the show?" Alex asked.

"In twenty minutes."

"Is there no rehearsal?"

"It's all impromptu."

Adelaide's head began to shake. Leland knew she was sensing something what with her eyes closed and her lips mumbling. The incantation was to a goddess of guidance as she lit an Open Road candle, set it on the windowsill at the far end of the warehouse. After, she performed a sage cleansing.

"I'll set up the paints for Dorian," Leland said.

"Rez and I will head downstairs. Addy, you're in charge of the candles, obviously."

Leland said, "This time no curtains. We need this venue for a long time."

18

Falling not into dream or nightmare, but her own dark thoughts. Imagine if the brain could be pulled from the skull, if we could peal back its greasy rind to reveal the hallucinogenic jelly. Only than could you dip a finger into the foundation of emotion and change the path of your life.

But consider that the brain is the seed of illusion rather than reason, and your mind the garden in which it will sow. Only the soul can spoil that loam. When a person finally accepts that they have taken life for granted, that every moment before conception was a gift, they become bitter.

Tyria knew this.

As the little germ inside her continued growing, she pondered the biological processes, the magic of zygote to embryonic meat. Thousands of cells uniting and dividing to the blueprint instruction of DNA, for the puzzle of flesh is nothing but a product of chemistry and physics.

In only a few weeks the soft cartilage would begin to calcify and bear weight. The spherical gob of connective tissue would soon house the brain. Limbs will sprout, the sex will be determined and the tiny heartbeat would deem it a living being.

From this moment forth every nutrient she ingests will be stolen. To know that the skin across her abdomen would puff, tear and scar; to know that her legs would swell and her tits would begin to hurt, was enough to make her want to rip it out herself. It will kill her to survive if it has to, and upon its grand arrival it will rain red between her legs.

That was the hardest part to accept.

"We have a lot to do," Dorian said.

Tyria snorted. "Tell me why I should even care."

"Because we made a commitment, because we're performers."

"I'm none of those things."

"Can you try to act somewhat human," pointing to the squalor of books, clothes and cigarettes. "You should care because I care."

The stage rung like home in her head; poetry was salvation. She knew it to be true as she held Anne Sexton's *The Book of Folly* and Walt Whitman's *Leave of Grass*, her nails sliding across the canvas covers, the battered pages speaking to her in tongues that warmed her heart.

"I'll be ready soon," placing the books down.

"You wanna shower?"

"Yeah."

"And eat?" Dorian was slipping on a new pair of wing-tipped boots; his hair hung over his face, concealing his eyes.

"I think I'm okay. Not too hungry."

"You don't want toast or anything?"

"I said I'm not hungry."

Not hungry because she was all of a sudden hearing voices. *What's inside you is mine*, it said. Tyria swung her fist toward the sound, felt the skin of her knuckles suck back as she released it from the wall. *I'll always be with you,* phantom fingers on her legs, a cold tongue on her shoulder. Tyria punched the wall again, and this time she felt the hot wire of pain burn all the way to her shoulder. Dorian caught her hand before the next blow, held it down.

"Don't fuck up the hand you write with, Ty."

"I want him out of my head."

Dorian bound her arms with his own. "Don't let your emotions get the best of you."

"But he won't leave me alone."

"Focus on the now. Look at all this shit I have to pack."

Paintbrushes like knives, tubes everywhere, and an array of portraits. Dorian had spread them all for show, vaginas filled with teeth and penises ripped in half revealing the scaly urethra. They seemed too dead to be so alive, their eyes watching, their voices the color of absolute insanity.

He had also switched on the television, an archaic device with bunny ear wires and a fully functional black and white screen; one knob to change the channels. Tyria heard the eerie music of *The Twilight Zone*, the credits showing that it was the "Howling Man" episode, one of Dorian's personal favorites. Wherever he was ciphering signal from remained a mystery as New York City was now a digital kingdom and received relatively no analog transmission.

"Which one do you prefer?" Dorian said.

Tyria stood at the kitchen sink washing her face. "Of what?"

"Of the paintings."

"Oh, all of them."

"I can't possibly bring everything. Which one speaks to you?"

"If I had to choose . . . that one."

She had eyes only for the triptych. It was a wrong thing. What kind of a haunt was Dorian trying to uncover? Though she knew that asking the artist for an explanation was bad juju, she still wanted to know. When the listener, the reader, or the viewer succumbs to art, they become God. There is no other way.

"I'm afraid of it," Dorian said.

Tyria knew that Dorian's portraits were so much a part of him that it was as if they were his own children. No doubt he had conceived them in a time of drunken rampage, tore the ideas out of his own psyche and drew them to completion. Could it be that his work was the spitting image of himself, like a child is to his or her parents? Or were they his visions of the real world, for when you take off the social costumes we wear, the true face of the society is bound to show.

"We have to go. Pack your shit."

The rags she had brought to his loft were stuffed back into her messenger bag; her books too. Smelly sneakers on

BLOOD KISS Daniel Stone

her feet, black jeans, ripped band t-shirt, a denim vest studded in spikes and layered with patches. She found her reflection before a mirror and was not satisfied until she put on her Ray Bans.

"I like that vest. Is it new?"

"No. Just haven't worn it around you."

"It's very punk rock."

Dorian towered over her, and Tyria noticed that she was somehow bowing before his marbled body like an altar. Though it was Dorian she was seeing, his face was different, his voice muffled. She saw a face made of wood the color of 4am; gold ringed its bold features and the long nose was like that of Pinocchio.

"Plague mask," Dorian said, all teeth and lips and wood.

"I know what it is," Tyria stood.

"Will you wear it?"

He placed it on her face softly. It smelled of glue and paint and poison. But when she looked at the world through its eyes, she found that it skewed everything. Behind the mask, she was free.

"You can hide yourself from them."

Hide, Tyria thought.

"I like it. Where did you get it from?"

"Treasures and pleasures are plentiful in this sterile city. You just have to go look for them."

"I know the adage. 'One man's trash is another man's treasure.' "

"That's exactly it."

Dorian returned to the maw of the studio, his shadow lingering with her like a spill of quill ink. But the mask made her brave. She dipped her pen into the liquid darkness and there came a sensation like a giant fish mouth had clamped her hand. When she pulled away the mask fell off of her face.

"Let's go," Dorian said. "Get your jacket on."

Outside was colder and darker than Tyria expected, but Dorian looked warm in his black denim jacket; she nearly froze in her cheap Hot Topic coat. The lighting scheme changed, as if the streets themselves were preparing for a show. Every other lamp post was smashed, and as they stopped beneath a skirt of light her shadow had come out to play again, but this time Dorian was on his knees trying to bite it.

"Come to me," he said in a tone that frightened her.

Teeth bared, the snakebites on his lip bleeding, and his hands curled into talons. *I want it*, over and over. *Gotta have it*. The smell of it was greasy and dank. As the anti-temperature enveloped her it began to spread apart her legs, tried to climb inside. Her vagina lurched, screaming so loud the cars began to lift from the ground—

—as Dorian stuck in his arm elbow deep until it let her go. "You okay?"

"I wanna get the fuck out of here."

"Look at what it did."

In his pale hands the triptych gleamed blade-like. The shadow had changed it, or had gone into it. Tyria studied the picture for a moment, let her eyes wander into the dark fairy tale it was telling. It was a graveyard of pain, a story of decay, growth and transformation. She saw the outer shell of a skull and the glittery burst of galaxies, saw whole cities in ruin and planets just being born. It was the story of life from the big bang to the big rip.

"What do you see when you look at my work?"

"Death . . . the journey of existence. How we all end up in the same place, how we all, essentially, come from the same elementary particles."

Dorian's black eyes like universes themselves, the kohl liner starting to clump. He folded the triptych carefully and said that tonight it would tell a new tale. The blocks they walked through were nameless, the streets too narrow, concrete tongues flecked with keloid ice. The pain in Tyria's hand was unbearable now that she was able to think straight, throbbing, bleeding.

"I'll never get used to the cold," Dorian said out of breath. "Never."

BLOOD KISS

"Can we just get on the train already?"

The stairs wanted to never end, but at the bottom the L train hummed soullessly, rocked back and forth to its metallic halt. Two NYPD drones at the far end of the station stared at Tyria and Dorian as if they wanted to stop and frisk them, but they boarded the train before the pigs had time to make a decision.

Wednesday was not a festive night, and it was far too cold for the real characters to come out. Tyria imagined they were huddled alone in their roach motels and basement hostels. Still, there was your local wino and your underground musicians and magicians on the train. And if one took in a deep enough breath they would be able to smell the dusty darkness of the tunnels. Just then Tyria kicked the floor.

"She's going to freak when she finds out."

"No one has to know." Dorian kissed her. He wanted the words to be a new mantra.

"I don't plan on telling her," Tyria said with her hands on her stomach. "But is this what it wants?"

Dorian's black eyes blinked once, twice. "I don't know what it wants."

"Somewhere in that fucked up head of yours, I think you do."

"All I know is that we belong on that stage. It's the only place where freedom is not taken for granted."

Tyria felt herself grin. "Sometimes it's that rush of a hundred other beating hearts . . . a hundred different brains that is a performer's stimulant."

The lights in the train fumbled; electric snapped and the brakes threatened to throw everyone to the other side of the car. Hands embraced the metal holders, graffiti shivered in time with the flickering fluorescence, *BrOoKlYn BaByl* and *DeAd LiNeS*. Tyria laughed after reading that last piece because she knew that it defined the train system itself in New York City. Then she closed her eyes, wondering how long she had before the thing inside of her was too big to flush out, but also if that small spasm in her uterus was its sinister smile.

IN THE DEAD OF NIGHT the girl named Delilah stepped off the L train and headed south on Bogart in search of Thames. She had just finished reading the advertisement placed on Electric Orchid's Facebook page, thus which enticed her enough to rise free from her Jäger slumber.

She knew the tawdry lines of the artwork, the careful right hand, the spirals and circles of the sloppy left hand. Alex. She also remembered that the girl and boy who ran this show had been at Death by Audio. Though hardly a place to remember faces, Delilah felt compelled to at least return the favor being they had supported her gig.

Bogart Street spread before her creepy and cold. Food trucks did not dot the sidewalks, hipsters could not be found, and the stores were closed. The sodium glow of the street-lights barely touched the enveloping night. Memories of wandering the streets of Queens and Manhattan came to her; the razor scars on her wrists burned. Old ghosts began to speak in tongues.

Delilah was a catalyst for darkness and pain.

Thames bore down on her left, the warehouses jutting into a black slate sky. She could smell the liquor permeating the air and the salvia smoke too sweet to enjoy. Her docs made awful sounds against the pavement; her hair swung like the limbs of dead tarantulas. Somewhere, out there in the dark, she saw the tall man standing, but then closed her eyes and counted to ten so that he disappeared like turning pictures in a book.

She found the building of choice, could not miss it. Long windows barred or loosely boarded and in need of serious repair. It was built as if a whole bunch of assholes cemented a pile of bricks together, filling the empty spaces with glass and a crappy door. And then she saw the ads.

BLOOD KISS

SyMbIoSiS.

She picked one off the window—such a strange hallucination to hold in her hands—and then opened the heavy metal door; fuck knocking. Delilah walked up the wavy stairs and found a group of pale faces gawked at her ghostly presence, candles everywhere like a starry séance and the odor of sage so thick, the strongest smoke of all.

ALL I WANT TO DO is stick my hand into the shadow to try and reassemble the girl she might have been. I would stitch the jagged shards of darkness together to make a new mind, a new body, a new soul for her to feel safe.

For us.

I thought how lovely it might be to have a family. I could make up for all the wrongs of my own childhood; Tyria and I dedicated not to art, but to our child. In this moment I traveled the slick thruways of sadism, to arrive at my most masochistic thought. Was fatherhood written in my destiny? Would it look like me?

Then another memory stole me.

The horror in Tyria's eyes was clear, to know that there is no escape from the past—that all haunts begin and end in one's head—is where the concept of true terror lies. I remember reaching into it—into her—hands slippery with nothingness, but my heart now in a protective state (I would not allow my family to be in danger . . . Goddess, what a word!) while at the same time I wanted to pry open Tyria's mind for the secrets to her universe.

I thought about what I had done.

It is utterly frightening to touch the flesh of a ghost. To be laved in all that gruesome ectoplasm, to face a thing greater than bone and teeth, mind and matter, is a hard reality to digest. The skin of a ghost is more dull sensation than that of wind chill. Its eyes are nowhere to be found, but you know that it is watching you . . . wants you.

Fear becomes us.

I've now come to realize that fear is nothing more than a mutated social construct rather than a genetic tool for survival. I do not know if I fear anything anymore, for what is there left to be afraid of when you have successfully passed along your own corrupt DNA? I am essentially born again.

But what happens when we do not want to face the destruction that lies within the fruit of our labor? All we do is create little deaths in procreation because nobody, as you know, lives forever.

The reaper is me.

And so the train hummed on. Tyria's head lolled gently against my shoulder; a tiny string of drool beaded her labret piercing. Her face was a plague mask of pain. A blank notebook lay in her lap, the pen still darting across the page. *WHY ME?* I read. *PARTING IS NEVER A SWEET SORROW BECAUSE IT IS BLISS.*

It was a most theatrical sleep. Her hands jerked, the pen scribbling more languid prose across the pages. Something about the silence in suffering, and now the cut on her hand bleeding again. I saw the flesh haphazardly part, saw the pen dip into the rich red reservoir to dab the pages in blood. I wondered if she was dreaming about its birth, about the three of us, the new Addams Family.

I looked at my hollow reflection from the train's window, bony mask of me, but out there beyond the reflection was the monster city, a mystery even to me.

I missed Landy.

I wondered what he would say when he found out and simultaneously cringed at the thought of Adelaide's reaction. But this is the price we pay when we want to play. It is so much easier for the gays when it comes down to the nitty-gritty, to not have to worry about being responsible for making more meat creatures. All we have to do is to make sure we don't kill each other with HIV, the celestial punishment for our sins.

BLOOD KISS

The train halted at Morgan Avenue and Tyria jolted awake. We took to the streets like big black birds. Every chance I had I looked for it, the color of darkness or the actual essence of it. I just wanted it to be mine. Why not make possible of the impossible?

The streets of Brooklyn are so very different at night. In this part of the borough there is no water for me to catch a reflection of the moon, and the clouds cover its enigmatic face. There is this impeccable sense of fright, for the area is so lonely your own breathing is too loud to comprehend.

We turned left on Thames to hear the rattle of zippo lighters, teeth clicking on gum and the rubbery thrum of Converse sneakers. The poetry of urbanites angry at the world or at themselves. Their music was strong; their wanton lusts bridged into a giant vessel leading to one universal heart.

I took a deeper look into them so that I could take a deeper look into myself. Drunks and metal heads, hipsters and Goths, goonies and bums and artfags. Tragic by all means. We all have a history, we all have issues. But some of us have it worse than others. Girls turn to cutting and eating disorders to make themselves feel better; boys turn to bullying to alleviate their insecurities. The queers turn to suicide and the quiet kids utilize gun violence.

But why does it always have to be that one side of the street is better than the other? Must one color always be superior to its antonym? Can it never be where everyone has a place rather than facing a judgment that doesn't need to exist?

"They want to party," Tyria said.

"I'm ready when they are."

Everyone was dressed in metal and black, the rogue fashion of long dead days. I wondered who in this crowd was the nameless writer making us famous. But all I caught was tangles of hair and every mouth busy with a fancy cigarette. The way they shaded their eyes certainly meant that they couldn't bear to be themselves anymore.

But they were the only ones who were listening.

"Look at them," I said.

"How many you think?"

"Over a hundred."

The line was two people thick and down the entire block. We cut through the crowd, to which a few hands rose guarding their spot, but one frightful jade glare from Tyria and they backed off. At the front of the line I caught a spicy whiff of Sour Diesel weed. The eyes that marked us were black, blue, red, green, gray; their fingers were all busy with trippy advertisements; their mouths all shot the shit about books, indie films and music.

A skinny thing said, "Is that her?"

"Her voice can crush glass," a girl snickered. "She's definitely possessed."

Tyria snarled, lifted her pen as if to stab, but I grabbed her hand and pulled her inside. I knew this crowd well enough to know that they meant no harm. In the end if no one talks about you . . . do you even exist? We hobbled up the long flight of stairs to the smell of ozone, clove cigarettes and something familiar. Tyria's nostrils flared near the metal door where I saw smoke rising. Sage.

"Addy," Tyria said grimly. "She's cleansing the room. Too bad she doesn't know that it's too late."

BLOOD KISS Daniel Stone

19

nto the room as if by magnetization, rising smoke inner-
vating the silence, and it was clear that some kind of séance
was taking place. A circle of bodies, palms facing the sky and
everyone's face alive with thought.

"You!"

Addy's arms opened as wide as her screaming mouth.
They latched onto Tyria and pulled her into the center where
she caught the pulse of pale eyes and the dark gleam of a
pissed off girl. They incanted to the goddess of crossroads,
mother of fire, moon and herbs. They unleashed the smells
of chaos and rot as they changed the positions of their hands
and feet to match that of a pentagram with Tyria in the
center.

"She made it," an unfamiliar voice said.

"Porcelain goddess."

The spell was done. Everyone was released from their
hypnosis. Tyria's chin hit her chest, but Adelaide would not
let her eyes avert. She brushed Tyria's hair back, kissed her
deeply on the lips, the kind of kiss that one waits a lifetime
for. Tyria leaned back slightly, getting ready for Adelaide's
outburst for abandoning her—more importantly for the thing
growing inside of Tyria—but she did no such thing. What
came about was just love, strong, abyssal, familiar; lizard
tongue and those hands so knowing, intelligent.

Tyria took back her rightful place as the center of the
universe, so nice to be worshiped by someone who truly
loves you. She clasped Adelaide's wrists gently and exchanged the sensual touching for an embrace. But Adelaide

would not stop caressing her, face and arms, the verdant terrain between her legs, and even her belly.

"Missed you," Tyria said.

"Missed you more," Adelaide kissed her forehead and cold cheek.

Adelaide had lost some weight. Tyria felt new plains and nudges; her bones shifted beneath her skin like never before. When Adelaide is weak, she goes in for the kill. Not others, but herself.

"Meet the crew."

"Hi," Tyria said.

Morgan, Leland, two boys who could pass for girls and one snake-haired wretch; a darkling that seemed the most out of place. Early patrons or new friends who simply respected art and magick?

"I'm Alex and this is Rez," shaking hands.

The snake-haired girl turned to meet Tyria's eyes. "Delilah."

When she took Delilah's hand a moment of complete and utter black took over her vision. Maybe it was the color of her sottovoce voice, or maybe it was her aura. But Tyria could never mistake another believer. There were so little of them, and this Delilah character was one of the powerful ones.

"You believe," Tyria said.

Delilah didn't budge. The dreadlocks seemed frozen in place. But then another voice broke her concentration.

"Where is he?" Leland didn't even say hello, and she didn't blame him. "Was he with you?"

"Yes," Tyria said. "He walked in with me."

Leland dashed for the door, pulled it open and stuck his head out. When he found that Dorian wasn't there, he turned paler and more worried than before. Tyria dropped her bag and pitched in the search for Dorian. Where the hell did he go? His paintings were all here and his coat was draped over the chair.

 BLOOD KISS

"Funny, I can smell him," Leland said. "But he's not here."

Adelaide snuck up behind Tyria, grabbed her wrists. "Come with me."

"No. I gotta find Dorian."

"Haven't you had your fill?"

"What?"

"He's still playing games, disappearing now."

"No, he ain't. Stop it, Addy."

"Oh gods! Something's wrong." Fear tainted Leland's voice.

"He came with me, I swear it," Tyria said.

"Ty!" Adelaide said.

"Not now Addy."

"I gotta call him." Leland raked a hand through his hair. "I hope he wouldn't just bail." Leland pulled out his cell phone and fell into a whole new world.

Tyria could feel the burn of Adelaide's stare from behind her, a stare laced with jealousy and one horrible question. Tyria knew what it was. Somehow girls can see the glow that men will never see. They are intuitive and rely on the truth of their emotions, and it's through this power that they can nearly read one another's minds.

"You're different," Adelaide said.

Tyria tried to grin. "Still me."

"No. Something's up."

Tyria shook her head. "Wrong."

"Where is that snake Dorian? I'm gunna give him a piece of my mind."

"Alright, alright. Calm down."

"I am calm," Adelaide said. "I just love you. I'd do anything for you."

"You know exactly what I could use right now."

Tyria had power over Adelaide, and it was felt throughout the entire room like a beam of light. Might it be the green charm of Tyria's eyes, or her velvet lips, but as Adelaide pulled out a pink baggie filled with fine white crystals from her pocket book, one could feel the ego being stripped away layer by layer.

Tyria took it with force.

"Wait! I gave you what you want. Now tell me what I want to know."

"I said drop it, Addy!" Heinous laugh; all she could do was laugh it off.

"You glow . . . but decay at the same time. Did *he* do it to you?"

At the height of the moment Alex squeezed between the girls and started a random conversation. Rez dressed himself in preparation for the cold; Delilah sat at the bar with Morgan. Her sapphire eyes never looked away from Tyria, not even as she walked in Tyria's direction, bull in a China Shoppe, her black spider hair imbued with pink and her face the silver of a knife. She placed a beer in Adelaide's hand and put her hand out for Tyria.

"Come," Delilah said.

She led Tyria to the stage. To step up they had to sturdy themselves on two stacks of newspapers and balance on one another, but once on top nothing could touch them. The vector microphone shined, and the stand was garnished in new expensive chains and silk that was long enough so that she could extend her arms like a great black angel. Delilah gave her the go ahead. Tyria touched the mic, then looked around the room.

"Don't let anything like girlfriends or petty human needs get in the way of art," Delilah said.

"I can try."

"You musn't *try*. You must execute, always. The stage is for you."

"How can you tell?"

"There's a special glow about you, Tyria. You believe, unlike so many others. I can feel the faith flowing through you."

BLOOD KISS

Delilah flipped her spidery hair out of the way to reveal the bird-like face, eyes filled with blue fire. Her aura was assertive for her own good. But it was every time that she opened her mouth that Tyria knew she was different. Her tiny voice was the color of an insubstantiality threatening to topple the universe.

"I am under the impression that you believe as well," Tyria said.

"I've no other choice but to give into *them*."

Delilah smiled.

"There's really no other way."

"I look forward to seeing you perform," Delilah began walking away. "And I don't say that about a lot of people."

To think such a strong girl—a girl who was just as pious in music and art—a girl who fronted a very successful underground band, was lauding her before she even saw the show, made Tyria smile inside. It made her world easier to live in.

"I guess I should say thank you."

"Just do what you do best."

Then Delilah faded away. Tyria noticed how the stage light beamed upon her as if someone had lassoed a star and brought it down to earth. From up here she could see the dark vista of the world. Below, Alex and Rez had their arms around one another; to the left Delilah smoked a black cigarette, her face wincing as if in pain, as if one could get their feelings hurt from a total stranger. Something wretched lived behind Delilah's rictus grin, and with that thought Tyria stepped down from the stage and joined the conversation.

"Ever hear of Electric Orchid?" Alex said in a voice so soft Tyria was almost certain she could taste the color of gold.

"Now I know why you look so familiar. I have a CD of yours."

"Do you like our music?"

"Hell yeah. Do you like poetry?"

"Of course. I came here to *see*."

There was a knock at the door, but before anyone could answer it swung open and someone came in kicking and screaming. It was Dorian. He was severely out of breath but a cigarette was in his hand; he looked like he had just seen a ghost.

"Where the hell were you?" Tyria asked.

"Out there with the fans. So many of them!"

Heavy footsteps ensued. Leland ran into Dorian's arms even before the sound of glee escaped his throat. The boys reunited as if they had been separated by war and famine and feuding families.

"I sooooo missed you," Leland said.

"Hug me tighter, baby."

Leland jumped up, wrapped his legs around Dorian's waist and they fell into the wall, against all the paintings, the brushes and the vials of blood. Tyria could still feel their stare numb as shadow. Leland's mouth was planted on Dorian's, his hand raking through the black oily mop of Dorian's hair. Tyria felt remotely jealous.

"Why does it feel like it's been forever?" Dorian said.

Their mouths touched again, eyes closed as romantic lovers do.

Leland leaned back. "You taste different."

"It's just my smokes. I switched to Newports."

When the boys finished searching for one another's heart after being separated for so long, there came another round of introductions. Alex and Rez stood back as if frightened by Dorian's dark grace, and *this is Delilah the scariest girl alive*, as Delilah offered nothing but a nod. Tyria had never seen Leland so excited, so giddy. His smile was natural, beautiful; nothing about this moment was forced. He had missed Dorian so much, and that made Tyria feel like utter shit. She had done him wrong, so wrong.

"Fraternal twins," Rez said in the color of autumn.

"But separated at birth," said Delilah

"So how did you two get back together?" Tyria asked.

"Oh, that's a long story!" Delilah said. "Better fit for another day."

BLOOD KISS

Now that Tyria had gotten a decent look at the sharp plains of their faces, the matching sapphire eyes and the small pale hands, she knew they were in fact twins. Delilah smiled, and so did Rez, as if they had read her mind.

"I like that necklace, Alex," Tyria said.

"An orchid," holding up the silver charm. "And yours is ohm."

"You must know about magick."

"I am openly Pagan."

"You're agnostic!" Rez said.

"Am so *Pagan*."

"Then why did you make me take Baphomet off our mantel?"

"Because Baphomet is represented wrongly! Idiots connect Baphomet with Satanism. I'm not into that shit."

"Neither am I," said Dorian.

"Speaking of Satan, why don't you tell me about your work."

Dorian laughed at the joke, but immediately opened his heart and his mind. The secret tongue of art-speak filled the room fast. Tyria understood some of it being she had spent so much time with Dorian, but a lot of it made her think about other things. When Dorian unraveled the triptych from its strings Delilah gasped; Rez's kohl eyeliner suddenly ran down his face.

The panels were more alive than ever. Black clouds simmered, and bones shivered. The skull-face had lips made of scales, and when it opened its mouth one could see down its abyssal throat. Delilah stuck her finger into it, and the thing clamped down. She screamed, kicked Dorian's leg, and the visage let go.

"That fucking hurt," she said.

"I'm sorry it did that to you."

"But I'm not." She sucked her bleeding finger. "Now I know I'm in the right place."

"A little spice and something not so nice," Dorian said

"Alex?" Rez said

He didn't answer, too transfixed upon a very poetic piece. Long strips of meat glittered wetly; the background seemed to be made of smoke and mirrors where the creature Baphomet stood in angst. *Something is watching me*, Alex said. Just then Morgan came down from his platform, but he refused to look at the paintings directly.

"I know all about their tricks," Morgan said.

Dorian rolled his eyes. "There are no tricks."

"Yo, I know what I saw."

"Why don't you go then?"

"Nah, yo, the money is too good."

"Hey, Morgan. Shut up," Delilah said. "These are like nothing I've ever seen. They're so . . ."

"*Alive*," Rez filled in the blank.

"They're just paintings," Adelaide said. "Stupid globs of jelly on a fucking canvas. They're not alive at all."

"Maybe you're afraid that *you* are the reason they're aching so," Delilah said, lighting a clove.

"I just don't care about the hocus pocus crap!"

"Don't disrespect my work right before I make you a whole lot of money," Dorian said.

"Half of those people are my clients," Adelaide said.

"They used to be your clients. Tyria and I are the ones they want to see. Do you really fucking think they came here for a good high?"

Adelaide's face turned crimson. "You prick."

"No more arguing," Tyria said.

"You can't put labels on people like that, yo," Morgan said. "People can be fans of whatever and whoever they want. They don't belong to any single group."

"He makes a lot of sense for a meth-head," Alex said.

Dorian scooped up some of his smaller pieces and hung them along the periphery of the room; if an easel was available he put up the bigger paintings. Delilah helped him set up the three panels directly next to the stage. She opened its folds as if she was spreading her own clit, tiny pale hand reaching out to touch something that just wasn't there; but

BLOOD KISS

Rez was doing the same thing. The two of them took on a moony glow

"What is it?" Rez whispered.

"Something is wrong," Delilah said.

Alex took his place behind the bar, a long table fronted by two huge lava lamps. Morgan put up banners of black and silver, dashed confetti all over the floor and placed glow sticks in buckets at the door. Rez headed outside as Adelaide and Leland discussed the rest of the plans.

"Everything's in order," Delilah said. "But one thing I know is that when I'm putting on a show I need curtains."

She had taken the liberty of wrapping a big black sheet around two poles sort of like a Chinese room divider. Tyria nodded in thanks, studied Delilah one last time. Something was odd about her, something much deeper than anyone she had met besides Dorian. She was a haunt made flesh.

STEP RIGHT UP. See the march of the pigs. Here they come in waves of smoke and song.

Queer boi and boy alike, transgender, transvestite and human detritus who divide the line between gender and sex. They come curious for the thrill, the avenge, and the madness. But every footstep gets them closer to the end of the beginning. Might it lead them into temptation or might it deliver them from evil?

They enter the room of choice. Each factory style window is laved in thin ribbons of ice. Green and purple glow sticks are donned like rave jewelry, or a fallen angel's halo. Faces change in the light of the candles; teeth glow like zombie infection. A young metal head touches the window and leaves behind the ghost of his handprint. A few girls complain about the feeling of fright.

But the bodies don't stop coming.

Their faces fall into shock and elation as they gaze into Dorian's art; it is a spiritual alchemy. Because each piece is a literal piece of Dorian, and it is too hard to turn away once the colors have latched onto you. Those splotches of dark red are truly his blood, that pale stain truly his semen.

"What madness is in his head?" A girl said.

"Something truly fucked up. Didn't you read the papers?"

"Ew! This one spit on me!"

More people walked in, pointing at the wall, and Tyria did not know how she had missed it before. *INNOCENCE LOST* and *I AM A MENTAL MOSH PIT . . . HE MADE ME LIKE IT* and *THIS IS HOW A GIRL MUST LEARN TO FIGHT BACK*. All scrawled in bright green chalk. Chalk the color of Tyria's eyes.

"Who did that?" Tyria said.

"Me," Dorian's elf smile.

"Why?"

"Because your words are eternal. And this."

He pulled out the plague mask. "To protect you."

"From what?"

"*Them*."

Outside, Thames Street was alive with bodies, reaching all the way to the Morgan Avenue station in a fleshy twist. She could smell their myriad scents of patchouli, ginger spice, incense and frankincense. The magic of throwing a good party lies in its patrons. Somehow when random people see a line around the block, they are naturally compelled to check out the place for themselves.

"We're going to become scars upon these people's minds," Dorian said.

He put his hands on her belly. Tyria removed them, but it was too late. Adelaide's mouth had fallen open. She could have swallowed the earth. But Leland was quick to distract her, opening her big messenger bag to start the sale of the night's fun. Tyria focused her attention back to the crowd to take in their growing energy; she could feel their minds becoming comfortably numb. And then Leland came back.

"I talked her into not going crazy . . . at least for now."

"Keep her that way," Dorian said.

BLOOD KISS

"She said that Tyria was pregnant, that *you're* the father, Dorian."

Dorian looked straight at Tyria who let her head hang down.

"You just had to, didn't you?" Dorian said.

Leland's face morphed into a most heartbreaking look. "Tell me she's fucking lying."

"It's not about who's to blame right now. We have a show—"

Leland interrupted. "Yeah . . . the show."

Tyria closed her eyes, did not want to see Dorian's face. The circle was complete. Everyone knew. What's done is done.

"We have to move on," Dorian said.

There was only one path to follow, and that was to the stage. Leland clapped his hands for silence, shed light upon the Chinese divider and set the smoke machine to full power. Tyria crouched down and Dorian as well, waiting on the cue of Morgan's experimental music.

Symbiosis.

Susurrations and cigarette smoke; the room is almost too dark to see.

Feedback rises and neon spirals downward; strobe lights melt over everything like a hallucinogenic sauce.

Tyria attached the chains and lace to her black gloves and then gripped the microphone. To her left Dorian and Leland were in a heated exchanged, confessing sins or repenting, she would never know. By the time they were done Dorian had begun to sweat and Leland entered the DJ booth with Morgan, dimming the lights like at the theater. Tyria watched the curtain sway, then whispered into the mic.

"Somebody has to crucify me."

At the sound of her voice the audience began to clap and whistle; not even a second later the music let loose. Morgan's fingers were daddy longlegs manipulating synthesizers and percussion beats. Tyria saw the green glow of musical notes like fireflies as a snare drum fronted her grand entrance. The soliloquy left her tongue.

"I am filthy." She slid a hand over her belly. "Because of what he put inside me."

The hands of the crowd rose in worship, their wrists marked by familiar swollen scars, necessary demons. Their bodies jived and dipped in motion. Something in the way they danced, feral, even tribal, inspired her.

"Where was God when he took me? Where was God when he poisoned my womb?"

When the curtain dropped she felt a holy light drizzle down her skin. Tyria pulled the phosphorescence into her body, saw that the shadow thrown behind her spread like bat wings. Her arms and legs defied volition; she swayed, hung her head down, and then put her lips against the mic.

"Darklings," she said softly. "I want you all to see with my words."

A power chord rang out as Tyria rumbled and roared. But before she could say her next line she caught sight of Delilah, Alex and Rez. They were pious and engaged; their eyes spoke of the seven wonders. Would she become the living, breathing eighth wonder?

"I want to tell you about a girl who's only dream was to be like everyone else, because it was so much easier to fit in than be herself."

Below her the crowd had come so close, their eyes sharp as their colored butane lighters. Green flames, blue flames, red flames, followed the by welcoming aroma of sweet and spicy grass.

"But one day she realized that there was no escaping her past. She could never be one of them because of it. And so she snapped and went on the attack."

The high notes of a piano crashed, a guitar strummed in drop D tuning. Then came the sound of trains and the hair-raising screech of nails down a chalk board, followed by wood snapping and bricks tumbling. Someone's murderous scream cut into the flesh of every listener. Tyria stomped to the rhythm and yelled throatily.

"It's not her fault, you know. She never knew any better! She had to learn how to fight in order to make everything right. But this world would not let her, so she gave herself to him, loosened up her hips . . . and allowed him to *stick it in*!"

Something tore inside her throat; she immediately tasted blood. But the momentum was too strong for her to stop screaming. She threw the Ray Bans off her face and replaced them with the plague mask. The world before her changed, plague doctor, executioner. She became the gloomy countenance.

The feel of the room evolved, inexorable, and the music blossomed into something of a new nature. Tyria saw how it commanded the crowd, their participation in the show now as important as her own. Flesh claws began tearing apart the glow sticks, throwing the neon juice everywhere.

"These are my secrets and my deceptions."

Down at her feet the smoke machine vomited sparks. She became enveloped in the mists of cool blue and the blood red of the stage lights, biting her lip and scraping her teeth across the head of the microphone in a ripping static force. The crowd took one step back.

"I am asking her to come . . . ignite, Goddess, we will unite!"

Dorian rose out of his dark corner, head lolling dangerously on that delicate stem of neck. His tattoos seemed alive in the heat and decadence. But it was his cue, and so he lit a bushel of sage, then dropped it into the bowl of offerings for the goddess Hecate: twigs of myrrh and saffron leaves for the crossroads.

"I bring this to you, for I seek your truth," Tyria said.

The crowd wailed, tongues drawn out and drool running down their chins. On the mark Tyria poured a fine white line of powder on her hand and snorted. The cocaine was a rip tide in her brain, a molecular cataclysm. She felt a flower that never was there bloom carrion as the growing womb-monster protested the drug no matter how much her cells craved it. If she had to get rid of it here, she didn't see the harm in reaching her hand all the way up her pussy and ripping it out herself.

"Take me," Tyria sung.

Her pose demonic as Dorian's was reverent. All around her the portraits were dripping blood and semen; a miasma of meat and feet and morning breath hit the air. Yet all attention was still on Tyria, bat-winged, black chains, a fallen angel in genuflection.

She clawed deeply into her flesh. Meat parted painfully, and instead of wiping her clean Dorian dipped his brush into the wound. When he drew the red arc across the triptych's landscape the slack jaw skull smiled horribly. Its mouth un-

BLOOD KISS

leashed a furred tongue that fell like rope across Dorian's boots. The smell of it was impossibly sweet as Tyria stole the mic again.

> *What's inside of me*
> *I do not accept as destiny*
> *It is the dark intricacy*
> *Of blaspheme*
> *That has infected me with complacency!*

The roar sent a shockwave down to the cornerstone of the building. The foundation split in two, everyone now divided by metal and dust; in the back the windows billowed with ice. But the crowd did not fear the unknown; they embraced it. They threw their hands up in a drunken dance; their bodies found a new way to gyrate, lips pressed together, teeth drawing blood and faces smeared in it.

"I refuse, I refuse, I refuse your temptation! I will not surrender. I am revolt."

Now her eyes were on the second panel. The xylophone ribs burst like brittle twigs in autumn, spraying the crowd in bone dust and blood and imploring each patron to take a seat. But rest was not for them; instead, they take turns playing with the proverbial fire, jumping over the chasm to levitate, as others fall straight into the darkness. But they do not stop, cannot stop. They are the true symbiosis, devouring the pent up energy as they allow the show to feed off their souls.

THE END TIMES ARE A SCHISM OF SILVER AND BLUE.

The stage is the final resolution.

Every eye was wide shut during Tyria's immolation. Were they too blind to see the brilliance?

Look at me, I heard something say.

I turned to see something far worse. The triptych was spreading itself in tandem to the music and poetry. Cadaverous wings and virginal legs, a beckoning throat, and as Tyria's lips kissed the microphone again, red as red can be, behind her the shadow grew as large as the room.

I knew that this was my final chance.

My eyes blazed with dead hope as I jumped to my feet to dipped my brush into its strange sensational depths. The triptych shuddered, demanding to have it as well. I could hear it making a grumbling noise, saw its vortex mouth swirl madly. In the back of the loft, separated by the crack in the foundation, Delilah and her twin Rez were trying to make sense of the commotion.

I thought maybe they were the catalysts for this madness, but then I also remembered what Rez had said about Adelaide. When I spotted her in the crowd she was crying, holding her bleeding ears and if something was churning her brain to jelly. There was this moment of guilt and pleasure, a feeling I knew all too well, but I let it slip away. She was of little distraction to my mission.

As Tyria's anger rose like volcanic smoke and with her blood on my brush, I knew what I had to do. The ectoplasm was thicker than expected as my hand grabbed it, and when I spread the liquid nightmare across the canvas I immediately became blasted with bad memories and poetry.

Memories are the shadows of life; they live in the dark spots in our mind—whether good or bad—and are the eternal facets of our existence because memories are what will stay with us until the end. They are the key to true salvation, that is, unless we give into our instincts. And that's what Tyria finally did with her words. She let go of everything, including me.

Too late for the disdain
She cannot change her fate
Because of the hell she was born in
Life is sprung from a thirty-eight week poison

BLOOD KISS

Tyria's voice metamorphosed into something insidious. The sort of sound that the ear raises itself to because it does not recognize the decibel, the kind of sound that you can feel all the way down to the marrow in your bones. A girl began to cry blood tears and the stage threatened to collapse.

In came the godsend.

She stood in gargoyle benediction as the daystar tore a hole into the sky and showered Tyria's body in gaseous light. A scintilla fell to my feet, and when I touched it the particles separated like mercury. I, as well as the crowd, was left confounded. The light had blinded us all. Had the angels come to take her away?

"Get up! Stand up," I yelled into the vector microphone.

But they would not listen. Everything was shaking; the music was unimaginably loud. I stepped off the stage, tripped over the furred tongue and took an unsuspecting seat within the xylophone ribs. Putrescent flesh caressed my face, slithered down my thighs. I began to fear the crowd more than the art, for it was the sea of needy bodies that could swallow me.

But then there came this heavy pang in my heart, a feeling like it was no longer beating, my lungs desperate for air and my brain beginning to shrivel. I was vicariously feeling Leland—joy or sorrow I did not know—as I saw his face white as powder, and the bruise forming beneath his left eye. I reached out to offer him help, fearing that he would soon become a victim of the masses, but he was so transfixed on something that he saw right through me.

I didn't expect it.

Tyria and the plague mask were intensely juxtaposed. She had it propped upon the microphone and was spinning it around. I caught the world through its eyes for a moment, thought how strange it was that a simple mask could change reality so. But the queerest thing was how much it resembled Tyria. When it stopped spinning I saw the mask smile.

"Stop! You're killing her."

Adelaide raced toward me. Her face was streaked in black tears and her eyes dangerous with rage. She grabbed my arm and clawed all the way down to my wrist. Upon instinct I shoved her deep into the crowd, thus which she could not swim her way back.

In my moment of freedom I heard a great dissonance. It spiraled through my nerves, threatening to crumble my focus. At this point I was not myself; my hunt for the shadow had reached its crescendo. I stepped upon the stage and thought I might have heard it speak, something like hate you or *she's mine.*

I took hold of it and pushed the darkness inside the accepting triptych. My arms followed it down the rabbit hole, and I thought to myself that I might stick my head in and find out what death might bring. I felt something like thorns, and my purest intention was to grab it. I didn't care what it was or could be—a skull, a ticket to doom, a cold black heart—I just wanted whatever it was willing to give.

When I pulled my hand out I was filthy with plasma, and I was cupping a living, breathing thing. No certain shape, about the size of football with four flaccid limbs curled into the fetal position. I smelled its infinitesimal bowels, felt the growing hunger. It was as if I'd dug my hand into Tyria's dead cavity and pulled out the bane of our existence.

I imagined that it called me Daddy, that it wanted me to protect it. And so I did what fathers for all eternity have been doing: I put the slippery umbilical cord between my teeth and severed it. I felt a smile stretch my face as little anthracite eyes locked onto my own.

"Son . . . Daughter," I mumbled.

But its hands reached for Tyria, the cradle and womb. I pulled my spawn close to me, studied the planes of its face, the tiny lips, the flaxen hair and vampire frown. This made me understand that procreation is a sort of like an art—all living things are created and are distinctively different—as is art itself.

"Don't you want to know?" I yelled at Tyria.

Now the little demon was gnawing at my hand, hard enough to rip the skin. I threw it down, threatened it with

BLOOD KISS

my raised boot, but it tore half the rubber sole away and ran toward Delilah, who kicked it straight into the breast of a young patron.

The androgyne screamed in sybarite relief. I stood fixated upon the sight of the neonatal monster cleaving its way down her torso, forcing her legs open to climb back inside. I'd never witnessed a live birth, but one thing I did know was that the baby should be pushed out rather than forced in.

Yet never had I seen such pleasure in one's face. Her hair stood up like she'd stuck her tongue in a light socket and her eyes rolled into the back of her head. She lay herself down, surrendering to her own passions. She was all too delighted to be sacrificed for the sake of art.

The crowd cleared a circle. Two kids held her legs open so that we could all see the red eye between her thighs blink once, twice, and then become a gumbo of gore as the demon burrowed deeper into its host. The poor girl died on the dance floor, but so did the demon.

With no soul to feed upon, it could not survive.

I grabbed the carcass and fed the triptych, its colors pulsating. Silver and black swam up my arm, nearly swallowed it. It filled me with feelings of joy and nothingness, and so I stuck my head inside. I felt a great pressure inside my head, brain cells smearing along the strange viaduct. When I pulled myself free the crowd watched aghast as I wiped the vitriol off my face.

Tyria and I had tested their limits. They became angry, scared. They convened, deciding their own strategy. Fists were raised up and teeth were bared. Spiked jewelry became their guiding light. They had formed an old school walking circle pit as Tyria belted out another line.

My skin is no longer my own
Didn't know this had to be written in stone
Destroyed for a blood kiss
Nightmare made flesh
I DESERVE THIS!

The miracle had arrived.

A bright ball of light divided the room, the triplicate road beaming right out of Tyria's ohm necklace. The turmoil showed no end as every painting began to cry out, to bubble; it made my skin flare up with gooseflesh. Then I heard glass breaking, real glass, and felt a cool breeze. Someone had thrown themselves right out the window.

I wanted to run but Tyria had taken the mic off the stand and raised it as if to bash me, but brought it back down and beat her stomach until her mouth was wide with pain and her teeth stained scarlet. When she collapsed the music cut out and Morgan was out the door without so much as a goodbye.

The applause was grand, smiles possessed by rictus. Pale ash exploded out of Tyria's fingertips, covering the room in warm snow. I knew it could only be the sacred Vibhuti ash that Jenny had prophesied.

Holy Reality.

Miracle.

Fate.

Then the need to escape kicked in. The death on the dance floor must have been too real a reality as the crowd filed toward the door. They would soon warn all of Brooklyn about human wreckage and the supernatural as each one of them tore off their dirty clothes, too scared to admit to their own culpable destruction.

BLOOD KISS

21

Someone call an ambulance!"

That was only the beginning of the screams. *She's dead*, the same kid cried out as he pointed to the broken window, and *he's badly hurt*. Leland had to slap himself to wake up from the horrible dream. What had he just seen? But no matter how much he wished, no matter how much he wanted things to have ended differently, nothing had changed at all.

"You can't all go out at once," Leland said.

They were pushing and shoving for the door, and Leland knew that they couldn't all possibly fit, but they were certainly trying. He could hear the desperate and wet glide of their muscles, smelled the fear in their breath and the urine in their pants. All this disorder was certainly a fire hazard; all it would take was one candle to set something aflame and they would all burn.

"Hey," Leland said to Dorian. "Say something."

He was dazed and confused, but somehow coherent in the way he stared. A weird, dry taste coated Leland's tongue, and when he looked deeper into the dark he realized that it was ash, and that it was everywhere. He looked past Dorian to see Tyria lying right side up, catching her breath, lips bubbling red and her hand absently coming up to wipe it clean. There was a long gash across her belly and the blood dripped from it in little red rivulets, the ash marking it black.

"Baby, get up," Adelaide said, wiping blood away with her bare hands.

Dorian turned. "Don't touch her."

"You fuck off!" Adelaide swung her hand around and blood hit Dorian's lips, to which he licked clean.

"You have the fucking nerve . . . you did this to her!"

"This was her choice."

Before Leland could intercept a girl protested loudly. Two tall guys began fighting, one drew out a pocket blade and the other a box cutter. Apparently Box Cutter had pushed Pocket Blade's girlfriend down and there was hell to pay. Box Cutter took a swing, and the blade whispered through the thick air, but Pocket Blade backed off fast, cowering into the cover of the crowd.

"I want everyone to back the fuck up!"

A drag queen took off her heel and hit a girl in the head. Beads rattled and filled the puddle of blood on the dance floor. A punk in a leather jacket spit in the face of a guy who was blocking the exit as another girl began to cry in fear of suffocating. They were all beginning to hate one another, soon there would be a rumble.

"Stop!"

Leland whistled and made them form a line. In times of panic, people surreptitiously seek a leader. But even in their calm state all the heads kept turning toward Dorian and Tyria; their faces were reverent.

"I saw oblivion," a girl with a choker collar said.

"It was more like the birth of death."

Dorian nodded, ran his hand through his black hair without saying a word. In the meantime Adelaide left Tyria's side, came up right being Leland. There was unexplainable rage in her face, and she dragged him to the window without saying a word. He instantly smelled the cold night air laced with cigarette smoke and diesel fumes. A most decadent odor.

"Look down there!"

"I don't want to see it," Leland said.

"I'm sorry, Landy, but you have to!"

BLOOD KISS

All of a sudden his eye ached. The ghostly memory of Adelaide's elbow making him see red, gold and neon sparks haunted his vision.

"I won't accept it, Addy."

"Fine. Stay ignorant."

They were quiet for a moment. "How much did we make?"

Adelaide's skinny body tensed. "Is that what you're concerned about, the money?"

"We put *everything* into this show. I don't feel guilty for wanting to get *paid* for it."

"A girl is dead, Landy. The one outside is likely to die as well."

"Oh, gods . . ."

"And I don't feel like getting arrested."

The moaning began as something faint, something that could have been coming from a loud television set a few doors down. But when Leland stuck his head out the window he followed the sound of the scream down into the street: a kid with both of his legs twisted horribly, the bones ripped through his jeans so that Leland spotted the jellied meniscus and the flaccid anterior cruciate ligament. Each head that surrounded the body turned toward Leland, their eyes connecting the dots.

"I'm calling the police, you fucking freaks," a hipster said, shuddering.

When Leland got his head back inside Adelaide was right in his face.

"I told you. Now come."

She forced Leland to inspect the dance floor. There was blood and paint and a strange sticky substance. Adelaide gasped at the sight of a tooth laying on the bar top. Leland picked it up reluctantly, and then threw it over his shoulder. When it hit the floor he noticed a rope of pink and black hair, hair that had been ripped from the root. That was when Delilah slithered out of the dark, holding her bleeding head. Alex and Rez were tending the wounds with bar napkins.

"It fucking bit me," Delilah said.

"Are you okay?" Leland's failed apology.

"I thought Electric Orchid was spooky, but you have us beat. Consider me a fan."

"You really put together something special, Landy," Alex said.

"We went out with a bang, literally."

Rez's eyes opened wide. "Art will always go on. Just like *her* black soul."

Adelaide snarled, but before she could get a word in Alex, Rez and Delilah were gone. They took with them the smell of clove cigarettes and Jägermeister. The room felt rather empty now, hollowed by the echoes of the patrons.

"That tall fuck bolted too," Adelaide said.

"We'll deal with him later. We have bigger fish to fry right now."

Thus the clean up had begun. Adelaide knew what to do. Leland started in the back, pushed all the detritus to the center, disregarding Dorian's tears and Tyria's exorcised state, her green eyes locked onto the ceiling.

"Why aren't you both helping?" Leland said. "You're not fucking rock stars. I'm not your roadie!"

Dorian didn't even turn toward him. "Just thinking about how we're going to fix this."

"Mother . . . mother . . . are they going to take me away?" Tyria sang.

All eyes were on the dead body. Leland gagged upon initial inspection, the young thing he remembered so full of life but now her flesh was slippery and gray, the inside of her thighs ripped to the glittering meat beneath. Her blood glowed black in the moonlight, and something else was there too. Its teeth were white and its eyes glowed like coals, but it was dead as her. Leland couldn't stop looking, thinking. Oh, how much trouble they were in. But then a hand on his shoulder, fingers like an arrow.

"We're fucking done for," Adelaide said. "I'm gunna kill him for doing this."

BLOOD KISS *Daniel Stone*

Leland didn't even turn around. "We're all in this together."

Adelaide huffed and puffed, curled her fists and hit herself on top of the head. "And you still protect him!"

"We're fucking fried no matter who's to blame," Leland said.

"Don't you think I know that? People like us, the junkies, we know death and become immune to the consequences."

"When will you all shut up!"

Now the Queen of Decay rising, face flushed in a horrible sweat, and *I felt it*, she said. *The Goddess came to me.* Dorian helped her down from the stage, lit a cigarette and took a step back. Tyria's dangerous jade eyes met Leland's, Adelaide's, then sailed upward as if looking for a star to wish upon.

" 'Then from his mouth the serpent spewed water like a river, to overtake the woman and sweep her away with the torrent,' " Tyria quoted. "The Dragon Persecutes the Woman. Revelation 12:15."

No one made any certain moves, too afraid to break her trance, too afraid she might kill everyone in sight.

"You wanted to scar yourself upon these people, Dorian. Well, you got your damn wish."

Her teeth and tongue were red, and she said that she could still taste the blood. Two beers later Tyria was righted, understanding of the destruction and of the guilt. But nothing seemed to make sense to her. There was a gap in her memory she couldn't figure out.

"What do we do about *this*?" Leland said.

"Get rid of it!"

"How do you suppose?" Tyria said.

"You're a believer ain't you?"

Dorian gripped the dead girl's hair, pulled her out of the muck that was her blood, shit and urine. It stained the dance floor darkly. There was this awful sucking noise as if her hair follicles were separating from the scalp, but as Dorian dragged her into the shadows everything came full circle. He lit two votive candles, placed one at the top of her head and one at the girl's bare pale feet.

"So they can *see*," he said.

Tyria moved closer to the body as if she'd seen something so huge, so impossible that it frightened her to stay. Dorian positioned the three panels in a triangular shape then took a step back, smirking. A tongue burst out of canvas like a tendril and wrapped around the girl's ankle, slowly pulling her into its gullet until it was as if she had never existed.

"And now there's nothing to worry about," Dorian said

Tyria smiled; everyone else's mouth was wide open, Dorian now the official king of hoodoo. Leland, for the first ever in Dorian's presence, felt fear. But Adelaide was the most shocked of all.

"I won't let him destroy me."

Leland reached out to grab her but she was too fast, too enraged. She slipped on the blood and fell down face first, the metallic smell rising fresh as a wound. When she righted herself her eyes were blowtorch nightlights attacking Dorian's triptych. She kicked down the easels with the intent to stomp on them, or maybe throw them out the window.

But only the easel fell. The paintings remained in the air.

Adelaide opened her mouth to scream but the slack jaw skull spit out its furred tongue and filled her mouth; the xylophone ribs creaked open like a wet coffin as it pulled her closer and closer.

"Make it stop, Dorian," Leland said.

He didn't react, rather, he enjoyed this hallucinogenic trip into hell. But Leland would have no more magic, gripped Dorian's face and demanded that he let her go as Adelaide's face was going blue. Dorian snapped his finger; Adelaide fell to the floor and pulled her knees up to her chest.

"It's amazing what you can do with a little faith," Dorian said.

Leland shook his head. "Why did you do that?"

"Because now I am the master."

BLOOD KISS

Tyria ran to Adelaide's aide and Leland pulled Dorian to the side.

"Real funny. You know she's sensitive."

"I don't know what you see in that joke of a human being."

Leland didn't want to argue here, not after the successes and the destruction, but Dorian had it coming. If he didn't open his mouth now maybe he would never understand.

"I keep her around because she doesn't want to betray or hurt me like you do."

"What do you mean?"

"I have no fucking clue who you even are anymore."

"Don't say that."

"I know it to be true. That thing inside of Tyria is *yours*."

"I don't want to hurt you, Landy." Dorian's finger caressed his hot cheek.

"Don't touch me," tears burning, so heavy on his face. "I've fallen for your tricks long enough. I smile and forget and brush them off because that's the healthiest way to deal with things. I forgive, because I know that it took a long time for the people I loved to forgive me for being a junky. But this . . . this is an atrocity."

"Landy please don't talk like that," Dorian's voice grew weak. "I need you."

Leland knew that Dorian didn't need anyone or anything accept his own ego. With this acceptance, he could let go of Dorian, could willingly let him transcend his own art and be with Tyria. She was the only one that brought out this new beast. They were better together than apart.

"You don't need me. You need power," Leland said.

"Don't walk away from me!"

Leland put his hand out to stop Dorian from following him. "You know, the strangest thing is that I thought I once needed you too."

Dorian's eyes began to fill with tears.

"I'm going home and packing my things. I'm done being played a fool."

He found the door and slammed it shut, but Dorian was already after him, ebullient in silent rage. Leland could not stop running, so fast, so wicked, so clear! He would not give anymore spooks his attention, not even the paintings that were levitating by the stairs. Organs oozed blood and penises dripped chemical come, but Leland kept going with no real mission in mind, no real plan, but anything was better than here.

IT WAS LIKE WAKING UP IN A NEW LIFE, as if some portion of her brain had been drained through her ears, the weight of emotion and darkness turned farce. Her stomach burned and her throat ached, but the divine light had touched her. There was a way out after all, she only had to see it to believe it.

For some reason she was thinking about Delilah. Had the light touched her too? Or had the shadow come down full force? Though she was gone—her brother and best friend too—and though she had only known her for a short period of time, Delilah had left quite the impression on Tyria. She hoped to one day see her again, sister of the moon, friend and foe.

Someone was yelling now, a voice that she knew, but sounded wrong when it got angry. Leland. His aura was no longer the cool blue that she was used to, but a fiery orange. She saw Dorian's head hanging down like a scolded child, which made his hair cover his face. Then Leland bolted for the door. Dorian looked at Tyria as if he needed some mystical permission, and so she nodded for him to go.

She pulled her head back into the room, letting her final thought of Delilah go out the window. It was still dark out, the sky black and pricked with stars like broken teeth. Tyria knew that millions of kids were wishing upon them, but what they didn't know was that when you wish upon a star your

BLOOD KISS

dreams can never come true. Every star you see is light-years away, and by the time your voice is carried to it that star is already dead, just like your dreams.

The stars were simply a tease.

She took in a great gulp of air and it felt like her lungs would freeze. There should have been no one on the street in this cold, but down there the kids were still careening, still threatening to call the cops. She saw the poor sod with his legs twisted to the other side of his body, felt his pain momentously. In some strange way Tyria wished that for herself, but then she looked up at the stars and flicked them off.

Back inside she pulled up her shirt and confronted her battle scars. The welts and scratches were still raw, bubbling with black blood from the ash that filled the room. The metallic taste in her throat was still fresh. To her right Adelaide was curled in a ball, afraid of Dorian or contemplating his doom. Either was a reasonable conclusion. In retrospect she thought that what Dorian had done was mean, but in the end it was necessary for self-expression.

Tyria kneeled. "Addy, get up."

"No. I'm scared."

"You're not scared. You're just defeated."

"I *am* scared. I don't know you anymore."

"But I love you, still." How does one go about telling their lover that they have someone else's child growing inside of them? How does one go about asking forgiveness for the unforgivable?

"There's not much to talk about," Adelaide said. "I hate him."

"What about me?"

Adelaide sighed. "A true disappointment."

The color of her words were too dark to see. "Addy, please. Hit me, tell me I'm a fucking cunt-whore! Anything but that!"

"I can't tell you that I hate you. That would be a lie. Dorian is hate. You are not."

"But Dorian—"

"You love him. I can feel it."

"Not in the same way I love you."

Adelaide lifted her head and for a second made eye contact. "Love is love, and you let him slide right inside you. The price is yours to pay."

"Are we lovers or enemies?" Tyria's voice was deep and throaty.

"You and Dorian are meant for each other."

"It's not like that at all, Addy."

"*Symbiots.*"

Tyria rolled her eyes.

"Yet for some sick reason I can't stop loving you. I'm an addict one way or another.

"Nothing's changed," Tyria said.

"Nothing has changed for *you*, but it's a whole new fucking universe for me, Ty. You broke my damn heart."

Tyria could not stop the blood from rushing to her face and the tears streaming down to cool it. This was the moment she feared her entire life: losing someone she deeply cared for.

"How can we fix this?"

Adelaide put out her hand for Tyria. Her familiar smell of sage and cigarette smoke wafted; memories filled Tyria's head like an ache she would never escape. She wanted to fold Adelaide up to keep her safe in her pocket. Tyria stroked her long black hair, kissed her soft lips, then cradled her head and rocked back and forth.

"Take off the sunglasses," Adelaide said. "I wanna see your beautiful face."

"You know how I feel about them."

"With me, you're safe."

When she took off the Ray Bans Tyria saw her own reflection and almost freaked. A ghost of pale green eyes and bright yellow hair stared at her through the lens. What she thought would be Adelaide's reflection was something fluid and black, but cellular.

BLOOD KISS

"What are you seeing?"

"Nothing," Tyria said. "It's nothing."

"Please tell me because I don't want to be crazy!" Adelaide shot right to her feet.

"Where the hell are you going?"

"I can't be in this room with *them*."

Tyria saw the paintings levitating, coming closer to Adelaide. They were all yawning, perhaps trying to protect their maker, or to see to it that Adelaide could not hurt him.

"Go away," Tyria said. "Addy close your eyes and count to ten."

"No! Rez said that I'm the beacon, that I'm haunted."

And then Tyria could see the true fear.

"You should go before the shit really hits the fan."

"I ain't going anywhere. You know I don't believe anyone but myself."

"But the way Rez knows things about the dark, him and Delilah might be darkness itself."

"That doesn't mean you're haunted."

"I *know* that I'm the catalyst to your ghost. But I also know it's only because you haven't dreamed of him," Adelaide said. "Your father. You haven't dreamed of him."

Tyria choked on her cigarette.

"Dorian dropped his seed inside and you didn't even put up a fight. Why didn't you at least stick a tube up there and suck it out?"

"I . . . I don't know . . ."

"When I saw Dorian push that dark thing into the painting I felt this anger boil over. I took it out on Landy, took it out on the crowd. I couldn't control myself. It was as if I was hoping it would devour him."

"What are you talking about?" Tyria said.

"It was oh, so surreal. But I knew that was the moment that you belonged to him. He saved you. I tried to do that for so long, and he stole my opportunity in front of my face."

Tyria didn't speak.

"I'll never forgive you for that."

"Why?"

"Because you allowed it. You betrayed me."

Tyria reached to bring her closer. "Addy, please."

"Don't touch me."

"But I need you!"

"This is where I say goodbye. This is where I walk out of here with my tail between my legs because you did me wrong."

Adelaide kissed Tyria on her cheek and found the door quickly. The sound of it closing was as loud as Tyria's heartbeat. With nothing left to turn to except the paintings, Tyria took in a deep breath and let out a roar so deep, so concentrated, it shook the entire foundation. The force pulled apart the paintings and blew every window clear out of the frame.

BLOOD KISS *Daniel Stone*

22

Leland blazed through the crisscrossing streets of Thames, Bogart and Flushing Avenue, a firefly burning out its effervescent light. He didn't stop to help the kid who'd shattered both of his legs, didn't bother with the girl yapping about the cops and club drugs. He was his own beast now, and he was hungry as the wind.

Being that I saw no ambulance or authorities in sight, I found it my duty to at least inspect the urchin out of child-like curiosity. The spectrum of pain on his face was clear; his makeup was smeared like my own palette. But by the time I kneeled down to offer my helping hand, he was no longer making any noise.

"You ruined something beautiful," I told him.

The boy's eyes rolled into the back of his head, but he said, "I needed to get out of there."

A great wave of ennui came over me, and I could think of nothing other than spitting in his face to alleviate it. Cruel and insulting, but the kid did not even blink as the mucus gormed his left eye; it was as if he was focused on something that I could not see. Then he lay his head on the cement and never looked back.

A passerby judged me in horror, but I ignored her as I had my own thing to do: find Landy. I hadn't seen which way he turned, but he had left a warpath in the snow, and I could smell his cigarette smoke that still lingered thickly in the winter air. I jetted toward Flushing Avenue, just in time to see him turning the corner.

"Leland, stop!"

He would not listen to me. He ran, as did I, and we passed horrible sights. Night is a time for introspection or dissection; the cover of darkness allows you to do such. But East Williamsburg *changes* at night, threatens to implode. Everything metamorphosed, the shivering horde of buildings, the rickety concrete. I looked for answers between the cracks while everyone else was just hopping over them, unaware of the hell below their feet.

I saw the outline of bodies making love in warehouse lofts, people in dives drinking well shots, craft beer and dropping tabs of street acid. Winos ravaged with cirrhosis—their skin yellow as the sun, eyes webbed horribly red—were on the hunt for the next quick fix. I saw a shadow—or maybe the memory of it was so fresh it stained my vision—spilled upon the tarmac. But it was so unlike Tyria's. It was lissome and bore no weight; nothing of true consistency. I could not hold it, could not fathom its depths. I realized that it was Leland's, feathery as his bones, a gentle adjunct to his heart.

"Landy!"

There was no sincere way I could apologize to him; no way I could scoff up the courage and suffer the proverbial "let me make it up to you." He knew this and I knew this, which is why he kept running. The truth enraged me so; it made everything in the world that I loved pointless.

"Stop!"

I thought of the billions of ways in which I could start the conversation. *I need you*, as I played out the ridiculous scenario in my head. *You are my all. Please forgive me for fathering a child you and I do not even want. Please take me back even though I stuck my dick in her.*

A sudden splash of light warmed my cold face. Flushing Avenue was full of cars and diesel trucks; hipsters played hacky sack and laughed loudly. Leland tore through the commotion, ran his hands along the windows of 983 Bushwick's Living Room and Catland esoterica. The abutting wall had a peeling sticker on it that said *SILENCE IS NOT DEFIANCE*. Naturally it made me think of Tyria.

BLOOD KISS

"I don't want to see you," Leland wailed.

We came full circle. He stopped, caught his breath. I saw little beads of sweat form at the top of his lovely brow. I found cover in the wavering crowd, fell headlong into a game of hacky sac as Leland scoured the block to make sure that he'd lost me. His chin hit his chest like a dog's tail between its legs as he was swallowed by the enchanting red glow of the closest bar: Wreck Room.

I kicked the hacky sac to the next vacant face and bulleted after him. The first thing that hit me was the bar-stink, the way a neglected beer smells after a few days, the way smoke settles atop wood floorboards. I admired the neon-emblazoned graffiti like a psychedelic dream. The music that played was spun by a DJ, which made me think of Morgan.

QUEER NIGHT said the bright banner.

A few stoners occupied the lounge area, tired limbs drooping over old car seats that gave off that great dirty stink that comes with aged polyester. Wreck Room was literally a wreck, and the music selection was always too outré for my taste.

"Leland," I said.

"Why can't you just lose me already?"

He didn't turn around, ordered a Genesee and a well shot, took down the whiskey like it was water—and I knew he did not like whiskey. I did the same, paid my lousy three dollars to loosen the cogs in my mind. That's when three girls walked in, stared me down, their clothes wet with a familiar substance, their pupils drug-dilated.

Gossip began: *Can you believe what we just saw?* one girl said. *He fell out of a window, high on molly. And that guy spit on him like he was gutter trash. Everyone's talking about magick and spooks. Maybe the people at Catland organized it.*

I said, "It was not that at all, you dumb fucks."

"You're the painter," one of the girls said.

I tsked. "The only thing you know about me is what I sold ya."

The girl was not happy. "Why would you do such a thing?"

"Because I can."

No one spoke for a good minute. So then I did. "Wanna see a magic trick?"

I smashed a glass on the bar top, fully aware of my new strength, and the pain did not hit me before I felt the warm spread of blood. *Watch this,* I said. Something sinister came to mind. A spiral, the wettest cigarette burn, my finger now a thing of its own mind. Circles into circles, a jubilee of red on the brick wall.

Ride the Spiral, I said, and grabbed the first head of hair I found—the girl with cat's eyes glasses and dreads down to her flat ass. Her hand broke through the brick wall as if it was a cobweb, her face delighted as the blood-spiral swallowed her limb whole. Her friends joined the camaraderie, testing the questionable vessel and drinking its metaphysical offerings—until the bartender screamed STOP!

"Take your hocus pocus next door. I'm sure they're worshiping Pazuzu as we speak."

"I want more," the girls said in unison.

Leland was not amused. His eyes were steady with impatience. I asked the girls to leave us and tended to my wounds with bar napkins, held so much pressure I thought I was going to pop a joint. Somehow the bartender went back to work like nothing happened as the gossip queens picked up their things and chivied to the pool table to play an innocent game.

"There was a time I'd run to your aide in a second," Leland said.

"And what's changed?"

"You're not the man I know anymore."

Too much red on the napkin, and so I used another. "I still love you."

"You didn't even have the decency to tell me yourself. I had to find out from Addy, which to me is a bigger punishment."

BLOOD KISS

"Why is that a bigger punishment?"

"Because I had to keep her sane when all I wanted to do was explode too!"

I reached out to grab that filthy twisted hair, wanted to kiss those flower petal lips so badly. *You are the only boy for me*, I thought. *You complete me*. But Leland was hardly into me, said that I was heading down a black hole, that I used to be somebody he knew, that the man he sees now is just a flesh-doll, a shadow. That stung.

"Leland—"

"What's the point of me loving you if you're going to stick your dick in the first pussy that crosses your path?"

Teeth gritting, jaw pain. "It's not like that at all."

"She's knocked up, ain't she?"

"I don't know anymore."

"Stop lying."

Then hands on his face, leaning into me so that I could smell his hair. He uncrossed his legs and flexed his waist either to tease me or show me what I was missing. I ordered a shot of Jäger and swallowed it down in one delicious brown burn until it took away the pain in my finger and in my heart.

"I *need* you."

"All you need is art, and power."

"*You*," I growled.

My hand placed itself upon his knee, and I could not stop its trajectory. I saw my fingers crawl up his strong thigh, then slip into his crotch. White-Knuckled and grabbing so hard that I ripped his jeans and drew blood. But Leland grew instantly hard, bringing his lips against my neck so that all of the room scolded us in jealousy.

But that did not matter. I had the love of my life back, my original muse. Gravity loosened itself from my bones and blood; the gods had no place in the whirling universe. Leland's touch sent an immediate charge to my soul and a fire set inside my heart. Our lips touched, our tongues darted for each other's, and for one divine moment everything seemed right.

"Not here," Leland said. "Downstairs."

The sound of his wingtip boots clacking against the floor was the most inviting thing I'd heard in a long time. My nose flared to his smoky trail of boy sweat, cheap soap and liquor. As we descended the stairs I found it to be the most frightening experience of my life; I might have been swallowed, become prisoner to peristalsis.

There was no light but the dull pulse of red neon like a dying vascular system, and it was so catastrophically cluttered with boxes and ephemera it was a wonder the propulsion of gravity didn't cause us to slip and fall. I recalled a scene out of *The Exorcist* when Father Karras threw himself out the window after beating the devil out of Regan, crash landing down the stairwell, splitting his skull in two and shattering his spine.

The walls were a freak show of graffiti, stickers and local art ads. *SyNeRgY* and *SyNtHeSiS* bisected the wretched *SyMbIoSiS* that seemed ready to burst like insect pupae; *EYE SEE NO END* and *ANGELS SPEAK, DEVILS BLEED* a horrible milieu of words leading us to the cramped bathroom stall.

"I want to feel you," Leland said, pulling me close. "Was she this crazy about you?"

"Must we talk about her?"

Leland's hand ran through my hair and his tongue left a slimy smear across my lips to mark his territory. If he was looking for atonement or retribution he need not seek it for I was always his from the start. His kiss was always the sweetest, his fuck the grimiest, but I'd never tell him how dangerous Tyria's love was.

When he let me go he arched his back against the sink, craned his neck and opened his legs for me to see the outline of his shaft. The wound spread furiously across his pale hairless thigh, and my bloodied finger outlined the small furrow like a mouse sniffing for cheese before I dug it into precious tissue. He did not squeal nor retract his leg; just sat there smiling, shivering with pleasure.

BLOOD KISS

"Everything you hate about me hides inside you," I said. "Let's get rid of it."

My finger deep dived, dragging until I heard his skin tear. I felt Leland in a way I'd never had before. No one tells you how buttery the tissues are beneath the surface, the red temptations of all that soft jelly, the taut muscles. I wondered how far I could dig until I found the secret pathway to Leland's heart.

"Fuck me."

My teeth were at the nape of his neck, my hand a vice-grip. Our reflection in the mirror was skewed with clouds of blood.

"You can't fool me." He laughed. "I know you better than I know myself. Your tricks are . . . I want the real thing."

"What are you talking about?"

"Fuck you, Dorian."

I'd never heard Leland growl like that before, never saw such evil gleam in his eyes. He pulled my finger out of the gauge and unbuckled his pants, down to the ankles; bright green underwear sailed off of his legs. I unbuttoned my own jeans and put one of his legs up to my shoulder, spit on my hand and slid quickly into Leland's cavity.

His eyes rolled into the back of his head, he began to cry. *I'm unable to carry your child*, he whispered. I almost lost my woody when he said that, but I focused my attention back on the moment. We made love as if it was the first time, holding one another so tight our bones could break, kissing hard enough to form scars.

"I am not her," he said, sounding broken.

In the heat of the moment he took control of everything. My subservient prince now the leader, pulling me down by the shoulders, his nails ripping into my shirt, stripping layers of skin clear off. I all of a sudden smelled sage and sweet grass, could see the feathery outline of yellow hair and Ray Ban sunglasses.

"You ain't focused," Leland said.

The strong-willed creature turned beautiful loser. We both were heading straight for the loony bin if we didn't think rationally. We were to be victims of an ill-fate.

"I want you," I said.

"You want *her*."

Leland kissed me again. "How do I taste? How does my body feel wrapped around yours?"

He ripped his shirt in half so that I could see his marbled torso. I counted all the beauty marks, rubbed my fingers against the slatted ribs and tiny nipples. *Am I as beautiful as her?* He repeated like a broken record. *Don't you love me anymore?* I ran my tongue down his smooth armpit, and then his sternum, my saliva stained red as paint to draw something vicious, something *alive*.

Then orgasm found us.

Leland's sphincter rippled and a fleeting, numb sensation claimed me at the height of my first portrait on flesh. There lay a great white and red clump on his belly, one that had been manipulated by my finger. Leland's eyes rolled back in shock at what I'd drawn: a little angry infant.

"Get it off of me!"

"Wait," I said. "I want to *see* it."

I held him down by his wrists to watch the muscles of his stomach bring my child to life. Crimson teeth and crenellated eyes, pale as Leland's skin. It cried inside of me, so much that I let Leland go in mid struggle. He crashed to the floor, wiped himself clean and then dressed as fast as he could.

"You piece of shit," Leland said.

It was in that moment I noticed that the smell of blood and come were one and the same, and it made perfect sense: the liquid that keeps us alive is born from the same smelly proteins that initially created us.

"I knew you wouldn't be able to do it."

"Doesn't mean I don't love you," I said sublimely.

BLOOD KISS

"There's a *big* difference between love and intimacy. If you wanna fuck her, go right ahead, but your heart is supposed to belong to *me*."

"Why can't I have both?"

The look on Leland's face was that of disgust.

Before he could answer someone was wrapping upon the door so hard I thought it would crumble. A boy looking to take a shit, long hair, big eyes and a leather jacket. Leland clawed his way up the stairs to play an innocent game of pool; half a dozen Wild Turkey's later, Leland wrecked as the bar's namesake, he gathered the strength to leave while I finished choking down my PBR.

"Don't you ever contact me again," Leland said.

I saw to it that he made it to the train safely just as my cell phone vibrated, a text from Tyria. *It's Gone*. I closed my phone and ran, actually ran faster than my legs could carry me to stop her before she did something she would regret.

I had become the expert juggler.

23

Tyria awoke to the smell of acrylic paint, alone and enveloped in the murky dark. Her body was seated in a prayer pose, her hands curled and on the attack like the goddess Kali. When she released her mind another tube of paint exploded and her body dropped to the floor. As she rolled lackadaisically across the paint it occurred to her that this is what Dorian's blood must be made of, and that she loved him, now and forever.

"I'm—"

Her throat was cracked and dried as dead leaves, the pain so great it stopped her from speaking. I am utterly alone, she thought. Adelaide had said that to her once, but that was when she was kicking the dope. Now that she was gone, now that she had no one, Tyria had no doubt that she'd be back on it. Rusty syringe nights would be commonplace, and that worried her. It was only a matter of time before her heart muscle would atrophy, until she would take her last breath.

But Tyria would not be around to see it happen.

There were two versions of guilt chasing each other in her thoughts: the destruction of Dorian's artwork by her own will and the fact that she had broken Adelaide's heart. The quiet didn't help her guilt along; it enhanced it. Nothing was louder than her thoughts and nothing was darker than from the place in which they were born.

She rose to her feet and paced the room, unsure if she should run after Adelaide or wait for Dorian to return. But he was busy tending to Leland, and Addy wasn't coming back, ever. Tyria opened a PBR and sat by the windowsill to pass the time.

A big white moon shattered against the clouds, and below it the outline of Brooklyn seemed like the first draft of a comic book sketch. The beer gave her gas, and when she belched the smell was that of rot and cigarettes. It disgusted her so much that she stuck her head out of the broken window for fresh air, reached as far as she could, vicariously calling Dorian back to the stage, the only place that brought them freedom from pain.

Something snaked up her arm and bit down. Winter had never felt so oppressive, but the ice had never looked so stunning. Big clusters of needles crowned every gutter. It was danger and beauty rolled into one. If but one icicle broke off its frozen nest it could jet down and pierce through the head of a passerby. Tyria broke a piece off the windowsill and launched it like a lance, saw it shatter on the street.

It's in you, a sexless voice said. *Belongs to him.*

A sensation ricocheted inside her; the revelation of motherhood a ticking time bomb. She lit a fancy black cigarette.

"This is my body," she whispered.

But he gave you the miracle.

The past that she recently let go of had returned. She didn't want to remember how she begged Daddy to take his dick out of her, or how she yearned for Dorian's. There was a love between them that was deeper than she knew how to give. Wasn't it natural to feel such a resistance towards it?

"I will take back what is mine," Tyria said to herself. "I control my own destiny."

Knees to the floor, hands up, and her eyes locked on the moon. Goddess, come. But the offerings were dry. All that was around her was sacred ash, the triplicate road now entombed, replaced with the image of a skinny spinster and a selfish screaming infant. Fate has a queer way of always telling you that it's so close, yet so far away.

But what if she could break that fate? What if destiny could be altered?

The scream erupted without warning. It ripped her throat into useless scraps of flesh, tore heavily into the air. The elements split into electrons, protons, neutrons and quarks; the floor cracked into patterns as intricate as a dream catcher.

Time was slow and golden as honey. An explosion of ice and glass spattered her with cold diamonds. She reached for the white light, clawing, hoping, but the aliens would not take her away. In all that vast universe, they did not want her. The only thing she was sure of was that she could not accept the value and privilege of motherhood as so many women do.

She had no need to be part of the greater paradigm that hypnotizes you to join before you can even choose. Think of the idiocy in any society that gives people freedom of choice, but with the expectation that one gender is to be dominant over the other. Women are free to live as they choose, acquire any form of education they want, but not to the point where it would threaten the ego that has seen men rise as the apex predator.

For a woman compromise is key. Ask that she give up her desires and her dreams, that she put her passions on the back burner to support a family, and you will find that nobody disagrees in protest. They will smile and nod and go about their lives instead of fighting for what's right.

Her thoughts were on fire.

Tyria wanted to catalogue her wisdom. She used the walls as her notebook. She wrote and wrote and wrote, could not find a reason to stop, not when the words were so clear. *IT'S TIME FOR ME TO GO HOME* in black, and *TO REMAIN IS TO DECAY*, literal blood into her words, because blood is forever.

Back on the dance floor she incinerated a bundle of sage and sweet grass, the smell of it like new beginnings laced with the finality of a dramatic ending. Retrospect became reality as she recalled getting rid of that first sac of poison planted inside her a decade earlier, the incredible *pop* she felt.

BLOOD KISS

It was a lonely memory. Those days were surely behind her, she had grown; the stage freed her of those chains. The only taste on her tongue was that of Dorian's blood kiss, so much regret but so much learning. You have to hit an all time low in order to rise. You have to break before you can heal.

Tyria walked over to Morgan's amplifiers, pulled out the chords and stepped up on the stage. She recalled the sea of faces, the winged dark, could feel the plague mask change her. She threw the chords across a metal beam and wrapped one part under to form a noose. The fall would not break her neck, but it would cut off the blood supply to her brain in no time.

Was this really the answer?

There was a new source of light coming to her: dawn. But she didn't want to see the sun anymore. Might Dorian find her here, might Adelaide regret leaving her this way, but they had done this to themselves. Escape was the only answer, because the responsibility of gestation was too great a curse to bear.

Then time sped up again.

There came the sound of metal hitting pavement, and at her feet something long and sharp, warm to the touch as if she had sent this through time for herself, to save herself. Parapsychologists called them *apports*.

It was a wire hangar daubed in blood. And on the sharp edge a throbbing little meat-bean.

Tyria knew what had to be done. She unzipped her jeans, legs open like she was thirteen-years-old again, and she sent the metal up inside, wound it through her cavity until she could push no further. A warm gob of blood surged into her throat.

Time slowed down again. Stars exploded behind her eyes, and when she pulled out the wire hangar freedom from pain and suffering rushed out in red. She placed her head into the noose, took a step forward, but then stopped. This was the most important decision she had ever made. It was for herself and only herself.

But the thought of Adelaide finding her this way was the crown of thorns, and Dorian the final spear to the side. She would not be told how to live her life, how to raise a child; she would not do it alone either. And then she stepped off the stage.

. . . to let a warm electric river swallow her.

THE STAIRCASE WENT ON FOREVER. When I reached the top I was ridiculously out of breath, sweating and full of regret. I lit a bogee and inhaled deeply. To my immediate left I saw that a portrait had been crushed and a gout of paint spilled from its depth. I reached out to touch the bleeding thing but was suddenly distracted by a noise. Heavy breathing, shadow, and a curlicue of smoke outlining an anomalous creature that I might have painted myself.

"You motherfucker."

Adelaide taller and darker than I remembered, her hair strung out like she had torn it from her own scalp. The tears in her eyes spoke of revenge, the Bowie knife proof of what she craved. She simply stared at me as I stared right back at her. The seconds didn't dare tick by.

"You put it into her head that you'd take care of her," Adelaide's voice sounded raw.

"I did no such thing," I said.

She began to cut small circles into her *Fragility Tour 2000* t-shirt. "You made her believe that she was going to be your pretty little wife."

"Tyria and I are friends."

Adelaide scowled. "Friends with *fucking* benefits."

"Get away from the door before I force you."

"No."

The cool blue light of dawn stretched into the hallway and brought about a sickly glow unto Adelaide's face. Her eyes were stone cold as Medusa's. Snot hung languidly off her

BLOOD KISS *Daniel Stone*

little nose as if she'd morphed back into that junky I had first met.

"You're scum."

"Thank you." I had no idea why I said this.

"At least there's no one here to stop me now."

She swung the Bowie knife but my senses automatically heightened. I heard it cut through the thick tension between us. Blood hit my lips and chin even though I felt no pain. My legs automatically took a step back, using the banister as a fulcrum to kick my boot into her torso. But her momentum kept growing like a boulder that rolls downhill and gains speed.

The Bowie knife came back for me.

I threw my cigarette at her face. She howled and bared her teeth; her lips tore and bled. I was certain that someone would come in and break up the fight being we were so loud, but no one did, and as the burn distracted her I knew that it was my only chance to grab the knife.

I failed miserably. She was too quick, even in her drunken state, pulling me back so that the exquisite metal sent a flood of pain up my entire arm. I fell against the wall and let the crimson rivulets soak into my pants and boots.

"You burned my eye," Adelaide said.

"I should burn something else."

The war was on. Adelaide gave up on the knife and went back to her mammalian roots, teeth and claws out for the kill. She pistoned her fist straight into my mouth and I felt my lips crush against my teeth. I noticed that the taste of her skin was not sweet and dangerous like Tyria's, but soured with malice. She proceeded to claw at my eyes and scalp, and I held her off as long as I could before I felt something in my brain snap.

The demon inside of me was set free.

"Gunna scar you so you *never* forget me," I said.

With my good hand I slammed her head into the wall, stunned her enough so that my bleeding hand could draw a Glasgow grin on her face. Not draw, but *claw*. Stretching her lips, splitting cheekflesh as my nails dug and tore, the transmogrification complete: Adelaide's perpetual frown now a grin. Then I heard the rush of footsteps and felt a sharp, threatening pressure in the small of my back.

"Let her go you crazy fuck!"

Leland was taut as a rope pulled on both ends. He edged the Bowie knife into me, threatening to plunge it. The predatory jolt of adrenaline that had taken over my conscious drained away. I was shocked into a momentary paralysis so that my arms fell to my side, thus releasing Adelaide. She collapsed to the floor, and I thought about kicking her down the stairs, her head would certainly split on the way down, which would match the new look of her face. But instead Leland held her, brushed her hair out of her face to make me feel stupidly jealous.

"What did you do to her?" Leland asked. "You sick fuck."

"Smile," I laughed.

"You can't put on your little magic show here," Leland said. "She doesn't believe in it."

"But you do."

"Not anymore."

It took me a second to understand what he meant. I had tried to draw her a new face, but in the end all I wound up doing was a portrait of mutilation.

"He hurt me, Landy."

"Shh. Don't speak."

"And he killed Tyria," Adelaide cried out.

I knew that junkies were chronic liars, and that they always need someone to blame for their condition. But the death of a loved one was something not even the lowest of the low would lie about; no one even in the wrong mind will use that to their advantage. My stomach dropped and my chest sunk in. If there was ever a feeling of absolute emptiness, like someone had split open my torso and excavated all my organs in one greedy sweep, that is how I felt when Adelaide said those words.

"What do you mean?" Leland said.

BLOOD KISS

I bolted through the door to see the destruction rather than hearing about it. The walls were shattered and the floor blighted. It was as if an earthquake had just taken place. I was greeted with the memories of the slack jaw skull and its furred tongue, amorphous sex organs and shadow. But in real time there was only the smell of sage and sweet grass laced with that of blood and bowels.

"Holy shit," Leland said in a lost voice. "You really fucking did it now, Dorian."

"No," I squealed

Tyria was swaying in front of the stage. It was indeed the death of a martyr, right upon the place that had freed her, and no doubt, had freed her again.

A spear of cold dawn sun divided the room into black and white. It felt wrong to be standing in light that was so frigid, but so bright. Reality settled in bleak and lonesome; I fell to my knees and raised my hands up to her. All I could do was worship her physical presence, knowing very well that her spiritual one was still in the room.

For some reason she wore the plague mask, maybe to hide herself from humiliation. I pulled it up, taken back how beautiful, fragile, but fierce she looked in death. I rubbed my finger against her stiff cheek, moved her hair to the side. The skin of a dead body is so much different from that of a living one. If you prod dead flesh the indent will remain for a long time like pressing your finger into hot candle wax; if you kiss the lips of a dead person all you taste is what *was* . . . what will never be. You see that the eyes remain the same as they stare at you, but soon they will shrivel like grapes left in the sun.

The blood had already left the upper half of her body and pooled in her extremities. Her hands were cold and colored a creepy gray-blue, her face paler than I can describe. But her eyes were still made of jade stone, and her tattoos remained vibrant.

I cried like a child wanting its mother. I was unable to imagine my life without Tyria. How could I grow as an artist, where would my art take me? No place was higher than the stage with her. That, and the fact that she was carrying my spawn, was salt in the literal wound of my heart.

"She used this." Adelaide held a wire hanger still sticky with Tyria's blood.

On the tip was a gleaming bead of meat that could have been my little boy, my little girl. Anger consumed me, made me destroy everything in my path; I threw beer cans, paint-brushes, streamers and chairs right out the window. I grabbed my triptych, thought about burning it alive, that it should feel the pain I feel.

"I didn't want it to be this way," I said to the ghost of my audience.

Leland's face was wet with tears. "You're a ruiner of the soul."

Adelaide pushed me out of the way and propped herself upon Tyria's body, Dahlia face to plague mask. She caressed and kissed her lips, leaving a red smear. There was a Tyria-shaped hole in her heart. She wasn't alone in that respect.

"My angel, ascend."

"Descend," I corrected her.

Something shot down from the sky and hit my cheek, a warm and wet wad of spit.

"I'm calling the cops," Leland said. "I won't clean up after you anymore. You're on your own."

"I never asked you to," I said.

"No, you never do."

Adelaide collapsed into a ball, took out a lighter, rusted spoon, and the old hypodermic. I wanted to aide her demise by switching the bag of rocks with something like baking soda, but as she injected the bore of the needle into her knee cap I knew I didn't need to have any part in her self-destruction. She would take care of that herself.

"Just let me die here," Adelaide said.

Leland took the needle away. "No."

"I-I told her that I was done with her. But I really w-w-wasn't." Adelaide's eyes rolled to the back of her head and she began puking.

BLOOD KISS

Leland pulled her toward the door and then walked over to me. I knew that this was the last time I was ever going to see him. I reached out my hands for his, but he would not take them. His black eyes were livid with tears and his teeth were clenched. There was no containing his emotions as he mouthed something I will never forget, because I knew he meant it.

"It's over."

Just like that they were gone.

I was left with nothing to show for my artistry but the radiating hum of Tyria's dead body. I crisscrossed the room and felt the skin of shadow, the dark slow churning of ecto-plasm. The triptych was only a few paces away, but I wouldn't play into its game. Instead, I kept vigil over my delicate angel, the mother of my dead child.

What could have been love consummate was wasted.

There was only but one thing left to do.

I cut Tyria out of the noose and lay her gently on the floor; she was so heavy in death. Her head snapped back and the mask exploded as hit the stage. Though she was at peace something in her uneasy shape translated into her notorious religion of resistance.

I kissed her lips for the blood, but tasted rot.

The thought of her body lying in the earth, alone and maleficent, betrayed me. She would be worm food before she could tell her carrion tale. I couldn't allow that to happen. My hands crawled across her shoulders, wrapping them around her as if my very own fleshy Christmas gift. I held tight—

—to never let go.

Tyria: my incubus in the dark. Without you I am a bag of bones, a vessel with no soul. I am stripped of passion and filled with gloom. I light an Open Road candle to set you on your mystical path and watch your earthly body bloom.

As the smell of you will forever haunt this room . . .

Did you enjoy the book?

We welcome all feedback and queries.
Villipede.com

"*Invention, it must be humbly admitted, does not consist in creating out of void, but out of chaos.*"

—**Mary Shelley**